ABARAT

ABSOLUTE
MIDNIGHT

ALSO BY CLIVE BARKER

The Inhuman Condition

Cabal

PLAYS

Forms of Heaven: Three Plays

Crazyface

Paradise Street

Subtle Bodies

Incarnations: Three Plays

Colossus

Frankenstein in Love

The History of the Devil

ANTHOLOGY

(Contributor)

Revelations

CLIVE BARKER

ABARAT

ABSOLUTE
MIDNIGHT

JOANNA COTLER BOOKS

An Imprint of HarperCollins*Publishers*

Abarat: Absolute Midnight

Copyright © 2011 by Clive Barker

www.epicreads.com

Library of Congress Cataloging-in-Publication Data
Barker, Clive.
  Absolute midnight / Clive Barker. — 1st ed.
    p. cm. — (Abarat ; [bk. 3])
  Summary: Candy Quackenbush of Chickentown, Minnesota, is the only person who
can stop the evil Mater Motley who, now that the hour of midnight has come, is pre-
pared to unleash the end of the world.
  ISBN 978-0-06-440933-9
  [1. Space and time—Fiction. 2. Fantasy.] I. Title.
PZ7.B25046Ac 2011   2010042665
[Fic]—dc22   CIP
                                                                              AC

Typography by Neil Swaab
13 14 15 16 17   CG/RRDH   10 9 8 7 6 5 4 3 2 1
❖

Revised edition, 2013

Johnny 2.0 Raymond
Mark Miller
Robbie Humphreys

There'll be no sun tomorrow morning.
There'll be no moon to bless the night.
The stars will perish without warning.
These lines proclaim the death of light.

CONTENTS

WHAT THE BLIND MAN SAW

Dream!
Forge yourself and rise
Out of your mind and into others.
Men, be women.
Fish, be flies.
Girls, take beards.
Sons, be your mothers.
The future of the world now lies
In coral wombs behind our eyes.

—A song sung in Paradise Street

O N THE EARLY COAST of Idjit, where two a.m. looked south over the darkened straits toward the island of Gorgossium, there was a house, its facade much decorated, set high upon the cliffs. Its occupant went by the name of Mr. Kithit, and several others besides, but none of the names were truly his. He was known simply as the Card-Reader. The cards he read were not designed for games of chance. Far from it. He only ever used the Abaratian tarot deck, wherein a reader as expert as Mr. Kithit might find the past murmuring, the present in doubt, and the future barely opening its eyes. A decent living could be made from interpreting the way the cards fell.

For many years the Card-Reader had served the countless customers who came there in search of wisdom. But tonight he was done with serving the curiosity of others. He was done with it forever. Tonight, it was not the future of others he was going to find in the cards. They had summoned him to show him his own destiny.

He sat down and took one slow, calming breath. Then he proceeded to lay out a pattern of nineteen cards chosen by the will of his fingertips. Blind though he was, each image appeared in his mind's eye, along with its name and numerical place in the pack.

There was *Fear*. There was *The Door to the Stars*. There was *The King of Fates* and *The Daughter of Curiosity*. Each card was not only to be read for its own values, but also calibrated against the cards surrounding it: a piece of mythological mathematics, which most heads could not fathom.

The Man Lit by Candles; *Death's Island*; *The Primal Form*; *The Tree of Knowing* . . .

And of course the entire arrangement had to be set against the card that his customer—in this case himself—had chosen as his Avatar. In this case, he had elected a card called *The Threshold*. He had put it back into the pack and then shuffled the cards twice before laying them out by instinct in the Naught Hereafter Spread, its name signifying that all things the Deck contained would be here displayed: all reparations (the past), all possibilities (now), and all risk (henceforth and ever).

His fingers moved quickly, summoned by a call from the cards. There was something here they wanted to show him. He quickly understood that there was news of great consequence here, so he neglected the rules of reading, one of the first being that a Reader waited until each of the number of cards required for the Spread had been laid out.

A war was coming; he saw it in the cards. The last of the plots were being laid, even now, the weapons loaded and polished, the armies assembled, all in readiness for the day when Abaratian history turned the final corner. Was this the cards' way of telling him what part there was for him to play in this last, grim game? If so then he would attend to whatever he was being taught, trust to their wisdom as had so many who had come to him over the years, despairing of all other remedy, seeking that which the cards would show.

He was not surprised to find that there were many Fire cards around his Threshold, laid out like gifts. He was a man whose life—and flesh—had been re-wrought by that unforgiving element. Touching the cards with his seared fingertip, it was impossible for him not to remember the merciless conflagration that had beaten him back as he tried to save his family. One of his children, the youngest, had survived, but the fire had claimed all the rest except his mother, and it had only granted her a reprieve because she had always been as pitiless and all-consuming as a great fire; a fire large enough to reduce a mansion and most of a dynasty to ashes.

In effect he'd lost everything, because his mother— crazed by what she'd witnessed, it was said—had taken the infant and disappeared into Day or Night, perhaps in her madness to hide the one survivor of her twenty-three grandchildren from the slightest hint of smoke on the wind. But the insanity plea had never been sufficient to quite calm the Card-Reader's unease. His mother had never been a very wholesome woman. She'd liked—more than was good for an unbalanced spirit such as hers—tales of Deep Magic, of Earth-Blood Doing and worse. And it had troubled the Card-Reader more than a little that he had lost track of both his mother and son; it troubled him because he'd not known what they were up to. But even more because they—the one who had borne him, and the one he had fathered—were out there somewhere, a part of the powers assembling for the labors of destruction that were signaled everywhere in the lay of the cards.

"Must I come and find you?" he said. "Is that what this is? Do you want a sentimental reunion, Mother?"

He judged by weight how many of the cards he had so far laid down. A little over half, he guessed. It was possible the half he still held carried news of his last connection with Abaratian history but he doubted it. This was not a spread of specificities. It was the Hereafter Naught, the last apocalyptic gospel of the Abaratian tarot.

He set the unplayed cards down, and went to the door of his house to bathe his scarred face in the cast of the silver starlight. The years when the children of the village of Eedo, which was at the bottom of the steep trail that zigzagged up the cliff to his house, had lived in fear of him had long since passed. Though they would playact terror to amuse each other, and he played the growling monster to feed the fiction, they knew he usually had a few paterzem to toss over the threshold for them to squabble over, especially when—as tonight—they brought him something they had found along the shore to give to him. Today, as he stood at the door of the house, one of his favorites, a sweet hybrid of Sea-Skipper and commonplace child, called Lupta, came squealing to find him with an entourage of children following closely behind her.

"I have flotsammi jetsammi!" she boasted. "I have many. Lookazis! Lookazis! All thrown up by Our Gracious Lady Izabella."

"You want to see more?" said her brother, Kipthin.

"Of course," the Card-Reader said. "Always."

Lupta grunted out instructions to her little gang, who noisily un-netted their catch onto the ground in front of the Card-Reader's house. He listened with a practiced ear to the noise the find gave off: the objects were large. Some clattered and clanged, others rang like sour-noted bells.

"Describe them to me, will you, child?"

Lupta proceeded to do so, but—as was so often the case for haggling in the weeks since the persuasive currents of the Izabella had invaded the Hereafter, flooded Chickentown in Minnesota, and returned carrying some trophies of that other dimension with them—the objects that the tide had thrown up on the rocky beach below were not easily described or pictured, having no equivalent in the Abarat. Still the Card-Reader listened intently, knowing that if he was to understand the significance of the deck half spread in the darkened room behind him then he would need to understand the nature of the mysterious Humaniticks, some of whose artifacts, their details hard to make sense of when a man had no sight, surely offered profound clues to the nature of those who might unmake the world. Little Lupta perhaps knew more than she thought she knew. And behind her guesses, she was plucking up truths.

"What were these things made for?" he asked her. "Are they engines? Or toys? Are they to be eaten? Or maybe to kill?"

There was some frantic whispering among Lupta's gang, but finally the girl said with absolute confidence:

"We don't know."

"They're much beaten by the sea," Kipthin said.

"I would expect nothing less," the Card-Reader said. "Even so, let me put my hands upon them. Guide me, Lupta. You needn't hesitate, child. I'm not a monster."

"I know that. If you were, you wouldn't look like one."

"Who told you that?"

"I did."

"Hm. Well, is there something here you think I might understand?"

"Yes. Here. Put out your hands."

Lupta put one of the objects into his proffered palms. As soon as his fingers made contact with whatever it was, his legs gave way beneath him, and he fell to the ground dumping the piece of trash Lupta had given him. He reached down and searched for it, seized by the same fervor that caught hold of him whenever he was reading the cards. There was one significant difference, however. When he read the cards his mind was able to make a pattern of the signs he was seeing. But there was no pattern here. Only chaos upon chaos. He saw a monstrous ship of war, with his mother, aged but still as much a harridan as ever, commanding the waters of the Izabella to burst through the divide between its natural bed and into the Hereafter, its crazed flood ripping apart what lay on the other side.

"Chickentown," he murmured.

"You see it?" said Lupta's brother.

The Card-Reader nodded. "Being ripped apart." He closed his eyes more tightly, as though he might blot out with a willed blindness the horrors he saw.

"Have any of you heard any stories concerning the people of the Hereafter?" he asked the children.

As before, there was frantic whispering. But he caught one of his visitors urging Lupta to *tell him*.

"Tell me what?" the blind man said.

"About people from a place called Chickentown. They're just stories," Lupta said. "I don't know if any of them are true."

"Tell me anyway."

"Tell him about the girl. She's the one everyone talks about," said a third member of Lupta's gang.

"Candy . . . Quackenbush . . ." the blind man said, half to himself.

"Have you seen her in your cards?" Lupta asked. "Do

you know where she is?"

"Why?"

"You have, haven't you?"

"What would it matter if I had?"

"I need to talk with her! I want to be like her! Everything she does people talk about."

"Like what?"

Lupta's voice became a whisper. "Our priest says it's a sin to talk about her. Is he right?"

"No, Lupta, I don't believe he is."

"I'm going to run away one day. I am! I want to find her."

"You be careful," the Card-Reader said. "It's a dangerous time and it's going to get worse."

"I don't care."

"Well, at least come and say good-bye, child," the Card-Reader said. He dug into his pocket and brought out a few paterzem.

"Here," he said, handing the coins over to Lupta. "Thank you for bringing the stuff up from the shore. Will you divide this between you? Fairly, now."

"Of course!" Lupta said. And happy with their reward she and her friends went off down the road to the village, leaving the Card-Reader with his thoughts and the collection of objects the current, the children, and circumstance had brought before him.

The urchin and her gang had arrived at an opportune moment. Perhaps with the remnants they'd brought he could make better sense of the Spread. The cards and the trash had much in common: they were both collections of clues connecting what the world had been like in a better age. He went back into the house and sat at the table again, picking up the un-spread cards. He had only laid down another two when the card representing Candy Quackenbush appeared. It was easily identified. *I Am They*, the card was called. He could not recall having ever seen it before.

"Well, well . . ." he murmured. "Look at you." He tapped her with his finger. "What gives you the right to be such a power? And what business have you got with me?" The girl on the card stared at him from his mind's eye. "Are you here to give me harm or happiness? Because I tell you I've had more than my share of sorrow. I can't take much more."

I Am They watched him with great compassion.

"Ah," he said. "It isn't over. At least now I know. Be kind to me, will you? If it is in your power."

It took him another six and a half hours from his speaking to Candy Quackenbush to finally deciding he was done with the Spread. He gathered up all of the cards, counting them to be sure he had them all, and then he went outside, taking them with him. The wind had picked up considerably since he'd been out here with Lupta and her little gang. It came speeding around the corner of the house, buffeting him as he walked toward the cliff edge, the pack of cards trembling in his hand.

The farther from his doorstep he ventured the more

unreliable the ground became, the solid earth giving way to loose dirt and pebbles. The cards were becoming more excitable with every step he took out there beyond the cliff edge. Events they'd been unable to share until now were imminent.

Suddenly the wind picked up its strength, and threw him forward, as if to cast him into the world. His right foot trod vacant air, and he toppled forward—seeing all too clearly in his mind's eye the waves of the Izabella below. Two thoughts came into his head at the same instant. One, that he had not seen this (his death) in the cards. And two, that he'd been wrong about Candy Quackenbush. He would not meet her after all, which saddened him.

Then two small yet very strong hands seized his shirt and pulled him back from the brink. Instead of dropping to his death he toppled backward, landing on top of his savior. It was little Lupta.

"I knew," she said.

"Knew what?"

"You were going to do something stupid."

"I was not."

"It looked like you were."

"The wind caught me is all. Thank you for saving me from losing my—"

"The cards!" Lupta said.

His grip on the cards was too weak. When the wind came gushing again it snatched them from his hand, and with what sounded like a ripple of applause as they slapped against one another, they were carried away, out into the naked air.

"Let them go," the blind man said.

"But how will you make money without your cards?"

"Heaven will provide. Or else it won't, and I'll go hungry." He got to his feet. "In a way it confirms my decision. My life here is over. It's time I went to see the Hours one last time before they and I pass."

"You mean they're coming to an end?"

"Yes. Many things will end soon. Cities, Princes, things foul and things fine. All will pass away." He paused, looking up sightlessly at the sky. "Are there a lot of stars tonight?"

"Yes. Lots."

"Oh good, very good. Will you lead me down to the North Road?"

"Don't you want to go through the village? Say goodbye?"

"Would you?"

"No."

"No. Just get me to the North Road. Once I have it beneath my feet, I'll know where to go from there."

PART ONE

THE DARK HOURS

Oh sweet children, my beloveds,
time to go to bed.
Oh sweet children, heavy-lidded,
you are bathed and you are fed.
Time for pillows, time for sleeping,
and fearless dreams to fill your heads.
Oh sweet children, my beloved,
time to go to bed.

—Anon.

1

TOWARD TWILIGHT

Candy's gang of Abaratian friends had plenty of plans laid to celebrate her safe return to the islands after the violence and insanity of the Hereafter. But they had barely finished welcoming her home with kisses and laughter (to which the John Brothers added an *a cappella* version of an old Abaratian standard) when Deaux-Deaux the sea-skipper, who had been the first friend Candy had made in Abaratian waters, came to find her, to tell her that word was being passed by every means in every direction, demanding her presence at The Great Head of the Yebba Dim Day. An emergency meeting of the Council of the Hours was presently assembling there to fully analyze the calamitous events that had taken place in Chickentown. Given that Candy had a unique perspective on those events, it was vital that she attend to give evidence.

It wouldn't be an easy meeting, she knew. No doubt, the Council suspected that she was the cause of the events that had wrought so much destruction. They would want her to give them a full account of why and how she had come to make herself such powerful enemies as Mater Motley and her grandson, Christopher Carrion: enemies with the power to override the seal the Council had put on the Abarat and force the waters of the Izabella to do their bidding, causing it to form a wave powerful enough to wash over the threshold between worlds, and to fill Chickentown's streets.

She quickly said her good-byes to those she'd only recently greeted again—Finnegan Hob, Two-Toed Tom, the John Brothers, Geneva—and with her geshrat friend Malingo for company she boarded the small boat the Council had sent and departed for the Straits of Dusk.

The journey was long, but went without incident. This was no thanks to the temperament of the Izabella, which was much stirred up, and carried on her tide plentiful evidence of the journey her waters had recently taken across the border between worlds. There were keepsakes from Chickentown floating everywhere: plastic toys, plastic bottles, and plastic furniture, not to mention boxes of cereal and cans of beer, pages of gossip magazines and broken televisions. A street sign, drowned chickens, the contents of somebody's fridge, leftovers bobbing by sealed in plastic: half a sandwich, some meat loaf, and a slice of cherry pie.

"Strange," Candy said, watching it all float by. "It makes me hungry."

"There's plenty of fish," said the Abaratian in Council uniform who was guiding their boat through this detritus.

"I don't see fish," Malingo said.

The man leaned over the side of the boat, and with startling speed, he reached down into the water and pulled out a fat fish, yellow dotted with spots of bright blue. He proffered the creature, all panic and color, to Malingo.

"There," he said. "Eat! It's a sanshee fish. Very good meat."

"No thanks. Not raw."

"Please yourself." He offered it to Candy. "Lady?"

"I'm not hungry, thank you."

"Mind . . . if I . . . ?"

"Go ahead."

The man opened his mouth much wider than Candy had thought possible, revealing two impressive parades of pointed teeth. The fish, much to Candy's surprise uttered a high-pitched squeal, which died the moment its devourer bit off its head. Candy didn't want to look revolted by what was probably a perfectly natural thing for the pilot to have done so she went back to looking at the bizarre reminders of Chickentown as they floated by, until finally the little vessel brought them into the busy harbor of the Yebba Dim Day.

2

THE COUNCIL
SPEAKS ITS MINDS

CANDY HAD EXPECTED TO be called into the Council Chamber, questioned by the Councilors about what she'd seen and experienced and then released to go back to join her friends. But it became apparent as soon as she presented herself before the Council that not all of the eleven individuals gathered here thought that she was an innocent victim of the calamitous events that had caused so much destruction, and that some punishment needed to be agreed upon.

One of Candy's accusers, a woman called Nyritta Maku, who came from Huffaker, was the first to present her opinion, and she did so without any sweetening.

"It's very clear that for reasons known only to yourself," she said, her blue-skinned skull bound so as to form a series of soft-boned sub-skulls of diminishing size that hung like a tail, "you came to the Abarat without invitation from anyone in this Chamber, intending to cause trouble. You quickly did so. You liberated a geshrat from the employ of an imprisoned wizard without any permission to do so. You roused the fury of Mater Motley. That in itself would be reason for a stiff sentence. But there's worse. We have already heard testimony that you have the arrogance to believe you have some significant part to play in the future of our islands."

"I didn't come here deliberately if that's what you're saying."

"Have you made any such claims?"

"This is an accident. Me being here."

"Answer the question."

"If I was to take a wild guess I'd say she's trying to do that, Nyritta," said the representative from the Nonce. It was a spiral of warm dappled light, in the midst of which flakes of poppy and white gold floated. "Just give her a chance to find the words."

"Oh, you really like the lost ones, don't you, Keemi."

"I'm not lost," Candy said. "I know my way around pretty well."

"And why is that?" said a third Council member, her face an eight-eyed, four-petaled flower with a bright-throated mouth at its center. "Not only do you know your way around the islands, you also know a lot about the Abarataraba."

"I've just heard stories here and there."

"Stories!" said Yobias Thim, who had a row of candles around the brim of his hat. "You don't learn to wield Feits and Wantons by hearing stories. I think what happened with Motley and Carrion and your knowledge of the Abarataraba are all part of the same suspicious business."

"Let it be," said Keemi. "We didn't summon her here to Okizor to interrogate her about how she knows the Abarataraba."

She glanced around at the Councilors, no two of whose physiognomies were alike. The representative from Orlando's Cap had a brilliant coxcomb of scarlet and turquoise feathers, which were standing proud in his agitated state; while the face of Soma Plume's representative, Helio Fatha, wavered as though he was gazing through a cloud of heat, and the dawning face of the Councilor from six A.M. was streaked with the promise of another day.

"Look, it's true. I do know . . . things," Candy admitted. "It started at the lighthouse, with me knowing how to summon the Izabella. I'm not saying I couldn't do it, I could. I just don't know how I did. Does it matter?"

"If this Council thinks it matters," growled the stone visage from Efreet, "then it matters. And everything else should be of little consequence to you until the question has been satisfactorily answered."

Candy nodded. "All right," she said. "I'll do my best. But it's complicated."

So saying, she began to tell them as best she could the parts that she did know, starting with the event from which everything else sprang: her birth, and the fact that just an hour or so before her mother got to the hospital on an empty, rain-lashed highway in the middle of nowhere, three women of the Fantomaya—Diamanda, Joephi and Mespa—had crossed the forbidden divide between the Abarat and the Hereafter looking for a hiding place for the soul of Princess Boa, whose murdered remains lay in the Nonce.

"They found my mother," Candy said, "sitting, waiting for my dad to come back with gas for the truck . . ."

She paused, because there was a humming sound in her head, which was getting louder. It sounded as though her skull was filled with hundreds of agitated bees. She couldn't think straight.

"They found my mother . . ." she said again, aware that her voice was slurring.

"Forget your mother for a moment," said the representative from Ninnyhammer, a bipedal tarrie-cat called Jimothi Tarrie, who Candy had met before. "What do you know about the murder of Princess Boa?"

"Boa."

"Yes."

Huh. Boa.

"Quite . . . quite a lot," Candy replied.

What she'd thought to be the voices of bees, was forming into syllables, the syllables into words, the words becoming sentences. There was somebody speaking in her head.

Don't tell them anything, the voice said. *They're bureaucrats, all of them.*

She knew the voice. She'd been hearing it all her life.

She'd thought it was her voice. But just because the voice had been in her skull all her life didn't make it hers. She said the other's name without speaking it.

Princess Boa.

Yes, of course, the other woman said. *Who else were you expecting?*

"Jimothi Tarrie asked you a question," Nyritta said.

"The death of the Princess . . ." Jimothi reminded her.

"Yes, I know," Candy said.

Tell them nothing, Boa reiterated. *Don't let them intimidate you. They'll use your words against you. Be very careful.*

Candy was deeply unsettled by the presence of Boa's voice—and especially unhappy that it should make itself audible to her now of all times—but she sensed that the advice she was being given was right. The Councilors were watching her with profound suspicion.

". . . I heard bits of gossip," she said to them. "But don't really remember much . . ."

"But you're here in the Abarat for a reason," said Nyritta.

"Am I?" she countered.

"Well, don't you know? You tell us. Are you?"

"I don't . . . have any reason in my head, if that's what you mean," Candy said. "I think maybe I'm just here because I happened to be at the wrong place at the wrong time."

Nice work, Boa said. *Now they don't know what to think.*

Boa's assessment seemed right. There were a lot of

frowns and puzzled looks around the Council table. But Candy wasn't off the hook yet.

"Let's change the subject," Nyritta said.

"And go where?" Helio Fatha asked.

"What about Christopher Carrion?" Nyritta said to Candy. "You were somehow involved with him. Weren't you?"

"Well, he tried to have me murdered, if you want to call that involvement."

"No, no, no. Your enemy was Mater Motley. There was something else going on with Carrion. Admit it."

"Like *what?*" Candy said.

She needed to lie now, Candy knew. The truth was that she was indeed aware of why Carrion had been drawn to her, but she wasn't going to let the Councilors know about it. Not until she knew more herself. So she said it was a mystery to her. And a mystery, she didn't neglect to remind them, that had almost cost her her life.

"Well, you survived to tell the tale," Nyritta remarked, his voice dripping sarcasm.

"So why don't you *tell* it, instead of meandering around explaining nothing at all?" Helio Fatha said.

"I've nothing to tell," Candy replied.

"There are laws defending the Abarat from your kind, you know that, don't you?"

"What will you do? Execute me?" Candy said. "Oh, don't look so shocked. You're not angels. Yes, you probably had good reason to protect yourselves from my kind.

But no kind is perfect. Even Abaratians."

Boa was right, Candy thought. They were a bunch of bullies. Just like her dad. Just like everyone else. And the more they bullied, the more she was determined not to give them any answers.

"I can't help it whether you believe me or not. You can interrogate me all you like, but you're just going to get the same answer. *I don't know anything!*"

Helio Fatha snorted with contempt. "Ah, let her go!" he said. "This is a waste of time."

"But she has powers, Fatha. She was seen wielding them."

"So maybe she saw them in a book. Wasn't she with that idiot Wolfswinkel for a time? Whatever she may have learned, she'll forget it. Humankind can't hold on to mystery."

There was a long, irritated silence. Finally Candy said, "Can I go?"

"No," said the stone-faced representative from Efreet. "We're not finished with our questions."

"Let the girl go, Zuprek," Jimothi said.

"Neabas still has something to say," the Efreetian replied.

"Get on with it."

Neabas spoke like a snail edging along a knife. He looked like iridescent gossamer. "We all know she has some affection for the creature, though why that should be is incomprehensible. She's plainly concealing

a great deal from us. If I had my way I'd call in Yeddik
Magash—"

"A torturer?" Jimothi said.

"No. He's simply somebody who knew how to get the
truth when, as now, it was being willfully withheld. But I
don't expect this Council to sanction such a choice. You're
all too soft. You'll choose fur over stone, and in the end
we'll all suffer for it."

"Do you actually *have* a question for the girl?" Yobias
Thim asked wearily. "All my candles are down and I don't
have any others with me."

"Yes, Thim. I have a question," Zuprek said.

"Then, Lordy Lou, *ask it.*"

Zuprek's shards fixed upon Candy. "I want to know
when it was you were last in the company of Christopher
Carrion," he said.

Say nothing, Boa told her.

Why shouldn't they know? Candy thought, and without waiting for any further argument from Boa she told
Zuprek, "I found him in my parents' bedroom."

"This was back in the Hereafter?"

"Yes, of course. My mother and father haven't been to
the Abarat. None of my family has."

"Well, that's some sort of comfort, I suppose,"
Zuprek said. "At least we won't have an invasion of
Quackenbushes to deal with."

His sour humor got a few titters from sympathetic
souls around the table: Nyritta Maku, Skippelwit, one or

two others. But Neabas still had further questions. And he was deadly serious:

"What was Carrion's condition?" he wanted to know.

"He was very badly wounded. I thought he was going to die."

"But he didn't die?"

"Not on the bed, no."

"Somewhere close by, you're implying?"

"I only know what I saw."

"And what was that?"

"Well . . . the window burst open, and all this water rushed in. It carried him away. That was the last time I saw him. Disappearing into the dark water, and then gone."

"Are you satisfied, Neabas?" Jimothi said.

"Almost," came the reply. "Just tell us all, without any lies or half-truths, what you believe the real reason for Carrion's interest in you was?"

"I already said: *I don't know.*"

"She's right," Jimothi reminded his fellow Councilors. "Now we're going around in circles. I say enough."

"I have to agree," Skippelwit remarked. "Though I, like Neabas, yearn for the good old days, when we could have left her with Yeddik Magash for a while. I don't have any problem with using someone like Magash if the situation really calls for it."

"Which this doesn't," Jimothi said.

"On the contrary, Jimothi," Neabas said. "There is going to be One Last Great War—"

"How do you know that?" Jimothi said.

"Just accept it. I know what the future looks like. And it's grim. The Izabella will be bloodred from Tazmagor to Babilonium. I do not exaggerate."

"And this will be all her fault?" Helio Fatha said. "Is that what you're implying?"

"*All?*" Neabas said. "No. Not all. There are ten thousand reasons why a war is bound to come eventually. Whether it will be the last war is . . . shall we say . . . open to speculation. But whether it is or isn't, it's going to be a disastrous conflict, because it comes with so many questions unanswered, many of them—maybe most, maybe all—are associated with this girl. Her presence has raised the heat under a simmering pan. And now it will quickly boil. Boil and burn."

What do I say to that? Candy silently asked Boa.

As little as possible, Boa told her. *Let him be the aggressor if that's the game he wants to play. Just pretend you're cool and sophisticated instead of some girl who was dragged up out of nowhere.*

You mean act more like a Princess? Candy replied, unable to keep the raw displeasure from her thoughts.

Well, as you put it that way . . . the Princess said.

As I put it that way what?

Yes. I suppose I do mean more like me.

Well, you keep thinking that, Candy said.

Let's not get into an argument about it. We both want the same thing.

And what's that?

To keep Yeddik Magash from taking us into a sealed room.

"So, if *anyone* has insight into Carrion's nature, it's our guest. Isn't that right, Candy? May I call you Candy? We're not your enemies, you do know that?"

"Funny, that's not the impression I get," Candy replied. "Come on. No more stupid games. You all think I was conspiring with him, don't you?"

"Conspiring to do what?" Helio Fatha said.

"How would I know?" Candy said. "I didn't do it."

"We're not fools, girl," said Zuprek, reentering the exchange with his tone now nakedly combative. "Nor are we without informants. You can't keep the company of someone like Christopher Carrion without drawing attention to yourself."

"Are you telling me that you were spying on us?"

Zuprek allowed a phantom smile to haunt his stone face. "How interesting," he said softly. "I sniff *guilt*."

"No, you don't," Candy told him. "It's just irritation you can smell. You had no right to be watching me. Watching *us*. You're the Grand Council of the Abarat and you're spying on your own citizens?"

"You're not a citizen. You're a nobody."

"That was just vicious, Zuprek."

"She's mocking us. Do any of you *see* that? She intends to be the death of us, so she mocks."

There was a long silence. Finally somebody said, "We're done with this interview. Let's move on."

"I agree," Jimothi said.

"She told us nothing, you dumb cat!" Helio yelled.

Jimothi sprang up off his chair and onto his haunches in one smooth motion.

"You know my people are closer to beasts than some of you others," he said. "Maybe you should remember that. I can smell a lot of fear in this room right now . . . a lot."

"Jimothi . . . *Jimothi!*" Candy stepped in the Cat King's line of sight. "Nobody's been hurt. It's all right. There's just some people here with no respect for those who are a little different."

Jimothi stared through Candy not hearing her, it seemed, or listening to anything she was saying. His claws curled into the table and raked the polished wood.

"Jimothi . . ."

"I have such high regard for the visitor. I admit that predisposes me to think well of her, but if I genuinely believed she would be—as Zuprek put it—'*the death of us*' there is no sentiment in the Abarat that would make me merciful."

"Well then, Zuprek," Nyritta said. "I think it falls to you to prove or not to prove."

"Forget *proof*," Neabas said. "This isn't about proof. It's about faith. We who have faith in the future of the Abarat must act to protect it. Sometimes we will be criticized for our decisions—"

"You're talking about the camps," Nyritta said.

"I don't approve of the girl hearing us discussing the

camps," Zuprek said. "It's none of her business."

"What does it matter?" Helio said. "People already know."

"It's time we discussed this," Jimothi said. "Commexo is building one on Ninnyhammer, but nobody asks questions. Nobody cares as long as the Kid keeps telling them everything's perfect."

"Don't you support the camps, Jimothi?" Nyritta said.

"No, I do not."

"Why not?" said Yobias. "Your family line is perfectly pure. Look at you. Purebred Abaratian."

"So what?"

"You'd be perfectly safe. We all would."

Candy sniffed something of significance here, but she kept her tone as casual as possible, despite the sickening feeling she had in the pit of her stomach. "Camps?"

"It's nothing to do with you," Nyritta snapped. "You shouldn't even be hearing these things."

"You make it sound like they're something you're ashamed of," Candy said.

"You're reading something into my words that's not there."

"Okay. So you're not ashamed."

"Absolutely not. I'm simply doing my duty."

"I'm glad you're proud," Jimothi jumped in, "because one day we may need to answer for every decision we've done. This interrogation, the camps. Everything." He was staring down at his paws. "If this goes bad they'll need necks for nooses. And they'll be ours. It *should* be ours. We all knew what we were doing when we started this."

"Scared for your neck, are you, Jimothi?" said Zuprek.

"No," Jimothi said. "I'm scared for my soul, Zuprek. I'm afraid I will lose it because I was too busy making camps for Pure-bloods."

Zuprek uttered a grinding growl, and started to get up from the table, his hands closed into fists.

"No, Zuprek," Nyritta Maku said, "this meeting is at a close." She threw an aside at Candy. *"Go, child. You're dismissed!"*

"I haven't finished with her!" Zuprek yelled.

"This committee has!" Maku said. This time she pushed Candy toward the door. *"Go!"*

It was already open. Candy glanced back at Jimothi, grateful for all he had done. Then she headed away through the door while Zuprek's cries echoed off the Chamber walls:

"She'll be the death of us!"

3

THE WISDOM
OF THE MOB

CANDY FOUND MALINGO WAITING for her among the crowd outside the Council Chambers. The look of relief that flooded his face when she emerged was almost worth the discomfort of the highly unpleasant interview. She did her best to hurriedly explain all that she'd just endured.

"But they've let you go?" he said when she was finished.

"Yeah," Candy said. "You thought they were going to throw me in jail?"

"It crossed my mind. There's no love for the Hereafter, that's for sure. Just listening to people passing by . . ."

"And the worst is still to come," Candy said.

"Another war?"

"That's what the Council thinks."

"Abarat against the Hereafter? Or Night against Day?"

Candy caught a few suspicious glances coming her way. "I think we should continue this conversation somewhere else," she said. "I don't want any more interrogations."

"Where do you want to go?" Malingo said.

"Anywhere, as long as it's away from here," Candy said. "I don't want to have any more questions thrown at me until I've got all the answers straight."

"And how do you plan on doing that?"

Candy threw Malingo an uneasy glance.

"Say it," he said. "Whatever it is you've got on your mind."

"I've got a Princess on my mind, Malingo. And now I know she's been there since the day I was born. It changes things. I thought I was Candy Quackenbush from Chickentown, Minnesota. And in a way I was. I lived an ordinary life on the outside. But on the inside, in here," she said, putting her finger to her temple, "I was learning what she knew. That's the only explanation that makes sense. Boa learned magic from Carrion. And then I took it from her and hid it."

"But you're saying that aloud right now."

"That's because she knows now. There's no use to play hide-and-seek, not for either of us. She's in me, and I know it. And I've got everything she knows about the Abarataraba. And *she* knows that."

I would have done the same thing, I don't doubt, Boa said. *But I think it's time we parted.*

"I agree."

"With what?" Malingo said.

"I was talking to Boa. She wants her freedom."

"Can't blame her," Malingo said.

"I don't," Candy said. "I just don't know where to start."

Ask the geshrat to tell you about Laguna Munn.

"Do you know somebody called Laguna Munn?"

"Not personally, no," Malingo said. "But there was a rhyme in one of Wolfswinkel's books about the woman."

"Do you remember it?"

Malingo thought for a moment or two. Then he recited it:

"Laguna Munn,
Had a son,
Perfect in every way.
A joy to see at work time,
And bliss to watch at play!
But oh, how did she come by him?
I cannot bear to say!"

"That's it?"

"Yeah. Supposedly one of her sons was made from all the good in her, but he was a dull child. So dull she wanted nothing to do with him. So she went and made another son—"

"Let me guess. Out of all the *evil* in her?"

"Well, whoever wrote the rhyme cannot bear to say, but yes, I think that's what we're supposed to think."

She's a very powerful woman, Boa said. *And she's been known to use her powers to help people, if she's in the mood.* Candy reported this to Malingo. Then Boa added, *Of course, she is crazy.*

"Why is there always a catch?" Candy said out loud.

"What?" Malingo said.

"Boa says Laguna Munn's crazy."

"And what—you're Candy, the sane lady? I don't think so."

"Good point."

"Let the mad find wisdom in their madness for the sane, and let the sane be grateful."

"Is that a famous saying?"

"Maybe if I say it often enough."

The geshrat talks a lot of sense . . . for a geshrat.

"What did she say?" Malingo asked Candy.

"How did you know she said anything?"

"I'm starting to see it on your face."

"She said you were very clever."

Malingo didn't look convinced. "Yeah, I bet she did," he said.

Their route took them back to the harbor via a selection of much smaller streets than those by which they had ascended to the Council Chamber. There was an air of unease in these narrow alleys and tiny yards. People were going about anxious, furtive business. It was, Candy thought, as though everyone was making plans for what to do if things didn't turn out right. Through partly opened doors that gave access into shadowy interiors she even caught a glimpse of people packing up in preparation for a hurried departure. Malingo clearly interpreted what they saw the same way because he said to Candy:

"Did the Council talk about evacuating The Great Head?"

"No."

"Then why are people getting ready to leave?"

"It makes no sense. If anywhere's safe, it's the Yebba Dim Day. Lordy Lou! This is one of the oldest structures in existence."

"Apparently old age isn't what it used to be."

They walked on in silence then, down to the harbor. There were a dozen fishing boats or more trying to find docking places so that the cargo of detritus could be unloaded.

"Bits of Chickentown . . ." Candy said grimly.

"Don't let it bother you. The people here have heard so many things about your people over the years. Now they've got something to actually hold in their hands."

"It looks like trash, most of it."

"Yeah."

"What are they going to think of Chickentown?" Candy said sadly.

Malingo said nothing. He hung back to let Candy go on ahead to examine the stuff the fishermen had scooped from the waters of the Izabella. Did the people of the Abarat think any of this was of value? Two pink plastic flamingos, washed away from somebody's garden, a lot of old magazines and bottles of pills, some bits of bashed-up furniture, a big sign with a stupid bug-eyed chicken painted on it, and another that announced the subject of the Sunday sermon at the Lutheran Church on Whittmer Street: *The Many Doors of God's Mansion.*

Somebody among the crowd, a golden-eyed, green-bearded individual lubricated by several bottles of the Kid's

Best Ale, had decided to take this opportunity to pontificate on the subject of how dangerous humankind and its
wicked technologies could be. He had plenty of support-
ers and friends among the crowd, who quickly provided
him with a couple of fish crates to stand on, from which
perch he let loose a venomous tirade. "If the tide carried
their treasures here," he said, "then it's going to bring some
of their owners too. We need to be ready. We all know
what the people of the Hereafter will do if they come back.
They'll be after the Abarataraba again."

He had only got that far when Candy heard somebody
nearby murmur her name.

She looked around, and quickly found a friendly face,
that of Izarith, who'd taken the trouble to look after Candy
when she'd first ventured into the chaotic interior of The
Great Head. She'd fed Candy, and given her a warm fire
by which to dry herself, even given Candy her first Abaratian garments to wear. Izarith was a Skizmut; her people
were born from the deep waters of what Izarith had called
Mama Izabella. Now she came through the crowd toward
Candy, wearing what looked like a homemade hat, sewn
from different kinds of seaweed. She was cradling her
baby Nazré with one arm and holding the little hand of
her daughter Maiza with the other.

She was very emotional about seeing Candy again. Her
eyes filled with silver-green tears.

"I've heard so much about you since you first came
to my house. About all the things that you've done." She
glanced at Malingo. "And I've heard about you too," she

said. "You're the one who worked for the wizard, right? On Ninnyhammer?"

Malingo made a little smile.

"This is Izarith, Malingo," Candy said. "She was very kind to me when I first got here."

"I did what anybody would have done," Izarith said. "Do you have time to come back to the house and tell me whether all the things I've heard are true? You both look hungry."

"Actually, I am a little," Malingo said.

But in the short time since Izarith had called to Candy the mood of the crowd had changed, influenced by the anger toward humankind pouring from the man with the green beard.

"We should hunt them down, every last one of them humans, and hang them," he said. "If we don't it's only a moment of time before they come looking to steal our magic again."

"You know, I don't think we have time to eat, Izarith, much as we'd liked to stay."

"You're worried about Kytomini aren't you?"

"Is he the one saying he'd like me hanged?"

"He hates everybody. Right now it's your people, Candy. It could be geshrats in five minutes."

"There's a lot of people agreeing with him," Candy said.

"People like to have somebody to hate. Me, I'm too busy raising the little ones."

"What about your husband?"

"Oh, Ruthus is working on his boat right now. Patching it up for selling. We're getting out of the Yebba Dim Day as soon as we have the money. It's getting too dangerous."

"Is his boat seaworthy?" Malingo said.

"Ruthus says it is."

"Then perhaps he'd take us to the Nonce, for a price."

"The Nonce?" Izarith said. "Why are you going there?"

"We're meeting friends," Candy said. She reached in her pockets as she talked, and brought out all the paterzem she had. Malingo did the same. "Here's all the money we've got," she said to Izarith. "Would that pay for the journey?"

"I'm sure it'll be more than enough," Izarith replied. "Come on, I'll take you to Ruthus. The boat's nothing fancy, just so you know."

"We don't need anything fancy," Candy said. "We just need to get away from here."

Izarith lent Candy her wide-brimmed hat, to keep anyone in the increasingly agitated crowd from realizing that they had a member of humankind in their midst, then led Candy and Malingo down the quay, past vessels large and small to one of the smallest of the lot.

There was a man on board doing some final work on his vessel with brush and paint. Izarith called her husband away from his work, and quickly explained the situation. Meanwhile Candy watched Kytomini's audience from the corner of her eye. She had a nasty feeling that she and Malingo had not passed through the crowd entirely unnoticed, a feeling that was lent weight when several of the crowd's members turned to look in Candy's direction, and after a moment, started to walk down the quay toward them.

"We're in trouble, Izarith," Candy said. "Or least I am. I think it would be better if you weren't seen with me."

"What, *them*?" Izarith said, staring back contemptuously at the approaching thugs. "I'm not afraid of them."

"Candy's right, love," Ruthus said. "Take the children quickly and go around the back of the fish market. Hurry."

"Thank you," Candy said. "Next time it won't be so rushed."

"You tell my husband to come back to us as quickly as possible."

"He will, don't worry," Candy replied.

The man with the green beard, who had first incited the anger with his speechifying, was now breaking through the approaching little mob of bullies to lead it.

"Are we going?" Ruthus yelled.

"Oh, Lordy Lou, are we ever," Candy said.

"Then *come on!*"

Candy jumped into the boat. Its boards creaked.

"If ye've cracked her boards and you drown, don't blame me." Ruthus grinned.

"We won't drown," Malingo said following Candy. "This girl has work to do. Great work!"

Candy smiled. (It was true. What, or how, or when—
she had no idea. But it was true.)

Ruthus was racing to the wheelhouse yelling to
Malingo as he did so: "Cut the rope, geshrat. Be quick!"

The dock was reverberating as the mob, its numbers
increasing, followed Green Beard's lead.

"I see you, girl!" he yelled, "and I know what you are!"

"Rope's severed, Ruthus!"

"Hold on, then! And pray!"

"*Go!*" Candy yelled to Ruthus.

"Your crimes against the Abarat must be punished—"

The last word was repeated by every hate-filled throat
in the crowd. *"Punished!" "Punished!" "Pun—"*

The third time, the threat was drowned out by the
raucous roar of Ruthus's little boat, as its engine came to
life.

A cloud of yellow exhaust fumes erupted from the
stern of the boat, its density blotting all sight of the mob,
just as its din had blotted all sound.

Ruthus's work was not over. They had got away from
the dock, but they were not yet out of the harbor. And
there were more opportunistic fishermen bringing in car-
gos of garbage all the time. If Ruthus's boat had been any
larger, it would have been caught in the confusion. But it
was a tiny thing, and nimble-like, especially with Ruthus
at the wheel. By the time the smoke trail had cleared, the
boat was out of the harbor and into the Straits of Dusk.

4

THE KID

CANDY'S ESCAPE FROM THE mob in the Yebba
Dim Day had not gone unnoticed. The greatest concentra-
tion of eyes spying her jeopardy were at Three O'Clock
in the Morning. At the heart of that extraordinary city
was a vast round mansion, and at the heart of the mansion, a circular viewing chamber, where the innumerable
mechanical spies that were scattered around the Abarat—
perfect imitations of flora and fauna so cunningly crafted
as to be indistinguishable from the real thing, but for the
fact that each carried a miniscule camera—reported what
they saw. There were literally thousands of screens in the
Circular Room covering the inner and outer walls, and
Rojo Pixler would have been there, watching the world
he had brought into being—its little tragedies, its little
farces, its little spectacles of love and death on full display—but today he was not riding around the room on
his levitation disc, surveying the archipelago. The team of
island-watchers was currently led by his trusted colleague,

Dr. Voorzangler, wearing his beloved spectacles which offered the illusion that his two eyes were one. It was he who was noting any significant comings and goings, one of which was that of Candy Quackenbush. Voorzangler ordered his second, third, and fourth in command to be sure that each reminded the other to remind Voorzangler to report the movements of the girl from the Hereafter to the great architect when he finally returned.

Though the phrase "when he returns" usually carried little significance, today it did. Today the great architect was surveying the site of his next great creation: an undersea city in the deepest trenches of the Sea of Izabella. Why? Voorzangler had asked Pixler more than once to which the answer had always been the same: to put a name to the hitherto nameless, and embrace the wonders that surely existed in the lightless deeps. And when innocent endeavors had been achieved and those creatures had been catalogued, then he would be able to undertake the true objective of this endeavor (one which he had only shared with Voorzangler): to lay in the hidden habitat of these unknown life-forms the foundation of a deep-water city so ambitious in scale and design that the blazing immensity of Commexo City would be as a rough sketch might be to the finished masterwork.

Even now, as Voorzangler watched Candy Quackenbush leave the Yebba Dim Day, Pixler was visible on an adjacent screen climbing into his bathyscaphe, giving the camera a confident wave as he did so. Inside he had only artificial intelligences beside him, but their cold company was all he needed.

His face appeared now in the fish-eye lens that relayed his presence at the master controls of the bathyscaphe. His voice, when he spoke, had a metallic tone.

"Don't look so worried, Voorzangler," Pixler said. "I know what I'm doing."

"Of course, sir," the doctor replied. "But I wouldn't be human if I wasn't a little concerned."

"Boasting now?" Pixler said.

"About what, sir?"

"About your humanity. There aren't very many employees of the company who could say such a thing." Pixler ran his hands over the bathyscaphe's controls, turning on all the vessel's functions. "Smile, Voorzangler," he said. "We're making history, you and I."

"I just wish we were making it on another day," Voorzangler replied.

"Why?"

"Just . . . bad dreams, sir. Every rational man is allowed a few irrational dreams, wouldn't you say?"

"What did you dream?" Pixler wanted to know. The bathyscaphe's door slammed closed and sealed with a hiss. An artificial voice announced that the winches were all fully functional.

"It was nothing of consequence."

"Then tell me what you dreamed, Voorzangler."

Voorzangler's single eye dodged left and right, looking for a way to avoid meeting the great architect's inquiring gaze. But Pixler had always been able to stare him down.

"All right," he said. "I'll tell you. I dreamed that everything went perfectly well with the descent except—"

"Except?"

"Once you got into the very deepest place . . ."

"Yes?"

"There was a city there already."

"Ah. And its occupants?"

"They'd gone, thousands of years before. Great scaly fins they'd had. And beauty in their faces. There were mosaics on the walls. Such bright, ambitious eyes."

"And what happened to them?"

Voorzangler shook his head. "They left no clue. Unless their perfect city *was* the clue."

"What kind of clue is perfection?"

"Well, you would know, sir."

Pixler was not so easily persuaded. "Why did you have to have that stupid dream? You may have cursed my entire enterprise."

"We're scientists, sir. We don't believe in curses."

"Don't tell me what I believe in. Find me the Kid."

"He's being searched for."

"And not found?"

"Not so far."

"Don't bother. I just thought he'd want to see me off."

The automatic doors of the bathyscaphe were closing. A flicker of anxiety crossed the great architect's face. But he would not be commanded by it. The three massive winches—one of them supplying power to the bathy-scaphe, the second delivering clean air, the third, and largest, bearing the weight of the immense vessel—were paying out steadily now. Voorzangler looked at the readings on the screens that surrounded the cabin. Hundreds of tiny cameras, like shoals of one-eyed fish, circled the descent column down which the bathyscaphe would be coming, their motion and their iridescence designed to draw out of the darkness every kind of mysterious creature that hunted in their oppressive depths.

"What happens if he never comes back?" said a forlorn voice.

Voorzangler looked away from the screens.

It was the Kid who had spoken. For once his smile had deserted him. He watched the bathyscaphe's descent with the expression of a genuinely deserted child.

"We must pray he does," Voorzangler said.

"But I always prayed to him," the Kid said.

"Then, my child, I suggest you think of another God, as quickly as you can."

"Why?" said the Kid, his voice tinged with a little hysteria. "Do you think Pops will die down there?"

"Now would I think that?" Voorzangler said, his response unconvincing.

"I heard you two talking about something that lives deep down in the dark. It's called the Recogacks, isn't it?"

"They, boy," Voorzangler said. "They are called the Requiax."

"Ha!" the Kid said, like he'd caught Voorzangler in a lie. "So they *do* exist."

"That's one of the things your father's gone down to find out. Whether they exist or not."

"It's not fair. He's mine. If he goes down into the dark and never comes up again what will I do? I'll kill myself. That's what I'll do!"

"No, you won't."

"I will! You see if I don't!"

"Your father's a very special man. A genius. He's always going to be looking for new places to explore and things to build."

"Well, I *hate* him!" the Kid said. He took out his catapult, loaded it with a stone, and aimed it at the biggest screen. He could scarcely have failed to miss. The screen shattered when the stone struck it, exploding in a shower of white sparks and Commexo Patent Glass fragments.

"Stop that immediately!" Voorzangler said.

But the Kid had already loaded his catapult again and was firing. A second screen went to pieces.

"I shall have to summon the guards if you don't—"

He didn't need to finish. The Kid had already seen something on the screens that made him forget his catapult. There was a girl being watched by the spy cameras: a girl who the Kid knew, at least by sight, because his father had summoned up her image for him the night he'd come back from Ninnyhammer, where he met her.

"Her name's Candy Quackenbush, my boy," the Kid

said, perfectly imitating his Creator's voice.

The sight of Candy put all of the Kid's rage toward Pixler out of his mind. Now he was consumed by curiosity.

"Where are you off to, Candy Quackenbush?" he said too quietly for Voorzangler to hear. "Why don't you come to the City and be my friend? I need a friend."

He went to the lowest of the screens that carried her image and, reaching out, he gently put his hand upon her face.

"Please come," he murmured. "I don't mind waiting. I'll be here. Just come. *Please.*"

5

REMNANTS OF WICKEDNESS

ABOUT THREE WEEKS AFTER the waters of the Sea of Izabella had crossed the threshold between the Abarat and the Hereafter, flooding many of the streets of Chickentown and demolishing in its force and fury the town's finest old houses along with the courthouse, the church and the Henry Murkitt Public Library, Candy's father, Bill Quackenbush began to take nightly walks through the town.

Bill had never had any enthusiasm for exercise before now. He'd always been happiest at his most sedentary, slumped in his leatherette throne in front of the television with beer, cold pizza and a warm remote control close at hand. But he no longer watched television. During the early evenings he sat in his chair drinking his way through a dozen cans of beer, smoking until every ashtray was filled, and on occasion eating slices of white bread. As the hours crept on, the members of his family would slope off to bed, not even his wife, Melissa, bothering to say good night.

Only once the house was finally still and silent, usually

a little after midnight, would Bill go into the kitchen, brew some strong coffee to wake himself up, and prepare for the trek ahead by putting on his old work boots, still crusted with dried chicken blood, and his dark blue windbreaker. The weather was becoming unpredictable, as autumn's grip deepened. Some nights there'd be rain in the gusts from the north, even sleet on a couple of occasions. But he didn't let the drop in the temperature change his rituals.

There was something he needed to do out in the streets of the town where he'd lived all his life: important work that his dulled mind tried to comprehend day after day as he sat in front of the blank television screen, the drapes drawn against the October sky; work that demanded he leave the comfort of his chair and venture out to wander through the town even though he had no idea what, or why, he was seeking. All he had by way of a compass was the deep-rooted conviction that one night he would turn a corner somewhere in the town and find before him the solution to this mystery.

But each night it was the same story: exhaustion and disappointment. Just before dawn he'd come home to the dark, silent house, with his hands empty and his heart aching as it had never ached: not in sorrow, nor in regret, and certainly never out of love.

Tonight, however, there was a strange certainty in him that had him so eager to start his search that he had headed out into the night as soon as he heard Melissa switch off the lamp beside the bed where they had once slept as husband and wife.

In his haste to leave the house he had not only forgotten to make some coffee, but also to put on his windbreaker. No matter. One evil canceled out the other: the cold so bracing he could scarcely have been more awake, more *alive*. Though his fingers rapidly became numb, and his eyes ached in their sockets, the anticipation of joy and the joy of anticipation were so powerful that he pressed on without concern for his well-being, allowing his feet to choose streets to turn into that he would never have chosen, or perhaps even seen, before tonight.

Finally his wanderings brought him to a little cul-de-sac called Caleb Place. The waters of the Izabella had done extremely devastating work here. Trapped within the basin of the cul-de-sac, they had thrown their destructive power around the ring of houses, completely leveling several of them and leaving only three with any hope of being rebuilt. The most coherent of the surviving buildings was the one to which Bill Quackenbush was drawn. It was heavily cordoned off with wide plastic tape on which was repeatedly printed the warning:

DANGEROUS STRUCTURE DO NOT ENTER

Bill ignored the warning, of course. Ducking under the tape, he scrambled up over the rubble and into the interior of the house. The moon was bright enough to spill through the stripped roof to illuminate the interior with a silvery wash.

At the front door he paused for a long moment and

listened. He could hear an unidentifiable sound from the interior: rhythmical, muffled. He listened carefully so as to at least locate its source. It was coming from somewhere upstairs, he concluded. He pushed open the front door, and waded through the litter of trashed furniture and bricks between the door and the stairs. The floodwaters had stripped virtually everything off the walls: the pictures, the wallpaper, even much of the plaster, which had fallen away in cobs making some of the stairs difficult to negotiate. But Bill had met and overcome many obstacles since Candy's time in the Abarat. He wasn't going to be dissuaded from this journey by a few littered stairs.

He experienced a few clammy moments as he gingerly stepped from one cracked timber to the next. But his luck held. He reached the landing, which was more solid than the stairs, without incident. He paused a moment to get his bearings, then he started down the passage toward the room at the far end, from which came, he was certain, the strange noise that had drawn him up here.

The room still had its door, which was open a few inches. He paused before it, almost reverentially, and then, using the pressure of just two fingers, he pushed. Creaking, the door swung open. The moon's brightness illuminated half the room. The rest was in shadow. On the moonlit boards he saw scattered the source of the sounds he'd heard. Dozens of birds, common creatures he couldn't have named even though he saw them on Followell Street whenever he'd gone out back. They were lying on the floor, as though some merciless force was pinning their heads to the boards, leaving them to flutter wildly, beating their wings so violently that the air was filled with flecks of feathers, which the constant updraft from the panicked wings below kept in circulation.

"What is this . . ." he muttered to himself.

In the dark half of the room, something moved. Something that Bill knew wasn't a bird.

"Who's there?" he said.

There was a second motion in the dark and something suddenly propelled itself out of the shadows into the wash of moonlight. It landed among the stricken birds no more than a yard or two from where Bill was standing, then leaped up again, so that with its second leap it struck the moonlit wall opposite the door. Bill got only a blurred impression.

It might have been a brightly colored monkey, except that he'd never seen a monkey move so fast. The motion drove the birds into a fresh frenzy, and some, in their terror, found the strength to escape their pinning. They rose into the middle of the room, apparently unwilling, despite the open roof above them, to depart the presence of whatever had attracted them here in the first place.

Their excited circling made it even harder for Bill to get a clear sense of the thing.

What was this strange entity pinned to the wall? It seemed to be made of fabric rather than skin: a patchwork of four, perhaps five, colored materials that ranged from livid scarlet to one of polished black with a dash of vibrant blue.

The beast didn't appear to have any recognizable anatomy; there was no sign of anything resembling a head or even any of the features a head might have carried: it had no eyes that Bill could make out, nor ears, nor nose, nor mouth. Bill felt profoundly disappointed. Surely this couldn't be the answer to the mystery of his nightly searches around town. The answer he'd been seeking had to be something more than some formless scraps of stained felt.

However, though there was little about the creature he found beguiling, he was still curious about it.

"What are you?" he asked, more to himself than anything.

The creature's response, much to Bill's surprise, was to stretch out its four extremities and draw all its power into itself. Then it kicked off from the wall and flew at Bill as though plucked by an unseen hand.

Bill was too slow, too surprised, to avoid it. The thing wrapped itself around him, blinding him completely. In the sudden darkness Bill's sense of smell worked overtime. The beast stank! It had the stench of a heavy fur coat that had been put away soaking wet and had been left in a wardrobe to rot ever since.

The stench oppressed him, disgusted him. He grabbed hold of the thing and tried to pull it off his head.

"Finally," the creature said, "William Quackenbush, you heard our call."

"Get off me!"

"Only if you will listen to us."

"Us?"

"Yes. You're hearing five voices. There are five of us, William Quackenbush, here to serve you."

"To . . . serve me?" Bill stopped fighting with the thing. "You mean, like, to obey me?"

"Yes!"

Bill grinned a spittle-grin. "Anything I say?"

"Yes!"

"Then stop smothering me, you damn fools!"

The five responded, instantly leaping off his head and back onto the wall again.

"What are you?"

"Well, why not? If he doesn't like the truth because it sounds crazy, then he's learned something hasn't he?" the thing said to itself. Then it addressed Bill. "We were once five hats, belonging to members of the Noncian Magic Circle. But our owners were murdered and the murderer then celebrated his getting what he wanted by having a heart attack. So we were left looking for someone to give our powers to."

"And you chose me."

"Of course."

"Why 'of course'? Nobody has ever willingly chosen me for anything."

"Why do you think, lord?"

Bill knew the answer without having to think.

"My daughter."

"Yes," said the thing. "She has great power. No doubt it comes from you."

"From me? What does that mean?"

"It means you will possess greater influence than you ever dreamed of owning. Even in your wildest dreams of godhood."

"I never dreamed of being God."

"Then wake up, William Quackenbush! Wake up and know the reality!"

Though Bill was already awake, his instinctive self understood the deeper significance of what he was being told. The expression on his face opened like a door, and whatever was behind it caught the attention of the creature that had once been several hats.

"Look at you, Billy-boy!" it said, its five voices suddenly changed and harmonized in admiration. "Such a radiance there is out of you! Such a strong, clear light to drive all the fear away."

"Me?"

"Who else? Think Billy-boy. *Think*. Who can deliver us from the terror that your child is about to call down upon the world if not *you* who made her?"

At the moment when the creature had talked about Bill's "radiance" the many silent birds Bill had seen rose into the air and circled around Bill in a vortex of bright black eyes and applauding wings.

"What are they doing?" Bill asked the shapeless thing.

"Paying homage to you."

"Well, I don't like it."

"What do you want me to do?"

"Stop them."

"Stop them dead?"

"Sure."

"Sure," the creature said, catching perfectly the tone of Bill's response.

"Are you making fun of me?"

"Never," came the reply.

A heartbeat later every single bird dropped out of the air and fell lifeless in the debris.

"Better?" the creature said.

Bill considered the silence.

"A whole lot," he finally replied. He laughed lightly. It was a laugh he'd forgotten he was capable of: that of a man who had nothing to lose and nothing to fear.

He glanced at his watch.

"Almost dawn," he said. "I'd better be going. What do I do with you?"

"Wear us. On your head. Like a turban."

"Foreigners wear those."

"You *are* a foreigner, Billy-boy. You don't belong here. You'll get used to wearing us. In our previous life we made very impressive hats. We've just come unglued of late."

"I know exactly how you feel," Bill said. "But that's all going to change now, isn't it?"

"Indeed it is," said the remnants of Kaspar Wolfswin- kel's five hats. "You've found us. Everything changes now."

6

UNDER JIBARISH

RUTHUS'S LITTLE BOAT CARRIED Candy and Malingo southwest down the Straits of Dusk and between the islands of Huffaker and Ninnyhammer to Jibarish, in the wilds of which a tribe of women called the Qwarv lived by preying on weary travelers, who they then cooked and ate. Rumor had it that Laguna Munn, the sorceress they had come to find, was sympathetic to the Qwarv, despite their appetites, tending to them when they were sick, and even accepting their offer to eat with them on occasion. Certainly the island was a fit place for such repugnant events to occur. It stood at Eleven O'clock at Night: just one hour from the horror of Midnight.

The islands were still, however, slivers of time sealed off from one another. Only sounds would find their way through for some reason, echoes of echoes, eerily remote. But it wasn't difficult to identify the sounds from the nearby Hour of Gorgossium. There was demolition going on. Massive land-clearing engines were at work, bringing down walls, digging up foundations. The noise echoed off the heights of Jibarish's west-facing cliffs.

"What are they doing over there?" Malingo wondered aloud.

"It's best not to ask," Ruthus said in a hushed tone. "Or even think about it." He stared up at the stars, which were so bright over Jibarish that the sum of their light was greater than even the brightest moon. "Better to think of the beauty of light, yes, than to think of what's going on in the darkness. Curiosity kills. I lost my brother Skafta—my twin brother—just because he asked too many questions."

"I'm sorry to hear that," Candy said.

"Thank you, Candy. Now, where do you want me to let you off? On the big island or the little one?"

"I didn't know there *was* a big one and a little one."

"Oh yes. Of course. The Qwarv rule the big island. The little one is for ordinary folks. And the witch, of course."

"By witch, you mean Laguna Munn?"

"Yes."

"Then that's the island we want."

"You're going to see the incantatrix?"

"Yes."

"You do know she's crazy?"

"Yes. We've heard people say that. But people say a lot of things that aren't true."

"About you, you mean?"

"I wasn't—"

"They do, you know. They say all kinds of wacko things."

"Like what?" Malingo said.

"It doesn't matter," Candy said. "I don't need to hear silly things people dream up. They don't know me."

"And you as well, Malingi," said Ruthus.

"Malingo," said Malingo.

"They say terrible things about you too."

"Now I *have* to know."

"You've got a choice, geshrat. Either I tell you some ridiculous gossip I heard, and while I'm wasting my time doing that the current throws us up on those rocks, or I forget the nonsense and do the job you're paying me for."

"Get us to solid ground," Malingo said, sounding disappointed.

"Happily," Ruthus said, and turned his attention back to the wheel.

The waters around the boat were becoming frenzied.

"You know . . . I don't want to be telling you your job," Candy said, "but if you're not careful the current's going to carry us into that cave. You do see it, don't you?"

"Yes, I see it," Ruthus yelled over the roar and rage of the Izabella. "That's where we're going."

"But the water's—"

"Very rough."

"Yes."

"Frenzied."

"Yes."

"Then you'd better hold on tight, hadn't you?"

Before another word could be exchanged, the boat entered the cave. The passage into the cave forced the foaming waters to climb and quicken, quicken and climb, until the top two feet of the boat's mast were snapped off as it scraped the roof. For a few terrifying moments it seemed the entire boat and those aboard would be scraped to mush and splinters against the roof. But, as quickly as the waters had risen, they subsided again without any further damage done. The channel widened and the racing current eased.

Though they had already been borne a considerable distance into the body of the island, there was a plentiful supply of light, its source the colonies of phosphorescent creatures that encrusted the walls and stalactites that hung from the roof. They were an unlikely marriage of crab and bat, their bizarre anatomies decorated with elaborate symmetrical designs.

Directly ahead of them lay a small island, with a steep wall around it, and rising in a very sharp gradient, a single hillock covered with red-leaved trees (that apparently had no need of sunlight to prosper) and a maze of whitewashed buildings arrayed beneath the garish canopy.

"We'll need rope to scale that wall," Malingo said.

"Either that or we use *that*," Candy said, pointing to a small door in the wall.

"Oh . . ." said Malingo.

Ruthus brought the boat around so that they could step out of the vessel and through the door.

"Give my love to Izarith," Candy said to Ruthus. "And tell her I'll see her again soon."

Ruthus looked doubtful.

"Are you sure you want me to just leave you here?" he said.

"We don't know how long we'll be with Laguna Munn," Candy said. "And I think things are getting cha-otic. Everyone's stirred up for some reason. So I really think you should go back and be with your family, Ruthus."

"And you, geshrat?"

"Where she goes, I go," Malingo replied.

Ruthus shook his head.

"Crazy, the both of you," he remarked.

"Well, if things go badly for us, you have nothing to blame yourself for, Ruthus," Candy said. "We're doing this in spite of your good advice." She paused, smiled. "And we *will* see you again."

Malingo had already climbed out of the boat and was squatting on the narrow step, trying the door. It opened without any forcing.

"Thank you again," Candy said to Ruthus, and stepped out of the boat, heading through the small and roughly painted door in pursuit of Malingo.

Before she stepped over the threshold, though, she glanced back down the bank. She had no chance to call good-bye to Ruthus. The possessive waters of the Izabella had already seized hold of the little boat and it was being carried away from the island, while the winged crabs applauded the boat's escape with a mingled ovation of wing and claw.

7

THE SORROWS
OF THE BAD SON

A STEEP, NARROW-STEPPED PATH WOUND
its way up from the door in the wall through the trees.
Candy and Malingo climbed. Though there was a wash
of visible brightness through the orange-red canopy, very
little of it found its way down to the path. There were,
however, small lamps set beside the steps to light the way.
Beyond their throw the thicket was dense and the darkness denser still. But it wasn't deserted.

"There's plenty of eyes on us," Candy said very quietly.

"But no noises. No birds chirping. No insects buzzing
around."

"Maybe there's something else here. Something
they're scared of."

"Well, if there is," Malingo said, speaking with a fake
clarity, "I hope it knows we're here to cause trouble."

His performance earned him a reply.

"You say you're here to cause trouble, geshrat," said a
young voice, "but saying it doesn't make it true."

"Why are you here?" said a second voice.

"The sons," Malingo murmured, the words barely audible to Candy, who was standing a single step away from him.

"Yes," said the first voice. "We're the sons."

"And we'll hear you," taunted the second, "however quietly you whisper. So don't waste your time."

"Where are you?" Candy asked them, slowly climbing another step as she did so, and scanning the shadows off to their right, from which direction the voices had seemed to come.

In her hand she quickly conjured a little ball of cloud-light; a cold flame she had learned to call up from Boa. It had been, Candy vaguely thought, one of the earliest pieces of magic Candy had filched from Boa's collection. Candy squeezed it tightly.

The moment would come when she had one of Laguna Munn's boys close enough to—

There! A shadowy form moved across her field of vision. She didn't hesitate. She raised her arm and let it go. It blazed yellow-white and blue, its illumination spilling only down at the figure Candy had willed it to illuminate. The cloud-light did its job and Candy saw the first of Laguna Munn's boys. He looked like a little devil, Candy thought, with his stunted horns and his squat body made of shadow and shards of color, as though he'd stood in the way of an exploding stained-glass window, which hadn't hurt him because his body was made of Dark Side of the Moon Jell-O.

When he spoke, as now he did, his voice was completely mismatched with his appearance. He had the precise, well-cultured voice of a boy who'd been to a fancy school.

"I'm Mama's Bad Boy," he said.

"Oh really? And what's your name?"

He sighed, as though the question presented huge difficulties.

"What's the problem?" Candy said. "I only asked your name."

There was something in her plain, unpretentious Minnesotan soul that was not taking to Laguna Munn's self-proclaimed Bad Boy.

"Oh, I don't know . . ." he said, nibbling at his thumbnail. "It's just hard to choose when you've got so many. Would you like to know how many names I have?"

She didn't.

"All right, I'm listening. How many?"

"Seven hundred and nineteen," he said rather proudly.

"Wow," Candy said flatly. Then, even more flatly, "Why?"

"Because I can. Mama said I can have anything I like. So I have a lot of names. But you can call me . . . Thrashing Jam? No, no! Pieman Hambadikin? No! Jollo B'gog! Yes! Jollo B'gog it is!"

"All right. And I'm—"

"Candy Quackenbush of Chickencoop."

"Chicken*town*."

"Coop. Town. Whichever. And that's your geshrat

friend with you, Malingo. You saved him from being the slave of the wizard Kaspar Wolfswinkel."

"You've certainly done your homework," Candy said.

"Homework . . . homework . . ." Jollo B'gog said, puzzling over the word. "Oh. Work given to students by their tutors in your world, which they attempt to avoid doing by any possible means." He grinned.

"That's right," Candy said. "On the nose!"

"On the nose!" Jollo B'gog said triumphantly. "I got it on the nose! I got it on the nose!"

"Somebody's enjoying themselves," said a woman, somewhere beyond the spill of the light that Candy had shed on Jollo.

The boy's good humor instantly died away, not out of fear, Candy thought, but out of a peculiar reverence for the speaker.

"Bad Boy?" she said.

"Yes, Mama."

"Will you find our guest Malingo something to eat and drink, please?"

"Of course, Mama."

"And send the girl up to me."

"As you wish, Mama."

Candy wanted to point out that she was also hungry and thirsty, but this wasn't the time to be saying it, she knew.

"All right, you heard Mama," Jollo said to Candy. "She wants you to go to her, so all you need to do is follow the silver eye." He pointed to a foot-wide eye, its pupil black, the lens of it silver, which hovered in between the trees.

"Should I come?" Malingo said to Candy.

"If I need you, I swear I'll yell. Really loud."

"Happy?" Jollo said to Malingo. "If Mama tries to eat her, she's going to yell."

"Your mother wouldn't—"

"No she wouldn't, geshrat," Jollo replied. "It's humor. A joke?"

"I know what a joke is," Malingo said without much certainty. He looked for Candy, but she'd already followed the silver eye off the path into the darkness of the trees.

"Come on, geshrat. Let's get you fed," Jollo said. "If you hear Candy call, you can go straight to her. I won't even try to stop you. I promise."

8

LAGUNA MUNN

Laguna Munn's island had seemed small when viewed from Ruthus's boat, but now that Candy was being led up through its darkened slopes it seemed far larger than she'd expected. She'd left the cloud-light behind her, but the silver eye shed its own light as it led her through the dense thicket. She was glad of its guidance. The ground beneath her feet was becoming steeper, and the trees she was moving between—sometimes having to force a gap large enough for her to get through—became steadily more gnarled and ancient.

There was a wind blowing up here on the higher elevations. It made the antiquated trees creak, and their branches shake down a dry rain of leaves and withered fruit. Candy didn't let anything distract her from her guide. She followed it as closely as the passage through the choked undergrowth would allow, until it led her to a place where the trees' lowest branches had woven their twigs with the bushes below, forming a wall of knitted wood. Candy stood before it a moment, while the eye cast its light upon the interwoven twigs. A few seconds went by and then a shimmer of motion passed through the wall, and where the eye had shone its light the wall unwove itself, opening a narrow door. The trees and shrubs were still parting when the voice that had spoken to Jollo said, "Either come in or be gone, girl. But don't just *stand* there."

"Thank you," Candy said, and stepped between the writhing branches.

She had come to the top of the island. The wind here moved in sighing circles, the freight of leaves it bore rising and falling as it was swept around her. It wasn't just leaves in the circling gusts, however. There were animals too, creatures of every size and shape moving around her, their flanks pale as the moon sometimes, sometimes red as a setting sun, their eyes blazing green and gold, and all leaving trails of motion on the shadowy air.

She couldn't be sure whether she was witnessing a joyous race or a life-and-death pursuit. Whichever it was, it suddenly turned in her direction, and she dropped to the ground, hugging her head with her hands as she felt the rush of life passing over her. It was loud now. Not only the rush of wind but the thunder of hooves and paws, and the screeches, roars, and howls of perhaps a thousand species, perhaps twice that.

"Do you not yet know the difference between a dreamed thing and a living one?" Laguna Munn said, her voice closer to Candy than the sound of the animals' passage.

"Dreamed . . . ?" Candy said.

"Yes, girl," Laguna replied. "Dreamed. Imagined. Conjured. Invented."

Candy dared a cautious glance up. Whatever the incantatrix was saying, the hooves and the claws that were still racing over the top of Candy's head looked real and extremely dangerous.

"It's an illusion," Laguna Munn said. "Stand up. Go on. If you don't trust me, how can anything I try to do for you have a hope of working?"

Candy saw the sense in this. She raised her head a little more. The violence of the living torrent galloped over the dome that protected her thoughts. It hurt. Not just her skull, creaking beneath the assault of the hooves, but the bones of her face, and the delicate tissues it protected.

If she didn't endure this assault she'd not find anyone else to tell her what Laguna Munn could.

She stood up.

Lordy Lou, the pain of it! Even though it was an illusion it was still strong enough to make blood trickle from her nose. She wiped it away with the back of her hand, but a fresh flow immediately followed. And still the animals thundered on, the violence of their passage buffeting her as they pressed on.

"I know you're there, Laguna Munn," she said. "You can't hide forever. Come on. Show yourself."

Still the creatures came, their passage through her as powerful as ever. The blood running from her nose was in her mouth. She tasted it, copper and salt. How much longer could her body survive this relentless onslaught? Surely the incantatrix wouldn't let her die because she failed?

"I'm not going to die," she told herself.

Again, she tried to force her vision through the conjuration. Again the conjuration forced its reality upon her.

You'll never do it without me, Boa said.

"Help me, then."

Why should I?

A wave of anger rose up in Candy. She was sick of Boa; sick of every egocentric woman with more power than compassion that she'd encountered, starting with Miss Schwartz, and finishing up with Mater Motley. She'd had enough of them—all of them.

And finally, her eyes started to prick the illusion that was battering her, giving her a glimpse of the mysterious Laguna Munn. She was what Candy's mother, Melissa, would have called a "big-boned woman," by which she'd meant fat.

"I . . . see . . . you," Candy said.

"Good," Laguna Munn replied. "Then we can proceed."

Laguna raised her hand, and made a fist of it. The tidal flow of living things ceased instantly, leaving Candy with aching bones, a buzzing head, and a bloody nose. Laguna spoke, her voice soft.

"I didn't expect to meet you, though I was curious, I must say. I thought the Fantomaya had your affections."

"The Fantomaya is the reason I'm here," Candy said.

"Ah, so somebody's been telling you stories."

"It's not just a story!" Candy snapped.

The anger was still in her, bubbling up.

"Calm yourself," Laguna Munn said. She seemed to rise from her chair and move toward Candy without taking a single step. "What did I see in your head, girl?"

"Something more than me," Candy said. "Another person."

Laguna's eyes, already huge, grew larger still, and brighter. "Do you know the name of this other in your head?"

"Yes. Her name's Princess Boa. Her soul was taken from her body by the women of the Fantomaya——"

"Stupid, stupid . . ." Laguna Munn muttered to herself.

"Me?" Candy said.

"No, not you," Laguna replied. "Them. Playing with things that they had no business with."

"Well, they did it. And now I want to undo it."

"Why not go to them?"

"Because they don't know I know. If they'd wanted us to separate eventually, they would have told me she was there, wouldn't they?"

"I suppose that's reasonable, yes."

"Besides, one of them has already been killed because

I came over to the Abarat——"

"So if any other witch was going to die you'd prefer it to be me."

"That's not what I meant."

"It's how it sounded."

"What is it about this place? Everybody playing stupid games! It makes me sick." She wiped her bloodied nose again. "If you're not going to help me, then I'll just do it myself."

Laguna Munn didn't attempt to conceal her astonishment or the seam of admiration that ran beside it.

"Lordy Lou. You would, wouldn't you?"

"If I have to. I can't find out who I really am until she's out of my head."

"And what happens to her?"

"I don't know. There's a lot of things I don't know. That's why I came to you."

"Tell me honestly, does the Princess want to have a life free of you?"

"Yes," Candy said with confidence. Laguna stared at her with intimidating intensity. "The problem is that I don't really know where I stop and she begins. I must have been born with her already in my head. And we've always lived together, her and me."

"I should warn you, if she truly doesn't want to leave, then you'll have a fight on your hands. A fight like that could be fatal."

"I'll take the risk."

"Do you understand what I'm—"

"Yes. It could kill me."

"Yes. And I'm assuming that you've also considered the fact that there may be parts of you that aren't you at all?"

"That are her? Yes. I've thought of that too. And I'd lose them. But if they were never mine in the first place—never me—then I'm not really losing anything, am I?"

Laguna Munn's gilded gaze softened.

"What a crazy conversation there must be going on inside your head right now," she said. "And I'm not talking about the one between you and your stowaway. It's a pity you and I have met so late in life," she said with what seemed to be genuine regret.

"I've only just turned sixteen," Candy said.

"I know. And that's young, I realize. But there are roads to revelation that should have been laid when you were just a baby, and laying them is going to be harder now. You came here in search of freedom and revelation, and I'm afraid all I can give you is warnings and confusion."

"So you can't separate me from Boa?"

"That? I can do that. I can't make any predictions concerning the consequences of the separation. But I can promise you that you will never be the same again."

PART TWO

YOU, OR NOT I

As thorn and flower upon a single branch sit,
So hate beside my love for her will fit.
Two pieces of one thing, that make a whole.
As you and I, my love, a single soul.

—Christopher Carrion

9

A NEW TYRANNY

IT WOULD HAVE COME as no surprise to the occupants of Gorgossium that the sounds of demolition were audible from the waters surrounding the island. Its inhabitants could barely hear themselves think.

The Midnight Island was undergoing great changes, all designed to deepen the darkness that held Gorgossium in thrall. It was not the darkness of a starless sky. It was something far more profound. This darkness was in the very substance of the island. In its dirt, in its rock and fog.

Over the years many had attempted to find the words to evoke the horrors of Gorgossium. All had failed. The abominations which that island had brought to birth, and nurtured, and sent out often across the islands to do bloody and cruel work defied even the most articulate of souls.

Even Samuel Klepp, who in the most recent edition of *Klepp's Almenak*, the standard guide to the islands, had written about Midnight in as brief and offhand a fashion as possible.

There is a great deal more, he had written, *which I will not sully the pages of the Almenak by relating, horrors that haunt the Night-Noon Hour that will only go on to trouble our minds the more if their horrid visions are dwelt upon. Gorgossium is like unto a fetid carcass, rotting in its own consumption. Better we do upon these pages what we would do were we to encounter such a thing upon a road. We would avert our eyes from its foulness and go in search of sweeter sights. Then so should I.*

There was worse to come, much worse. Whatever the fear-flooded mind might have imagined when it thought of Midnight—the unholy rituals performed there in the name of Chaos and Cruelty, the blank-eyed brutalities that took the sanity or the lives of any innocent who ventured there; the stink out of its gaping graves, and the dead who had climbed from them, raised for mischief's sake, and left to wander where they would—all this was just the first line in a great book of terror that the two powers who had once ruled Gorgossium, Christopher Carrion and his grandmother, Mater Motley, had begun to write.

But things had changed. In an attempt to track down and finally slaughter Candy Quackenbush (who had caused her endless problems) Mater Motley had stirred up the Sea of Izabella and used their maelstrom to carry her warship, the *Wormwood,* into the Hereafter. Things had not gone well. The magic she had unleashed in that other world, contained perhaps by laws of matter that had no relevance in the Abarat, had lost its mind. The warship had been torn apart in the water—pieces of the Izabella and countless numbers of her stitchling warriors torn up the same way. Her grandson, Christopher Carrion, had drowned there too. Mater Motley had returned to Gorgossium alone.

Her first edict as the sole power now ruling Midnight was to summon up six thousand stitchlings—monsters filled with the living mud that was only mined on Gorgossium—to begin the labor of demolishing the thirteen towers of the Iniquisit. In their place, she would let it be known, there would be just a single three-spired tower built, far taller than even the tallest of the thirteen. From there she would rule, not only as the Sovereign of Gorgossium, but in time as the Empress of the Abarat.

She was a dangerous potentate.

Even among her hundreds of seamstresses—some of whom had known her for the better part of a century—there were few who trusted her affections. As long as she had need of their services (and at present she did) they were safe from harm, for without seamstresses there were no new stitchlings, and without stitchlings, no new legions to swell her army. But if that situation were to ever change, the women knew, they would be as disposable to the Old Mother as any stitchling.

Her weapon of choice when summarily executing one of her mud-men was her snake-wood rod, a simple but immensely powerful wand made of snake-wood that had been burned, buried, and raised up again on three consecutive midnights. It shot black lightning, destroying its target in an instant.

On several occasions, while surveying the work of demolition, she would catch sight of one of the stitchlings failing to labor as hard as the rest, and would summarily execute the brutish thing where it stood. The lesson: life and death were Mater Motley's gift to give or take as she saw fit, and only a fool or a suicide walked where she walked without caution.

With such a powerful overseer, work on the demolition and removal of rubble proceeded at great speed, and in a matter of days the plateau where the many towers of the Iniquisit had stood there now stood a monumental structure. A single tower, designed by an architect of genius, incantatrix Jalafeo Mas, who used her knowledge of magic to defy the laws of physics and raise up a tower taller than the sum of the thirteen that had once stood there.

It was here, in the red-walled room at the top of the tower, that Mater Motley assembled the most trusted of her seamstresses: nine of them.

"The years of labor and faith are over," Mater Motley said. "Midnight approaches."

One of the nine, Zinda Goam, a seamstress half a thousand years old who had arranged to have her familiars raise her from the grave after her death so that she might continue to serve Mater said, "Are we not at Midnight now?"

"Yes, this is a time called Midnight. But now it's Absolute. There is a greater Midnight than any in the making.

A Midnight that will blind every sun, moon, and star in the heavens."

Another of the women, whose emaciated body was draped with veils of fine cobwebs, could not silence her incredulity.

"I have never understood the Grand Design," said Aea G'pheet. "It doesn't seem possible. So many Hours. So many heavens."

"Do you doubt me, Aea G'pheet?"

The seamstress, though her skin was pale, became paler still. She hurriedly said, "Never, m'lady. Never. I was just astonished is all—overwhelmed, really—and misspoke."

"Then be careful in the future lest you find yourself without one."

Aea G'pheet lowered her head, the cobwebs shimmering as they shook.

"Am . . . am I . . . forgiven?"

"Are you dead?"

No, m'lady," Aea said. "I'm still alive."

"Then you must have been forgiven," the Old Mother said without humor. "Now, back to the business of Midnight. There are, as we know, many forms of life that have taken refuge from the light. Even the light of the stars. These creatures will be freed when my Midnight dawns. And they will make such mischief . . ." She paused, smiling at the thought of the fiends unleashed.

"And the people?" said another of the nine.

"Anyone who stands against us will be executed. And it will fall to us to spill their blood when the time comes, without hesitation. And if there is any woman here who is unwilling to fight this war upon those terms let her leave now. No harm will come to her. She has my oath on that. But if you choose to stay, then you will have agreed to do the work before us without fear or compromise.

"The labor of Midnight will be bloody, to be sure, but trust me, when I am Empress of the Abarat, I will raise you so high all thought of what you did to be so elevated will seem like nothing. We are not natural women, henceforth. Perhaps never were. We have no love of love, or of children, or of making bread. We are not made to tend fires and rock cradles. We are the unforgiving something upon which despairing men will break their fragile heads. There is no making peace with them, no husbanding them. They must be beneath our heels or dead and buried beneath the earth upon which we walk."

There was a ripple of pleasure around the chamber at this remark. Only one of the younger seamstresses murmured something inaudible.

"You have a question," Mater Motley said, singling her out.

"It was nothing, lady."

"I said speak, damn you! I won't have doubters! SPEAK!"

The seamstresses who had been surrounding the young woman now retreated from her.

"I was only wondering about the Twenty-Fifth Hour?" the young woman replied. "Will it also be overtaken by Midnight? Because if not——"

"Our enemies could find sanctuary there? Is that what you're asking?"

"Yes."

"It's the question to which, in truth, I have no answer," Mater Motley said lightly. "Not yet, at least. You are Mah Tuu Chamagamia, yes?"

"Yes, lady."

"Well, as long as you are so curious about the state of the Twenty-Fifth, I will put two legions of stitchlings at your disposal."

"To . . . do what, m'lady?"

"To take the Hour."

"Take it?"

"Yes. To invade it. In my name."

"But, lady, I have no skill in military matters. I could not."

"Could not? You dare say COULD NOT to me?"

She stretched out her left arm, the fingers of her hand outstretched. The killing rod she used against the stitch-lings flew from its place against the wall into her hand. She grasped it in a white-knuckled grip and in one sweep-ing motion pointed it at Mah Tuu Chamagamia.

The young woman opened her mouth to offer some further word of defense, but she had no time to utter it. Black lightning spat from the rod in her direction, and struck her in the middle of her body.

Now she made a sound. Not a word, but a cry of horror as her ghastly undoing spread out from her backbone in all directions turning her flesh and bone to flakes of black ash. Only her head remained untouched, so that she might better witness every moment of her dissolution.

But it was only long enough for her to see what her young beauty had been, and to turn her eyes up toward her destroyer one last time. Lone enough to murmur: "No."

Then her head went to ashes, and she was gone.

"So dies a doubter," the Old Mother said. "Any further questions?"

There were none.

10

THE SORROWS
OF THE GOOD SON

LAGUNA MUNN CLIMBED DOWN from her chair and called for her second son, her Good Boy.

"Covenantis? Where are you? I have need of you, boy!"

A joyless little voice said, "I'm here, Mother," and the boy Laguna Munn had reputedly made from all the good in her came into view. He was an unfortunate creature, as gray and dull as his Bad Boy brother had been glamorous and charismatic.

"We have a guest," said Laguna Munn.

"I know, Mother," he said, his voice colorless. "I was listening."

"That was rude, child."

"I meant no disrespect, Mother," the boy replied, his mother's chiding only serving to increase the sum of hopelessness in his empty eyes.

"Lead her to the Circle of Conjurations, boy. She has come here to do dangerous work. The sooner it's begun, the sooner it's safely over."

"May I stay and watch you teach her?"

"No. You may not. Unless you want to witness something that might well be the death of you."

"I don't much mind," Covenantis said, shrugging.

His whole life was in that shrug. He seemed not to care whether he was alive or dead.

"Where will *you* be?" Candy asked the incantatrix.

"Right here."

"So how are you going to help me with the separation?"

Laguna Munn looked at Candy with lazy amusement.

"From a safe distance," she replied.

"What happens if something goes wrong?"

"I'll have sight of you," Laguna Munn said. "Don't worry. If something goes wrong I'll do what I can to fix it. But the responsibility for the outcome falls on you. Think of yourself as a surgeon delicately separating twins born joined together. Except that you are not only the surgeon—"

"I'm also one of the babies," Candy said, beginning to understand.

"Exactly." Laguna looked at Candy with new admiration. "You know, you're smarter than you look."

"I look dumb? Is that what you're saying?"

"No. Not necessarily," she said, and then raised her hand, which was a fist, and opened it.

Candy put her hand in her pocket and took out the photograph she and Malingo had taken in the market in the port city of Tazmagor, on Qualm Hah. In it, she was wearing the same clothes she was wearing now. She had purchased those clothes on a whim, but now that she took a closer look, she realized that she resembled her mother to an astonishing degree. She quickly put the photo back in her pocket. Laguna Munn was right: when this was all over, she was going to get a change of clothes as quickly as possible. She'd dress like the Nonce, she decided, all color and happiness.

Before she had fully broken from her thoughts, Candy saw something bright move toward her from Laguna Munn's palm. It came too fast for her to make sense of what it was, but she felt it strike her like a gust of cold wind. There was a flicker of light in her head and by the time it was extinguished Laguna Munn had disappeared, leaving only poor, gray Covenantis at Candy's side.

"Well, I suppose you'd better come with me then," he said, showing not the least enthusiasm for the task.

Candy shook the last reverberations of the light from her mind, and followed the boy. As he stepped in front of her, she caught her first glimpse of his lower anatomy. Until now, she had been so caught up by the pitiful expression on his face she hadn't realized that below the belt, he looked more like a child-sized slug than a boy. His legs were fused into a single, boneless tube of gray-green muscle upon which the upper portion of his body, which was simply that of an ordinary boy, was raised up.

"I know what you're thinking," he said without looking back at Candy.

"And what's that?"

"Can that *really* be the son she made from the *good* in

her? Because he doesn't look very good. In fact he looks like a slug."

"I wasn't—"

"Yes, you were," the boy said.

"You're right, I was."

"And you're right. I do look like a slug. I've thought a lot about it. In fact it's really the only thing I think about."

"And what have you found out, after all that thinking?"

"Not much. Just that Mother never really loved the good in her. She thought it was boring. Worthless."

"Now, I'm sure—"

"Don't," he said, raising his hand to stop her trying to pamper the hurt. "That only makes it worse. My mother's ashamed of me. That's the truth, plain and simple. It's my evil little brother, with his glittering smiles, who gets all the glory. That's what they call a paradox, isn't it? I'm made from good, but I'm nothing to her. He's made of all the evil in her and guess what: *she loves him for it. Loves him!* So now he's the good son after all, because of all the love he's been given. And me, who was made from her compassion and her gentility, was left out in the cold."

Candy felt a flicker of anxiety run through her. She understood Covenantis's words all too clearly. She knew the glittering beauty of evil. She'd seen it, and been in some ways attracted by it. Why else had she felt so sympathetic to Carrion?

"Stay here while I light the candles," Covenantis said.

Candy waited while he moved off into the shadows. It was only when he'd gone that Candy's thoughts returned to the strange gesture Laguna Munn had made before she had gone from view. And with the memory came other recollections, stirred up by the woman's gift and Candy realized exactly how many coincidences, instinctual maneuvers, and twists of fate were really pieces of Boa's magic at work within her.

She remembered it all now with uncanny clarity: she remembered the words that had come unbidden into her throat on the *Parroto Parroto—Jassassakya-thüm!*—and once spoken, they had driven off the monstrous Zethek; she remembered instincts, when Mama Izabella had come at her across the grasslands, that had allowed her to relax in the grip of the sentient that might well have drowned her if she'd caused any trouble; and she remembered the way she'd fallen into a pattern of bittersweet exchanges with Carrion, who would have slaughtered her in a heartbeat if he hadn't sensed something inside her that he knew. No, *that he loved.*

For the first time, Candy realized just how much of Boa there might be in her. A spasm of panic seized Candy.

"Oh no," she said. "I don't think I can do this."

Of course you can. You've come this far, haven't you?

"Do you think it'll hurt?"

Hurt? Boa replied. *HURT? A cut finger hurts, girl. A cracked rib. But this is the end of a union of souls that has defined you since the day you were born. When the connection between us is severed you'll lose forever pieces of your mind you thought were yours.*

"But they were yours. They were you."

Yes.

"So why would I want them?"

Because it'll be an unspeakable agony to lose them. You see, I know what it's like to be alone in my head. I'm used to it. But you . . . you have no idea of what you have invited down upon yourself.

"I know perfectly well, I think," Candy said.

Do you? Well, for what it's worth, I doubt you'll keep your sanity. How could anyone stay sane when you can no longer recognize the face in the mirror?

"That's *my* face!" Candy protested. "A *Quackenbush* face!"

But the eyes.

"What about the eyes?"

You'll look at your reflection and the mind you'll see staring back at you won't be yours. All the memories of glory that you thought belonged to you, all the beautiful mysteries that you believed you'd discovered for yourself, all the ambitions you hold dear—none of them are yours.

"I don't believe you. You're lying now the way you lied to Finnegan and Carrion."

You keep Finnegan out of this, Boa said.

"Oh, feel a bit guilty do you?"

I said—

"I heard you."

There were a few moments of extremely strained silence between them. Then Boa said: *Let. Me. Out. Of. This—PRISON!*

Covenantis appeared and looked at Candy with round, terrified eyes.

"Did you hear that?" he said softly. "A human's voice, I swear. Tell me it's not just me."

"No, Covenantis, you're perfectly sane. Will you get the conjuration underway please, before she gets murderous?"

"It's already begun. I'm going into the labyrinth to prepare the site of separation. Follow me there. But first repeat the sacred word nineteen times."

"Abarataraba?"

"Yes."

"Does that one count?"

"*No!*"

Then the last thing he said before disappearing into the maze, leaving Candy to feel as though at the very moment she was making a life-changing decision for herself—a very adult thing to do—he'd reduced her to a kid in the school yard.

She smeared the last six Abarataraba into a single Abarrrarababa, and without alerting Covenantis to the fact that she was done counting and was coming, ready or not, she plunged into the maze, entering as Two-in-One and hopefully exiting as simply two.

11

SEVERANCE

CANDY TOOK FOUR CAUTIOUS steps into the darkened trees, each step delivering her into an even profounder darkness. On the fifth step, however, a flying creature appeared at the periphery of her vision. It buzzed like a big insect, and the brightness of its colors—turquoise and scarlet, speckled with flecks of white gold—defied the darkness.

It darted around her head for a while then sped away. Candy took a fifth cautious step, then a sixth. Suddenly the creature reappeared, accompanied by several hundred identical beasts, which surrounded her with so much color and movement that she felt faintly nauseated.

She closed her eyes to seal off the sight, but the chaotic motion of the creatures continued behind her eyelids.

"What's happening?" she said, raising her voice above the noise of the buzzing cloud. "Covenantis? Are you still there?"

"Patience!" Candy heard the boy say.

He's frightened, Boa said, a distinct undercurrent of amusement in her words. *This isn't an easy thing to do. If he messes up, he'll sacrifice your sanity.* She let the laughter surface; there was undisguised malice in it. *Wouldn't that be a pity?*

"Covenantis," Candy said. "Stay calm. Take your time."

"He never was very good at that, were you, brother?" said Jollo B'gog.

"Stay out of here!" Covenantis said. "Mother! *Mother!*"

"She was the one who said I could come and help," the Bad Boy replied.

"I don't believe you," Candy said, opening her eyes again.

As she did so she saw the Bad Boy run through a wall of the colored creatures, who had assembled ahead of her in an intricate jigsaw of wings, limbs and heads. He yelled as he ran, scattering the assembled creatures. They rose up in front of her, the motion of their wings causing a gust of wind to come at her face, tasting of metal on her tongue.

"Stop that!" Covenantis yelled, his voice shrill with anger.

The Bad Boy just laughed.

"I'll tell Mama!"

"Mama won't stop me. Mama loves everything I do."

"Well, aren't you lucky?" Covenantis said, unable to entirely disguise his envy.

"Mama says I'm a genius!" the Bad Boy crowed.

"You are, darling, you are," Laguna Munn said, entering the space as little more than a shadow of herself. "But this isn't the time or the place to fool around."

All it took was the sound of Laguna Munn's voice and the creatures that had been scattered by the Bad Boy's cavorting came back down on the instant, knitting themselves together—wing to claw to beak to coxcomb to fanning tail—forming a small prison around Candy.

"*Better,*" Laguna Munn said, her voice all-forgiving. "Pale Child?"

"Yes, Mama?" Covenantis said.

"Have you secured all the locks?"

Oh yes, Boa said. *Got to have plenty of locks. I like the sound of that.*

"What are the locks for?" Candy said aloud. "What are you keeping out?"

"Nothing's being kept out—" Covenantis said, stopping only when his mother yelled his name, and dropping the last part of his reply to a whisper. "It's you she's keeping *in.*"

"*Covenantis!*"

"I'm coming, Mama!"

"Quickly now. I haven't got much time."

"I've got to go," the Good Boy said to Candy. "I'll be right outside."

He pointed to a narrow slit of a door in between the wings and claws of the big bugs, and for the first time Candy realized that a solid little chamber had formed around her. The walls were draining of color even as she watched, and every last crack or flaw in the knitted forms sealed. What had been a colorful room made of flittering wings was becoming a silent concrete cell.

"Why are you locking me in?" Candy said.

"Conjurations this strong are unstable," Covenantis said.

"What do you mean?"

"They can go wrong," he whispered.

"Covenantis!" Laguna Munn shouted.

"Yes, Mama!"

"Stop talking to the girl. You can't help her."

"No, Mama!"

"She'll probably be dead in under a minute."

"I'm coming, Mama," Covenantis said. He gave Candy a little shrug, and slipped out through the door, which closed, leaving no trace of its presence, not a crack.

Well . . . Boa said softly. *You got us here. Better finish it. If you've got what it takes.*

"I've got what it doesn't take," Candy replied, without hesitation.

Oh? And what's that?

"Don't be stupid," Candy said. *"You."*

And suddenly, the fear drained from Candy and she turned on the spot, addressing the cold, gray walls.

"I'm ready," she told them. "Do whatever you have to do. Just get it over with. If you can avoid spilling blood, that'd be great. But if you can't, you can't."

She didn't have to wait very long for the cell to respond. Six shudders passed through its walls, ceiling and floor, like tides of life moving in its dead matter, resurrecting it. She understood now why she'd been given a peripheral glimpse of what the cell had been in its last incarnation: the flock of winged beings. She saw them haunting the gray walls still. One life inside another.

Was the lesson here that she would have been gray and lifeless as the walls if Boa's soul had not come into her? Was she being warned that the life she was choosing would be a cell: gray and cold?

She didn't believe it. And said so.

"I'm more than that," she told the shimmering gray. "I'm not dead matter."

Not yet, Boa crowed.

"Are you ready to do this?" Candy said and thought to both wall and Princess. "Because I'm getting bored with all these stupid threats."

Stupid? Boa raged.

"Just do it," Laguna Munn said, her voice quickening the powers in the walls. *"Quick and clean."*

"Wait!" Candy said. "I just wanted Boa to know I'm sorry. If I'd known she was there I would have tried to set her free years ago."

If you're looking for absolution, Boa said, *you won't get it from me.*

"Then that's an end to that," Laguna Munn said, her response making Candy realize with a shock that the old

woman had been listening in on her thoughts from the beginning. *"Let's get this done, one way or the other. Candy! Palms to the wall. Quickly!"*

Candy lay her palms on one of the walls. Instantly she could see the creatures dancing in the solid air beyond. Their wings and bodies shed the flakes of white gold that decorated them. They converged on Candy's palms, the fragments flowing together into two gilded streams.

She felt them against her palms, breaking into deltas, spreading along the dry watercourses of the lines upon her hands, and then sinking deeper, dissolving her surface in order to flow into her veins. Her hands became translucent; the brightness inside her flesh was so intense she could see the strong simple lines of her finger bones, and the complicated design of her nerves.

The brightness quickened once it got to her elbows, like a fire blown by the wind into a thicket many summers dry. It raced up her arms, and across her body.

She felt it, but it didn't hurt. It was more like being reminded that *this was her.*

She was real: and being real, and her, was—What? What was it? Who was it?

That was the big question, wasn't it? When all the fireworks were over: Who was she?

You're nothing, Boa said quietly.

Candy wanted to counter Boa's insults. But her energies were focused elsewhere: on the rush of awakening that was passing through her body, down from her neck, over her torso, and up, filling the twice-souled vessel above.

Did you hear me? Boa said.

"Keep your petty insults to yourself, Boa," Laguna Munn said. "You may have suffered a little, trapped in the child's head. But Lordy Lou, there are worse deaths to suffer. Such as the real thing. Oh . . . and while we're talking, I know what you're thinking: that once all this is over you'll have my sons running around doing your bidding!"

Boa said nothing.

"That's what I thought. Well, forget it. There's only room for *one* woman in the lives of my beautiful sons."

Please, Boa protested. *I'd never try to compromise the sacred relationships between you and your sons.*

"I don't believe you," Laguna Munn replied plainly. "I think you'd try anything if you thought you could get away with it."

I wouldn't dream of it. I know what you're capable of.

"You might think you do but you don't have the first idea, so be careful."

Understood.

"Good. Now, I should leave this chamber."

"Wait," Candy said. "Don't go yet. I'm feeling dizzy."

"That's probably because I'm still here gabbing. I should leave you to give birth to Boa."

The image Laguna Munn's words conjured was grotesque. It made Candy feel sicker than ever.

"It's too late to feel queasy now, girl. This is dirty magic we're doing. It's not the kind of work sanctioned by the Council of the Yebba Dim Day. If it was, you wouldn't be here. Do you understand?"

"Of course," Candy said.

She understood perfectly well. It was the same in Chickentown. There was a Dr. Pimloft whose offices were above the Laundromat on Fairkettle Street. He'd do certain operations people were too embarrassed to talk to their regular doctors about. Sometimes that was your only choice.

"I'm going to get out of here," Laguna said, "before I throw the conjuration off balance."

"Where will you be? In case there's a problem?"

"It'll be fine," Mrs. Munn said. "You want to be separated, after all. So . . . here comes the conjuration. I designed it to do what you require. So let it do its job."

There was a sound like someone chopping with axes from behind Mrs. Munn, and a shadow-bird—or something like it—rose from the darkness and flew in and out through the intricate pattern, wall to wall to wall to wall, before disappearing into the darkness behind Mrs. Munn.

"What was that?" Candy said.

"The chamber is getting impatient," she said. "It wants me gone."

The phenomena occurred again, exactly as before.

"I should go," Laguna Munn said. "Before this gets any worse."

Candy suddenly felt weak and her legs buckled beneath her. She tried to make her legs respond to her instruction, but she realized she was no longer the mistress of her body. Boa was.

"Wait . . ." Candy started to say, panic rising in her chest. But even her tongue wouldn't do as she instructed. And it was almost too late. Laguna Munn had turned her back on Candy, preparing to leave.

It's over now, the Princess said.

Candy didn't waste energy trying to reply. She was seconds away from losing herself forever. She could feel rhythmical thundering that no doubt Boa had set to work. It was eating at the corners of her world, consuming her consciousness with ever-larger bites.

Through a haze of white noise she saw Laguna Munn open up a door in the wall.

No. Candy tried to say. But no sound came out.

This would be a lot easier if you just gave up and gave in. Let go of Candy Quackenbush. You're going to die. And you won't want to be alive when I start feeding.

What? Candy thought. *Feeding off me? Why?*

Because I've got to grow myself a body, girl. That requires nourishment. A lot of nourishment. Did I forget to mention that?

Candy wanted to weep at her own stupidity. Boa must have shaped these plans no more than a few thoughts away from where Candy had been hiding her own thinking. But she'd hidden her intentions totally. There hadn't been a moment when Candy had been suspicious.

But you know now, Boa gloated. *If it helps, think of this as punishment for stealing my memories of magic. I know death may seem a very strong punishment, but it was a terrible thing you did.*

I'm . . . I'm . . . sorry?

Too late. It's over. It's time you died, Candy.

12

ONE BECOMES TWO

FAR OFF, SOMEWHERE IN the darkness, Candy Quackenbush thought she heard the sound of Laguna Munn's voice.

"Covenantis? Did you lock the chamber? *The lock, boy!*"

There was no answer from the child. All Candy heard was the chorus of strange noises her dying body was making. Her heart hadn't stopped entirely. Every few seconds it still managed to beat; on occasion it even managed two or three beats strung together. But what little life her body still possessed was more like a memory than the real thing: like a vision of the Abarat even as it slipped away. All gone now. All forgotten.

No, not *entirely* forgotten. Some portion of her eyes' ability to form images still existed. Though she could no longer see the walls of the Separation Chamber, she *could* see, with eerie specificity, a stain of smoky gray air appearing in front of her face. She knew its source. It was coming from her own body.

It was Boa's soul she was looking at. At least the haunted shadow of it, finally liberated from the cell into which the women of the Fantomaya had put it. Freed from Candy. And now gaining strength.

It was pushing itself, spreading itself, extruding rudimentary legs from its torso, and something that had the potential to become arms, while from the top a single thread of gray matter sprouted. From this fragile stalk, two leaves had formed and on them, the undeveloped shape of a mouth and nose. And above the leaves, two white, slim petals grew, each with bursts of blue and black upon them, as if blessed with sight.

It was a simple illusion, but it quickly gained credibility as new stalks sprayed upward in their dozens, forming intricate laceries of vein and nerve that began to conjure the shape of their possessor's face. Though it was still little more than a skinless mask knitted of pulsing threads, there was a glimpse, even there, of the young woman who would soon come into being. She would be beautiful again, Candy thought. She would break hearts.

Candy hadn't lifted herself up off the ground since her knees had buckled beneath her. She still knelt in the same spot, watching the vestigial form of Princess Boa attract to it the detritus of the life-forms shed by the chamber walls: withered flower housings, leaves, living and dead, all adding their sum to the patchwork that was slowly giving the Princess more substance. The surrounding flora and fauna were nourishing Boa's body, and it was by their sacrifice alone that Candy's life had been spared. But the process was going too slowly.

Candy could sense Boa's frustration as she received these pitifully inadequate contributions to the body she was trying to grow again.

She opened her lips, and though her throat and tongue were unfinished, she managed to speak. It was light, more than a quiet whisper, but Candy heard it plainly.

"You look . . . nourishing . . ." she said.

"I'd make bad eating right now. You should find something healthier."

"Hunger is hunger. And time is of the essence. . . ."

This time Candy forced her throat to form the question, though it was barely audible.

"Why is that exactly?" she said.

"Midnight," Boa said simply. "It's almost upon us. You don't feel it, do you?"

"Midnight?"

"Midnight! I can feel it. The last darkness is coming, and it will blot out every light in the heavens."

"No . . ."

"Saying no will change nothing. The Abarat is going to die in the dark. Every sun will be eclipsed, every moon blinded, every star in every constellation extinguished like a candle flame. But don't worry. You won't be here to suffer the consequences. You'll be gone."

"Where?"

"Who knows? Who'll care? Nobody. You will have

served your purpose. You had sixteen years of life, going places you would never have gone if you hadn't had me hidden inside you. You have nothing to complain about. Now your life ends. And mine begins. There's something quite pleasing about the balance, isn't there?"

"I'm not done living . . ." Candy murmured.

"Well, I'm sorry," Boa said, mocking Candy's gravity.

"You don't . . . understand," Candy said.

"Trust me. There's nothing you know that I don't."

"You're wrong," Candy said. Her voice was gaining strength as she drew upon the clarity Laguna Munn's gift had given her. "I know how you played Carrion along all those years, making him think you loved him, when all you really wanted from him was the Abarataraba."

"Listen to yourself," Boa said. "To hear you, people might think you actually knew what you were talking about."

Candy sighed.

"You're right," she said. "I don't know much about the Abarataraba. It's a book of magic——"

"Stop! Stop! You're embarrassing yourself. Don't waste your last minutes worrying about something you'll never understand. Death has come for you, Candy. And when it leaves it's going to be taking you along with it. You, and every thought you ever had. Every hope, every dream. All gone. It'll be like you never lived."

"The dead don't disappear. There are ghosts. I've met one. And I'll be one, if necessary. I have energy and power."

"You have nothing," Boa said with a sudden burst of rage.

She reached out and seized hold of Candy. The effect, in both directions, was immediate. Now, as she drew power out of Candy directly the smoky air began to solidify into gray bone behind the latticework of veins and nerves that had first defined her features.

"Better," Boa said, smiling through gritted teeth. "Much better."

Every part of her body was speeding toward completion now. The fluids in Boa's eye sockets bubbled like boiling water. Even in her diminished state Candy could still see the bizarrity in the sight before her.

"Oh, I like this," Boa said, luxuriating in the bliss of her reconstruction.

This time there was enough of her flesh and bone in place that Candy could see a hint of the beautiful woman whose image Finnegan Hob had kept above his bed. But every sliver of Boa's recovered beauty was being purchased at the expense of Candy's life. Each time Boa's greedy fingers touched Candy they left her more impoverished, more exhausted. And this was not the kind of exhaustion that she could sleep off in a few quiet hours. This was the other kind: the sleep from which there was no waking.

Death has come for you. Boa had uttered the words just a few minutes ago.

She hadn't lied.

13

BOA

WEAK THOUGH CANDY WAS—THE convulsions wracking her body with increasing frequency, her legs so exhausted she doubted they'd support her for more than two or three strides—she had no choice. She had to get out of the chamber quickly, or Boa's appetite for her life force would be the death of her. In one small detail, luck was on her side.

Candy remembered hearing Laguna Munn's voice. It felt ages ago, but the incantatrix made mention of the lock. Suddenly Candy realized that despite his mother's instruction, Covenantis had failed to lock the chamber door. It had opened, just a crack. But it was sufficiently wider than the narrow shadow it cast. Without it, Candy would have had little or no chance of locating her escape route. But here it was!

She only allowed her gaze to linger on the shadow of the door for the briefest moment. She was afraid of giving anything away to Boa. Then, directing her gaze to the opposite wall—as if it was there that she'd guessed the door to be—she slowly started to haul herself to her feet.

Boa's relentless appetite had robbed Candy's body of strength and flexibility. It felt like a dead weight, which took every bit of willpower to get moving and *keep* moving. Every part of her seemed close to failure. Her lungs were like two stones inside her, while her heart fluttered like a torn paper bird. Her body would have to be stirred from its torpor if Candy was to have any hope of escaping this chamber. She would have to force her enfeebled arms to make her torso collaborate in its own survival.

"Come on," she told herself through gritted teeth, ". . . move."

Reluctantly, her body responded. But it hurt. Her heart-bird got panicky. The rest of her innards started to close down. She could taste something disgusting in her throat, as though her entrails were backed up like choked sewer pipes. She tried not to think about it, which was in fact quite easy because her mind was failing along with everything else.

She didn't need much brainpower to recognize her mortal enemy, however. Boa was with her in the chamber, and she was a distressing sight. Without bones, Boa's anatomy was a ragged mass of possibilities that had not yet congealed. Her fingers dangled like empty gloves, her face a long mask of lost intention, and her mouth, a hole without a tongue or teeth.

Boa's appearance was so appalling that Candy forgot

her exhaustion and scrambled to get out of her way. With a sudden rush of energy, Candy pushed herself up off the chamber floor, catching Boa off guard, and knocking her to the floor.

"Be still, witch!" Boa yelled. "Let's have this over with, once and for all!"

Candy lurched toward the door, avoiding the coils which, had they encircled her and tightened their grip once more, would have ground her ribs to powder and her guts to meat and excrement.

She reached out to the shadow, which marked her destination, and slid her fingers around the door. It was no illusion. It was solid and real in her grip. She pulled, half expecting the door to protest its opening, but no. Despite its massive size, it was served by some kind of counter-weight, which allowed it to swing open with only the most modest of effort on Candy's part.

Her surprise made her careless. As she pulled the door open, Boa's forefinger wrapped itself around her throat, tightening with the efficiency of a noose.

Candy instantly let go of the door, and forced her fingers down between neck and noose. But it wasn't enough to keep Boa from putting so much pressure on Candy's windpipe that she could no longer draw breath.

Candy's thoughts were already in swift decay thanks to Boa's theft. Now the sudden loss of oxygen robbed her mind of still more functions. Her thoughts became increasingly confused. What was she doing in this place?

And the woman with the hole for a mouth; who was she?

Boa's skills with her body were growing as fast as Candy's body was drained. She spoke now, her voice crude.

"This is no way to die," Boa said. "Where's your dignity, girl? Stop struggling, and let me take what's mine. You lived a fine life because of me. Brief, yes, but full of my insights. My lessons. My magic."

Somebody outside the chamber walls, but close enough to have heard Boa's speech, apparently found it very funny. Her mockery echoed around the chamber.

"Listen to yourself." It was Laguna Munn. Again, the laughter ignited. "Such pretension. And from what? A cannibal. Yes, that's the truth of it when you get down to the facts. You are able to devour the life of a girl who gave you sanctuary from those who had taken yours and would gladly have extinguished your soul. Let Candy go."

"Oh no . . . there's no letting go."

"Is there not? We shall see about that."

As she spoke, the wall opposite the door began to fold in upon itself, and the incantatrix came into view.

She was pointing at Boa, as she continued her accusations.

"Whatever was good in you, and bright, has gone to corruption."

"You can say whatever you like, old woman," Boa replied. "Your time's over. There's a new world about to be born."

"Funny. I hear that a lot," Laguna Munn said, her voice

thick with contempt. "Now let the commoner go, Princess. If you really want to dine on flesh, you shouldn't be eating the hoi polloi."

The expression on Boa's face suddenly cleared.

"Oh my. She is, isn't she?"

"She's not of noble birth, like you, Princess."

"No," Boa said, her tone deeply grateful. "If you hadn't stopped me——" She released Candy from her grip. "I could have tainted myself."

"And what a sad day that would have been for all those poor suffering aristocrats like yourself who would have lost a beloved sister."

"Oh me! Oh, poor beloved me."

As Candy stumbled out of Boa's hold she turned and the subtle signs of deceit upon Boa's face caught Candy's attention. Boa didn't wait to let Candy speak. She quickly was gone, out of the chamber and off up the wooded slope. Candy did her best to recover her equilibrium, but it was difficult. Boa's thefts had left her body weak, and her thoughts ragged. She was only certain of one thing.

"She would have killed me . . ."

"Oh, I don't doubt it," Mrs. Munn replied. "But this is my rock, girl, and she has no——"

"Mama!"

The cry came from Covenantis. And as heart wrenching as his wails were, the terrible howl of anguish that followed was infinitely worse.

Laguna was clearly torn between her responsibilities

to her injured guest, and those she had to her son. Candy simplified things:

"Go to the boy! I'll be fine. I just need to recover my breath." She looked up at Mrs. Munn. "Please," she said, "don't worry about me!"

Her plea was lent force by another sobbing cry from her son.

"Where are you, Mama?"

Laguna Munn looked at Candy one more time.

"Go!" Candy said.

Laguna Munn didn't put up any further argument. Instead, she addressed the walls of the chamber.

"This girl is here as my guest. She's hurt. *Heal her.*" She turned her attentions back toward Candy for a moment. "Stay here and let the chamber do its work. I'll be back with my boys."

"Be careful . . ."

"I know, girl, I know. Boa's dangerous. But believe me, so am I. I've got a few tricks she wouldn't want to see. Now heal. The dark Hours that are coming won't wait for you to put yourself back together. Hurry up. The beginning's been a long time over. And the end always comes sooner than you expect."

And so saying, she left the girl who was truly Candy Quackenbush, nothing added or taken away, to the healing hush of the chamber.

14

EMPTY

NEVER IN HER SIXTEEN years had Candy felt as alone as she felt now. Though she'd tried many times to imagine what it would be like without Boa in her head, her attempts had failed miserably. Only now, alone in the vastness of her thoughts did she sense the horror of such solitude. There would never again be a presence to silently share the state of being as Boa had. She was utterly, unconditionally alone.

How did people, ordinary people like those on Followell Street—even her own mother, even her *father*—deal with the loneliness? Did her dad drink himself senseless every night because it made the emptiness she was feeling right now hurt a little less? For them, was it the constant chattering of the television that helped them through the bad times? Or hurtful little power games like those Miss Schwartz played that helped them forget the hush in their heads?

Candy suddenly recalled the big billboard outside the

Presbyterian Church on Munrow Street in Chickentown that had carried the same message for as long as Candy could remember:

THE LORD IS WITH YOU ALWAYS. YOU ARE NOT ALONE.

Well he's not with me now, Candy thought. *Nobody's with me. And I just have to live with things being like this from now on, because nobody's going to step in to help change it. All I can do is—*

A shriek interrupted her thoughts. Laguna Munn was shouting one word, its force fueled by horror and rage.

"NO!"

She stopped only when she ran out of breath. She inhaled and began again.

"NO!"

Finally, she let the word fall off into silence. Several seconds passed and then Candy heard her say, "My son. What have you done to my son?"

Candy didn't wait for any more clues as to what had taken place. She got up and headed for the door, realizing as she did so that while she'd been contemplating her loneliness, the sentient chamber had obeyed Laguna Munn's instructions and begun the process of healing her. She was no longer shaking as she had been just a few minutes earlier. And her weakened legs had recovered some of their strength. Even her thoughts, which had been left muddied by Boa's attacks, were clearer now.

Exiting the chamber, she didn't need any further cries from the incantatrix in order to discover her whereabouts. The powers she feared she'd lost to Boa's devouring were unharmed. Once the chamber had washed from her thoughts the grime of Boa's appetite, she remembered without effort how to locate Mrs. Munn in the darkness. All she had to do was follow the vibration that moved ahead of her, trusting it to choose a safe path up the slope.

The temperature quickly warmed up as she ascended; the air carried with it a smell like rotted meat that had been burned on a barbecue.

Bad magic, she thought.

Then she heard Mrs. Munn again, speaking softly somewhere ahead of her.

"What's she done to you, child? Now you hush your weepin'. I'm right here. Where does it hurt?"

"Everywhere, Mama."

Candy saw a light now, no brighter than two candle flames, hovering in the air a few feet above the ground. The scene illuminated was a grim one.

Mrs. Munn was kneeling on the ground, tending to her favorite son, Jollo B'gog. He was in a terrible state. All the dark beauty he'd possessed when Candy and Malingo had first met him had gone. He was emaciated now, his bones jutting through his withered skin. His teeth were chattering, his eyes rolled up behind his lids.

"Listen to me, Jollo dear," Mrs. Munn was telling him. "You're not going to die. You hear me? I'm here."

She stopped talking, and looked up in rage, her gaze instantly locating Candy. There was a flicker of lightning in her eyes.

"It's only me," Candy said. "Don't—"

The lightning receded, and Laguna Munn looked back down at her son. "I want you to stay here with him. Keep him from any further harm while I find her."

"Boa . . ." Candy growled.

Laguna Munn nodded. "She took from the child what I stopped her taking from you." She tenderly stroked her son's cheek. "You just stay here, sweet one," she said to him. "Mama will be back in just a few moments."

"Where are you going?"

"To find her. And take back what she took from him."

She got to her feet, rising with surprising ease for so large boned a woman, looking down at Jollo all the while. It was only with the greatest difficulty that she finally separated her gaze from him.

"I'm so sorry," Candy said. "If I'd known what she was capable of doing—"

"Don't," Mrs. Munn said, waving Candy's apology away. "We have more urgent business than talk. Will you please stay with him, maybe talk to him a little so his spirit stays near?"

"Of course."

"She's not a *real* Princess, you know," Mrs. Munn said with an odd deliberation in her voice, like an amateur actor reciting lines. "She may have a crown and a title but they mean nothing. True royalty is a state of the soul. It belongs to those who have the gift of empathy, of compassion, of vision. That's how people are led to do great things, even in cold, brutal times. But this . . . *Boa* . . ." Her lips curled when she spoke the two syllables: Bow-ah. ". . . attempted to first take your life, and then my Jollo's, just to put some flesh on her spirit. That's not the act of a Princess. To attack someone who had been her sanctuary? And then a child? Where is the nobility in that? I'll tell you. There is none. Because your Princess Boa is a fake! She has no more royal blood in her than I do."

There was a furious shriek from overhead—

"Liar! Liar!"

—and the branches shook so violently that a green rain of torn leaves fluttered down.

"There you are," Candy heard Laguna Munn mutter under her breath. "I knew you were up there somewhere, you vicious little—"

A branch overhead creaked loudly, drawing Candy's gaze up through the knotted branches to the place where Boa was squatting, her form delineated by narrow rays of violet light that passed up through her body from her soles to her scalp and from her head to her heels, throwing off a loop of incandescence when they crossed at her waist. She rocked back and forth on the branch, and then suddenly spat on Laguna Munn's now upturned face.

"What are you staring at, you fat, old buzzard?" Boa said.

Mrs. Munn pulled a large handkerchief out of the sleeve of her dress. "Nothing of any worth," she replied as she wiped her face. "Just *you!*"

And with that she sprang up from the ground into the canopy where Boa was squatting, leaving her handkerchief to drop to the ground.

"Take care of Jollo!" she yelled to Candy as she disappeared into the shadowed canopy. Then the nearby trees shook as Boa attempted her escape into it, and the chase overhead moved off up the slope, leaving Candy alone with the sick child.

15

FACE-TO-FACE

"MAMA?" JOLLO SAID WHEN Candy sat down beside him. She didn't need to correct his error. "Wait, you're not Mama."

"Your mom won't be long," Candy told him. "I'm just here to look after you until she comes back."

"Candy."

"Yes."

"She came out of you, didn't she? The girl who killed me."

"You're not dead, Jollo. And your mom's not going to let you die."

"There's some things even Mama can't control," Jollo said. His voice was getting weaker, word by word.

"Listen to me," Candy said. "I know what the Princess did to you was horrible. She tried to do the same thing to me. But hold on. *Please.*"

"What for?"

"What for?"

"Don't worry. You don't have to answer that." He raised his head off the ground and squinted at Candy. "Tell me about the Constrictor."

"The what?"

"Boa," he said, his face suddenly becoming a playground of mischief. "Get it? Ha! I just made that up."

At the moment death was forgotten, anything was possible. Candy grinned. There was such sweetness in him she saw, hidden behind his melancholy.

"She was there inside you all the time?"

"Yes, she was there."

"But you didn't know what a monster she was, did you?"

Candy shook her head. "I had no idea," she said. "She was part of me."

"And now? How does it feel?"

"Empty."

"You feel alone?"

"Yes . . ."

"Still, it's better that she's gone."

Candy took a moment to consider this before replying. "Yes. It's better."

Before Jollo could ask any further questions, a welcome and familiar figure appeared between the trees. "It's only me!"

"Malingo!"

"Same old geshrat," he said. "But who's this?"

"You remember Jollo? Mrs. Munn's boy?"

"He remembers me the way I was," Jollo said. "Before Boa got to me."

"So it worked," Malingo said.

"Yes, she's gone," Candy said. "But she almost killed poor Jollo."

"And you."

"Well, yes. And me."

"Where is she now?"

"Up in the trees somewhere," Candy said.

"She's running away from Mama," Jollo said. He looked up at Candy. "Isn't she?"

"That's right."

"But I want her back now. Just to say good-bye."

"Maybe I should go and look for her," Candy said.

"Yes . . ." Jollo said.

Candy took hold of Jollo's hand. His fingers were sweaty but cold. "What do you think, Jollo? If I have Malingo stay with you, will you promise not to . . . not to . . ."

"Not to die?" Jollo said.

"Yes. Not to die."

"All right," he said. "I'll try. But bring Mama back soon. I want her here with me if . . . if I can't stay any longer."

"Don't say that," Candy said to him.

"It's the truth," he replied. "Mama says it's bad to tell lies."

"Well, yes," Candy said. "It is."

"So hurry," he said, slipping his fingers out of Candy's grasp. "Find her." He turned to Malingo. "You were a slave to a wizard once, weren't you?" he said.

"I was," Malingo said.

"Come closer. I can't see you in the darkness. There. That's better. Tell me about it. Was he cruel? I heard he was cruel."

Jollo's interest in Candy had already slipped away; all his focus was now entirely upon Malingo. Candy got to her feet and left the two of them to talk, happy the boy was diverted.

"So how did you become a slave?" he said to Malingo.

"My father sold me . . ." Malingo began.

Candy didn't hear any more. She retreated until she no longer had sight of Jollo, and he had no view of her. Only then did she turn her back on the place where he lay and face the tree-covered slope. This time she didn't need any magic to plot a course to Mrs. Munn. She could hear the chase going on through the densely knitted canopy farther up the slope. Candy could even hear echoes of the incantatrix calling after Boa.

"There's no way off this island, Boa."

"Let me alone, will you?" Boa yelled back as she sprinted over the treetops. "I didn't know the boy was your son. I swear I didn't. I mean, how could I? There's no family resemblance."

"Liar! Liar!" Candy yelled right back, her interruption echoing that of Boa, minutes before. But she had more to say. "You knew *exactly* who he was, Boa. Because I knew. And if *I* knew then——"

"Stay out of this, Quackenbush!" Boa hollered. "Or you'll be sorry!"

"I'm already sorry," Candy yelled back. "I'm sorry I ever let you out of my head."

"Ah, the sting of regret!" Boa crowed. "Well, it's done, girl, and it can never be undone. So you'd better get used to it. I'm in the world now. Everything changes from now on. *Everything.*"

"Stay away from her, Candy!" Mrs. Munn hollered. *"She'll hurt you!"*

"I'm not afraid of her," Candy said.

"Liar, liar, funeral pyre!" Boa chanted.

"Well, one of us is going to have to tell the truth sooner or later," Candy replied.

Boa finally reached the tree beneath which Candy stood, and looked down through the leaves, shaped in their fullness, like planets with golden rings around them. That Boa's body was defined by the dual motion of bright rings was no accident. Her new skin—bought with the coin of Jollo's suffering—had taken for inspiration the design of the foliage all around it.

"You want the truth," Boa said, squatting on a branch so as to peer down at Candy through the canopy. "Then here: have it. I would have taken all the life force in you to heal me completely. But I was denied the total sum of you by that fat witch. And then when I do the only thing left to me—take her son—she comes howling after me as though I'd committed a crime. Ridiculous woman!"

"I heard that!"

"So? You think I'm afraid of you?"

"I know you are. I can smell the fear off you!"

There was a great commotion in the trees behind Boa. The branches were cracking as they were shaken and their motion becoming more violent as it got nearer.

"You are dead, you vile creature."

"No. Death is what you will all inherit now. I am returned with life. But you . . . you will follow the child into oblivion, come soon, come late. No exceptions for children or lost girls. Everybody dies, come soon, come late. And you—"

She leaped off the branch where she'd been perched, heading for Candy as she descended. She grabbed hold of Candy's face, throwing them both back through the barbed thickets to the ground. Her hand went from Candy's face to her throat.

"You, I say *soon*!"

16

LAGUNA MUNN ANGERED

IF CANDY HAD NOT had the sight of the Princess's face to look up at, she would have quickly succumbed to her death grip. But luckily she only had to look up at Boa's beautiful, hateful face to keep fighting, even though Boa's hold on her throat had cut off most of her air. She just kept beating at Boa's face, over and over and over, determined not to let the waves of darkness that lapped at her sight overwhelm her. But even with her fury at Boa to help keep her conscious she couldn't hold back the black tide forever. Her blows were getting weaker, and Boa was showing not the least sign of being hurt or dissuaded from further attack. She stared down at Candy with the implacable gaze of an executioner.

And then, behind her joyless face, there was a blur of color, too chaotic for Candy's weary eyes to make sense of.

But the voice that came with the colors was a different matter. That made perfect sense.

"Let go of the girl right now," the incantatrix said, "or

I swear I will break every bone in your body, Princess or no Princess."

A moment later Boa's hands let go of Candy's throat and she gratefully inhaled two lungfuls of sweet, clean air. It took her body a little while to push back the tide that had come so close to drowning her, by which time the struggle between Laguna Munn and Boa had already taken the two of them some distance from the place where Candy lay. When she got to her feet and looked around she saw them a long way up the slope, standing several yards apart but locked together by several cords of conjuration—those pitched by Mrs. Munn, digging their blazing fingers into Boa, while the cords Boa had cast danced vicious tarantellas around Mrs. Munn. The cords had shed bright flakes of energy—some no larger than fireflies, others the size of burning birds—that littered the darkness around and above the circle of ash and blackened timber that the powers of the combatants had burned into being.

Candy knew when she was out of her league. These two were exchanging blows from a magic she had no comprehension of, much less the means to conjure. Even as she watched, each of the pair called out more incandescent hurts and harms, yelling their furies at each other in what Candy recognized as Old Abaratian, the mother tongue of time itself. She understood not even a syllable of what they were hurling back and forth. But there was strange proof of its potency in the branches and on the ground all around the fire-formed grove.

While most of the scraps of power remained in the arena's zone of influence, a few escaped, and finding living subjects up among the branches and down between the roots, remade them. It was the sweet-songed capellajar birds that shed light on the spectacle, the magic transforming them into beasts that had something of the bat about them, and something about the lizard, their once modest beaks became snouts the length of their bodies, which pierced the dense lattice of branches, twigs and leaves as they descended from their high perches. The cavern's crystalline roof threw down shafts of rainbow silver, lighting the shadow world below.

For a few seconds Candy was enraptured by the eccentric life-forms that were appearing from the trees and thicket: bizarre relatives of creatures that would have still had a certain strangeness to Candy, even in their unaltered state, but were even more extraordinary now.

The spectacle held her in thrall so completely that she failed to notice that the two women were no longer fighting in the burned-out grove, and were making their way back down the slope toward her, until she heard Mrs. Munn's voice:

"Take it, girl!"

Candy persuaded her gaze to look away from the animals, and found that Laguna Munn was approaching her through the trees at an extraordinary rate, fearlessly careening through the thornbushes, no more than seven or eight strides from where Candy stood.

And again she shouted, as though the sense of what she was saying was utterly self-evident.

"Take it, girl!"

And as she shouted, and raced toward Candy, she offered up her right hand, which was partially open and completely empty.

"Be quick, girl. The vicious thing behind me means to take our lives!"

Candy looked back over Mrs. Munn's shoulder and saw that Boa's recently acquired flesh wore an expression of almost insane fury: her eyes gaping, her mouth gasping, and her lips curled back like those of a crazed dog, exposing not only her teeth but her gums too. Her body, though it was still without clothes, wore a pattern of shadowy stains that moved under the surface of her skin, dividing into smeared spots in one place and gathered into a single ragged shape in another, all constantly changing.

Even her face was stained: with a swarm of blots, then with rows of rising stripes, then a single black diamond, one form becoming another without lingering in any state for so much as a moment.

For some reason the display touched a nerve in Candy. It was literally sickening; it made her stomach rebel, and it was all she could do not to keep herself from puking.

Mrs. Munn's half-opened hand was now in front of Candy.

"Take it!" Mrs. Munn said. "Just do it!"

"Take *what*?"

"Whatever you see in my hand."

"It's empty."

"Look again. And be quick." Candy was aware of Boa's shape rising up behind Mrs. Munn, and beating at the air above her. "I can't hold her off for long. The power in her!"

Candy could hear Boa calling to her as she beat at the Air Armor the incantatrix had put up to keep her from finishing the chase. The Armor, a conjuration Candy knew of but couldn't wield, made Boa's voice slurred and remote, but Candy could still comprehend enough to know what Boa was doing. She was trying to sow seeds of doubt in Candy concerning Mrs. Munn.

"She says you're crazy," Candy said.

"She's probably right," Laguna Munn replied. "Did she make you want to vomit when you saw the Sepulcaphs?"

"Is that what they're called? Yes. It was horrible."

"If she tries it again, you run, put your eyes out, bury your head in the ground, just don't look at the patterns. If she's strong enough to keep them in her skin, which she is, she can make you puke yourself inside out."

"That's . . . that's not possible. Is it?"

"I'm afraid it is. She almost had me doing it two minutes ago, up the hill. Me? On my own rock! Where she got power to wield Sepulcaphs is . . ." She shook her head. ". . . unbelievable."

"She was taught by Christopher Carrion."

"Interesting. And of course the question remains:

where did *he* get it? The Hereafter doesn't have power. That's why you did business with us. But even the Abarat doesn't contain wieldings that powerful."

There was a sharp stinging sound, as more pieces of the Air Armor behind Laguna Munn shattered beneath Boa's assault.

"Lordy Lou. How did you ever live with her?"

"She wasn't like this."

"Or she was and you suppressed it."

"Huh. I never thought of that."

"No wonder you were a dull little batrat of a child. All your energy was going into keeping this monster from breaking out."

"Who said I was a dull little ratbat—"

"Batrat."

"—of a child?"

"You did. Who you are is the stone on which you stand. Now no more—"

There were two more brutal stings in quick succession. Then another three.

"She's breaking through. Take your weapon!"

Once again she was offering her hand to Candy, and once again Candy was seeing nothing but an empty palm. There was a desperate urgency to the problem. Boa and her nauseating Sepulcaphs were a cracked plate of air away.

"Look again!" Mrs. Munn insisted. "Look away. Clear your head. Then look again. It's right there!"

"What is?"

"Whatever you want."

"Like a poisonous snake?"

She had but to ask, and there it was in Mrs. Munn's hands: a seven-foot-long snake, its colors—a toxic yellow-green with a band of glistening black running along its length—designed to tell anyone that it was a venomous thing.

"Good choice, girl!" Mrs. Munn said, in a tone so ambiguous Candy had no idea whether she was serious or not. "Here! Take it!"

She tossed the snake at Candy, who, more out of instinct than intention, caught it in both hands.

"Now what?" she said.

17

SNAKE TALK

"JOLLO?"

There was no response from the wizened figure on the ground. His eyes were closed, and his pupils were motionless behind his gray, papery lids. Malingo kneeled down beside him, and spoke to him again:

"Are you still there?" he asked.

For several seconds there was no response. Then his gummy green eyelids opened and he spoke. His words were slurred, his voice watery.

"I'm still here. I just needed to rest. Everything was too noisy with my eyes open," he said.

Malingo glanced up at Covenantis, hoping he'd know the significance of Jollo's confusion of senses, but Covenantis's focus was neither with his brother nor Malingo. Covenantis was turned away from his brother in the direction of the sound of—

"Shattering air," Covenantis said.

"I didn't even know air could shatter," Malingo said.

"Glass can be poured like treacle if it's hot enough. Did you not know that either?" Covenantis replied. "Are all geshrats so stupid?"

The noise came again. And again. Malingo was now looking in the same direction as Covenantis, curious as to what shattered air looked like. Suddenly, Jollo seized hold of Malingo's arm, first with one hand then with both, pulling himself up into a sitting position, his eyes opening wide.

"She's there," he said, staring with eerie accuracy in precisely the same direction as his brother.

Malingo didn't need to ask Jollo of whom he was speaking. There was only one "she" in the boys' universe. And all Jollo wanted right now was the comfort of her presence.

"Mama . . ." said Jollo. "Find her, Covenantis."

"She's coming, little brother."

"Hurry her up. Please?"

"I can't hurry her when she has such important work, brother."

"I'm almost dead," Jollo said. "I want to see her one last time . . ."

"Hush, Jollo. No more talk of death."

"Easy to say when it's not your life that's . . . fading away." His face became a tragic mask. "I want my mama."

"She'll come as soon as she can," Covenantis said, only this time much more quietly, his voice filled with sorrow as though he knew, however fast she came it would never be fast enough.

"Don't look up!" Mrs. Munn yelled over another round of shattering air. "Just be ready!"

"What do you mean?"

"You wanted the snake. Get ready to use it!"

Candy felt stupid and angry and confused all at once. She'd never imagined letting Boa go would escalate into such chaos: the Princess nearly killing Mrs. Munn, her firstborn, and Candy, and now breaking through Mrs. Munn's defenses, still no doubt wearing the Sepulcaphs. The mere thought of them was enough to stir up nausea, so Candy concentrated on the snake.

Its body was too thick for her to get her hand around, but it didn't seem to want to escape her grip. Quite the reverse. It slid the cool, dry length of its tail twice around one of her arms and then, raising up its large head so that it could look down imperiously at Candy it said, "I think myself a very fine snake. Do you not agree?"

Its speech, which was as elegant and smooth as its motion, came as no great surprise to Candy. It had been the greatest disappointment of growing up—far more wounding than finding out that there was neither an Oz nor a Santa Claus—to discover that though animals talked often and wisely in the stories she loved, few of them did so in life. It made perfect sense then that a creature she had fashioned in a moment of blind instinct would possess the power of speech.

"Are you the one who called me into being?" the serpent inquired.

"Yes, I'm the one."

"Lovely work, if one may be so bold," the snake said, admiring his gleaming coils. "I would have done nothing different. Not a scale. One finds oneself . . . perfect." He looked a little embarrassed. "Oh dear, I think I'm in love," he said, kissing his own coils.

"Aren't you poisonous?" Candy said.

"Indeed. I can taste the bitterness of my own poison. One is of course immune to one's own toxins, but if a single drop fell on your tongue——"

"Dead?"

"Guaranteed."

"Quick?"

"Of course not! What's a poison worth if it's quick?"

"Painless?"

"No! What's a——"

"Poison worth if it's painless?"

"Precisely. My *bite* may be quite swift, but the consequence? I assure you, it's the very worst. It feels like a fire is cooking your brains and your muscles are rotting on your bones."

"Lordy Lou."

Hearing the animal speak so lovingly of the agonies it could cause made Candy think of Christopher Carrion. Much like the snake's poison, Carrion's soup of nightmares had been lethal to others. But to Carrion, they'd been companions, trusted and loved. The similarity was too strong to be a coincidence. Candy had laced her invented snake with a little of Carrion's essence.

The chat with the snake, along with Candy's recollection of Carrion, had taken but a few seconds, during which time the sound of Boa battering on the last plate of air had grown steadily louder.

"Does your snake know what to do when Boa gets in?" Mrs. Munn yelled over the noise. "Because she's a vehement one. She's going to be through very soon, and you'd better be ready."

"Oh, I think my snake knows his business," Candy yelled back.

"*Your* snake, am I?"

"As long as you don't object," she said, doing her best to reproduce the snake's imitation of high birth.

"Why would one mind?" the snake replied. "In truth, lady, one is both honored and moved."

It raised its finely formed snout a little way, in order to deepen the bow that followed. Candy did her best to conceal her impatience (what part of her, conceiving of a snake, had created one with such humorless formality?) but it was difficult. The only thing that kept her from losing her composure was the serpent's genuine commitment to her.

"You've won me over entirely," it said to her. "I would kill the world for you, I swear I would."

"Candy . . ." Mrs. Munn said. "Be quick or it's ended."

"I hear you," Candy replied. "We're ready."

"Is it to be the world then?" the snake said.

"Thanks for the offer, but no, I just need you to stop one person."

"And who's that? The fat woman?"

"I heard that, snake!" Mrs. Munn yelled.

"No, snake," Candy said. "*Absolutely not.* That's our friend."

"It's not the world and it's not the fat one. So who?"

"The one on the other side of the air," Candy said.

"Why her?"

"Because she's a bad piece of work," Candy said. "Trust me. Her name's Boa. Princess Boa."

"Oh, now wait," the serpent said. "This one's royalty? No. No no. One has one's limits. She's one of my own!"

"Look at her! She's no snake."

"I don't care to."

"You were ready to kill the world for me just a minute ago!"

"The world, yes. Her? No."

Mrs. Munn had not heard a single word of this. She'd been too busy using her strengths—mental, physical and magical—to keep the final plate of air, which was already badly cracked, from shattering completely.

It was a struggle she was going to lose very soon, Candy feared. Boa's power was now so formidable that despite all the incantatrix's years of wieldings, she had run out of energies to oppose her. In desperation she had reached into her very soul for strength. But even that had not been sufficient. Its fuel had been almost entirely burned through in seconds. When it was gone, her life would be over.

"I'm sorry, Candy . . ." The thundering of Boa's forces beating against the final plate of air almost drowned her out. She drew a deep breath and tried again one last time. "I can't hold her back. I've used everything I have. There's no life left in me."

"No! Mrs. Munn, you can't die. Just get out of her way."

"If I move, it's over," she said. "Boa will be through and we'll both be vomiting."

"You know what?" said Candy. "Let her come. I'm not afraid of her. I've got a killer snake right here at my side."

"You *don't* have me," the snake said.

Candy had neither the time nor the temper left for debate. She raised the snake still coiled around her arm. "Now you listen to me, you pretentious self-loving, empty-headed worm—"

"Worm? Did you call me a *worm*?"

"Shut up. I'm shouting! You exist because I made you. And I can unmake you just as easily." She had no idea whether this was actually true, but given that she'd brought the snake into being, it was a reasonable assumption.

"You wouldn't dare!" the snake said.

"What?" Candy said, not even looking at him.

"Unmake me."

Now she looked. "Really? Is that a request?"

"No. No!"

"Are you quite sure?"

"You're crazy."

"Oh, you've seen nothing yet."

"And I don't want to, thank you very much."

"Well then, do as I say."

She met the snake's beady black gaze, and held it. And held it. And held it.

"All right!" it said finally, breaking his gaze. "You win! There's no dealing with insanity."

"Good choice."

"I'll bite her, but then you let me go."

Before Candy could reply, Boa unleashed a shriek, which was drowned out seconds later, overwhelmed by the crash as the final plate of air shattered. The blast of energy slammed into Laguna Munn, who shielded Candy and the snake from the worst of its force. She, however, was picked up, despite her weight, and thrown like a straw doll, off into the darkness between the trees.

The snake's instant response was to escape from Candy's grip, the entire muscular length of its body writhing around in panic.

"So sorry. One has to leave. Look at the time."

"Nice try, worm," Candy said, reaching out and grabbing hold of its body, somewhere, she guessed, close to its head. She was loathe to open her eyes too wide to check on where she'd fallen in case an exploratory glance, however brief, gave her a lethal glimpse of Boa and her Sepulcaphs. On the other hand she wasn't going to be able to use the snake against Boa unless she knew where the enemy was standing.

Suddenly the snake's frenzied twists and turns stopped, and seizing the chance its sudden passivity offered, Candy slid her hand up along its body. She'd seen how real snake handlers worked. They seized hold of the animal right behind its head and held on with all their strength so that the snake couldn't whip around and bite them.

But Candy's snake showed no intention of doing so. It didn't move at all. In fact, the reason for its sudden stillness was clear just a few inches farther along its body. A shoeless foot was pressed down upon the snake's head.

"So . . ." Boa said. "I think it's time you looked at me, don't you? I can make you if I want to."

18

AN ENDGAME

MALINGO WAS STILL STARING off between the trees, hoping to catch some sign of Candy's return—so far no luck. What he did see was a flock of perhaps ten or twelve winged creatures, which looked through the trees in his general direction, barking and squealing, chattering and howling with the stolen voices of a dog, pig, monkey and hyena.

"What's that noise?" Covenantis said.

"You need to see for yourself," Malingo said, his vocabulary too impoverished to do the sight justice.

"I can't look right now," the slug-boy replied. "I'm . . . *concentrating* on something. It's not something I can take my eyes off."

"You need some help?"

"No," the boy said. "This is for me to do and only me. Why don't you just keep watching for Candy and Mama? And please . . . don't watch me while I'm doing the wielding."

"Are you going to do some magic?"

"I'm going to try. Just a verse and a chorus."

"What?"

"They're songs. Mama wrote down all the spells she learned or created as songs. They're harder to steal that way, she says. I've been listening to Mama's songs as recordings since I was about two. So I know all her magic because I could sing all her songs, every single one."

"Did you understand them?"

"We're about to find out, aren't we? That's why I don't want anyone watching. If something goes wrong, at least you'll have your back to it."

"What are you going to do?"

"Nothing too ambitious. I'm a horrible singer. But I'd like to ease Jollo's pain if I can."

"Isn't your mother going to go crazy when she finds out you've been stealing her magic?"

"Probably. But she'll go even crazier if she gets back and finds Jollo's dead. It'll break her heart. And what kind of son will I be if I don't try to stop my own mother's heart from being broken? I'll tell you. A bad one. I've disappointed her enough. This once I'm going to get it right."

"Couldn't you just wait a few more minutes?"

"Don't ask me. Ask Jollo."

Malingo glanced back at Jollo, and had his answer. If it hadn't been for the very subtle rise and fall of Jollo's chest, Malingo might easily have assumed the life had already left Jollo's body.

"I have to start," Covenantis said. "You keep looking for Mama or the Quackenbush girl."

"They'll come," Malingo said, and turning his back to Covenantis he did as the boy had requested and stared off between the trees.

As he studied the corridor of shadow before him and ever-deeper shadow ahead of him he became aware that he, the studier, was himself being studied. He let his gaze follow his instinct up into the lower branches of a tree close by. There sat three members of the pale-feathered flock that had made such noisy passage between the trees only a couple of minutes before. They were silent now, hushed perhaps by the melancholy scene below. He watched them watching him, unnerved by their scrutiny.

And then, from behind, came the sound of Covenantis's voice, singing with unnerving accuracy, in a falsetto, a song his mother had obviously written to sing herself. It had the lilting rhythm of a lullaby. These were the primal sounds of an Abarat that was holding the Hours in trust for humankind to one day possess. Sounds that were about light and darkness, sky and sea, rock and fire.

> "Kai tu penthni,
> Kai tu ky,
> Hastegethchem
> Smanné fy."

And death. That was the subject waiting behind all the other immensities. Death the merciless, death the irrevocable, the enemy of all things tender and easily broken:

cracked like an egg dropped from a high place; burned black when lightning turned the forest to fire; killed by the cold, huddled in the cleft of a rock.

And still the ancient words came, flowing so fearlessly the boy might have been reciting his own name.

> *"U Tozzemanos,*
> *Wo th'chem*
> *Wo Kai numma*
> *Jeth yo yem."*

What was he doing? Malingo's curiosity grew more insistent the longer the recitations went on. What kind of comfort could he possibly be offering his brother that required the uttering of words so ancient and alien?

Malingo was in the process of instructing himself not to turn, not to look, when his body acted upon a demand far deeper than his instruction.

He turned and looked. Again his body overtook his mind, this time to simply expel a word—

"No!"

—not once but over and over and over—

"No! No! No! No!"

Candy didn't waste time wondering why Malingo was shouting. She simply seized the moment, and with it, the snake. Boa's foot was still on the animal's head, but neither her full attention nor her weight were with it, so when

Candy pulled on her invented beast it slid out from under the Princess's foot without a struggle.

The serpent gave out a most unserpentine din of mutinous rage, writhing fiercely. She tried to grab its twisting coils with her free hand, but she was concentrating so hard on doing so that all thought of Boa and her lethal designs went out of her head. She half turned carelessly, and realized too late that her eyes had grazed the shape of Boa, moving toward her. Worse, they would not now let go. She tried to detach her sight from the form of the Princess—and worse, from the sight of the designs, moving up and over her face, forming their nauseating symbols in the air around her head. Signs to make a body recoil against itself: to make it turn itself inside out in a frenzy of disorder, to work against nature, against purpose, against life, and destroy itself.

So much destructive power was encoded in the patterns playing on Boa's face. Even though Candy knew the harm they would make her do to herself, their enchantment had more power than her will. She couldn't force it from her, even when she felt her stomach turning over—

"*Don't! Look!*" Laguna Munn shrieked.

She didn't have a gentle voice, a voice of calm or contemplation. No, her voice was rude and raw, which was just what the moment needed.

Much to Candy's relief and astonishment, her eyes had obeyed the instruction. As soon as she looked away, her will was her own again.

"Good!" Mrs. Munn said. "Now quickly, girl! Give that damnable beast to me."

Candy began to offer it, but Mrs. Munn was impatient.

"Give the beast to me!" she said. She appeared from within the trees and reached out to take hold of the animal. "Next time, call up an ax!" she said as she dragged the creature out of Candy's arms. "Snakes are all teeth and talk!"

"I'll make you regret—" the snake began to say, but Mrs. Munn was in no mood for its threats.

She wrenched its tail off Candy's arm, and all but bundled the creature into a ball of black-and-yellow coils.

Then she told it: *"Go bite a Boa!"* and threw it at the Princess.

Grabbing hold of Candy's sleeve, Mrs. Munn dragged her off between the trees, leaving Princess Boa and the conjured serpent to take out their lethal rage upon each other.

19

THE PRICE OF FREEDOM

"A WALL OF BLUE FLAME Thorns is going around those two," Mrs. Munn said as she hurried Candy away from the spot where they'd left Boa and the snake to match their venomous skills. The incantatrix was no longer the figure of calm power and confident abundance she'd been when Candy had first met her. The colors in her dress had been somehow removed, and one of her feather antennae had been torn out. Everywhere there was evidence of how hard the last few minutes had been. She was scratched, bruised, and sweating: an exhausted fighter still standing, but only by sheer force of will.

"When will the wall go up?" Candy asked her.

"It's already up. No, girl, *don't look back*! Lordy Lou, when are you going to learn some caution? You're not playing games. The Boa girl may have been a civilized tenant when she was sharing your head, but that simply testifies to the power of your influence. You must have kept her villainy subdued, without knowing you were doing it. But she's loose now."

"What about the wall of Flame Thorns?"

"Oh, that's not going to detain her for very long. Nor is that ridiculous snake of yours."

"You were right. I should have made an ax—"

"It would have been no more use than . . . the . . . snake." As Mrs. Munn's words slowed down so did her pace until she was standing still, Candy beside her, staring off into the trees. Candy looked for some sign of Malingo, or of Jollo and Covenantis, but the shadows between the trees seemed particularly dense directly ahead of them: almost clotted.

"What's wrong?" Candy said.

"One of the boys," Mrs. Munn said. "Something's happened to one of my boys."

She started to pick up speed again, moving swiftly, parting the darkness ahead of her like a curtain with a few muttered words. Candy kept up, but there was no longer room for them to walk side by side: the trees and the shadows were too tightly packed. She could only follow after Mrs. Munn as she wove between the trees.

Finally, a figure appeared from the darkness ahead of them. It was Malingo. Even before Mrs. Munn had reached him, he began to apologize:

"I didn't know how to stop him. He had these words . . . from one of your books—"

"Jollo was doing magic?"

"No, Mrs. Munn. It was Covenantis. He started reciting some sort of conjuration—" He put his hand up to his face, which was wet with tears. "I tried to stop him, but he took no notice. He wasn't reading from a book so I couldn't take the words away from him. He had them all in his head."

"Oh, I'm sure," Mrs. Munn said. "He's a very intelligent child. That's a piece of the good I put in him before he was born." She studied the clogged darkness that lay ahead of them. "Where is he now?" she said.

"He's still with Jollo. But I don't know exactly where." He frowned, and shook his head, confounded by his own stupidity. "They should be right there behind me, because almost as soon as I went off looking for you both— I couldn't have taken more than two or three paces—I thought: this is wrong. I should do as Candy said and stay with them. So I turned back, and there was shadow, thick shadow, where there hadn't been any before."

"You know why."

"Me?" Malingo said.

"You don't have to say it," Mrs. Munn replied, her voice softer than it had been until now. "Maybe you didn't even realize you were running from it."

"I wasn't running *from* anything. I told you. I didn't even know what was happening."

Laguna Munn moved past Malingo, advancing toward a place from which all light had been driven. "But you heard it in the words he was saying."

"It wasn't a language I understood."

"Even so, you heard it," she said.

It wasn't a question. She was merely stating what they both knew. He didn't attempt to avoid admitting the truth any longer.

"Yes, I heard," he said.

"Heard what?" Candy asked.

"Death," he said.

And as if responding to that summoning word, the shadows ahead of the incantatrix tore themselves apart as though they were made of wet newspaper. Malingo didn't want to see, at least not yet. He slipped between two trees, allowing Candy to follow Mrs. Munn, who had now passed beyond the shredded shadows, and was looking at what lay between the trees directly ahead of her.

The boy was dead, no doubt of that. His body had withered considerably more since Candy had last seen him, his flesh so drained of its vital juices that the bright, dark creature he had once been had gone entirely. What was left looked like a dwarf lying in a baggy shirt made of skin.

He looks so small, Candy thought: small and colorless. Jollo's skin had been as black as the night sky, with fireworks streaking through it. Where had all that darkness and color gone? Death had scoured Jollo's remains so completely clean that it looked more like his brother's body.

Either that or—

Or what?

"I don't think that's Jollo, Mrs. Munn," Candy said very quietly, as though the news might disturb the dead.

"I know," Mrs. Munn replied.

The fact that the corpse was so very small now made sense. The remains before them weren't those of the beloved and well-fed Jollo B'gog. It was Covenantis's body, Candy realized, which lay in the grass.

"What happened to him?" Candy said, her voice hushed with horror. "Did the magic he was wielding backfire?"

"No. The wielding worked exactly as he wished it to," Jollo said.

As he spoke he emerged from between the trees on the far side of his brother's body. All trace of the damage Boa had done to him in consuming his life force had been healed, and Jollo was once again the gleaming, glorious creature he'd been when he'd first introduced himself to Candy and Malingo: his mother's pride and joy. All he lacked was his dazzling grin.

"He used the Old Magic, Mama. I had nothing to do with it, I swear. He just gave me his life. I didn't even know you could do something like that."

"You can't. Not easily. You have to find the right conjuration, and learn it perfectly, speak it perfectly. And then, of course, you have to be ready to give up your life."

"That's what he did, Mama. I didn't even know he was doing it. I swear I didn't."

"So your brother gave up his life out of the goodness of his heart?"

"Not of *his* heart, Mama. Yours. That's what you made him out of, isn't it?"

Mrs. Munn stared hard at Jollo, clearly assessing his honesty. "And you, boy, I made from all the wickedness in me. My capacity for cruelty. And for vengefulness. And for *lies*."

"Are you saying I'm a liar, Mama?" Jollo said. He literally bristled at the idea. His glossy black coat, which had lain so perfectly flat that Candy hadn't even realized Jollo had fur until this moment, now stood up in three parallel ridges that went from the front of his head to the back, and described a spiral on his belly, centered where a normal child had a navel.

"Don't you raise your hackles at me, boy!"

"Then don't call me a liar when I'm not."

"Your brother is dead, Jollo. I need to know why!"

"Then ask the geshrat!" Jollo said. "He saw it all!"

Mrs. Munn looked to Candy. "Where did your friend go?"

"He's not gone far. I think he's just keeping a respectful distance."

She looked back over her shoulder, sensing Malingo there rather than seeing him, then quietly telling him:

"She's not angry. She just wants to know——"

"Yes, I heard," Malingo said, coming out of the shadows between the trees. "And it all happened pretty much as Jollo said it did. The little kid used a conjuring in Old Abaratian. I could feel the power in the words. And I saw the life, like a stream of light and water, running out of him and into Jollo, who was just lying there, near enough dead. He didn't say anything to make it happen. It was Covenantis's doing. The whole thing."

"Did you try to stop it at least?" Mrs. Munn said.

"Of course. I started yelling at him. But that didn't work. And he wouldn't let me get close to him to stop him by separating them. When I tried, some force just threw me back, and I hit the ground. I kept trying but eventually there was no point. Covenantis just withered away. All he said was that he knew you'd understand. His exact words were: 'Tell Mama: She'll understand.'"

"Stupid," Mrs. Munn murmured.

"I did what I could," Malingo replied.

"Not you, geshrat. My boy. My firstborn."

"It's too late to say that now!" Jollo replied. "I mean, look at him! He's gone forever, Mama, and he's never coming back."

Mrs. Munn nodded.

"If he wanted to punish me," she said, "then he succeeded."

"Punish you?" Candy said. "Why?"

"Because I was not the loving mother I should have been. Because I loved the darkness in me more than the light." She approached the tiny body in its shroud of oversized skin, and went down onto her knees beside it. "Forgive me, child," she said softly. There were tears in her voice.

"I think we should go," Candy said.

"Yes, I think maybe you should," Laguna Munn said,

not turning to look at Candy or Malingo, just staring down at the dead boy.

"I'm . . . sorry," Candy said.

"It wasn't your fault. The error was mine. Be well, Candy Quackenbush. The struggles ahead of you will test you to the limits of your endurance. Beyond them, perhaps. But if you are in need of further healing . . ."

"Yes?"

". . . don't come here in search of it." Tears thickened every one of her words. "Jollo," she said. "Take them down to the harbor and find them a boat."

"Thank you," Candy said.

Mrs. Munn did not acknowledge her thanks, or say so much as a single word in reply. She had laid her hands on the body of her dead child, and her tears fell on it.

That was Candy's last image of the great incantatrix, Laguna Munn: kneeling beside the body of the boy made from all the good in her, with her tears falling and falling.

Once out of his mother's presence, Jollo became very talkative, keeping up a monologue of chatter about one subject only: himself. *Was this a necessary part of evil?* Candy wondered as she listened to him: this utter self-absorption, as though nothing else in the world mattered but Jollo and his boredom, Jollo and how he'd suffered during Boa's attack, Jollo and what he was going to do when he left the rock and went out into the Abarat.

"There's a time coming, Mama says, when someone with my genius for wicked things will be really useful.

I mean, I'm going to be a King, at least. Probably something more than a King. What's more than a King? Oh, like someone who kills a King. That's what I'm going to be. Because if you kill something you're more important than whatever you killed. Mama didn't tell me that. I just thought it up myself. Because I have these dreams, see, where it's the future, and everything boring and good is being lined up to be killed. They'll have their heads chopped off. I might do the chopping, but no, that'd be boring wouldn't it? I hate being bored. That's why I'm going to leave very soon. . . ."

And so he went on, an endless speech about Jollo, Jollo and more Jollo. When they eventually emerged from the trees they saw before them a shallow bay with a short, wooden jetty that jutted from the steep beach. Candy and Malingo exchanged looks of relief. They were going to be out of the boy's company very soon.

Jollo, however, had one subject left to pontificate upon.

"When I leave here," he told Candy, "I'm going to be taking all of Mama's magic books with me, because she's got books that there's only one of, and I could get thousands of paterzem for a magic book that there was only one of, right? So do you want me to bring them to you first? I know the geshrat's too stupid to read a big book, but you're famous aren't you? Mama told me before you arrived—" They were on the jetty now, the boards creaking beneath them.

"She knew I was coming?" Candy said.

"Excuse me," Jollo snarled. "I was still talking. How *dare* you interrupt me? You know what? I'm not going to bring Mama's books. Not when you're so rude. I can't believe that! Ignorant peasant! Don't try groveling because that won't get you anywhere. Grovelers are pathetic. Like my brother. He used to grovel when I kicked him really hard. I'm going to miss him. I won't have anyone to kick. I just had a brilliant idea! I'll forgive you for being rude, and I'll bring you the books like I said I would. All you have to do is leave the geshrat here. I won't hurt him badly. I'll just do the same stuff I did with my brother. You know, kicking and spitting and stuff. That's a good deal, right? I mean, when I'm King you're going to be so glad I forgave you because otherwise your life won't be worth living." He grinned. "Like my brother. I got his life because I'd made his so miserable." The grin broke into squalid laughter. "That's the stupidest thing anybody ever did, isn't it? When I'm King I'm going to make him a saint. He's going to be Saint Covenantis, the Patron Saint of Stupid People! Ha! I love that! He'll have his own Holy Day. Today, the day he died. Nobody will work. They'll just say stupid prayers for a stupid saint of stupid people. Wait! What's your geshrat doing."

Candy didn't answer.

"Tell me! Oh. Oh, I get it. You need permission to speak, right? You may now speak. Tell me what your geshrat's doing."

"Are your eyes bad?" Candy said.

"No. My eyes are perfect."

"Then you can see what he's doing. Standing in the small boat, untying the rope."

"Well, tell him to get out of the boat. We made a deal, you and me. The geshrat stays and when I'm King—"

"*Shut up.*"

"What?"

"Are your ears as bad as your eyes? I said: *shut up*. You'll never be King of anything. You're a nasty maggot-brained little nobody. You think of nothing but yourself, and the only thing you'll ever be King of is something you'd find on the bottom of your shoe."

"Enough, Candy . . ." Malingo said quietly. He was reaching out to take hold of Candy's hand, but she wasn't quite finished.

"King *Turd*," she said. "That is the most you'll ever be."

Jollo's hackles were rising, and he was giving off a vile bitter odor, which she hadn't smelled earlier, perhaps because she'd been farther away from him. The acrid smell made her eyes water, and it was that fact more than Malingo's summons that made her give up telling Jollo what she thought of him. She didn't want him to have the satisfaction of believing he'd reduced her to tears so she turned her back on him and went to catch hold of Malingo.

The smell of Jollo's rage suddenly became a lot stronger, and she knew without looking back that the little monster was right behind her reaching up to dig his claws into her neck. But that was another satisfaction he wasn't going to get. She didn't have time to grab Malingo's hand. She just leaped off the jetty and into the boat, falling face-down in the stale water that had collected at the bottom. By the time she got up, Malingo had already gotten the oars in the water and was rowing the boat away from the jetty where Jollo B'gog was still standing, bristling and spitting, his wads of spittle expelled with such demonic force that they could be heard as they hit the stern of the boat.

That, however, was the worst he could do, at least for today. Perhaps tomorrow he would get his throne and crown. Stranger things had happened. Until then Candy would remember him as a frustrated brat standing on an antiquated jetty, spitting and spitting, until his target was out of range.

As soon as Malingo's rowing brought the boat clear of the boy's protection, it was collected by a current of surprising swiftness, which carried them off. The current moved with the speed of an instructed messenger, carrying the boat through a tunnel that in no way resembled the cavern through which they'd entered. It curved sinuously, first left, then right, then left again, the motion almost hypnotic. As she was rocked in the cradle of the boat, Candy allowed herself a moment of happiness.

I got rid of her, she thought to herself. *The bitter monster who was in my head, killing my joy, has gone forever. And I'm a little different, maybe: but I'm still Candy Quackenbush, the way I always was.*

"You're smiling," Malingo said. "It's because she's gone, isn't it?"

"You know me so well," Candy replied.

"I like that. Knowing you. It's the best thing that ever happened to me."

"And from now it's going to get better and better," Candy said.

They said no more, but lay content in their well-earned fatigue, as the boat moved on through the long, winding cavern, until its waters brought them out into the waters around Jibarish, which lay calm under a sky so bright with stars that they could see to the mists where this Hour faded and became another.

"Where now?" Malingo asked.

PART THREE

MANY MAGICS

The magic of the circle,
The magic of the eye,
The magic of the vortex,
The magic of the cry.

The magic of the head bone,
The round which bounds the mind,
The coin of gold which buys the bait
The ouroboros will find.

The worm surrounds the human heart,
Our hearts surround the world;
And sleeping, in the beating womb,
The naked babe is curled.

Chant your courage round the child,
Make joy its root and rhyme;
And we, my love, will wander freed
Of Loss and Fear and Time.

20

TOMORROW, TODAY

As is true of all prophets, the prediction merchants of the Abarat were egotistical and combative, contemptuous of any other seers besides themselves. The fact that each of them worked in radically different ways to achieve their results only intensified the antagonism. One might see signs of futurity in the eighty-eight cards of the Abaratian tarot; another found his own vision of tomorrow in the dung of the yutter goats that grazed the golden fields of Gnomon; while a third, having witnessed the way the music of a Noncian reed pipe had induced the lunatics in a madhouse on Huffaker to dance, had then discovered evidence of how the future would unfold in the footprints the patients had left in the sand.

Thus, separated both by their methodologies and by a dangerous sense of their own importance, none of the soothsayers ever compared their predictions with those of others. Had they done so they would have discovered that each of them—however unlike their methods—was receiving the same news. Bad news.

A darkness was coming. A vast and implacable darkness that would pinch out every star and eclipse every moon that lit Night's skies and extinguish every sun that blazed in the Heavens of Day.

Had the prophets of Abarat put aside their vanities and self-importance when these presentments of darkness had first crept into their minds and shared their fears with one another instead of clinging to them like the lethal possessions they were, they might have avoided the tragic consequences that had come as a result of that envy and covetousness.

The tragedy lay not only in the waste of those prophetic minds, doomed to descend into madness and self-destruction, it lay in the fact that the Abarat was to be plunged into a waking nightmare that would change it forever.

21

BOA AT MIDNIGHT

BOA AND THE SNAKE, finding they both were of royal blood, parted amicably. And, rather than waste any more time with Laguna Munn or her sorry excuses for children, Boa fled Jibarish for Gorgossium. Something became apparent to her as soon as she set foot on Midnight's earth: Gorgossium had changed. There was a new urgency about the island that she couldn't remember ever sensing when she'd come here before. At the Todo Mines there was a steady stream of miners, thousands of Abaratians of every species from every island, some marching down to work in the open seams, which were illuminated by banks of lights fiercer than the noonday sun on Yzil, while other gangs of workers—many among them members of the Kooth nation, whose four huge eyes naturally produced strong beams of parchment-yellow light—were crowding into iron elevators, each big enough to carry two hundred workers, so as to be taken to work in the labyrinth of tunnels below. The noise of drilling and cursing and blasting made Boa's head throb. She'd overtaxed her new body with the demands of the Sepulcaphs. It wouldn't be an incantation she'd be using again any time soon.

Away from the mines she headed toward the forest of Ancients, trees of half wood, half stone. They were massive pillars that kept her from seeing her destination—the thirteen towers. It was there that she encountered further evidence of Gorgossium's furious new appetite. A large group of merchants, who'd been traveling ahead of Boa by a half mile or so, had been attacked by a number of Corruption Flies, the form and color of which was exactly that of the flies Boa had seen crawling on rotted food in the alleyways of Chickentown, except that Gorgossium's species were the size of cars.

She didn't have to wait until the last of the merchants had perished to get past the place where the flies had found them. While the screams of those being plucked up and carried away was still going on, a wave of Old Red, which was the islanders' nickname for the crimson mist that curled around the island like a gargantuan scarlet snake, appeared nosing its way between the stone-still Ancients. She cursed it under her breath. She had no choice: enter the mist, which wasn't a pleasant thought, or contend with a pestilence of agitated Corruption Flies.

More than once Carrion had teased Boa by telling her that he knew of references in the Abarataraba, the most rare and powerful magical work of the Hours, concerning the true nature and purpose of Old Red. She wanted to know the details, but Carrion had refused to share what he knew.

"In time," he'd said.

That had always been a favorite trick of his: putting off telling the juicy stuff until later, always later.

Well, *later was here.* She wanted knowledge and she would have it, even if it meant stepping into the skin of Old Red itself. She didn't let her unease slow her down. She plunged into the churning mist and kept walking. Rather than allow her mind to dwell on her fears, she kept her thoughts on the future. She would have to be careful from now on. She had lived beneath the mask of an innocent Princess when she'd been here before. She no longer had such cover. Word of what had transpired on Laguna Munn's island would surely have reached Gorgossium by now. And given that her rise to power in Carrion's world had meant that others, who had doubtless expected to be elevated long before her, had seen those dreams dashed, there would be many here at Midnight who would gladly see her dead.

Carrion had been a man on the rise when she'd carefully orchestrated their "accidental" meeting. He had quickly made it plain to her that his ambition was almost limitless. He intended to go everywhere, know everything, and have knowledge of every state of being. She knew a man destined for power when she saw one.

Word was that he'd perished in the Chickentown fiasco. And she'd seen him, through Candy's eyes, carried away by the Izabella, and lost in the flood that had overwhelmed Chickentown, but she could not bring herself to believe that he was dead. He had been badly injured, no doubt. But he'd been wounded many times before, often grievously, without forfeiting his life.

No. Her precious Christopher, who had taught her so much, was alive. She was certain of it. Somewhere she would find him. And somehow they would mend what had been broken between them.

The clammy folds of Old Red thinned and parted, and through its bloody veil Boa could see one of the towers ahead. She was almost there! The tower was being worked on, she saw, the old stone being replaced with polished plates of quamighto in the silvery surface of which reflected objects were fantastically distorted.

Despite her exhilaration at knowing she would soon be in Carrion's presence she couldn't help but feel a twinge of unease. If Carrion was indeed alive, and had come back to Gorgossium—where else would he go?—then she was perhaps but a minute or two from being in his presence. She brought an image of him into her mind's eye. That almost naked head, with barely sufficient flesh to stretch over his jutting bones, and the two pipes that had been surgically implanted in the back of his skull, causing his nightmares to be siphoned off out of his brain and swim freely in the fluid that he breathed, allowing him to live in the company of his own darkest vision. But for all that was monstrous in his appearance, there was a tenderhearted creature within.

And she had betrayed that tender heart. She had used him for her own advancement as a magician, and then cast him aside to marry Finnegan Hob. For that crime against love, Carrion had hired an assassin to murder her at her own wedding. So, they were evenly matched. A heart for a life. Who could argue with that? They'd both paid terrible prices for what they'd done. If she could persuade Carrion of that—if she could make him understand that it was time to forgive and move on—then perhaps there was a chance he could forgive her betrayal. Words of love would no longer suffice, of course. He would want her closer than words: much, much closer.

But if that was the price of winning his devotion again, of healing the hurt she'd done him, then it was a tiny price, and she would gladly pay it. And it certainly didn't hurt her case that she was returning to him with knowledge of the Hereafter; a world she knew he had long hoped to subdue with wieldings of unimaginable scale. Now she was familiar with that idiot world. She'd studied it for almost sixteen years through the eyes of Candy Quackenbush. She had witnessed in nauseating detail how the human world worked: its rituals of comfort (television, food, religion); its appetite for poison (television, food, religion); and for the monstrous edifices of desire (television, food, religion): she understood them all. What might she and Carrion, the apprentice and her sometime master, not do if they went to work in that stupefied world with the intention of bringing it to its knees?

Oh, by A'zo and Cha:

WHAT MIGHT THEY *NOT* DO?

And then, as she came to the edge of the trees, Old Red dispersed completely, and Boa barely suppressed a cry of shock seeing how the scene before her had changed. She had seen only one three-spired tower through the mist. The rest had been demolished completely, their rubble removed and the ground where they'd stood pummeled flat, so as to make the size of the new tower seem even more prodigious. The spires had no windows for ninety-eight percent of their height.

Only at the top of the immense central spire, which was needle-fine, were there windows; a row of them, shaped like narrow eyes, all around the crown of the structure. As she studied it, however, she saw that there were vertical rows of symbols etched into the stone, which had the sheen of mercury. They were indecipherable to Boa, but she knew their origins. They were pieces of ancient Abaratian, the language of the Thread as it was sometimes known, meaning that it had been used to encode and connect all things beneath the Twenty-Four Hours and One that hung above the islands. In these sigils, every piece of the Abarat, from a dew drop to a mountain, from a flea to the Requiax, from a second of unendurable grief to an infant's first smile—all written and entwined in the thread that ran unbroken through Time and Time Out of Time, connecting it all, forever and always.

But oh, she thought, *what a fine and terrible thing it would*

*be to cut that sacred cord! To sever all from all, in perpetuity and
visit the despair that no prayer or calculation could cure. . . .*

The thought of doing such sublime harm filled her
with joy. A Princess capable of such ambition was inviolate. She had died, but lived again. No harm could
possibly come to her. And, in thinking so, she stepped
out from beneath the Ancients and started across the
open grounds toward the Needle Tower. No one was
guarding the tower for a very simple reason: it had no
door. Boa circled the tower twice examining the wall
for the slightest hint of an opening, however narrow or
small. But there was nothing. Of course it was perfectly
possible the door was concealed by a Seemi Feit, but
she was in no mood to search for any trailing threads
of Seemi Rope to carefully pull it apart. She was out of
practice with decoding, and impatient to see what was
inside the tower. So she gave her blood a charge of power
by whispering three syllables—v'aatheum—against her
wrist, then immediately biting into the meat, drawing
off a mouthful of blood, and before it had time to dissolve on her gums and tongue, spat it with all possible
force against her distorted reflection.

The reflecting seal bubbled, smoked and dissolved.
She stepped inside, too curious to wait for the melt to
stabilize, preferring instead to endure the sting of metal
droplets on the top of her skull and on her shoulders as she
entered.

Her impatience was quickly rewarded, the little

hurts inconsequential compared to the astonishment that awaited her inside.

There were no stairs spiraling up the great heights of the Needle. Nor was there any kind of mechanical device to carry her up. Instead the walls of the tower were covered with elaborate growths of yellow, gray, and blue-purple tissue, which erupted into sentient blossoms of exquisite complexity and beauty, their membranes swelling and contracting, their intertwined stems flushed with speeding iridescence as they aspired to reach the moon-lit chamber at the top. Very cautiously Boa reached up and touched a censer-shaped knot of multicolored matter, which hung at the intersection of several lengths of shiny-wet cord.

The Needle's anatomy responded to the touch instantly. The ground beneath Boa's feet rolled, and she might have been thrown down had it not instantly compensated by rolling in the opposite direction, allowing her to recover her equilibrium. She caught hold of a loop of knotted gut to prevent herself from being caught off guard again, but she had barely done so when the entire system of flowering entrails and light-bearing veins into which she had stopped began to raise her up on a platform of petal-flesh stretched over bone, rising at a breath-stealing speed, overtaking swift-seeded organs that oozed hon-eyed sap, and that raced ligament vines around the walls, fruited motes and glands bursting in celebration of her presence, spilling their luxurious juices upon her, staining her with their life (she, who had been a creature without form just a few hours before, expelled from solidity) blessing her with new ways to live this life After death.

She was almost at the top of the tower now, and she could see that the chamber was not only illuminated by moonlight. There were other sources of light up there as well, and they were moving.

"Carrion?" she said. There was no reply. "It's me. It's your Princess. I'm back."

Being an island that saw the transportation of the living and the dead (along with many travelers who could not fall into either category), Gorgossium had need of three harbors.

The harbor equipped for the construction and launching of vessels of great magnitude was at Kythevai, in the northeast. This was the harbor from which Mater Motley's newly commissioned warship, the *Wormwood*, had set forth to wreak havoc in the Hereafter, only to meet an undignified end on the flooded streets of Chickentown.

For sheer volume of vessels docked and unloaded, however, the commercial harbor at Uznak, in the south of the island, was the more important.

But it was from the third and smallest of the three harbors at Vrokonkeff, that the Old Mother was presently preparing to make her departure.

The voyage she was about to take was not of enormous length; she was merely crossing to the pyramids at Xuxux.

The voyage may not have been of great consequence, but it was one of great significance, and she had prepared for it by fasting for nine days, and during that time, not uttering a single word. Even now, as she dismounted from the mummified hand that had long been her preferred mode of travel, and approached the simple vessel that would carry her to the pyramids, she did not speak. Nor, out of deference to their doyen, did the seamstresses who accompanied her.

She was halfway up the gangplank when there rose a commotion farther down the quayside.

"Lady! Lady!"

It was a girl called Maratien, who for some years had attended upon the Old Mother in the tower, who came racing along the dock to speak with her mistress. Several seamstresses broke ranks to stop the girl from reaching Mater Motley for fear that Maratien's intentions might be violent.

But the Old Mother had no fear of the girl.

"Let her go," she instructed. "She may approach. What is it, Maratien? What's distressing you, child?"

"There's somebody in your tower."

"Yes, of course. I left—"

"Not any of your seamstress sisters."

"Who then?"

"I didn't recognize her."

"You were sufficiently concerned to race down and warn me?"

"Yes, my lady."

"You do know how important this voyage is?"

"I know. Of course. And forgive me for having delayed you in your great work. I meant no disrespect. Please—"

"Ssh, ssh, ssh," Mater Motley said with an almost loving indulgence in her voice. "You did well."

"I didn't think—"

"I said you did well, Maratien. And so you did. There will be another tide. I will return to the tower with you."

"What if I'm wrong?"

"Then you will have made an error and you'll learn from it, won't you?"

"Yes, lady."

"Now let's see who has come to visit me."

22

TURNING AWAY

ONCE THE SMALL ROWING boat had delivered Candy and Malingo out of the maze of caves beneath Jibarish, and into the open waters of the Izabella, it had lost all power of self-will.

"Do you have any idea of what direction the Nonce is in?" Malingo said, gazing about confusedly in all directions.

Candy considered this for a long moment. A chill wind came across the waters. She shuddered.

"I can't focus. I'm all alone in here," she said.

Her hand went to her face. Behind it, tears came. And once they came, could not be quelled. Malingo just sat, an oar in each hand, watching her. Though his head was dropped, he kept his eyes on her.

"I would have thought you'd be happy to be rid of her," he said.

"I am," Candy replied. "At least I was on the island. And she's a vile piece of work. But still, in here . . ." She tapped the middle of her forehead with her finger. "In here there's just me and a lot of space. Too much space."

"Everybody's in the same situation."

"Yes?"

"Of course."

"Lonely?"

"Sometimes very."

"I didn't realize how strange it would feel, with her gone. You're right. I'm just feeling what everybody else feels."

She wiped the tears from her cheeks with the heels of her hands, but she'd only just done so when her sorrow overwhelmed her again and more tears came. It was as though she, Candy, was weeping for the first time, without another presence in her thoughts to help her shrug off her grief. She didn't try to stem the flow now. She just let the tears come, talking through them.

"I thought there was enough of the real me just spread out to fill my head. That's how it felt at first."

"And now?"

"Now it's like I'm sitting by a little fire in the middle of . . . in the middle . . ." The tears almost silenced her, but she pushed on through them. ". . . the middle of a huge gray *nothing*."

"Is it solid? The gray, I mean."

"Does it matter?" she said, looking out over the dark waters.

A single squid, its body no longer than her foot from the tips of its tentacles to the top of its head, propelled itself past the boat, its body decorated with waves of color.

"Maybe it's just a gray mist," Malingo said. "Maybe it's not empty. Maybe it's full of things that you just haven't seen yet."

Candy glanced up at Malingo, who was studying her so intensely, his face so full of love she could feel its presence, a living thing, coming in to drive off her solitude. Whether he intended it or not, that's how she felt.

"I hate girls who cry at every little thing," she said to him, wiping her tears away for a second time, "so no more blubbering from me."

"It's not as if you didn't have a reason," Malingo replied.

"There's always reasons, aren't there? I'm sure all kinds of things will go wrong before I get home."

"Back home to the Hereafter? Why go back there? You said you hated it."

"It wasn't that bad," Candy replied without much conviction. Then, looking back at the sea, she said, "I love being here, Malingo. Nothing would make me happier than to stay forever."

"Then stay."

"I can't. The price is too high."

"What price?"

"People's lives. Not just Covenantis. But Mrs. Munn . . . she was almost killed too. And there've been plenty of others. Some of them perhaps you'd say deserved it. Kaspar Wolfswinkel. The Criss-Cross Man. A lot of stitchlings on the *Wormwood*, and Mater Motley's seamstresses. All of them would still be alive if I'd stayed in Chickentown. What just happened with Laguna and her boys is the last straw."

"And what about the other ones whose lives you've changed? The people who love you? What about me? What will *I* do when you're gone, Candy? I thought we were going to be friends forever."

Candy sighed.

"You'll come visit," she said.

"I'm sure I'd be *very* welcome in Chickentown," Malingo said. "They'd probably put me in a zoo."

"But suppose something were to happen to you right here, because of me? You know it could. I couldn't live with that."

"Nothing's going to happen to me, I swear. I'm going to live forever. We both are."

"Oh, and how long have you had this planned?" Candy said.

"Since we got out of Wolfswinkel's house. I thought then: this girl has miracles at her fingertips. Nothing's beyond her. That's what I believed then and I believe it even more strongly now."

"Miracles? No. That wasn't my doing. That was Boa, staying in practice for the day when she finally got out."

"So if you'd have come knocking on Kaspar Wolfswinkel's door without Boa—"

"We'd both be slaves right now."

Malingo shook his head.

"You're wrong. I remember very clearly looking in your eyes that first time Wolfswinkel summoned me."

"You were hanging upside down from a roof beam."

"That's right. And I looked in your eyes—I remember

this so, so clearly—and you know what I saw?"

"What?"

"Exactly the same person I'm looking at right now. Candy Quackenbush, of Chickentown, Minnesota. Come to save my life—"

"But—"

Malingo raised a finger.

"I'm not done yet," he said. "You'd come to save my life from the hell Wolfswinkel had turned it into. Maybe you didn't realize that was what you'd come to do, but it was. Now you can make lists of people who got hurt because you crossed over from the Hereafter, but I can make just as many lists of people who are still alive, or whose lives are better, because of you. Think of all the people who lived in fear of Christopher Carrion. You took that fear away."

"Did I? Or did I just leave room for something even worse to take his place?"

"You talking about Mater Motley?"

"For now. But there's probably somebody out there even worse, whose name we don't even know yet."

"You're right. The Abarat's got its share of bad. Just like the Hereafter, right?"

"Right."

"But you didn't put them here. Can you really blame yourself for every twisted, poisoned soul in the Abarat?"

"No. That'd be stupid."

"And you're not stupid," Malingo said. "You're anything but. Even if you were to leave right now the Abarat would never be the same. There'd always be this brief, golden time we'd remember. The Age of Candy."

That broke Candy's dark mood, at least for a moment.

"The Age of Candy!" she laughed. "That's the silliest thing you've ever said."

"I thought it had quite a poetical ring to it," Malingo replied. "But if you think it's silly then there's only one way to stop us all from making idiots of ourselves."

"Which is—"

"You can't leave. Simple as that."

Candy's laughter died away and she thought about things for a long while. Finally she said, "I tell you what. I'll stay until this whole business with Boa is cleared up. How's that?"

"It's better than you leaving us right now. And of course there's a possibility that the mystery of Princess Boa will never be completely solved. In which case you'll just have to stay with us forever." He grinned. "What a terrible thing that would be."

There was a moment of silence between them, and then Candy's eyes drifted back over the edge of the boat. The lone squid she'd seen before had found a companion.

"Oh no!" she said, with sudden urgency. "Finnegan!"

"What about him?"

"Boa's going to go to him the moment she gets away from Jibarish. And he'll be so happy he'll believe whatever story she tells him."

"Perhaps some of it'll be true."

"Like what?"

"Well . . . maybe she still loves him."

"Her? *Love?* No."

"How can you be so sure?"

"Because I know what she is inside. I went and spied on her, in her dreams. And there's only room for one person in Boa's heart."

"And that's Boa?"

Candy nodded.

"Do you think she'd hurt him?"

"I think she's capable of anything."

"Then we should find him."

"Agreed," Candy said.

"I suppose I row now," Malingo said unenthusiastically.

"We'll each do some," Candy said.

"So . . . we'll head for Qualm Hah, yes? That's where the John Brothers said they'd be. We'll find them with the help of a little magic, and then catch another ferry to the Nonce."

"Right now I think I've had enough playing with magic."

"Understood," Malingo said. "We'll just find them the old-fashioned way. And we can talk about whether you're going or staying later . . ."

"I'm not going to change my mind, Malingo."

He gave her a sly, sideways smile.

"Later," he reiterated.

23

COLD LIFE

ON THE WESTERN EDGE of the Isle of the Black Egg, where the Pius Mountains formed a grim wall between the Izabella and the island's interior, was a stretch of coastline known as the Shore of the Departed. It had earned the name from a grim, grotesque phenomenon. Owing to some peculiarity in the way the submerged coastline was configured, whatever litter the waters of the Izabella had gathered as they moved along this part of the island was here shunned and pitched up onto the shore by a current too languid to carry it any farther.

Thus, borne up and deposited on the Shore of the Departed, were the remains of humble fishing skiffs and massive ironclad war vessels, foundered upon the reefs of the Outer Islands, many of which remained uncharted. Sometimes there was little more than a few planks painted red, or a crow's nest, perhaps a sail; but on occasion entire vessels, which had survived the assault of the belligerent surf, had borne up onto the shore, breaking open their hulls as wave upon wave threw them against the massive black boulders—the magma children of Mount Galigali—which formed the steep, brutal beach.

Today, however, there was nothing of any great size to see. Just a bicycle wheel, a tangle of old fishing nets in which several rotted carcasses were caught up, plus a great deal of trash that had been in the water so long it wasn't really recognizable. There was one other thing, however, that the sluggish tide had delivered to the shore this day, something that lolled back and forth for a long while in the shallows as the teasing waters carried it up a little way and then claimed it again, only to roll it still farther with the next wave, until the sickly surf lost the strength to torment its plaything any further, and withdrew, leaving the ragged sack it had thrown up onto the black stones to remain where it was.

There, amid the fly-swarmed seaweed and the broken bottles and pieces of sea-worn wood (along with the occasional reminder that the Izabella had not returned empty-handed from the Hereafter: a very drowned chicken; a street sign bitten in half by one of the Izabella's more aggressive occupants; a wooden crate containing several boxes of expensive whiskey; even—of all things—a laughing plaster pig, standing three feet tall and dressed in a chef's regalia, while carrying a silver platter on which the pig was apparently quoted as saying: "Eat more pork!") lay the body the waters had cast up on the Shore of the Departed.

It was the remains of a person, though the extensive damage that had been done to the body both from hungry fishes below and hungry birds above, did not at first make it easy to distinguish its gender.

But the signs were there, had there been anybody on that abandoned stretch of coast to see. It had the large hands of a male, and there was still an Adam's apple in its much decomposed throat; its hips were narrow, and its shoulders broad. There were even a few signs of how this man might have looked in life. For some reason much of his face had been left untouched by the birds that had pecked at him as he floated, and it was still possible—if someone had cared to study his features closely—that at some time in his life somebody had sewn up his mouth.

The body had not gone unnoticed. Already some of the smaller scavengers that lived along the beach were appearing from under the stones they used as doors to their hideaways and cautiously venturing out to investigate the newcomer. The crabs that had been foraging in the rotting seaweed were now scuttling over the rocks toward this new meal. Most of them were small, their blue-gray shells barely as broad as the length of a thumb, but no sooner had they appeared than the bigger crabs, some of them twenty, thirty times larger than the foragers, appeared, pushing aside stones which then rolled or skipped down the shore and into the scummy water.

None of this sudden activity was missed by the bittamu birds that lazily circled the shore, huge scavengers that resembled the offspring of albatross and pterodactyl. They loosed full-throated shrieks of appetite and, making the subtlest of modifications in the angle of their wings, began a steady spiraling descent. But while they were still descending, a new claimant for the meat the Izabella had washed up came into view.

It had perhaps once been a crab, perhaps a crab of common dimensions. But it was much changed now, by something or someone who had corrupted it into this monstrous form with careless magic. It was albino, its shell marked with a symmetrical design of maddening complexity. It had no less than seventeen shiny black eyes, sitting atop twitching stalks, while its mouthparts worked in ceaseless finicky motion, as its massive claws rhythmi-cally delivered the morsels it constantly picked up into the machine of its maw with a delicacy that their scale belied.

Scuttling sideways, like all of its clan, it approached the body. Several smaller birds, sharp-beaked mekaks who seldom took flight, preferring to dine, breed and die on the shore, were already dancing over the corpse in their delight at having so many treats to pick from. And in their squawking enthusiasm they failed to notice the approach of the albino. The creature, for all its size, was quick. It came at the frenzied mekaks at a rush, catching one in each of its scissor claws, and snapping each bird in half before they even had time to struggle.

The others, shrieking in panic, attempted to depart, flapping their ill-oiled wings in an attempt to get beyond the range of the crab's claws. But no. *Snap!* And a third bird fell down headless. *Snap! Snap! Snap!* And a fourth dropped, quartered, to the stones.

Now the albino had the feast to himself. Even the bit-tamu birds delayed their descent, and circled above the beach unwilling to take on the beast below, however tempting the meal.

The crab assessed the body with its pincers and eyes, seeking out the best place to begin. It elected the hand of the corpse, taking hold of the wrist in its left pincer and lifting it up in order to snip off its fingers. But as it did so a long thread of life, its length spilling a sickly light, slid from the entrails of the body, where it had been nesting.

It let out a high-pitched squeal as it appeared; the strongest sound that shore had heard in many an age. It climbed up the corpse's arm so fast that the crab had no time to prepare for its attack. The creature coiled around the claw, which still held the dead man's hand. Livid bursts of brightness, more intense by far than the light its body spilled, now burst from it. They caught the shell of the crab's claw in a web of lightning, which instantly tight-ened. The claw cracked wide open, shards of shell and pieces of its meat flying in all directions.

The crab did not have a mouth with which to voice its pain. It simply scrambled wildly to be away from its muti-lator, its pincer legs sliding on the rot-slickened stones. But it wasn't given a chance to escape. A second lightning thread had appeared from the coils of the corpse's gut, and gathering itself into a coil had launched itself at the monster striking its eyestalks then dropping to the stones in front of the immense beast.

It instantly zigzagged beneath the crab, and drove its lightning-wreathed length at the crab's belly with such force that the unthinkable happened. The crab—which had ruled the shore for a decade, slaughtering indiscriminately, even when there were rich pickings among the dead—was thrown over onto its back. Its barbed legs struck out wildly in an attempt to right itself, but could only pedal the air, which was suddenly thick with flies. For the first time in its life the crab made a thin whine of complaint, tinged with fear.

It had reason. It had only been on its back for a few seconds when its enemies slid up over the rim of its shell and onto its underside. There they rose and fell, rose and fell, their motion perfectly matched, until some invisible signal turned their dance into death. Together they drove their lightning-bathed heads into the crab's segmented belly.

The crab's whine became a shriek. Not of pain—the crab knew little of that—but of profound terror. This was its nightmare, its *only* nightmare: to be lying helplessly on its back while something that it had intended to make a meal of, devoured it.

But it was not a crabmeat dinner the bright thread sought. It was the fear itself, which it fed on, fattening on its cream, rich and thick then bearing its bounty, returning to the body from which it had come.

In the brief time that had passed since the waters of the Izabella had relinquished the corpse, rain clouds had blown in from the northeast. They were the first sign of a storm that had formed in the wildly unstable air above the edge of reality itself, where the sea dropped away into oblivion. Within two or three minutes the rain shower had become a deluge, which drove all but those few caught in the life-and-death struggle on the shore back into their hiding holes beneath the stones.

The crab, of course, had no hope of retreat. Exhausted by its panic it lay inert as the rain roared down on it. The storm hadn't slowed the threads that were feeding on its terror. The bright threads came and went, harvesting the fear that suffused every part of the animal's anatomy. They didn't need the nourishment for themselves. It was their deceased creator, whose body they had never deserted, that they sought to reclaim with these gleanings of fear.

Had they been rational creatures with an understanding of death's implacable hold, they would never have attempted to resurrect their host. He was dead, beaten and broken by the waters of the Izabella as they returned from the Hereafter. They had borne a chaotic freight of detritus from the streets of Chickentown. Storefronts, lampposts, cars, parts of cars, people in cars (some alive), roofs, doors, windows all stripped from houses, and innumerable remnants of the lives lived inside those houses: chairs, fridges, magazines, rugs, people, toys, clothes, and on and on; junk and life all thrown together in a soup of things lost forever. The threads' host had been dashed against so many sharp, heavy, twisted pieces of trash that he might have died half a hundred deaths if he'd had them to die.

But finally a calmer current—the one that delivered his body to the Shore of the Departed—had claimed him. And now, in contradiction to the Shore's very name, and in defiance of all the laws pertaining to the dissolution of the flesh, the devoted labor of the threads, carrying the food that the crab's terror provided back to their maker's corpse over and over, bore fruit.

The dead man moved. The crab did not see the miracle its nightmares had made possible. At some point in the coming and going of its fears' devourers, the crab let go of life. The sluggish motion of its legs ceased entirely, and its whine sank away into silence.

The albino didn't see the corpse it had almost dined upon twitch on its bed of black stones, nor its eyelids flicker open as the rain danced down on its all but fleshless face. As one life ended another began.

Nor was it for the first time. Christopher Carrion had drawn his first breath many, many years before, as a baby prematurely born. Now he took that breath again: a second first. This time, however, it was not a frail inhalation. This time, though the rain was still beating a tattoo on the stones as loudly as ever, the sound of the dead man drawing breath reverberated all along the shore, its resonance causing the stones beneath the stones, and those layered still deeper, to rattle against one another, the sum of their percussions so loud that the din of the deluge seemed inconsequential.

And as if driven off by that greater thundering, the

storm clouds rolled inland, to pour their waters upon a place they had some hope of cleansing: someplace where the laws of life (and death) still held sway. The shore lay silent, except for the breathing of the dead man, and the sound of the Izabella as it threw its waves upon the stones.

The drumming of the stones finally ceased, its task complete. Carrion lived. His body was no longer the wretched, colorless thing it had been. Myriad forms of light were spilling into the air around it, memories of a life he almost lost. They seethed around him blazing with a living light this shore had not witnessed in many an age. In the flux of memories, Carrion began to whisper ancient incantations, designed to heal his broken body. In the time it took for the tide to turn, retreat, and turn again to once more climb the shore, the healing was complete. Healthy tissue spread over his wounds, sealing them and causing the rotted flesh to fall in strands and scraps onto the hard bed where he still lay.

The smaller crabs, the tiny, green sea lizards that had taken refuge beneath the stones, and the mekaks that had seen several of their kind killed by the Albino, returned now to the proximity of the man so as to feed on the putrid meat that the healed body had sloughed off. They had no fear of this man or his bright agents. He didn't even see them as they scuttled over the stones around him, cleansing the shores of every last scrap of the death he had taken off in order to dress in life again.

After a time, he got to his feet. His memories still played in the darkness around him, their meaning—having been put to the purpose of Carrion's rebirth—eaten away, leaving the darkness surrounding him swarming with the remnants of a life he'd lived once, died too. It was well lost. He would not make the same mistakes again.

The screech of metal on stone stirred him from his ruminations. He looked toward the water, and found there the source of the raw sound. The incoming tide had brought another souvenir of Chickentown to the Shore of the Departed. An entire truck, missing three of its wheels but still containing the slumped body of its driver, securely held in his seat by his seat belt, was being delivered to the shore.

Carrion's face had betrayed no trace of feeling until now, when the subtlest of smiles appeared on a mouth still marked, even after his revival with the scars of his grandmother's handiwork: the lines where she'd sewn his lips together for speaking the word *love*. He raised his hand to his mouth and ran his fingers over the scars. The smile died, not because Mater Motley had done him harm, but because she'd been right. Love was sickness. Love was self-slaughter. Love was poison and pain and humiliation.

He was reborn to be love's enemy. To destroy it, utterly.

The thought gave him strength. He felt the power in his body surge, and with it a sudden desire to celebrate his return into the living, tender, fearful world.

He lifted his arm and pointed at the truck that was still in the water, the surf surging around it.

"Rise," he told it.

The vehicle obeyed instantly, lurching violently as the water poured out of its engine. The driver lolled around like a drunkard at the wheel, as the truck continued its ungainly ascent. At Carrion's feet the loyal nightmares, which had masterminded his return to life, fawned and cavorted as they watched their naked lord at play.

Carrion dropped his right hand to his waist, palm out, and the nightmares sprang to meet his fingers, coiling themselves up and around his wrist and arm so as to reach the precious place where they had been made: his head. Once they had swum in a collar filled with a soup of sibling terrors, which he had drunk and breathed. They would again, soon. But for now they made two blazing rings around his neck, and were in their heaven.

Carrion watched the truck ascend for a little while longer, and then uttered a syllable ordering its immolation. It instantly blew apart: a fireball of yellow-and-orange flame from which the burning fragments fell like tiny comets, meeting their reflections and extinction, in the sea. Carrion turned his gaunt, tragic face heavenward to watch the spectacle, and a single bark of laughter escaped his lips.

"Ha!"

Then, after a moment:

"What's a resurrection without fireworks?"

24

AT THE PREACHER'S HOUSE

MALINGO ROWED THE LITTLE boat in the direction of Ninnyhammer. It wasn't an Hour with the happiest of memories for either of them, given that Malingo had been Kaspar Wolfswinkel's slave there for many years and Candy was very nearly murdered by the wizard in the process of escaping. But dark as their associations with Ninnyhammer were, the island was still the closest place to find a ferry that would take them to the massive harbor in Tazmagor on the Hour of Qualm Hah, which would ultimately lead them to the Nonce, and therefore to Finnegan Hob.

When they had reached Ninnyhammer, they decided upon a ferry called *The Sloppy*. And once they had bought their tickets, waited in line to board, and finally found chairs on the upper deck of the small steamer, the stresses of recent events took their toll, and Candy very soon began to doze.

"If I sleep . . ." Candy said, already halfway there, "I

might go dream walking."

"You mean *sleep*walking?"

"No. This is that thing I told you about."

"Ah. I remember. The Hereafter. Are you sure you're safe there?"

"Yes. Of course."

Malingo smiled. "Good."

The ferry's captain blew three blasts on the horn, sending plumes of white steam into the night sky. That was the last thing Candy knew of their departure. As the third plume floated to darkness, so did Candy. A blanket of sleep came down, and the ship, the sea, and stars all went away.

She didn't rest in a dreamless state for long. By the time *The Sloppy* was out of Ninnyhammer's harbor, Candy's dreaming soul had gone home to 34 Followell Street.

She woke in the kitchen. It was daytime in the Hereafter. She glanced up at the clock above the fridge: a little after three. She went to the sink and looked out into the garden, hoping that her mother would be out there, sleeping in the rusted chair, her back turned to the house. Chance—or something like it—had arranged things perfectly. Her mom was indeed sitting in the old garden chair just as Candy had pictured her, asleep, which meant that this was indeed one of those precious times when they could talk together, dreamer to dreamer.

The first and only time they'd met this way before, Candy had left the encounter with a new determination to understand the mystery that had brought her into the Abarat in the first place, an impetus that had led, finally, to her separation from Princess Boa. Now she wanted to tell her mom all that had happened on Laguna Munn's rock. Knowing that this dreamtime was unpredictable, and that they might be interrupted at any moment, she went straight outside.

She found her mother in exactly the same place she'd been when they'd met before, staring up at the sky. Melissa Quackenbush didn't need to look around to know that Candy was with her.

"Hello, stranger," she said.

"Hi, Mom. I missed you. I hope you're not angry with me."

"Why would I be angry?"

"Because I haven't been home to see you since the battle."

"No, honey, I'm not angry," Melissa said, turning around now, and smiling at Candy. A true smile, full of love. "You've got a new life in the Abarat. And that day when the water came through—"

"The Sea of Izabella."

"Yes, well, if what I saw that day is anything to go by, you've got your hands full. So no, I'm not angry. I worry about you. But things happen for a reason. I've always believed that. We don't always know the reason. We just have to get on with things."

"Everything's going to be fine, Mom."

"I know. I trust you. But"—she stopped and stared at Candy hard, her head turned slightly—"you're different somehow."

"Yes I am."

There was a long moment of silence between them. Finally Melissa said, "So tell me everything."

"It's not very easy to explain."

"What's so hard about it?" Melissa replied with a little shrug. "You got rid of her."

Candy laughed out loud, in part at her mother's plain way of saying something that had seemed so difficult to put into words, and in part out of surprise that she knew.

"Who told you?" Candy said.

"About the Princess? Diamanda told me. The one with the long, white hair. The oldest of the women of the Fantomaya."

"What did she tell you?"

"Not much really. Not about the Princess herself. But that you wouldn't need to know anything."

"She's gone now. It was hard. Somebody died because of it. But I had to have her out. She's bad, Mom. And I never knew. I never realized she was there inside me. And now she's gone—and what she did when I let her go—" She shook her head, knowing she'd never find the words. "Seeing her clearly. This . . . monster who'd been inside me all that time." She took a deep breath. "Did you ever see that in me? Any sign?"

"Of what? Of something bad in you?"

"Evil?"

"Lord, Candy, no. Never. Of course you had your little secrets. And you were always quiet. There was something special about you. I think even your dad felt that. But evil? No."

"Good. I was afraid . . . you know how you hear about how people repress things? Bad things? So bad they can't admit that they did them so they forget them?"

"Well, I wasn't with you every minute of every day for all those years, but if you'd really done something bad—"

"Evil."

"—I think I would have at least had some clue."

"But nothing?"

"Not a thing. If this Princess is as bad as you say she is, I think I would have known if she'd shown herself."

"But she did, Mom."

"When?"

"All the time. She was part of who I was. Otherwise how would you have known that something was different? You felt it as soon as you saw me, didn't you?"

"Yes." She studied her daughter again, with eyes full of love as before, but tinged with a hint of fear. "But now you and she are separated. You'll stay out of her way, I hope."

"As long as she leaves me and my friends alone, I hope I never lay eyes on her again."

"Good. Nobody needs bad people in their lives."

"Mom, you don't need to worry. Because when I've seen all my friends and I'm sure they're okay, I'm coming home."

"Home *here?*"

"Yes."

"To stay?"

"Yes, to stay. Why do you sound surprised? This is my real home. With you and Dad and Ricky and Don . . ." Now it was Candy who did the face watching. "You don't seem very happy about it," she said.

"No. Of course I'm happy. To have you back home would be wonderful. But . . . things aren't the way they were before the flood. A lot of people blame you. If you came back, they'd arrest you and interrogate you until they could find something to accuse you of. You opened their eyes to another world, darling. They'll never forgive you for that. I know they won't. There are a lot of cruel people in this town. There always were. But now there are a lot more."

"I never thought about that," Candy said. Her mother's response had blindsided her. She'd always assumed there'd be a way. "People can forgive, right?"

"I'm afraid this is only the beginning, Candy. Something really terrible's going to have to happen before ordinary folks come to their senses."

"Where's Dad?" Candy said, changing the subject.

"Well . . ." Melissa took a deep breath. "He's at church."

"He's *what?*"

"At church. He's preaching, believe it or not. He does it every day now."

Candy wanted to laugh; of all the strange things she'd heard recently, the idea of her father heading to church to deliver a sermon was by far the strangest.

"I know how ludicrous it all sounds," Melissa said. "Believe it or not, Ricky goes too. He has a lot more respect for your father these days."

"What about Don?"

"He doesn't have any interest in any of this. He stays in his room a lot these days."

"This is too weird. Where does Dad preach?"

"He calls it The Church of . . . wait, let me get this right . . . The Church of . . . The Children of Eden. It's on Treadskin Street, where the old Baptist Church used to be. They painted it green. It's a really ugly green. But he's really changed his ways, Candy. And people like what he has to say. Look. On the windows."

Melissa pointed. There was a poster taped to the dining room window. And two more of the same design upstairs. Candy took a couple of steps back toward the house, so as to read what they said.

COME IN!

NO CONFESSIONS!

NO CONTRIBUTIONS!

ENTER AND YOU SHALL BE SAVED!

Candy was suspicious.

"He used to watch those TV evangelists just to laugh at them! And now he's a believer?"

"Well, he isn't drinking as much, which is a blessing.

So maybe it's doing him some good." Suddenly, Melissa halted and the look of concern she already had on her face deepened. "You have to go now," she said.

"Why?"

"I heard the front door. Your father's back."

"He can't see me, Mom. I'm here in your dream."

"I know that's the way it was before, Candy, but like I said, things have changed."

"No *that* much."

As she spoke she felt a strange tingling sensation at the top of her spine, and slowly, slowly—almost as if in a nightmare—she turned back to see something her soul told her not to look at. Too late.

There was her father, coming out of the house. And he was staring right at her.

25

NO MORE LIES

CANDY HAD FACED MORE than her share of monstrous enemies in the last few months: Kaspar Wolfswinkel in his prison house on Ninnyhammer; the Zethek, crazed in the holds of the humble fishing boat *Parroto Parroto*; and the many Beasts of Efreet, one of whom had slaughtered Diamanda.

And not forgetting, of course, the creature who'd waited for Candy in the house where she'd taken refuge after Diamanda's death: Christopher Carrion.

And the Hag, Mater Motley.

And Princess Boa.

But none of these monsters prepared her for this confrontation, with her very own father. Here he was, and he could see her.

Things had changed, just as her mother had warned.

"You thought you'd slip in here and spy on good Christian people without being seen? Think again. I see witches very clearly." He held up the Bible he was carrying in his hand. "Thou shalt not suffer a witch to live!"

This sounded so utterly preposterous coming from her father's mouth that she couldn't help but laugh. His face, which had always gone red when he flew into a temper, instead became pale, draining of blood.

"You mock me, you mock the Great One," he said. His tone was calm, remote. "Do so if you wish. Laugh yourself into the flames of perdition."

Candy stopped laughing. Not out of fear, but out of puzzlement. Her father *had* changed. The puffiness had gone from his face, and there was a new intensity in his eyes, replacing the blur of beer. He was leaner too. The extra pounds that had softened his jawline had gone. Nor was he combing his last few hairs over his head from side to side in a pitiful attempt to conceal his loss of hair. He had shaved it off. He was now completely bald.

"I don't know what your mother's been telling you, but I'm sure it's lies," he said.

"She just said you and Ricky go to church together."

"Oh, indeed we do. Those of us with brains in our heads have seen the light. Ricky! Come out here! We've got a visitor."

Candy threw a glance up at her mom. There were so many contrary emotions fighting for Melissa's face that Candy couldn't figure out what she was really feeling.

"Your mother can't help you," Bill said to Candy. "So I'd put her out of your head, if I were you. There's only one man of vision left in Chickentown these days, and you're looking at him. *Ricky!* When I tell you to get out here, you do it!"

While her father was looking toward the house, Candy glanced down at the vest he was wearing. Even by Abaratian standards it would have been thought outlandish. It was made from a patchwork of various thick fabrics—one striped, one polka-dotted, one black—but possessing an odd iridescence. She knew she'd seen this odd combination of colors before. But where? She was still puzzling over the mystery when Ricky appeared from the house. Her brother's hair had been shaved off as well and he looked skinnier than ever. His eyes looked huge, like an anxious baby.

He's so afraid, Candy thought. *Poor Ricky. Afraid of the man who's supposed to be his protector. No, not afraid: terrified.*

"I was getting a clean T-shirt, Dad—I mean, Reverend, sir."

"I don't care what you were doing," Bill snapped. "When I call you, you've got how long?"

"Ten seconds, Dad. No. I mean—sorry, sir. Reverend. I mean, Reverend."

"Finally, the boy says something I can bear listening to. Now, I want you to take a deep breath, boy. And I want you to rest that stupid, stupid, stupid brain of yours. Do you understand what you need to do?"

"I guess so."

"It's real simple, son. Just don't think."

"About anything?"

"About *anything*. I just want you to close your eyes. That's good. You're perfectly safe."

Candy threw a puzzled glance toward her mother,

but Melissa was watching her husband. There was not so much as a flicker of affection on her face. If she had ever really loved him, it seemed, that love had been poured away, every last drop of it. In its place, there was only fear.

"Our eyes deceive us sometimes, son," Bill was telling Ricky. "They make us see things that aren't really there. And sometimes they hide things that *are* there."

"Yeah?"

"Oh yes. I wouldn't lie to you. You know that."

"Of course."

"So it's time your eyes told you the truth, don't you think?"

"Sure."

"Good," Bill told him. "Now . . . are you ready?"

"For what, sir?"

"To see what the world really looks like, Ricky. Your attention is wandering. You're not *focused*. Listen to me. We have a force of evil that will destroy us, right here in our midst."

"Do we?"

"Open your eyes, and see for yourself."

Ricky's eyes flickered open and it was clear from the instant his eyes focused that his father's tutelage had worked.

"Candy?" he said. "Where did you come from?"

"I'm not—"

"Shut your wicked mouth!" her father said, jabbing the air just a couple of inches away from her face. "Don't listen to anything she says, boy. I told you they're full of lies, didn't I? It comes so easily to them. They open their painted red lips and the lies just start tumbling out! They can't stop themselves."

"What are you talking about, Bill?" Melissa said.

"You, woman."

"Woman?"

"That is your gender, isn't it?" Bill replied.

Candy saw the look of mystification on Melissa's face. This sounded like her father, only worse.

"I don't know what the hell—or *who* the hell—has got into you, but you are not my husband . . ."

"What's happening?" Ricky said, with an edge of panic in his voice.

Bill pointed at Candy.

"You're the reason this town has lost its way. Lost its mind. You brought freaks onto our streets so they can gain a hold on our world."

"That's ridiculous," Candy said. "Whoever is still here was just left behind when the waters receded. I'm sure they all want to go home."

"Home? Oh no. These deviants are never leaving this town. Except in coffins."

"What?"

"How much plainer do I need to be? We are fighting a war against these invaders. My foot soldiers are ordinary men and women, who come to worship at my church, and have heard me speak. They've seen these freaks with their own eyes. They know they exist. Demons, from the bowels of hell!"

"No, Dad, they're just lost people who want to get back home to the Abarat. Let me go back there and talk to the Council. They'll find some way to peacefully get all the folks who were left behind out of your town without blood being spilled."

"Did you hear her, Ricky? *Folks*, she called these demons. As though they were the most natural things in the world."

"Yes, sir. I heard."

"What's to be done, Ricky? She's *your* sister. If you tell me to be merciful, I will be. But be very certain. I don't want to turn my back on her and find she's using her magic against us. Just look at her. There's nothing natural about her."

"Why are you so interested in magic all of the sudden?" Candy said to her father. "You would've said anyone talking about that was crazy."

"That was before I found my vest of many colors." He ran his palm over the garment, and it responded to his touch. A ripple of pleasure ran through it, causing its designs to intensify.

"Hats!" Candy said, suddenly remembering where she'd seen all the pieces of the patchwork before. "It was five beaten-up hats."

Bill's expression was glacial.

"Clever," he said.

"I knew the person who owned them, Dad. Now he *was* bad. He murdered the people who owned those hats just so he could have them for himself."

"Disgusting. You're making all this up as you go along. Just like your mother. Lies, lies, and more lies. That's all you women are capable of."

"I swear," Candy said. "That's why he's talking all weird, Mom. He's got a little bit of Kaspar Wolfswinkel in him, because that was where his power was. In the hats he stole from the dead."

"You're not frightening me, if that's what you're trying to do," Bill said. "Your sorcery won't work on me. I think we should take her to the church, Ricky."

"Yes, sir."

"I don't need your religion, thank you," Candy said.

"You're not getting any. You see, I've been having visions. Imagine that. Your drunken lump of a father, who everyone laughed at behind his back——"

"I never laughed, Dad. It was sad."

"*Shut your mouth! I don't need your pity!* I've built a machine." He tapped the middle of his forehead. "It came from a vision. And I couldn't understand what it was for. But now I know. It all fits."

"Bill!" Melissa broke in. "Maybe we should listen to her."

"No. A greater voice speaks to me. And I listen to it." He paused, and for a moment closed his eyes. "Even now, it speaks. It's telling me what it needs."

"Oh yeah? And what's that?" Candy said.

Bill's eyes opened in an instant.

"You."

PART FOUR

THE DAWNING OF THE DARK

No need to fear the beast
That comes alone to your door,
For loneliness will be its undoing
Nor need you fear those beasts
That hunt in packs.
They will die when divided from their clan.
Fear only the one
That does not come at all.
It is already here, standing in your shoes.

—The last sermon of Bishop Nautyress

26

THE CHURCH OF THE CHILDREN OF EDEN

"CANDY? WE'RE ALMOST THERE."

Even though Candy had told Malingo not to wake her, she surely couldn't have meant him to leave her sleeping once they'd arrived. Still, he'd learned to be delicate when he was rousing her from sleep.

There was no great urgency. The ferry had only just sailed into Tazmagor Harbor. It would be several minutes before they docked. Even so, there was an unease among the passengers that was nothing to do with their arrival. Their voices were shrill, their laughter forced. Malingo knew why. There was a mysterious sense of foreboding in the air. Something was coming: something that wasn't welcome. He had no more idea of the approaching some-thing than the passengers who hurried past him. But it wasn't good. His stomach was tied in knots, and there was an itch behind his eyes that he first remembered feeling the day his father took him to be sold. He did his best to put the itch and the unease out of his mind so as to concentrate on waking Candy. He put his hand on hers, and shook her gently.

"Come on, Candy. Time to wake up." There was no response. He shook her again. "Come on," he said, leaning toward her now. "You'll have to finish this dream another time. Wake up."

"I'm just dreaming this," Candy reminded her father. "I don't have to listen to you. I can wake up at any time."

"Well you'd better not, because if you do"——he pointed to Melissa——"*she* is going to be the one who suffers."

"Stop it, Bill," Melissa said.

"Why? Because you think I don't mean it? I mean it. Ask your daughter."

"There's stuff in his head right now he can't control, Mom," Candy said. "Somebody stronger might have fought against it. Dad just didn't want to."

"You're going to regret that," he said.

"Candy? What's wrong?" Malingo asked her.

The expression on Candy's sleeping face was no longer calm. A frown furrowed her brow, and the corners of her mouth were turned down.

"You're starting to scare me," Malingo said. "Why won't you wake up? Can you even hear me?"

Did she nod her head? If she did, it was the tiniest of motions.

"Oh, Lordy Lou. What is going on? Please wake up."

Now it seemed she shook her head, though the motion

was as subtle as her nod. So subtle he wasn't sure she'd moved her head at all.

"Is it that you don't want to wake up right now?"

And again she nodded. Or at least he thought she did.

"All right . . ." Malingo said, doing his best to sound calm. "If you want to stay asleep, I guess that's okay. There's not much I can do about it anyway. You just keep dreaming. I'll deal with things on this end."

There was neither a nod nor a shake by way of response. Her face simply became more intensely troubled.

It was strange to be walking the streets of Chickentown again, even stranger to be walking them at her father's side—though of course she was invisible to everyone but him—and to see people's responses to him and how his reputation had changed in the time she'd been away. A few people were openly afraid of him. They either crossed over the street to avoid him or hurriedly ducked into stores. But others, seeing him coming, made sure to pay him their respects. Some simply nodded or offered a quick "good afternoon." But not one of them was able to entirely conceal the unease they felt in his presence. A few of them actually called him Reverend, which Candy knew she'd never get used to. Reverend! Her father, the brutal alcoholic who beat his wife and children: Reverend! Her mother had been right: things had certainly changed in Chickentown.

Once they were off Main Street and there weren't so many people to see him apparently talking to himself, he said to Candy, "Did you see how much respect I get?"

"Yes, I saw."

"Surprised you, didn't it? *Didn't it?*"

She wanted to defy him even now. She wanted to tell him that it was all an empty illusion, and she knew it. But then she thought of her mother. The man at her side was capable of doing terrible things, she didn't doubt it. So she answered him, "Yes. I guess it did surprise me."

"But what you don't understand is that these people are frightened. They can smell the freaks: the things that got washed into the streets and left here. And they're afraid. What I do is take the fear away."

"How?"

"None of your business. Salvation's a very private industry. They pay for the privilege, I can tell you that. I don't take a cent of it. All their contributions go back into the church. And everybody's glad to give. I'm bringing some comfort and maybe some happiness back into their lives. That's worth a few dollars of anybody's money. Here we are. Home sweet home."

He was talking about a plain, one-story brick building, now painted a garish green, which Candy must have walked past hundreds of times in her life. It had a big bulletin board on the small lawn at the front which bore a single message:

THE CHURCH OF THE CHILDREN OF EDEN

REVEREND WILLIAM QUACKENBUSH

WELCOMES ALL SINNERS IN NEED OF SALVATION

The member of *The Sloppy*'s crew who found Malingo and Candy still aboard fifteen minutes after the ship had docked, was, much to Malingo's surprise and relief, another geshrat. Talking to one of his own people made the complicated business of explaining their situation a little easier. It became easier still when the ferryman said, "You're Malingo, right?"

"Do we know each other?"

"No. I've just heard all the stories. My sister, Yambeeni, follows everything you and the girl do as best she can. There's a lot of rumors. People invent things about you I'm sure, just so they've got something new to talk about."

"I didn't realize anybody cared."

"Ha! You're kidding? You and Candy—is it okay if I call her Candy, or should it be, like, Miss Quackenbush or some-such?"

"No, I'm sure Candy would be fine."

"I'm Gambittmo, by the way. Bithy, Mo, but usually Gambat. Like Gambittmo the geshrat, only shortened. Gambat Yoot."

"It's good to meet you, Gambat."

"Can I ask you something?"

"Of course."

"Could I get your autograph? It's for my sister? She will *flap her fins*!"

Gambat demonstrated what was obviously a family

trait by flapping his own orange fins, which were uncommonly large.

"Your sister would want *my* autograph?" Malingo said.

"Are you kidding? *Of course*. She's a big fan. I am too, only it's really the girls who go crazy. She knows all the details. How you saved Miss Quackenbush—sorry I can't call her Candy, it just doesn't sound right—from that crazy wizard guy, Wolfswinkel. We went to the house on Ninnyhammer, my sister and me. Saw all the stuff in the story. I mean, you can't touch anything. It's all roped off. But there's the proof. It all happened. Oh, and maybe on the next page just something for me?"

Malingo accepted the notebook and then the pen, which had a small carved and painted copy of the Commexo Kid's head on the end of it, grinning from ear to ear.

"Sorry about the stupid pen. A passenger left it. I hate the Kid."

"Yeah?"

"That toothing grin. Like everything's just dandy."

"And it isn't?"

"You ever met one of our people with money? Didn't think so. We don't have power, or money, or people to lead us. Why do you think we're all talking about you?"

Malingo looked up at Gambat, searching his face for a hint of mockery. But he could find none. Candy's head lolled around as she slept.

"Is Miss Quackenbush okay? Does she need maybe a doctor?"

"No, I don't think so. She'll be fine. She's just tired. What do you want me to write?"

"Oh . . . I don't know. Anything you like. Her name's Yambeeni. Y-A-M-B-Two Es-N-I." While Malingo signed, his new friend chatted on. "Just between us, you two can stay up here for as long as you like. We're not heading back to Ninnyhammer for five or six hours. We've got to clean up the trash the passengers left. Oh, *you are the gesher*. Look at that! She gets a drawing too?"

"It's not much, but—"

"You drew that so fast! That's amazing!" There was a pause. Then he said, "What is it?"

"Just something I see in dreams," Malingo told him. "It's a huge baby in a very small boat."

"What does it mean?"

"I don't know. I just dream it."

"Well, she's going to flap so hard she'll fly. Thank you. That is spaf, gesher, totally spaf." Grinning a grin that was almost as broad as the Kid's, he studied the autograph and drawing, and went on his way.

Brief as the exchange had been, it left Malingo with a lot to think about. It was a huge shock to discover that there were members of his beleaguered nation who not only knew of him, but were proud of having him numbered among them. For as long as there'd been books written, the Geshrat nation had been judged to be a lower order of being. They were menials, tradition stated: scrawny, dull-witted creatures without a maker of trinkets, trousers or trouble, in their tribe's history.

Was it possible that he, who had come to believe over the years that his father's lack of grief when he sold him had been perfectly understandable? He was a worthless thing that no one, not even his own father, would be sorry to lose. Perhaps he judged himself too harshly, and too soon.

Candy groaned in her sleep, shaking Malingo out of his stupor. What was he doing thinking about himself, when Candy was still *lost* in slumber? For the first time in this journey at Candy's side he felt the need of some of the others. Two-Toed Tom, Geneva Peachtree or Finnegan Hob. Someone he could talk this problem through with. Anyone but the John Brothers. They just had too many opinions.

But wishing he had their company wouldn't make it so. He was on his own, in the silent company of the person who meant more to him than anyone ever had. Suddenly, he was afraid for her.

Bill told Ricky to stay outside the church and keep watch. He then led Candy inside the church which was as unremarkable on the inside as it had been on the outside. The pews were rows of cheap wooden chairs, the altar a table covered with a plain white cloth. There was no cross.

"As you can see," Bill Quackenbush went on, leading his dreaming daughter down toward the altar, "we don't go in for anything fancy here. The message is what's important."

"And what is the message, Dad?"

"Don't call me that anymore. There's nothing between us."

"Like love, you mean? Because I don't think you've felt that for any of us. Maybe Mom once, before you had us to hit—"

"Enough," he said, his voice thick with old rage.

They were just a few yards from the altar now, and Candy saw six or seven other people in the darkened corner of the church. Her father had seen them too. That, she thought, was why he wanted to end their conversation.

"I've no interest in going over old errors, old sins."

"Whose errors, Dad? Whose sins?"

She went on, pressing her father in the hope of getting him to really show his temper. Maybe some of the members of his congregation would think twice about their smiling Reverend if they saw the real Bill Quackenbush. The one she knew. The one that was vicious and violent.

Bill stepped in between the folks gathered in the corner, and very quietly said, "You've changed. I can feel the stench of your corruption, and it sickens me to my soul. I will do anything in my power to protect the good people who worship here from your perversions and abominations, the filth that you brought from that Other Place—"

"The Abarat, Dad. You can say it."

"I won't soil my tongue!"

He wasn't quiet any longer. His fury echoed off the plain whitewashed walls.

"Listen to yourself, Dad!" Candy said.

"Don't call me—" He stopped himself, as his rant came to meet him from the far wall of the church. He stopped, and once again dropped his voice. "Clever little witch, aren't you? You still know how to anger me. But I'm not falling for it." He took a deep breath. "If you defy me one more time I will make your mother suffer. Do you understand me? Look at me, girl, when I'm talking to you. I want you to know who I really am."

"The enemy," Candy said.

Her father smiled.

"Finally we agree on something," he said. He turned his back on her and called out to his followers. "Is the machinery all warmed up and ready to go?"

"I did it all exactly like you told me to, sir," one of them said.

"Good. Very good."

27

INTERROGATION

AROUND THE TIME GAMBAT was leaving Malingo and Candy on the upper deck of *The Sloppy* (now the happy owner of two autographs from the hand of the most famous geshrat alive) a convoy of five vessels was about to depart from the harbor at Vrokonkeff, on Gorgossium. The largest of these five, the *Kreyzu*, was flying a smoke flag in the billows of which the stylized image of a needle and thread had been worked, marking it as the bearer of the presumptive Empress of the Hours, Lady Midnight herself, Mater Motley. The four ships that accompanied the *Kreyzu* were armed from waterline to crow's nest with cannons and stitchlings, all in service of protecting the Lady Midnight.

Her departure had been delayed, of course. She had returned to her tower with the girl, Maratien, to find that Taint Nerrow, the seamstress she'd left to clean the mosaic map of the Abarat that was laid into the floor of her chamber, had been thrown out of one of the chamber windows and lay dead at the bottom. Mater Motley had liked the Seamstress Nerrow; the woman had been loyal and zealous. It didn't please her that circumstances obliged her to now interrogate the dead woman, which would cause the deceased profound anguish. Mater Motley was certain that, had she been able to offer her opinion, Taint Nerrow herself would have volunteered her suffering in return for the name of her murderer.

Events many years in the designing were about to come to fruition: events that would transform the islands and all that lived upon them forever. She—who would be the mistress of that transformed world—could not afford to let a force as powerful as Taint Nerrow's murderer go uncaught. She needed to know who the trespasser had been, and quickly. She bent down and turned Taint's corpse over. Her face had a crack down the middle. But there was little blood. Ordering the rest of the women to retreat a few steps, Motley threw up a Dome of Diligences around herself, the body, and Nerrow's spirit, which was hovering over the corpse, attached by a decaying cord of ectoplasm.

"Calm yourself, woman," Motley said. "I don't need more than a minute or two of your time."

"I don't want—"

"You have no choice."

"—to go back—"

"You have no choice."

"—into the flesh."

"You have no choice. Hear me, witch?"

Taint's spirit, a smudge of a panicked shadow,

repeatedly flew against the inside of the Dome of Diligences like a fly trapped in a jar.

The Empress quickly became weary of Nerrow's panicked cavorting.

"Enough," she said.

She reached out and caught hold of her seamstress's
spirit. The shadow flailed, desperate to be free. Several of
Nerrow's sisters watched on in silent horror.

"Neysentab," said the Old Mother, and with these
three syllables she unmade the Dome. "If any of you find
necromancy hard to witness, then I suggest you avert your
eyes."

Several did exactly that, one or two of the sisters even
walking away from the body of Taint Nerrow entirely so as
not to even hear what was happening. Meanwhile, Mater
Motley went down on her knees beside Taint Nerrow's
corpse, telling one of the remaining sisters, "Fathoon?
Open her mouth wide and hold her head."

Kunja Fathoon, who was a big-boned woman with
huge hands, did as she was instructed.

Mater Motley swiftly placed the spirit between Nerrow's lips and ordered Fathoon to close the dead woman's
mouth and keep it closed whatever happened. Kunja Fathoon pinched the dead woman's mouth to stop the spirit
from exiting that way. She kept it pinched closed for as
long as a minute. Nothing happened. And nothing. And
still nothing. Then, suddenly, the woman's leg twitched.
Its motion was followed by an eruption of thrashings and
kickings.

"Calm, Taint Nerrow. Calm," Mater Motley said. "I know this must be horrible for you coming back into your broken body, but I only need a few questions answered." She glanced up at Fathoon. "Are you ready?" Fathoon nodded. "Don't weaken."

"I won't."

"No," Mater Motley said, her certainty confirmed by something in Fathoon's eyes. "No, you won't. Then let's be done with this, shall we?"

"At your instruction, my lady."

"Now."

Fathoon uncovered Nerrow's mouth.

"Cease this, Taint Nerrow! RIGHT NOW!"

The woman's cries became less pitiful. Her contortions dwindled.

"That's better," the Old Mother said. "Now, answer me quickly and truthfully. Then I can let you go, and you can go to your death."

Taint drew a second phlegmatic breath and then spoke, her voice unequivocally that of a dead woman: flat, thin, joyless.

"What did I do to deserve this?"

"The fault wasn't yours, Nerrow. I simply want to know who murdered you." Mater Motley leaned forward a little to catch the answer when it came. "Who was it, sister?"

"It was the Princess Boa."

"Impossible!"

"I swear."

"She's been dead sixteen years, sister."

"I know. Yet it was she."

"And you have no doubt?"

"None. It was she. It was Boa. It was! It was!" Her reanimated body was beginning to defy her control. Her face was riddled with tiny tics and seizures. They seemed to give her pain, even though her nerves had only a ghost of life left in them.

Mater Motley studied the corpse at her feet without replying. Nerrow's despairing eyes stared up at the woman who held her spirit hostage. "I've told you all I know. Let me go to death. It will be kinder than life was."

"Well then . . ." the Old Mother said. "Let go, Fathoon. Peace in the Void, woman. *Be gone.*"

She had barely finished her sentence before the seamstress's spirit had fled its confinement and was rising away from her prison and her imprisoner. Then the shadow-smudge had gone from sight, lightless against a lightless sky.

Mater Motley's return to the Needle Tower, and her subsequent discoveries and dealings there, had delayed the departure of the *Kreyzu* a little over two hours. But once the immense vessel was out in the open waters it moved with extraordinary speed, the engine that blazed in the belly of the vessel—a brutal delirious conjoining of the harrowing with the depraved, the unforgivable with the insane—propelling the *Kreyzu* through the Izabella, defying every current.

The Izabella did not protest the vessel's brutal power.

The sea knew what dread influence had wrought the vessel, and had given it authority. She knew the monstrous power the Old Mother wielded. Simply by reading rumors and toxins in the streams that poured down the slopes of the islands into her tides, the Izabella knew how much worse things were soon to get. It would serve the myriad life-forms who dwelt within her waters no good to oppose the Midnight Empress for she was capable, the waters knew, of practically limitless acts of destruction. Not flesh nor wood nor stone nor dust was inviolate. She had it in her, this woman and her allies on high, to do death to every Hour of Day and Night if she did not get her way.

So for now, the Izabella decided, she must seem to do so. To have her will, however wicked.

Thus, untroubled by the sea's enmity, the woman who would very soon change the Abarat out of all recognition speeded toward her destination.

On board the *Kreyzu*, the girl Maratien came into the Old Mother's darkened cabin, her head reverentially bowed. She didn't dare raise it until the Old Mother murmured, "What is it, child?"

"We are approaching the pyramids, my lady. You told me to come and tell you."

Mater Motley rose from the hovering stone on which she sat and descended the air to come to the place where Maratien stood.

"Are you excited, child?"

"Should I be?"

"Oh yes. If you have the courage to stay with me today and for the days to come, I promise you that you'll see such rare sights as will change forever the way you imagined the world to be. And of your place in it."

"So I may watch?" Maratien said cautiously, not entirely certain that she had understood the invitation correctly.

"Of course. Right here at my side. And if you are as wise a child as I believe you to be, then you will take note of everything you see. Every detail. Because there may come a time when someone will ask you what it was like to have been there, and you will want to answer them truthfully."

"Yes, of course."

"Now go to Melli Shadder, one of my sisters—"

"I know her."

"Tell her that I ordered you be given my warmest coat. It will be bitterly cold when all the suns go out, Maratien. Go on. I'll wait for you."

"You will?"

"Of course. I've waited for the better part of six centuries for this Hour. I can wait a few minutes more while you find yourself a coat."

28

ALTARPIECE

"CANDY? MALINGO? ARE YOU up there?"

It was a familiar voice that instantly lifted Malingo's spirits.

"John Mischief? Is that you?" Malingo said.

"Yes——"

"We knew you'd be on one of these ferries sooner or later——" said John Serpent.

"A ferryman told us where to find you——" said John Pluckitt.

"And we're all here!" said John Drowze, eager to share the good news.

As he spoke, the brothers rose up the stairs from the deck below, followed by Two-Toed Tom and——

"Even Geneva!" said John Fillet.

"It's good to see you all again. But please, keep your voices down. Candy's still asleep."

"Should we wake her up?" said a rather heavily armed Geneva.

"I don't think that would be a good idea right now," Malingo said.

"Why not?" Two-Toed Tom asked, emerging from behind.

"There's something weird about the way she's sleeping," Malingo said.

"What do you mean?" Geneva said.

"Well, look for yourself. But put your weapons down first."

"Why?"

"They make such noise."

"I'd only do this for you," Geneva said, unbuckling her belt and handing it, with sheathed swords, to Tom. "If anybody but me unsheathes those . . ."

"We wouldn't think of it," Mischief said.

"No, no, no, no, no . . ." the brothers all murmured. "We're just concerned for our Candy."

"Keep your voices down, please," Malingo said. "She mustn't be disturbed. Don't ask me why, because I don't know. She just shouldn't, I think."

"Look at the expression on her face," Geneva murmured. "She's in pain."

Malingo nodded.

"Yes. I think she probably is."

"If she's having a nightmare, shouldn't we wake her?" Geneva said. "Look at how troubled she is! How pained!"

"I know," said Malingo. "I don't like seeing her like this either. But wherever she is right now, and whatever she's doing, it's something important. And I think we're better leaving her to do it. When she dreams like this she goes to Chickentown to see her mother."

"She doesn't seem very happy about it," Geneva remarked.

The frown on Candy's face deepened.

"Lordy Lou! She looks terrible," John Serpent remarked. "Are you sure she isn't dying?"

"No," Malingo said after a length of silence, "I'm not."

Candy counted eleven people, including her father, but not herself, now assembled within the church. They had emerged from the shadows and they could all see her, a feat no doubt made possible by her father's stolen magic. Candy recognized almost all of their faces, though she could name only a few. One was Norma Lipnik, who had once (a long time ago, in another life) showed Candy the haunted room in the Comfort Tree Hotel. It was she that had told Candy about Henry Murkitt, the ghost of Room Nineteen. Seeking out his legend was what brought Candy, for better and for worse, to the spot where she now stood. Now, Norma was dressed in all her best Sunday clothes. She even gave Candy a smile as though there was nothing remotely odd about seeing Candy's dreaming presence.

Also among the small group were two of Melissa Quackenbush's friends. One, she remembered, was called Gail, an overweight woman who always wore an excessive amount of sweet perfume in an attempt (which failed) to mask the unpleasant smell that her body exuded. The other was a woman, named Penelope, who lived a few doors down from them on Followell Street. She knew by sight several of the others too; one was the janitor at her school, though like all the others she didn't know his name. Each one of them in turn locked eyes with her, unblinking, and smiled—puppet smiles, painted on puppet heads.

"Today is a special occasion. My daughter is here in her dreaming state," Bill was explaining to the small gathering of his worshipers, "but it should be no more difficult to get what we need out of her in this form as in her real body. Knowledge is shared between the dreamer and the dreamed, after all. They're still connected. Norma, the curtain please."

Norma Lipnik offered Candy one last forced smile, then went to do as her minister instructed, drawing aside the milky blue curtain behind the altar. There was a peculiar kind of machine standing nine feet tall, perhaps ten, behind the altar.

"I know what you're wondering, witch," said Bill. "You're thinking: who made that impressive piece of machinery?"

"You're right," said Candy, doing her best to fake an appreciative smile. "I mean, who else . . . ? It's . . . amazing!"

Behind the flattery, she was all panic. This was bad. Very bad. She had no idea what this monstrous machine did, but if it was Kaspar Wolfswinkel's brain-child—and it certainly wasn't her father's, so that only left the wizard who had stolen the hats her father now possessed—then its purpose could not be benign.

"I can't take all the credit," Bill said. "I was inspired by this." He stroked his vest of many colors. "But my mind understood it instantly. You know why?"

Candy shook her head.

"Because you were born for greatness, lord of lords."

The speaker was a woman whose presence Candy had missed until now. Now, however, she stood up. Her head was bowed, but Candy recognized her immediately: it was her former teacher, Miss Schwartz. Oh, how she had changed. Her hair was no longer scraped back from her face and held hostage behind her head. Instead it fell free, long and shiny, framing her pale face.

"Nicely put, Miss Schwartz," Bill said.

The woman looked in the direction of Candy's father, but did not raise her head.

"I'm glad it pleases you, sir," she said.

Her passivity—her downcast eyes—her pitiful gratitude—were distressing. This wasn't the Miss Schwartz Candy had despised. Her father had broken her. Broken her and stuck her back together again so that she was fragile and afraid.

"Mr. Thompson, Mr. Elliot, why don't you prepare my daughter for our little science experiment? And be quick about it. I want this over and done with."

29

MIDNIGHT HAS WINGS

As Mater Motley ascended the steps of the Great Pyramid at Xuxux, her thoughts turned briefly to her grandson. They had worked for many years devising the plan that was about to come to fruition, and while she'd had no time for sentimentality—it was a spineless, sickly feeling—she couldn't keep a wave of regret from breaking over her. She'd done her best to warn her grandson about the vicious power of his affections. She'd forced the lesson upon him by sewing up his lips with needle and thread when she'd first heard him use the word *love*; the scars that her handiwork had left were still upon his face the last time she'd seen him, which had been on the deck of her death-ship, *Wormwood*. The scars, however, had failed to inspire contrition in him.

She let the regret have its useless moment, then let it go. Carrion had been a fine coconspirator, but once the taint of love had touched him, he'd become a danger to himself and to their great enterprise. So she was alone as she climbed the steps to the doors of the Great Pyramid.

She paused. This was a great moment. She wanted somebody with her to witness.

"Maratien," she said quietly.

"I'm here, m'lady," Maratien said behind her, but nearby.

She couldn't conceal the unease in her voice. The Old Mother sensed it.

"There's nothing to fear, child," she said. "The creatures behind this door—they are the sacbrood—and are all in my service."

"There are many?"

"Numberless, at least."

"All in this pyramid?"

"They are in all the pyramids, and below all the pyramids, beneath the Izabella, spreading out and down great distances." Mater Motley waited for all this to register with the girl. Then she reached into the fold so her dress, its fabric weighed down by captive souls, and brought out a key. It was a strange, restless form. "Here," she said. "You open the door. See for yourself."

Tentatively, Maratien accepted the key.

"Take courage, child. There are powers waiting upon you. Look back. See for yourself."

Maratien glanced over her shoulder. In the short time since they'd stepped off the *Kreyzu* and onto the steps of the pyramid, massive numbers of sea creatures had risen to crowd the surface of the Izabella, many of them giving off luminescence from their scales or shells.

"See how impatient they are?" Mater Motley said, directing Maratien's attention to the bottom step, where the dozens of monstrous forms were emerging. "You'd better get on with it."

Maratien needed no further words of encouragement. She returned her gaze to the door, and slid the key into the lock. She didn't have to do more than that; the key knew its business. It slid out of her fingers and into the lock, disappearing completely.

"Good," Mater Motley murmured. "Very good."

There was a noise from within the pyramid now, as the system of counterweights that operated the doors was set in motion. The lock was turning, but so was an entire portion of the door surrounding the lock. And the motion was spreading, forms turning within forms, until the entire triangular door was moving, the design dividing, opening onto the darkness within.

A rank smell came to greet the Old Mother and Maratien, fouler by far than that of excrement or rot, though the worst of both was contained within it. Maratien put her hand up to her face, disgusted by the stench. Mater Motley was indifferent to it.

"How I have waited . . ." she breathed.

The triangular door was completely open now, and from inside, carried on that foul air, was the voices of the sacbrood: clicking, hissing, ticking; its volume steadily rising as news spread from hive to hive that the Hour of

Hours had come. Mater Motley reached into the folds of her skirts again, and brought out her slim, black wand. Then quietly instructing Maratien to follow her and stay close, she entered the Pyramid. The only illumination within was the moonlight that had entered with them. It did nothing to define the mysteries of the interior.

"Be ready," Mater Motley said to Maratien.

Then she lifted the wand above her head and its tip suddenly blazed. It was a tiny source, but it threw off tens, then hundreds, then thousands of beads that flew in all directions, each as bright or brighter than its creator, and each trailing a filament of light that did not diminish, but hung in the air like the threads of a luciferian spider. And as this web of brightness spread, it began to unknit the darkness, and offer Maratien and her guardian a glimpse of what the Pyramid contained. The Old Mother had not remotely prepared the girl for what she now saw.

The sacbrood were everywhere, each its own invention. Were they vast insects, or winged reptiles, or an unholy marriage of both? Some had limbs numbered in the hundreds, and eyes in clusters, like bright black eggs, and bodies that coiled upon themselves like nested snakes. Some were swarming with parasitic creatures whose bodies were in turn leeched upon by bloated mites; some hung in loops from the heights of the Pyramid, their translucent bodies containing jellied spawn; and others skittered over the floor, moving with such speed they left only an impression of their barbed bodies.

But none of these details distracted Mater Motley from the business she had here.

"I know that many of you here have waited years for this Hour," she said, using that voice that, though it was barely conversational in volume, was somehow heard everywhere. *"The waiting is over. Rise, all of you! And give me my Midnight!"*

She did not pause for a response from the brood. She simply pointed her black rod at the apex of the Pyramid. One last bend of brightness flew from it, and struck the top of the Pyramid. Unlike those messengers of light she'd previously unleashed, it was, however, instantly extinguished. It had done its work, triggering a mechanism somewhere in the Pyramid's belly. A profound growl shook the structure, punctuated by something akin to the beating of a vast drum.

"What's happening?" Maratien said.

"They are being freed to do what they were born to do," Mater Motley replied. "See?"

She directed the girl's attention to the spot where she had sent the triggering pulse. Moon-silvered clouds were now visible with a litter of stars between them. The pyramid was opening, its sides no longer touching at the apex, but parting like a three-petaled flower. To move stone walls of such immensity was no easy task, and the blossoming above was slow. But the sacbrood sensed their imminent release.

Waves of agitation passed through their prodigious

numbers. A few of those close to the roof fluttered up to the three-pointed aperture and flirted with the moonlight; some even flew up fearlessly into the night. Their escape encouraged other members of the brood that were clinging to the walls lower down the Pyramid to also take flight, so that soon the Pyramid was filled with the clamor of wings.

The shafts of moonlight were broadening as the Pyramid continued to open, but the sight of the sky only caused word to spread into the deeper and deeper hives. The floor of the massive structure, though built by masons who had known how to move blocks of stone the size of mountains, vibrated from the motion of a billion wingbeats, each striking the air with no great violence.

Midnight had arrived.

30

DRAINING THE GHOST

THE DEVICE THAT BILL Quackenbush's technicians, Elliot and Thompson, had hooked Candy up to was very obviously not of any parts its builder had available in the Hereafter. The portion secured to the wall behind the altar curtain was a large, messily constructed device made of equipment that had probably been taken from the big pharmacy on Main Street mingled with stuff that might have come from a garage or perhaps from the wreckage of the chicken factory, or both.

At its heart, however, were magical mechanisms that had not, she thought, been found in Chickentown, unless by chance the floodwaters of the Izabella had conveniently brought them here. More likely, Candy thought (no, *feared*) they had been supplied to him by somebody in the Abarat, which meant that trade between the two worlds had begun again. Perhaps it had never been fully eradicated in the first place and all that her father needed to do to find the parts for his machine was ask the right people.

There were two parts of the device that really carried the stamp of Abaratian technology. One was a globe of pulsing power about three feet across—the glass it was made from, full of flaws—that was set at the center of the device. It made the air smell like summer lightning: sweet and metallic. The second piece of Abaratian design was the bizarre mechanism that the globe was set upon. It looked like the innards of an old television, only slightly melted and then given to a family of tiny, white bugs to nest in and that now lived inside the guts of the thing and moved at such speed through the machine that they were blurs.

There was a third piece: a chair.

"Sit," her father said. "Go on. And before you try any of your tricks, just remember: your mother is back at home, fast asleep. Defenseless. Do you understand me?"

Candy nodded.

"Say it."

"I understand," she said quietly as she sat in the chair.

"Sir, may I step outside and take a breath of air?" one of the men said, as Elliot and Thompson each uncoiled lengths of the needle tubing. "I've always been a little squeamish around medical things."

"No, Futterman," Bill Quackenbush snapped. The nervous man, who Candy only now recognized as the manager of the supermarket on Riley Street, reluctantly obeyed the preacher's instructions. Bill grabbed him by the arm, and pulled him closer. "You will stay right *there*—"

"Must I? I think—"

"I don't care what you think. I'm the minister of this church and if you want to stay in the Lord's good graces then you'd better do as I damn well say!"

Meekly, Futterman remained where he'd been told to stand. All the color had drained from his face, leaving him pasty white. Candy felt sorry for him. He looked so afraid. He seemed to feel her watching him, because his eyes flicked in her direction. Candy desperately wanted to give him some hope. She wanted to throw a thought into his head to say: *It's going to be all right. The preacher's just a bully who found some magic hats. He hasn't got any real power.*

Candy's concern for him distracted her from her own problems, until at a little nod from her father, Elliot and Thompson, working with well-rehearsed synchronicity, went down on their haunches to either side of the half-melted television with the white bugs in it, and unraveled from either side of it long black and yellow cables. They had at the end of them small discs with lids that the two men cautiously unscrewed.

"Now we just have to get this thing going," Bill said.

He reached behind Candy and flipped one switch, which started a deep, regretful moan in the machine. Thompson and Elliot knew their cues. They each opened one of Candy's hands without any need of force, and placed the discs on the palms of either hand.

"The Silter nests are in place, sir. We're ready."

Bill flipped two more switches, and Candy felt a creeping sickness climb through her body. The Silter nests broke through the flesh of her translucent palms and began to send fine tentacles up into her hands. She instantly started to feel the hunger of the voracious things called Silters. At once she felt weaker, as though her very life force was draining from her.

"Dad, please . . ." Candy muttered in her sleep.

"Did you hear that?" Malingo said. "She's talking to her father?"

"Lordy Lou," said John Moot. "That man's psychotic."

"She knows how to deal with him," said John Fillet.

"Does that sound like somebody who's dealing with things?" John Serpent said.

"She sounds as if she's dying," Geneva said.

"She's just dreaming," Mischief said.

"Look at the poor girl," John Serpent replied. "They're *tormenting* her. We have to do something!"

"I think he's right, for once," Tom said. "She's obviously in pain."

The expression on Candy's face was becoming more and more agitated. Malingo glanced up at the faces of the John Brothers, Tom and Geneva, all looking down at Candy with echoes of her pained expression on their faces.

"You have to wake her," Geneva said.

"But what'll happen if we do? She's never been like this," Malingo said.

"Oh, Lordy . . ." she murmured. "Now you've got me

doubting my own instincts."

"What do you think, Malingo?" Tom said.

"I think . . ." he said softly. Then, drawing a deeper breath, ". . . I think we have no choice but to trust that she knows what she's doing."

"Doesn't look that way," John Serpent said.

"She'll be okay," Malingo said. "I believe in her."

31

THE FLOCK

*E*XACTLY WHEN DID *I get to be so appetizing?* Candy asked herself. She seemed to be on a lot of menus lately. The first clue, now that she thought about it, was the attack of the Zetheks, who would definitely have bitten a sizeable chunk out of her if she'd not kept out of his way. Then, of course, Boa, who'd been determined to get a new body out of Candy's energies. And now, the unlikeliest thief of all: her own father.

The machine, she could see from the corner of her eye, was devouring her visions. No, not visions—visions were simply sights, passively admired—no, it was *experiences* she was having leeched from her: glorious experiences.

All her beautiful experiences, and the memories of these experiences, were being stolen, drained into large phials that sat in the center of the machine. And it wasn't just one life the device was sucking out of her, it was all the lives that she'd seen or felt in the Abarat. Her ever-inquisitive soul had touched them all in its way, made them her spiritual kin. They had stayed with her long after their physical forms had gone from sight: the dream-bedecked occupants of Marapozsa Street, Jimothi leading an army of tarrie-cats in battle against the bone beasts on Ninnyhammer, the Sea-Skippers on the tide of the Izabella. She'd confronted Zetheks, the Beasts of Efreet, not to mention Carrion and his grandmother.

Some of the memories had been nightmarish visions but she had kept hold of them in her mind for a reason. They were hers, for better or worse, and she wanted them all back. Experiencing them, in all their strangeness, she had come to better understand herself. If her father took them from her, then the Candy she had become—the true Candy—would also disappear.

" . . . not . . . going . . . to happen," she said.

"Reverend?"

"What is it, Norma?" he said as he studied the readouts from the Thieving Machine.

"The girl said something, Bill."

"You are to call me Reverend, do you understand, Norma? And I heard her. I just didn't care."

"I think you should."

"I told you, I couldn't care—*wait. Wait!* These readings aren't right!" He looked up at Candy. Her body pulsed with light as the Silters flailed about riotously in her etheric body. "Stop! You can't do this!"

"You'd . . . be . . . surprised . . .

—◦—

". . . what I can do."

"Look! She looks better. I think whatever was happening to her before . . . she has it under control," Malingo said.

"You're supposed to die now," her father said. "Stop fighting it!"

"My memories of the Abarat don't belong to you!"

"She's getting agitated again," Geneva said. "Look how wildly her eyes are moving behind her lids. She's watching something."

"Yes," Malingo said. He watched the motion of her eyes closely. "It looks like she's looking down."

"At her hands, maybe?" Betty said.

Candy, asleep on the boat, continued to clutch at nothing. The sinews in her fingers taut like harp strings.

"Lordy Lou, what is that monster doing to her?" Tom said.

"I was born with a piece of Abarat inside me," Candy shouted. "I was *meant* to be in the Abarat."

"Well, you can take comfort in this: soon you won't even remember the word."

"I'll remember it forever," she said defiantly. "Abarat. Abarat. You'll never take it from me! Abarat. Abarat. Abar—"

Her recitation of the three syllables was interrupted

by a yell from the other end of the church.

"Dad! I'm bored! Nothing's happening outside," Ricky said as he entered the church and walked down the center aisle toward the altar.

"Ricky, I told you to stay outside. Get the hell out! Why have I been cursed with idiotic children?"

Ricky stopped short at his father's insult. His eyes welled with tears.

"Dad?"

"I said get out of here, boy! This isn't for your eyes."

It was then that Ricky saw Candy, strapped to the machine, the slimy Silters creeping up her arms and into her chest, draining her of life and essence.

"What are you doing to her?" An expression of profound disgust came over his face. His question became an outraged yell. *"What are you creeps doing to her?"*

"It's none of your damn business, boy!"

"Look at her! Oh, God. You're torturing her!"

"Go home, boy!" Bill said, a dangerous growl in his voice. "If you don't, you'll be sorry."

"I already am. I thought you'd changed, but you haven't. You're . . . bad. Rotten inside! That's what you are."

"Thompson, grab him!"

The burly Thompson pushed through the other witnesses to go and grab Ricky. But Ricky had no intention of being caught. He backed up along the center aisle, picking up one of the folding wooden chairs from the end of the row and throwing it at Thompson, who was quick enough to swat it away before it struck him, but not fast enough to see the second chair coming. It struck him hard, and it was he who folded up, not the chair, taking several more chairs with him when he went down.

Candy knew she would not get another chance to undo the harm her father had done. She let her head loll as though she was barely conscious, and the ruse seemed to work. She caught a sideways glimpse of her father glancing up at her and—apparently deciding she was in no state to cause him problems—turning his back on her and starting to clamber over the litter of overturned chairs to get Ricky.

"I need some help here!" he yelled to his little congregation. "He's just a kid! He can't hurt you!"

He'd no sooner spoken than Ricky made a liar of him, picking up one of the folded chairs in both hands and swatted at Miss Schwartz with it. She was thrown off her feet by the blow, knocking over the man called Elliot on her way to the ground.

Candy needed to pull the wretched Silters out of her, she knew, and be quick about it. Bill wouldn't be distracted for long. In a matter of seconds he could be back to finish his work. She lifted her hand up toward her mouth as far as the restraints allowed, and bent so that she could remove the invading Silters with her teeth. But she had to be quick. There was no time to be squeamish.

Do it! she told herself, and giving her mind no chance

at second thoughts, she bit down, taking off their heads.

They tasted like rotting, slimy flesh, but as soon as she bit into them, the flowing tentacles shrieked and withered. She pulled them out with her teeth and spat them onto the ground.

The machine was not happy with this sudden change in events. In the few seconds it took Candy to remove the Silters she'd glanced back to see that just about every element of the device capable of motion was registering this unexpected reversal; its gauges fluttering, its warning lights ticking, and the phials in which the loot of Candy's mind was stored, rattling in their metal cages. Her luck could not hold for very much longer. It was only a matter of time before her father took his eyes off the messy struggle going on in the pile of folded chairs, and saw her escaping.

It was not Bill Quackenbush who raised an alarm, however. It was Mr. Futterman, who had been crying, forgotten on the ground in his faint until now. When he opened his eyes he saw Candy biting into the slimy Silters and spitting them out.

"I'm going to be sick!" he said, his comment by chance finding a window in the general racket of shouts and chairs that echoed around the church.

Candy slid off the edge of the altar and by the time the soles of her feet were on the ground the clatter of conflict died away almost entirely. She looked up. Her father was turning, his eyes already fixed upon her. Candy couldn't make any sense of the string of curses he then unleashed, but there was no doubting the raging fury that fueled them. Bill drew back his right arm, at belly level, to the side of his body, his hand raised, palm out, fingers bent. He made a quick counterclockwise flick of his wrist, then reversed the motion. As a result, the overturned chairs that lay between father and daughter divided. The chairs squealed on the polished boards and were whipped away by an invisible force, thrown up and over one another by the power of Bill's gesture.

There were shrieks from several of the minister's flock (the shrillest from Mr. Elliot) as they apparently decided that they'd witnessed quite enough for one day. They started to walk, then race toward the front door. They weren't fast enough. Bill turned his back on the altar and threw the force of his attention at the exits. Candy did not know if he made another gesture or if it was simply his will that caused the huge doors to slam shut and the bolts to slide noisily home to seal the contract.

Norma Lipnik had been closest to the doors when they closed. Now, shaken by the noise, she retreated from the entrance, calling to her minister as she did so.

"Please, Reverend!" she said, putting on the warm, unflustered voice she always used when things went awry at the hotel, "I really have to go."

"It doesn't work that way, woman!"

"But you don't understand . . ."

That's it, Candy thought, *keep talking, Norma.* Every

second that Norma Lipnik wasted distracting Bill Quack-enbush was another second Candy could devote to figuring out how to undo the theft of her treasured knowledge.

She stumbled, her legs weak and aching, around the altar to the device itself. The phials that contained her memories seemed to already know that she intended to reclaim them, as though some tenuous thread of thought between her mind and these stolen experiences still existed. The substance in the phials—was it liquid or gaseous? Perhaps both—sensed her proximity and it raced around the glass. It had been colorless, but it had darkened in its agitated state, until it was the purple-gray of a thunderhead, in the belly of which multicolored lightning rods bloomed.

She was still staring at it in dazed wonder when she heard the voice of her father from across the church: *"If you touch my machine, I'll kill you where you stand!"*

32

SACRILEGE

CANDY LOOKED BACK AT her father, just in time to see him conjure a trinity of thin, silver-tipped arrows. With their silver tips glinting, they flew at her and she felt a nauseating tug in her belly, as though they were homing in on her innards.

She let them get to the other side of the altar before she made her move, forcing her less-than-eager legs to shift her out of their path at the very last moment. The needles were too close to change direction, and struck at the spot where she had been standing seconds before. The first needle hit the middle of the device, causing an arc of yellow-green lightning to leap from it, while the other two struck the phials causing a few of them to explode instantly. Their contents emptied like flowering clouds, the colors they contained suddenly blazing like glorious fires. They returned instantly to their owner, performing a celebration dance of liberation by circling Candy three or four times, then without warning, leaping back into her.

Oh, the bliss of that! The unadulterated joy of being reunited with herself. Her head was like a pail into which a dam was pouring its contents, images that she had forgotten she'd owned blazing for a tiny perfect instant in her mind's eye before another came to show its beauty to her. A bird, a tower, a slave, a face, ten faces, a thousand faces, a moon in a tree, a glass of water, a wave, a tear, a laughing moth, her mom, Ricky, Don, Diamanda, Carrion, the Dead Man's House, the Yebba Dim Day, a bottle of rum, Kaspar, Malingo—oh, Malingo, Malingo, Malingo—

She was laughing now, in her sleep, and saying his name.

"Malingo! Malingo! Malingo!"

"I think the worst might be over," Geneva said cautiously.

"Let's hope so," said John Mischief. "Because my heart can't take much more of this."

"*Your* heart?" said John Drowze. *"What about mine?"*

His complaint started them all going.

"—and mine!"

"—and me!"

"Shut your nattering traps!" said Two-Toed Tom. "It isn't over till it's over."

Candy threw her will against the other phials. There was no anger in it. The pleasure of the reunion had washed her clean, and her cleanliness gave the blows greater force. All but one of the phials blew, and Candy's memories and meditations, prayers, dreams, and revelations, came back to her in all their chaotic, glorious profusion.

"You stupid cow!" her father yelled.

He surged at the mass of obstacles between them—both chairs and people—sweeping them aside. Then he came at her. She could see on his face what he intended. He wasn't going to trust magic to punish her. It was apparent that he intended to deal with her the old-fashioned way—with his hands. He was coming at her quickly too. Moving much faster than expected, given his beer gut and his lumbering gait. His face was beet red with fury, his gritted teeth yellowish, the color and light in his eyes completely extinguished, leaving two black slits, without so much as a highlight to relieve their eerie veracity.

Keeping her gaze fixed on him she fumbled for the final phial, and pulling it out of its holder she lifted it above her head and with all the strength her beleaguered limbs could muster, she threw it to the ground at her feet. There was a satisfying noise of breaking glass erased almost immediately by a soft *whump* as the contents burst into a ball of smoke and flowers, doubling its size with every passing second, spitting out riotous smears of color that graciously curved upward until they were a few feet from their source, and climbed at a giddy speed to explode a second time when they struck the ceiling. There was a loud, sharp crack, followed by several splintering sounds, as one of the support beams cracked. Globs of white plaster dropped to the floor where they shattered.

"How dare you!" Bill said, his tone so ludicrously theatrical she almost laughed. *"This is sacred ground."*

Candy let the thoughts from the final phial, having burst against the ceiling, come down into her. She was almost complete. She had her memories back, but she was running out of tricks. Under her breath, she muttered, "Diamanda, if you can hear me . . . please help . . ."

On the shores of the Twenty-Fifth Hour, walking with her sometime husband, the love of her life (and afterlife)—the once-pitiful ghost in Room Nineteen, Henry Murkitt—Diamanda heard her name called. She recognized the voice instantly.

"Candy's calling me," she said. "We have to go. She's in danger."

Bill lunged and caught hold of Candy. His hands were huge and heavy, as though he had lead for bones. He struck her across the face.

Almost as a reflex, Candy channeled her shock and turned her thoughts from her father's twisted face to something even less pleasant: the Fever Gibe, one of the Beasts of Efreet, leaning up on its back legs, the purple-blue spines on its hide standing on end. She cast the image out into the air behind her father, continuing to add details to it as she did so. Its forelimbs with their razor claws. And worse, its head, which opened like a grotesque flower with but one petal, red and moist, which spread and stretched, uncaging the vast tooth-lined maw at its center. Though it was made of dust, light and memory, touched into life by the powers she'd reclaimed, it had sufficient self-intent to immediately turn its fury on the panicking fools stumbling among the overturned chairs. It loosed a roar, and the church's stained-glass windows blew out.

"Reverend!" Futterman said. He had crawled away from the place where he'd fallen, and was at the minister's feet. "Forget her! Please! You're a man of God. Summon up an angel. Make this thing go away."

"There's nothing there," Bill Quackenbush said, still holding Candy. His fingers had gone to her neck, his thumbs pressed against her windpipe, cutting off the flow of air. "It's just something my idiot daughter gave birth to."

"Well, tell *her* to make it go away."

"You heard the man, Candy. Make it go away," Bill said, and he squeezed tighter.

". . . can't . . ." Candy said.

"Can't or *won't?*"

Despite her desperate situation, Candy managed a tiny smile.

"Say good-bye," her father said to her. The tone of his voice was matter-of-fact. He was simply stating the truth. "You're not my daughter. I don't know whose you are, but you're not mine."

He pressed his thumbs down even harder on Candy's neck. She fought for breath, but none was coming. All she could think to do was to summon the Efreetian Beast she'd conjured back to her. It came. She saw it rise up behind her father's head, the veins in the stretched flesh around its mouth throbbing. He saw its reflection in her eyes, it seemed, because he turned and, an instant before she lost consciousness for want of breath, his grip on her throat loosened. She gingerly extracted herself from his hands and slid down the wall, gratefully drinking the air.

The Fever Gibe was leaning over her father. A string of saliva ran from its gaping mouth and landed on his face. It must have stung because he cursed, then retaliated against the Gibe with his own silver-tipped darts. When they struck the beast, it curled and eddied like smoke, only to recover its form once the dart had passed through it.

"How dare you bring your filth into this holy place!" he yelled.

He turned to face the mirage, firing his bolts into it over and over. The coherence of the image could not hold in the face of such a consistent assault. The holes in the creature grew larger, its matter growing thin and finally dissolving completely. There was a long moment while everyone recovered from the events. Candy didn't wait for her father to renew his attack. She moved around the side of the altar and then began to race toward the door.

"No way out!" her father yelled behind her.

She'd seen him close the door and bolt it to keep Norma Lipnik from leaving, but that couldn't keep her from unbolting it, and getting back out onto the street.

"*Catch her, you fools!*" her father shouted. "*Don't let her get out of here!*"

They had seen what their Reverend was capable of and

out of blind fear they did as he instructed. Candy kept her eyes fixed on the door, but from the corner of her eyes she could sense her father's people closing in on her from both left and right. She wasn't going to make it to the door before they laid their hands on her, she knew. She forced her weakened legs to work till they throbbed, but there simply wasn't enough speed in them.

"Bring her down!" Bill yelled. "The first one with their hand on her gets to drink from the cup of her power. After me, of course."

Her own father giving a piece of her away, as though she was his to give? It was too much! She stopped running, and turned on her heel.

"You're right!" she yelled across the church at him. "I'm not your daughter! You don't know me! You never did and you never will! I belong—

"—to the Abarat," Candy said in her sleep.

"That's my girl," Malingo said softly.

"It's a fine sentiment," John Mischief murmured. "I just hope it isn't the last thing she says!"

Candy didn't try to retrace her steps to the altar. She knew she had no hope of getting there. The minister's mob was just a few steps from seizing hold of her. She raised her arms, openhanded.

"If you're going to take me," she said, looking at them with naked contempt, "then take me. But be careful. I bite."

"Take no notice of her!" Bill said. "She has no real power!"

Five of his flock did as their shepherd instructed, and reached out to grab hold of her. As they did so the front doors rattled violently, and the screws securing the iron bolts flew off. Seconds later so did the bolts.

The five brave souls who'd seized hold of Candy changed their minds, and let go of her. Only one, the father of Deborah Hackbarth (Candy's one-time friend and, later, school-ground nemesis), stepped in to do what the others had declined to do. At school, his daughter had always boasted about her noble origins; hence, she said, her delicate bones and perfect manners. To the extent she had such qualities at all, they did not derive from her father, who was a fat-bellied thing of a man, who took no little pleasure in squeezing Candy's arm to achieve the maximum discomfort.

Candy felt a rush of wind against her face and a welcome voice said: "Let go of the girl this instant."

Candy looked toward the front door, whence the voice had come. It was still closed. But Diamanda and Henry Murkitt had passed through it, and were standing inside the church.

"I said, let go of her," Diamanda said. "Don't make me force you."

"I'd like to see you try," Deborah's father laughed.

"As you wish."

She started to whisper something, the words she was speaking forming an agitated cloud in front of her face, which with a tiny flick of her forefinger she dispatched toward Hackbarth. The words were upon him in an instant, circling his head. He tried to swat them away with his free hand, but that didn't work, and they quickly began to sting him, resulting in a burst of obscene language from Hackbarth. He let go of Candy in order to employ both his hands to ward off the attack.

"You can wake up now!" Diamanda insisted.

"What about my mom? I can't leave—"

"I'll take care of her. Get back to the Abarat! *Now!* They need you there."

Candy began the process of waking herself. She heard Diamanda speak again.

"Defend them, child! You're the only one who has a hope of stopping it."

"Stopping what?" she muttered.

"The war, child! The war between Night and—"

Candy opened her eyes, as the last syllable Diamanda uttered "—Day!" fell away into the no-man's-land between sleeping and waking. She looked up and saw her friends, Malingo, the Johns, Geneva, and Tom.

"It's all right," she said. "I'm back."

33

NO STRANGER NOW

VERYONE HAD QUESTIONS, OF course. Where had Candy been in her dream travels? And who (or what) had she encountered on her journey that had caused her to struggle so desperately while she slept?

"It's complicated," Candy told them all. "And I'm hungry. Could we go find some food and I'll tell you while we eat?"

There was no disagreement on that. Everybody was hungry.

"Let me and the boys lead the way," Mischief said. "We'll find somewhere to eat. Eight pairs of eyes are better than one."

So saying, he and his brothers headed down the gangplank and onto the dock, leaving the others to follow at a more leisurely pace. As she walked Candy was struck by the peculiar hush that lay upon the harbor. Though it was far from deserted—there were people working on board the fishing boats that were moored along the quay, and the streets that led up into the town were busy—everyone was talking very quietly. There was no shouting or cursing from the fishermen, nor laughter and chatter among the women in the market. Even the large Abaratian seagulls, which were usually even more raucous than their brethren in the Hereafter, were not making their usual demands. In fact all but those few too ancient to fly were in the harbor. The rest had gone; the only sign of their numbers was the white droppings all along the seawall where they'd perched.

Candy surreptitiously snagged Malingo's arm.

"There's something wrong here, isn't there?"

"I was just thinking the same thing," he said quietly. "But what?"

In search of an answer Candy scanned the streets of the town, which was built on the flank of a steep hill, its whitewashed houses neatly arrayed on its zigzagging streets. Many of their windows were shuttered and their drapes drawn. Clearly, a lot of the residents in the town had no desire to even look outside, much less step.

"Oh, Lordy Lou," Malingo murmured.

"What?"

She glanced at Malingo. He was staring at the sky. She did the same.

There was a wind blowing up there, carrying before it, in a northerly direction, a great flotilla of clouds. It wasn't the clouds, however, that had caught Malingo's eye. It was the birds that were flying through them. A mass migration was underway, not just of the seabirds that had vacated the harbor, but of hundreds of species—no thousands—many of which challenged the very definition of a bird. There was a flock of what looked to be winged boars, and several flights of feathered dragonflies. Their size was hard to gauge, but if the boars were the size of pigs, the dragonflies were the size of seagulls. The giants of this chaotic flock, however—creatures as big as airships, and kept aloft by the same bloated bodies, but trailed streams of flickering tentacles, like the tails of countless kites intertwined with quarter-mile strings of Christmas tree lights.

"So many," Geneva said, amazed. Then, more darkly, "But where are they all going?"

"Have you seen anything like this before?" Candy asked.

"No, nothing," Malingo said. "Even as a kid."

"Me neither."

There were shaken heads from everyone.

"There's plenty of eating places along the harbor front," Mischief and his brothers had already returned to report.

"It's mostly fish," said John Slop.

"It's all fish," said John Fillet.

"There's crab," said John Moot, "and squidling."

"It's still fish," countered John Fillet.

"A crab isn't a fish," John Drowze said.

"Let's just eat," said Tom.

Candy looked at Malingo. The massive migration of birds had passed out of sight. With their disappearance there wasn't much else to discuss.

"Agreed," Candy said.

They wandered along the small cafés and restaurants along the harbor front, consulting the menus on view outside. But their harassed proprietors quickly appeared to offer them some bad news. Tonight's dining would be delayed. It had yet to be filleted, battered and fried because it had yet to arrive. Everyone tried to make the delay sound quite inconsequential, a common occurrence. But they didn't fool Candy.

"Where were they fishing?" she asked one of the café owners.

"To the west," the owner replied, "in the straits between Gnomon and Gorgossium."

West, Candy thought. *The direction from which the birds were flying. What was going on? Something out of Gorgossium, more likely than not.*

With all the premises along the harbor front proving useless, they decided to head up into the town in search of other sources of sustenance. The cobbled streets were steep, and the climb was hard work. But the reward was the sound of laughter, mainly where children were playing. Busy though the market street was, it was hard to miss the sight of the green-skinned man with piercing eyes towering over the crowd. It was an odd sight, considering the green man was shorter than he was green.

"Well, look who's here," Candy said with a smile. "Legitimate Eddie!"

"Where?" said Malingo.

"Straight ahead. And he's standing on Betty Thunder's shoulders."

"Eddie and Betty?" said Two-Toed Tom. "Are you making this up?"

"They're actors," said Malingo. "They put on a play about us once. It was very funny."

"I don't see anyone," said John Mischief, who was the shortest of his brothers.

Tom peered ahead and nodded.

"I see them. Oh, look at that. She looks so glamorous. All those sequins. All those muscles."

They emerged from within the crowd and everyone could now see that they were accompanied by their playwright friend, a five-foot ape named Clyde, who was waving.

"Well, well, well," said Legitimate Eddie. "If it isn't Qwandy Tootinfruit and her friend Jingo."

Everyone except Candy and Malingo looked extremely confused.

"Oh, I love reunions," Candy said, and proceeded to make a round of introductions.

Once everyone had become acquainted, everyone decided that eating would be the next order of business, and proceeded up through the streets of Qualm Hah. At the top of one street, a market with all manner of things for sale: the produce of an Hour blessed by sun and showers; the endless balm of late spring morning; there were even some fruits here Candy knew and could name—Abaratian specialties like tuntarunts and doemanna rotts and kuthuries—but there were far more that she did not know.

"Forbidden fruits," Legitimate Eddie said, plucking one very lushly shaped fruit from a pile. "She's a big girl, this one," he said with a mischievous grin. "Looks like you, Betty."

The fruit did indeed resemble a very curvaceous woman. Betty was not offended.

"If it's me then I'll take it," she said.

"They're the best moriana we've had in a very long time," the stallkeeper said.

"What's the big deal?" Candy said.

"You tell her," Betty said, biting the head off the moriana, then the upper body. The smell that spread from the coral-pink flesh of the fruit was so delicious it made Candy dizzy with pleasure.

"Oh wow," she said.

"Aren't they good? And no you can't have a bite. Ask Eddie to buy you one," said Betty.

"Why should I—?"

"You bought *me* one," Betty said.

"I'm paying for that?"

"You'd better," the wood-toothed stallkeeper said.

"I'll pay for *one*," Eddie said, putting up a single, stubby green finger.

"Uno moriana is seven paterzem."

"Seven?" said Candy. "That's ridiculous!"

"Where have you been?" the stallkeeper asked. "Paterzem ain't worth what they used to be."

As Eddie paid for Betty's meal, Candy searched her pockets. She had two paterzem and some change.

"Where's Malingo?" she said more to herself than anyone. "He's got all our cash."

She told everyone that she was going to look for Malingo and headed off along the line of stalls, assuming he'd wandered on ahead. She was surprised to find that he wasn't just a few paces farther on, but had apparently gone on to explore the more elaborate stalls farther on, and more particularly, knowing Malingo, he'd headed for the marionette show that was playing for a crowd of adults and children at the very end of the street. She started to make her way through the throng toward the puppet theater, standing on tiptoe now and then or jumping up and down on the spot in the hope of catching a glimpse of him.

The third time she tried jumping she saw him. He was no longer on the street, however. He'd had a bad experience in Babilonium when he and Candy had been separated from each other. It had scarred him, causing him to feel uncomfortable in large crowds, and he'd apparently decided to get out of the press of people for a little while. Now he was standing in a narrow alleyway, barely more than a vague form beckoning to her from the shadows.

"There you are!" she yelled to him as she made her way across the street. Once on the other side she slid cautiously between two stalls piled high with produce. Then she stepped out of the bright, noisy street into the hushed, shadowy alley.

"I thought for sure you'd be watching the puppet show," Candy said to him.

"I took a quick look," Malingo said. "But it was the same old story. You know . . ."

"Not really," Candy said, a little mystified.

"Yes, you do. Love and Death. It's always Love and Death. Though at least with puppets you see things the way they really are. Everything has strings attached."

It was unusual for Malingo to make a joke. And this one actually made Candy laugh, though there seemed to be some significance in the remark that she couldn't connect with Malingo and his life.

"Is there something you're not telling me?" she asked him.

It was Malingo who laughed now: though there was something about the echo in the alleyway that made the sound darker and deeper than it should have been. Candy slowed her approach. Now she stopped.

"What secret would I have from you?" Malingo said. "You of all people."

"I don't know," Candy said.

"Then why are you asking?"

"Just that you were talking about love."

"Ah," he said softly. "Yes, and I was talking as though I'd actually experienced it. Yes. As though I knew how it felt to fall for somebody. And then to hear them making all the right promises. That they'd love you forever if you'd just give them . . ." He shrugged. "Oh, I don't know. Something inconsequential."

Candy felt an icy nail run down her spine. This wasn't Malingo.

"I'm sorry," she said, doing her best to keep her voice from betraying her fear. "You're not who I thought you were."

"It's not you who needs to apologize, Candy," the figure in the shadows said. "You've done nothing wrong."

"Well that's good to hear," she said, still attempting to sound as though there was nothing of great importance here, simply a misunderstanding. "I have to go. I have friends . . . waiting . . ." She made an attempt to look back, but her gaze returned to the stranger.

Except, of course, he *wasn't* a stranger.

"I thought you were dead," she said very quietly.

"So did I," Christopher Carrion replied.

34

UNFINISHED

"I WOULD HAVE DIED," HE said, "except that I knew you were still here, Princess. I think that's what kept me from giving up completely. The thought of finding my way back to you. Oh, and my nightmares, of course."

As he spoke, two of the filament creatures slid out of hiding among the tattered robes Carrion was wearing, and encircled his neck. Though they were not as bright as they'd once been, the phosphorescence they gave off was still enough to offer her a glimpse of Carrion's face. He looked like something that had been thumbed out of mud and excrement, his eyes little more than pits in which there were slivers of light, his lips ragged strips of dirt and sinew that could not conceal his dead bone smile.

"Don't look at me, Princess," he said. He tried to turn away from her, to conceal his diminished state but he did so too quickly for his mismade legs. They failed him, and he stumbled. He would have fallen in the filth underfoot had he not reached out and forced his fingers—which for all their crude form, did not lack strength—into the rotted plaster and fractured stone.

"I'm ashamed that you should see me like this. But I needed to be in your presence, just for a little time. When you next see me—"

"She isn't here," Candy said.

"What?"

"We parted ways."

"You drove her out?"

"Not all by myself. I needed help to be sure I had the details right. But she is gone. See for yourself. Look in my mind." She approached his hunched-over figure as she spoke to him, raising her arm as she did so, offering contact. "Go on. Do whatever you need to do. I'm not afraid of you anymore."

It was true. The Lord of Midnight who'd stalked her in the Dead Man's House was nowhere visible in this frail shadow figure that stood before her now. He glanced at her face, his raw features riddled with suspicion. Then he reached out and touched her, fingertips to fingertips. She felt his inquiring presence in her, like ice water swallowed on a baking-hot day.

"She'd used you up," she said to him. "So she left."

She seemed to hear him calling for his Princess in her head. Just her name. No endearments. No filigrees. Just that plaintive crying out.

"You loved her, didn't you?" Candy said. "You still do."

Carrion raised his head a few inches and turned to

look at Candy. There was such despair in that broken face, and such rage there too, mingled with it.

"Yes, I love her," he said. "Of course I love her."

"And she promised she'd love you, if you gave her what she wanted."

Carrion made a tiny nod of his head.

"Which was . . . ?"

"Magic, of course. Nothing significant at the beginning, she just wanted to find out whether she had an aptitude for it."

"Which she did."

"Yes. Then of course she wanted more."

"When was all this? Before I was born?"

"Of course, years and years. These things don't happen quickly."

"What do you mean: *these things*?"

"I mean I fell in love with her. She was a very powerful creature. But this was long before you were born, Candy. I was a very young man. I couldn't resist her. I gave her access to the Abarataraba. And I think she probably started to steal secrets from it immediately. So many secrets. I let her steal whatever she wanted as proof of my love. I even built her a place where she could practice what she'd learned."

"Where was that?"

"On the Isle of the Black Egg. Building her that place was my first big mistake. She told me she wanted her privacy, and I could only step foot there if she invited me.

Which I didn't do much. Sometimes I'd wait maybe two or three months before she'd deign to let me see her."

"But you put up with it."

"I loved her beyond all reason."

"And she knew . . ."

"She knew."

Before Carrion could reply, Candy heard John Mischief calling her name. Then Drowze. Then Serpent. She glanced back toward the market. There was no sign of them. But it was only a matter of time before one of them came looking.

"It's time we parted, Carrion. If any of my friends see you they'll assume the worst and you'll get hurt."

"Do you really care?"

"I suppose . . . yes. I suppose I must. Seems to me you've been hurt enough one way or another."

"I've taken a lot of lives in my time. I don't suppose that comes as any surprise."

"Not really."

"But you still wish me no harm? I find that . . . unusual, to say the least. It's not as though you're a sentimental girl."

"I thought I saw you die once already," Candy said. "And that was enough. Nobody needs to suffer that twice."

"One life, one death . . . ?"

"Yes."

"If only things were that equitable."

"Well, aren't they? You live a life, you die. That's it."

"No, Candy, that's not it. We each of us die countless

little deaths on our way to the last. We die out of shame and humiliation. We perish from despair. And of course we die for . . ." He stared at the garbage-strewn ground, the word he wanted to say defying him.

Candy said it for him.

"Love."

He nodded, still looking at the ground. "Nothing else wounds so deeply and irreparably. Nothing else robs us of hope so much as being unloved by one we love."

"Why can't you let her go?"

"Because if I did, I'd have no reason to live."

"Come on," Candy said with a smile in her voice. "It can't be that bad."

"Have you ever loved, then lost your beloved?"

"No. I haven't."

"Then let us remember to talk again, when things are different."

Candy heard her name called again.

"Somebody is looking for you?" Carrion said.

"Yes. I have friends here. They'll come looking for me soon."

"And—"

"Well . . . they wouldn't . . ." She struggled for the words. "I haven't . . . I mean, what we . . ."

"What we?"

"We have a strange . . ."

"Go on. Say whatever it is you were going to say."

"Friendship. We have a strange friendship."

"That we do," he said. "Are you ashamed of it? Of me?"

"No. It's just . . . when people talk about you—"

"You don't need to go on. I know my reputation. After all, I earned it."

"Please," Candy said. "*Go.* I'm going back to—"

"Wait. Before you rush off. You need to know something."

"Well, be quick."

"Go back to the Hereafter. *Now.* And go quickly. Take your friends if you want to save their lives."

"Why?"

Carrion sighed.

"Why can't you just take my word this once?"

"I'm me. I ask questions. And try to stop you from getting killed."

"And now I'm returning the favor."

"Are you saying that if I stay in the Abarat I'll be killed?"

"Not just you. Most of the Abarat is about to change forever."

"How? Why?"

Carrion drew an aching breath and spoke.

"You may as well know, I suppose, if it'll persuade you to go." He took another breath, deeper still. Then came the answer to her question. "I've reconnected with a few of my spies. I used to pay them to inform on my grandmother. The Old Hag has a few tricks up her sleeve. She's creating something called a stormwalker."

"I don't like the sound of that."

"No. You shouldn't. Second, an army of stitchlings has been assembled. Enough to provide 'a knife for every heart,' was the phrase my employee used."

"Lordy Lou," Candy whispered.

"And—"

"There's more?"

"Much. Absolute Midnight, Candy. That's what my grandmother calls it. She plans to block out the light. No moons, no suns, no stars. The sky will be dark over land and sea. And it will be *cold*."

Candy felt dizzy. This was a lot of information to process in far too short a time.

"She has enough power to blot out the suns?"

"Not personally. She's unleashed a living darkness. A species called the sacbrood, who've been growing in number for years. Now there are millions of them. Enough to cover the heavens from one end of the Abarat to the other."

"And you were part of this?"

"She raised me to release them. I was to be the one she knew she could trust. After the fire, there was only she and I. Everything I had I owed to her, starting with my life. And she never let me forget it."

"So the sacbrood cover the skies? There's no light? No warmth? It's like the end of the world?"

"That's right."

"But they can't stay up there forever, can they?"

"No. They'll die off after a time. But it'll only take a few days of darkness for the real trouble to show itself. There are fiends all across the Hours who have been waiting for this Midnight. Enemies of the light, waiting for a chance to strike down those who loved the sun, moon, and stars. These enemies are monsters of every kind, but they have hatred in common. They're all outcasts, pariahs; fiends who've escaped the gallows or the guillotine, and want revenge. Ghouls, Malefics, Wrathaki, Babelites; fifty kinds of monsters you could maybe name, and three times as many you could not. They've been out of sight for so long, living with the dead, or in thunderheads, or in places where the waters of the Izabella are all bruise and blood. So they've been hiding. Waiting. Waiting. Waiting until this Midnight, when they will finally get their chance to slaughter everything that smells of happiness."

"A plot like this can't have been completely unseen. What about the Council? Or people who see the future?"

"If anyone saw the truth and spoke it, then that was the end of them. My grandmother has never needed the law to get a judgment. She is her own judge, and her seamstresses her executioners. One needle, driven into the eye, or one knife—"

"All right," Candy said. "I get the idea. I wish I knew you for a liar."

"But I'm not."

"No. You're not. They're coming out of the west, aren't they?"

"How did you know?" Carrion said.

"The birds," Candy replied.

It wasn't much of an answer, but it seemed to be all that Carrion needed.

"Well, now it's no longer a secret. There's no need for anyone to move carefully. So it'll spread quickly."

"So what's to be done? How do we defend ourselves?"

"That's what I've been trying to tell you. There is no defense, Candy. Just go back home while you still can. And be grateful that you've got Chickentown to go back to."

"Back to Chickentown? *No.* I love the Abarat. I won't give up on it."

"So love it from afar. Sometimes it's better that way."

"There you are!"

She looked back down the alley. The John Brothers were heading toward her.

"Go," she murmured to Carrion.

"Who's your friend?" John Drowze wanted to know.

Carrion gave her one last puzzled look, then he started to stumble back away down the alley. She watched him take a few steps, then she turned back to face the brothers.

"Who was that?" Mischief said.

"It doesn't matter, at least not now. We have more urgent problems. Where is everyone?"

Half the brothers were still looking back into the shadows where Candy's mysterious friend had gone, while the rest were trying to follow Candy and there was an absurd moment when they went neither one way nor the other.

"Mischief, will you get your brothers in order? We have to ready ourselves."

"For what?" Mischief said.

"The End of the World," she replied.

35

STEALING AWAY

THERE WERE TIMES, CANDY knew, when it was best to be honest. But not always. Sometimes telling the truth, the whole truth and nothing but the truth brought nothing but trouble. And truth, like lies, often just got worse if you tried to clean up the mess with more of the same. She was in that very situation now.

When she'd emerged from the alleyway following her conversation with Carrion, and found her gang of friends, she had something very urgent to tell them: information given to her by Carrion. Midnight was on its way: a darkness that was clearly designed to kill everything in its path. But she couldn't tell them such news and not expect them to ask her how she'd come by it. They'd want to know. She could scarcely blame that. In their position, faced with the same news, she'd want to know its course too. But that's where the lies had to be told.

If she told them she'd spent the last few minutes in conversation with Christopher Carrion, they'd be debating whether he could be trusted until Midnight came and blacked out everything. So she reported the story as Carrion had explained it, but told them the information had come from one of the women of the Fantomaya. It was difficult enough reporting such bizarre news in the midst of the market crowd, doing her best to make herself heard over the din of the stall-owners yelling their prices. Candy told them only of the sacbrood. For once, John Serpent believed her. The rest thought this woman from the Fantomaya was either crazy or an impostor.

"I don't believe it," John Mischief said. "You can't plague the whole world with darkness. It's not plausible."

"Why not?" Candy said. "Because it hasn't happened yet?"

"Do you trust these women?" Betty Thunder asked her.

"Yes. I think what I'm telling you is the truth. It doesn't help much"—she looked at Mischief—"to say it can't be done because it's being done. Right now. It certainly explains the birds."

"Oh, Lordy Lou," Malingo murmured. "The birds."

Now the doubt began to melt.

"We saw them too," Legitimate Eddie said. "All flying east . . ."

"Away from the sacbrood," Tom said. "That makes sense. I've certainly never seen a migration like that before."

"There's never been one," Malingo said.

"All right," John Mischief said, "so this thing is happening: what do we do?"

"As much as I hate to say it, I think we should go to the Yebba Dim Day," Candy said, "to that Council that hates me so much."

"My mother's on Babilonium," Betty said. "I've got to go to her."

"I'm going with you," said Tom. "My Macy is there. We should be together if the world is going to end."

"I think Babilonium might already be in the dark," Candy said.

Silent tears ran down Betty's cheeks. Clyde hugged her.

"It doesn't matter," he said. "We're going. The three of us."

"Why is Mater Motley doing this?" Tom wanted to know.

"Because she's a venomous piece of work," John Serpent said. "And yes, I do realize a man called Serpent shouldn't be tossing words like venomous around, but I've plenty more. She's a vicious, loathsome, life-hating monster. I vote we skip the trip to the Yebba Dim Day and go straight to Gorgossium and call her down from her tower."

"And what do we do if she comes down?" John Slop said.

Serpent didn't offer up a reply.

"I think we should start walking down to the harbor while we talk," Candy suggested. "We have to find a boat."

"We should get three boats, then," Geneva said. "I'll go to the Nonce and find Finnegan."

They had emerged from the market by now, and on the quieter street that took them back down toward the harbor. They were about to talk at a more natural volume, though Candy dropped her voice to a whisper and shared the other piece of information regarding Mater Motley's plans: the part about the beasts.

"Lordy Lou," Geneva said. "This is very bad."

"And the part about the darkness wasn't?" Mischief said.

"Are there a lot of creatures hidden away in the darkness?" Tom said.

"Oh yes," said Eddie.

"How do you know?" Candy said.

"I wasn't always a great actor," Eddie said. "Before I took to the stage I made a nice business out of tracking down the Ziaveign and putting them out of their misery."

"Zia-what?" Candy said.

"Ziaveign. Eight Dynasties' destroyers and fiends."

"This gets worse and worse," said John Slop, looking rather pale.

"Did you say you put them out of their misery?" Mischief said.

"I worked with my two brothers," Eddie said, "and yes, we *did* kill them when we were able to do so. Of course that was much more expensive. Much too expensive in the end. It cost my brothers their lives."

A heavy silence fell on the company.

"I'm sorry," Candy said finally. "That's terrible."

"They were fine, brave men. But the Eight Dynasties are strong. They may have been in hiding a long time, but that doesn't mean they're dead. They'll rise up. That's what Mater Motley is counting on."

"She didn't do all this alone," John Mischief said. "She had help from that wretched grandson of hers."

"Well, at least he's dead and gone," Geneva said.

Candy couldn't bring herself to keep the truth from these people, who had done so much for her, any longer.

"Actually . . . he's not," she said.

"You know this for a fact?"

Candy nodded.

"How?"

"It's complicated," Candy said.

"What's complicated about a man who lives in a fish-bowl, pickled with his own nightmares?" Mischief replied. "And who has almost taken your life on several occasions? He's dreck, dirt, *excrement*."

Candy remembered her first glimpse of him in the alleyway. She'd thought something very similar: that Carrion was indeed made of filth. But in the end that was the fate of all flesh, wasn't it? Everything decayed, went back to dirt, to the earth. But that wasn't the whole story. People weren't just walking sacks of meat. Unlike Carrion, she'd started to understand that there was something eternal, *underlying*, in everyone, perhaps even every*thing*. A soul, for want of a better word, which—even when time had dimmed her sight and dulled her memories—would burn as brightly as it burned now.

Even if her memories seeped away, the sweet and sour of her life stolen from the meat of her mind, her soul would know its way to the net of remembrance that was being cast out over her life and all that touched it, gently retrieving the details of every moment. Cast out over and over, world without end. It wasn't so surprising that these thoughts were being discussed in the room at the back of her head, while in the front of her mind the part of her that was in the here and now continued to talk with her friends. If ever there was a time in her life that she needed the comfort of this faith in the Eternal, it *was* Here and Now. She was part of a struggle that was older than life: the battle between Light and Darkness.

She was certain she belonged in this moment, in the company of these loving friends. She was here, in this world she loved so much, to play a part in its future. She didn't understand, nor even particularly care to, how she had come to have a part in the approaching struggle. But everything she'd done since she'd first come here—her meeting with Malingo; with Wolfswinkel; her visit to the Time Out of Time; her pursuit of her own secret history that she'd pieced together from many sources; her strange relationship with Carrion; and her final liberation from the Princess Boa—all of it had been a preparation, an education, for being alive at this moment.

"What are you thinking about?" Malingo inquired.

"Everything," she replied.

The atmosphere down at the harbor, which had been so odd when they'd got off the ferry, was even odder now. Some of the seabirds were still there, sitting in silent rows like bored jurists awaiting the beginning of a trial. But most of the people had left, and those who remained were gathered around a makeshift pulpit from which a crazed minister with long white hair and one ragged wing was preaching to them.

Candy listened to the creature talk about how the righteous would find their way to the light and the rest go into darkness; that was all she could stomach. She blocked its voice out, and looked in the opposite direction only to find that the missing seabirds had also found themselves a spiritual leader. Having forsaken their perch along the harbor wall they were now gathered in front of one of the shuttered restaurants, attending with many a beady black eye to a very large but very antiquated bird that looked like an albino vulture with a touch of pterodactyl in its blood. It was addressing its congregation in a language of crawings and chitterings, which was a great deal more complex, even eloquent, than the screech of a seagull.

As for the captains and crews of the small fishing boats that were tied up alongside the quayside, they had all departed, presumably to be with their families at this troubling time, or to drink in solitude.

"So now what do we do?" said Malingo, surveying the deserted dock.

"We choose boats that look sturdy and are fueled up, and we take them," Eddie said.

"Just take them?"

"Yes! Lordy Lou, this isn't the time to be arguing the moral niceties of the thing. There's nobody here to barter with anyway."

"Do we have to take boats?" Clyde said. "What about one of your glyphs?"

"I think we could probably conjure up a glyph between us but trust me, we don't want to be in the air right now. Not with those things up there."

"We're safer on water," Tom said.

"I trust Mama Izabella," Candy said. "She's not afraid of the dark. So we take some boats, yes? We can apologize when the lights go on again!"

"I wish there were some weapons we could lay our hands on too," Geneva said.

"Maybe some harpoons?" Eddie suggested.

"It's worth a look . . ." Geneva said. "I'll take whatever we can find. We don't know what we're going to be up against."

"The worst of the worst," Eddie said grimly. Since he'd confessed his monster-trapping past, and the grim price it had cost his brothers, Candy realized that Eddie had nothing left to lose. The sight of his pain made her speak up.

"We're all going off in different directions," she said, "and who knows when we'll see one another again. Or even if. So I just want to say that I love you. And I've been blessed to have this time with you. I want you to know you're the best friends anyone could have."

She looked from face to face as she spoke, not even attempting to put on a smile. If she'd understood Carrion correctly, then this Midnight would mark the end of the Abarat as they'd all known it. And what would be left? An archipelago ruled over by the monstrous Empress, Mater Motley? Or simply a wasteland, destroyed by the poisonous work of the fiends this darkness would unleash?

As Malingo and Clyde searched for weapons, boats were chosen. Geneva, who was traveling in search of Finnegan, chose a small, sleek vessel that looked to have been designed for sport rather than commercial fishing. It was called *The Loner*. Two-Toed Tom took the helm of a vessel called simply *Big Boat*, which he, Betty, and Clyde chose for its size, given that they were hoping to evacuate more than just one person. Candy chose for sentiment's sake a boat that reminded her of the harrowing journey on the *Parroto Parroto*: Malingo, Legitimate Eddie, and the Johns agreed to join her. John Mischief instantly had his brothers democratically vote him the Captain.

All three boats had lanterns hanging from their masts and from the eaves of their wheelhouses, but at Candy's suggestion they went aboard several other vessels moored in the vicinity and borrowed their lanterns too. If they were truly going to meet a wave of darkness out there then they needed to be carrying as many light sources as possible. There was some debate as to whether they should go back to the market and get some provisions to sustain them, but before they could come to a conclusion on the matter it was taken out of their hands by the fact that six or seven of the potbellied minister's righteous congregation had noticed Candy and her friends. They broke away from the assembly, yelling: "Thieves! You get away from those boats!"

"I'll be going then," Geneva said briskly. "I'll see you all again soon. Travel safely."

So saying, she fired up her boat and sped away from the dock.

The *Big Boat*, carrying Betty and Clyde, and captained by Tom, was right behind. The only thing holding up the departure of the third boat, *The Piper,* was dissention among the John Brothers about who was going to be second-in-command.

"We don't have time for this!" Candy said. "Get moving! *Right now!*"

Her intervention had an immediate effect. The brothers grabbed the wheel and readied themselves.

The fastest member of the minister's congregation was a young man with mottled purple-and-white skin and a very fierce look on his face. Without waiting for the others to catch up with him he leaped into *The Piper*, and went straight for Malingo, who was attempting to untie the rope that tethered the boat to the dock. Candy reacted straightaway, catching hold of the collar of his jacket and pulling the young man toward her. He wasn't any taller than she was, but he was lean and strong and, despite the fact that he was trying to stop them, there was something in his eyes that—

He wrenched himself free and turned on Candy, yelling: *"Stop! Right now!"*

"Got no time!" Candy said, shaking away whatever it was she had felt a moment ago. *"And no choice!"*

There were yells meanwhile, from other members of the minister's congregation.

"We're coming, Gazza!" one of them yelled. *"Don't let them go!"*

In a few more seconds, Candy knew, all would be lost. They'd never get away.

"Mischief!" she yelled.

At that very moment, *The Piper* shuddered as the engine turned on, and then jerked forward with such violence that Malingo, the piebald Gazza, and Candy were all thrown down onto the mess of nets and floats that littered the deck. Eddie, who was much shorter and therefore steadier, was the only one not to fall. He had found a large machete somewhere, and holding it aloft, he raced to the stern of *The Piper* where the rope still kept the boat from departing the dock. Candy sat up, throwing off a net stinking of fish in which she'd landed, only to see Legitimate, wielding the machete like a man who'd done it many a time and brought it down with all his strength, severing the rope that kept them from making their escape.

He did so with not a moment to spare. The rest of their pursuers were a stride or two from boarding *The Piper*. One of the men attempted to leap aboard the boat even as the rope was severed. *The Piper* sped forward, and the leaper landed in the water.

They were away! The only problem was their extra passenger: the youth called Gazza. He was still in a fighting fury.

"You!" he said, pointing his mottled finger at Candy. "I know who you are! The girl from the Hereafter!"

"Candy Qua—"

"I don't care to know your name. I demand that you order your thugs to turn this boat around."

"We can't," Candy said. "If you want to get off, you'll have to jump and swim."

The youth called Gazza pulled a short-bladed knife out of a sheath hanging from his belt.

"I'm not swimming," he said.

"Well, we're not turning back."

"We'll see about that," Gazza said, and shoved Candy aside. Then, knife in hand, he headed toward the wheelhouse.

Malingo yelled a warning to Mischief, but the roar of the engine surely kept the brothers from hearing it. Gazza opened the wheelhouse door, and would have been through it, his knife raised, had Candy not lunged at him throwing one arm around his neck and slamming her fist down on the hand that held the knife. He didn't drop it. But she managed to pull him away from the door, at which moment, by sheer chance, the boat cleared the harbor and hit the heavy swell of the open sea. The boat was briefly lifted into the air as it crested the first big wave, throwing Candy, with her arm still around Gazza's throat, back onto the deck. He fell with her. On top of her, in fact.

This time he did lose the knife. And by the time all the blushing and scrambling and cursing and struggling to stand up again was over, Malingo had picked the knife up and Eddie, looking a lot more serious, indeed dangerous, than the short, green, egotistical comedian Candy had first met, had his stolen machete pointed at Gazza's navel.

"I will gut you, sir," he said, betraying a trace of actorly flamboyance in that last syllable only, "if you make any further attempt to do harm. I mean it. I can and I will. You can let go of him now, Miss Quackenbush. Unless of course, you feel there's a reason to hang on to him that I hadn't fathomed."

Candy stared briefly into Gazza's eyes.

"No," she said, averting her gaze and feeling embarrassed but not entirely sure what she had to be embarrassed about. "He's . . . fine. He's not going to be stupid about this once we explain—"

"Never mind the explanations. All I wanted you to do was turn the boat around," Gazza said.

The purple patches on his face had turned a very pale

blue, and his eyes, which had shards of gold in them, were no longer fierce.

"You can still jump in and swim back."

"I can't swim."

"We don't have *time* for this," Eddie said impatiently. "We've got work to do."

"If he goes in the water," Malingo said, "he'll drown. I can't have that on my conscience."

"I don't give two hoots about your conscience. The whole world is being overtaken by darkness and the dynasties—"

"We heard it, Eddie," Malingo said.

"I know their names! All eight of them: Tarva Zan, the Binder, and Lailahlo, who sings babies to their graves. And Crawfeit and Quothman Shant, and Shote, who leaves plagues wherever he walks—"

"Is he okay?" Gazza said, looking at Candy, the colors in his eyes reeling around.

"No," she said.

"—there's Clowdeus Geefee, who killed my little brother. And Ogo Fro, who killed my big brother. Sent him down into a despair he never rose up from. And last—but very far from least—there's Gan Nug, who talks to the creatures that are in waters, deep down below us right now."

Mischief and the brothers had emerged from the wheelhouse to hear Eddie offer up his list.

"What's going on out here?" John Slop said.

Gazza stared at Mischief and his brothers, and for the first time in the considerable while Candy had known the Johns, she saw them do something that was curiously eerie. All of them shifted their gazes and looked at Gazza at the same speed and the same moment. And then, all at the same time, they said: "What are you lookin' at, kid?"

It was too much for Gazza. He dropped to his knees, presenting the diminutive Eddie with an easier target.

"All right," he said, "I won't fight. I won't cause any trouble. I believe you. Whatever you say, I believe you."

Candy laughed.

"That's good to hear. Eddie, put down the knife. We already know he's trustworthy."

"Me?" Gazza said. "Absolutely. Totally and utterly. I'm with you."

He looked up at her, the pastel motes in his eyes settling into blue irises in pale yellow eyes. They looked straight up at Candy, meeting her gaze and quickening her heart.

36

THE SHADOW-SHROUD

DESPITE THE CURRENT DEFYING power of the *Kreymattazamar*, which returned Mater Motley and her entourage back to Midnight's island faster than any other vessel in the Abarat, and despite the speed with which she was transported from the harbor to the circular room atop her Needle Tower, the shadow shroud of the sacbrood had already begun to spread in all directions from the pyramids.

Such was the passionate bloodlust of the brood to be out and doing their murderous duty, that when the path to the sky became blocked they set upon one another with unbounded brutality. Very quickly the areas surrounding the exits of the pyramids were littered with the remnants of the weak or unlucky, who had perished before reaching the stars they had been born to extinguish.

But such wastage had been factored into the calculations from the beginning. They did as they were programmed to do. They rose up and they spread across the sky. They went east to darken the skies over Babilonium, southeast to cover Gnomon's wilderness, in the midst of which stood its Great Ziggurat; and northeast to Scoriae, where the darkness overhead seemed to encourage Mount Galigali to stir up the fire in its belly and spit streamers of liquid rock into the starless heavens. North it went to Pyon, where the lights of Commexo City burned so brightly that its apocalyptic effect was not felt. On other parts of the island, of course, places so far uncivilized by Pixler's influence, the peasant community thought the blanking out of all the stars was just one more show of power by the great architect, and resigned themselves to finally giving up their independence and going to the bright streets of Commexo City where they would add to the sum of beggars there. The same northerly advance also encompassed Idjit, where that island's incessant lightning storms became even more violent, stirred up by the blinding of the heavens. Finally the cloud spread west, southwest, and south, erasing the moon and stars from the skies over Jibarish, and Ninnyhammer, and extinguishing the late afternoon sun that bathed Gnomon where there had been many oracles, all of whom were quite capable of seeing this approaching catastrophe.

Notwithstanding the egotistical attitude that had silenced most of them, a few had been foolhardy enough to speak of what they'd seen. All had been dead within the hour. The rest, having quickly got the message that this was a future that would be fatal to talk about, kept what they knew to themselves, or left Gnomon entirely thinking they'd be safer talking about the approaching apocalypse on some other island. But wherever they went—some to the Yebba Dim Day, in the hope of talking to the Council, a few to Yzil or farther—it all failed to change their own futures. Those who spoke their fears aloud were murdered within the hour, leaving the others two options: to live in silent anticipation of the world's end, or to take their own lives before it came.

So the secret of Absolute Midnight had remained secure. And when the sacbrood rose up in their millions, the noise of their innumerable beating wings was like no sound those hearing it had ever heard before, nor would again. They were out. Out and up, covering the sky. And it wasn't only the bodies and wings of the brood that were blocking the light. They exuded a thick juice called broodgrume from their abdomens, which dried to a dense, hard, shell-like substance within a few moments of being exposed to the air. They had been programmed generation upon generation that, once they were up above land and water, they were to completely empty their sacs of this broodgrume. The consequence? That they all would become helpless prisoners of their own secretion; countless millions of their insectile brains too simple to understand that the instruction to void themselves of the grume would be the first and only act they would perform in the world outside their hives.

There had been times when Mater Motley had trouble

believing that such a massive number of living things, however simplistic their thinking, would do as they had been
programmed to do so blindly. At such times she went to
a secret and sacred place that she had never named aloud.
Its name was Zael Maz'yre, and from it all dark blessings
flowed. She had bathed in those blessings for many years,
and in due course she would pay the price, gladly. But
for now, there was pleasure to be had hearing creatures
of every kind raising their voices in panic as the erasing
darkness spread across the sky, wiping out star after star,
blinding moons and blotting out suns. Even the constellations had gone. Every last star had been like candles in a
hurricane.

People offered prayers to the divinities of every Hour,
but outweighing the prayers offered to gods and saints
a hundred to one were those prayers offered up to the
most ubiquitous force for happiness in the Abarat—the
Grinning Boy himself—the Commexo Kid. He was
the savior to whom countless terrified souls called out
as the shadow-shroud moved on, its layers of living brood
and their excreted grume two or even three layers thick
in some places. Jibarish was plunged into utter darkness.
So too was Ninnyhammer, and the Rock of Some Distinction called Alice Point; and the Nonce, and the Isle of the
Black Egg, and Huffaker, and Orlando's Cap, and Hobarookus . . .

Cries of terror and panic still rose up out of the islands
that were newly overtaken by darkness. But out of those

that had first fallen under the influence of the shadow-
shroud the fear was punctuated with a new and very
particular sound: that of accusation. Who had done this,
and why? *Why?* Somebody needed to own up to this crime
and do so quickly or there would be consequences. On
island after island, in Hour after Hour, people started to
seek out anyone that was in some way odd, and found, in
mere distinctions, evidence of guilt. The signs were usually
very small—a harelip, a slow eye, a tic, a stammer—but
all that mattered was that the voices of accusation were
able to rouse a mob into believing that these innocents
were in some way responsible for this terror.

Mater Motley watched all of this with gluttonous satisfaction. She had reports from Nightseers, seamstresses
whose eyes were powerful enough to pierce the darkness
even at its densest. On Gnomon she was shown a crowd
of three hundred or more, having lit fires to illuminate
an ancient place of judgment, start the business of dealing
with those that their collective madness had decided were
responsible for the death of light.

The leader of the mob was a little man with some
Skizmut blood in him somewhere. His name was Dyer
Mere, and he had elected himself as the leader of the court
among the trees. He demanded that the three prisoners
the mob had selected—two sisters, Juup and Namena
Chantamik, and a sometime tax inspector called Theopolis Kalapao—confess their guilt. The mob was convinced
that it was they who had brought this calamity upon the

islands. The two sisters were sobbing and quite beyond saying anything coherent, so it fell to Theopolis to reason with the crowd.

They all knew him, he reminded them. Had he not always been honorable in his dealings? Had he not possessed a sense of what was fair and right? He had no knowledge of the monstrous powers that had been used to blind the heavens. He was a victim of this catastrophe, just as they were. Unfortunately for him, Theopolis the tax inspector stammered, and the more he realized he wasn't winning the argument against his accusers, the worse his stammer became, until his words of self-defense, reasonable though they were, could not even be understood.

The crowd didn't listen. The deaths of Theopolis and the sisters were swift.

"Now the culprits are dead," Dyer Mere declared. "Their spell will be undone very soon. Unless, of course, there are more conspirators we have not yet rooted out."

By now the darkness had reached the eastern limits of the Abarat, as it had to the north and south. It was as though the Abarat was a vast coffin and the sacbrood its lid. And still, when Mater Motley turned her gaze toward the pyramids, she saw the brood emerging from their hives like a black snake, their numbers apparently undiminished, rising to extinguish every last light in the skies, their programming so powerful, and their hunger so vast, that they cared not at all that those of their species who'd emerged an hour earlier were now trapped in a vault of bodies and solidified grume. All that mattered to each was the task they'd been programmed to perform. To any other subject—such as the suffering of their own kind (which they would soon share)—they were as blind as the Abaratians on the islands below.

Within forty minutes, the number of innocents accused of causing the darkness to descend, and summarily hanged for their wickedness, had risen from three to eighty-five. Among that number was Dyer Mere himself, who had overseen the executions of his own wife and son-in-law before the finger of suspicion had turned on him. Now he was dead. Strung up from the same branch from which his first victim, the stammering tax inspector, Theopolis Kalapao, had been hanged.

The same insanity had possessed mobs of frightened souls on every island. The spectacle of their panic turning to judgment and slaughter was not something Mater Motley had considered when she'd been calculating the way that the events of this Midnight would play out. But what came next she *had* foreseen: the arrival of the Ziaveign. The eight families of monsters and their vile hybrids who had been hiding all across the island, harboring their hatred, waiting for a long-promised darkness to spread across the Abarat, now came out of hiding.

The Old Mother had made it her business over the years to reach as many of them as possible herself, finding them in their grim sanctuaries, hidden from the light and its servants. So she knew many of the demonic creatures that now rose up to sew havoc among the tribes who had hunted them when their sacred suns and moons had been high and mighty. Now the skies were black, and the light-givers gone. In the dark the hunters were about to become the hunted.

There were creatures in this rising multitude that were as ancient as the elements. The Crawfeit, for instance, whose bodies were bone cages filled with flocks of burning birds; their heads black iron pots brimming with a vile stew of venom, angel's grief, and human meat; their limbs lengths of burned muscles held together with hair and hooks, and arrayed with dagger fingers. They were not demons. The Abarat had no known hell. The Crawfeit, like the other seven Ziaveign from which root all forms of night-beast, each corrupted in its own particular way, sprang from the presence of cruelty, pain, and loneliness among the Hours.

The Old Mother caught sight of all the Fiends she'd hoped to discover as she scanned the islands. On Scoriae she found the Abarat's first executioner, Quothman Shant, at his bloody work. On Soma Plume, she saw Lailahlo, the Queen of Murderous Song, leading a chorus of tiny Pulcinellas. The Binder, Tarva Zan, who wrapped the hearts of her victims in fire, was walking the silent boardwalk of Babilonium. Gan Nug was still standing at the highest point of The Great Head calling forth more horrors. At his feet, gazing up at him in adulation, were nine of his Preyers, or priests. Clowdeus Geefee she found on a boat, alone, the Izabella stained bloodred all around, while Shote, the Plaguer, she discovered seeding diseases in the fields of the Nonce, and on Huffaker, caught sight of Ogo Fro, who was entropy and fatigue incarnate, among a crowd of the wanderers lost in the dark.

It was a triumph for darkness. All eight of the Great Fiends had risen up and shown their faces. And if *they* were here, then their children would surely be here too. And their children. And theirs. None of them as powerful as their legendary forebears to be sure, but they still possessed the genius to terrify. The Old Mother was happy—at least as happy as she knew how to be. She had thrown a party in the name of darkness, and all the guests she'd most wanted to attend had done so.

The Twenty-Fifth Hour, however, had been entirely unaffected by the invasion of the sacbrood. It not only protected itself at sea level, effortlessly repelling the darkness that attempted to touch the shore, but it also defended the air above with a sheath that reached up into the stratosphere, and instantly cremated those sacbrood who, in their thoughtless conviction, treated the air above the Twenty-Fifth Hour like any other. It was not. The rules of physics were inverted over that timeless place.

Air that should have been lightless was instead pale yellow, while the stars, whether they were fixed or falling, blazed black against its brightness. The Twenty-Fifth had no intention of allowing the brood to invade its sacred air. Though the forces encircled the island, throwing wave after wave of forces against it, the power that the Hour emanated was too unpredictable to be overwhelmed. Finally, the brood seemed to comprehend that this was not a battle they could win, and left off the attack to move on to new conquests: some breaking north to the Outer Islands, others around the island to follow an easterly course.

The fact that the Twenty-Fifth had not succumbed irritated Mater Motley.

"You hear me make this oath, Maratien," she said when word reached her that the brood's attempts to get onto the island had failed. "Before very long, you will follow me as I walk up from the water's edge into the heart of the Twenty-Fifth. And I will stand there as its owner, and I will sink it if I so choose."

"And it will be the same with Commexo City?" Maratien said.

Mater Motley made a snort of contempt as she strode toward the mosaic of the island of Pyon, and set her foot upon the spot where Rojo Pixler had built Commexo City.

"The stars no longer shine over Pyon," she said, "but the city still burns as brightly as ever."

"Is Pixler there?"

"Why would he not be?"

"He went down into the Izabella."

"So he did. An odd coincidence. Something vast happens in the heavens, and Pixler is down in the deep . . ."

"I heard a rumor," Maratien said.

"Go on."

"That he came back, but he's not himself."

"Really?"

"Yes. He supposedly went in search of a Requiax. Those don't really exist, do they?"

"Everything exists at some depth, Maratien."

"Everything?"

"Yes. Everything," the Hag replied. "Perhaps he's come back suffering from deliriums of the deep." She took one of the needles from her dress; needles forged in cold fires that Zael Maz'yre itself had called up. She gave the needle to Maratien. "Take this down to General Axietta. You know which of the women she is?"

"She's the bald one with the birthmark?"

"That's her."

"She's beautiful," Maratien said.

"Well you take the needle down to her as proof that these orders came from me."

Maratien took the needle.

"What orders, m'lady?" the girl said.

"She's to take four warships, with six legions of stitchlings in each vessel. Head straight for Pyon. There'll be plenty of distraction to keep Mr. Genius Pixler from expecting an attack from the sea. When she gets into the city she's to take it—destroy it if she's in the mood. I don't care. But there are two things I need her to do without fail."

"Yes, m'lady?"

"Kill every light that burns in that damn city. And make it her personal business to bring me back the heads of Rojo Pixler and the boy."

"The boy . . . ?"

"The Commexo Kid."

"Is he a living thing?"

"We won't know until we have his head in our hands, will we?" Mater Motley said. "Now go. I want Commexo City dark in two hours."

37

LOVE AND WAR

MATER MOTLEY WASN'T THE only one who had a comprehensive view of the sacbrood's advance over the Abarat. At the heart of the Commexo Company's headquarters, in the Circular Room, reports came in from the innumerable mechanical spies, perfect copies of species from the tiny tiger tic to the enormous Rashamass (which resembled a cross between a whale and a millipede). They weren't programmed to seek out events of any great moment. But there were so many of Pixler's spies out in the world that at any given Hour one of them would be certain to catch witness of a scene of tragedy or celebration, were it to occur.

But in all the years the cyclopic Dr. Voorzangler, whose genius with Abaratian technologies was responsible for making Rojo Pixler's visionary dreams into practical realities, had traveled the immense circle on one of the gravity-negating discs that carried him wherever he willed them to take him, he had never witnessed anything as momentous as the events unfolding on the screens now. He had watched as the pyramids at Xuxux had been unsealed, silently awed—though he would never have admitted it— by the sheer power of the hidden engines that had opened the pyramids up. But their opening had only been the first part of the spectacle. What followed had been more incredible still: the outpouring of a life-form Voorzangler was not familiar with, that had been hidden away in the tombs, and now rose like six black rivers flowing heavenward, where they converged to become a sea of darkness that spread over the sky and above the pyramids, blotting out the constellations above Xuxux then moved outwards: east toward Babilonium, south toward Gnomon, west toward Jibarish, and north toward the island of Pyon, at which Hour, of course, Commexo City stood.

Voorzangler surveyed the sight for a few minutes, trying to get a grasp on what he was seeing, then he summoned his assistant, Kattaz to his side.

"What's Mr. Pixler's status?" he wanted to know.

"I was just with him," Kattaz replied. "He says he feels fine after 'the problem.' That's what he calls it, sir. The little problem with the bathyscaphe."

Voorzangler shook his head. "Really, the man is fearless. We nearly lost him . . ." He stared at the spreading darkness again. "I'm going to start making a report on this . . . this phenomenon. I'd like Mr. Pixler to see it for himself when he's feeling well enough. Would you inform him that we have a very immediate problem? This . . . darkness is going to cover the city within the next ten minutes."

"What is it?" Kattaz asked him.

"According to my records this is a species, I believe they are sacbrood. They predate Time, and therefore these islands. But what we know of them from fossil records suggest that they were significantly smaller than these creatures we see now."

"Genetically altered then?"

"That's my assumption."

"By science? Magic?"

"Possibly both. Look at them!"

He directed Kattaz's attention to the screen behind her. One of the creatures reporting this cataclysm, a balloon fox, had risen dangerously close to the sacbrood, risking its existence in order to report every detail of what it was witnessing. The sacbrood were a study in diversity: no two of them were alike. Their heads were complex arrangements of black, insentient eyes, which were sometimes assembled in glistening bunches like ripe fruit. Some had immense barbed jaws, some complex arrangements of mandibles. Some had heads that almost resembled that of the common Hereafter housefly, which had quickly established itself in the Abarat having come between worlds in the early years of trading.

"Oh by the Kid! Look at this, Doctor Voorzangler! This one . . . the eggs it's carrying! That's disgusting. Lordy Lou, look at all those little maggoty . . . oh, that's horrible."

"Do you really think so?" Voorzangler said, looking at the image with a detached curiosity. "It's just more life, isn't it? We can't be judgmental. At least I can't."

"Well, I'm sorry, Doctor. You're probably quite right.
It's just another species."

She was about to say more to him when the door to
Rojo Pixler's private chamber opened and the great architect appeared.

"What's going on, Voorzangler?"

"I was just about to alert you, sir."

"No need. You're being watched too, remember?"

"I wasn't aware——"

"That some of the screens you're looking at are looking at you?"

"Yes."

"Well, they are."

He closed the door to his suite behind him and then,
moving very slowly, his limbs exhausted, he stepped up
onto one of the discs and, taking up his familiar posture,
hands cupped left in right behind his back, he allowed the
disc to carry him the long way around the room, examining the screens as he went.

Such was the immensity of the chamber, and vastness
of the numbers of screens, that it took him several minutes to come around again to the place where Voorzangler
and Kattaz were standing. When he finally did so, and
Voorzangler got an opportunity to look at his mentor very
closely, he was troubled. Pixler appeared very much the
worse for wear following his descent into the depths of the
Izabella. His skin was white, and beaded with sweat. His

hair was pasted to his scalp with the moisture.

"I wish you'd let me examine you, sir. Just a brief checkup?"

"I've told you, Voorzangler, I'm perfectly fine. Never better."

"But weren't you in the bathyscaphe when the Requiax took hold of it?"

"Oh yes. Oh, I've been closer to death than I ever care to be again. But the Requiax is an ancient entity, Voorzangler. It has no interest in whether a man lives or dies."

"You're not a man, sir. You're Rojo Pixler. You're the father of the Commexo Kid."

"Yes. Yes, I am. And I am not going to die. Now, or ever."

"Or *ever*, sir?"

"You heard me, Voorzangler. Or *ever*. The future is mine to own. It's bright, Voorzangler, and full of possibilities. I can't afford to die."

"I want to believe you, sir—-"

"But—?"

"But these sacbrood, sir . . ."

"Is that what they are?" Pixler said matter-of-factly. "Fascinating."

"Our records report—"

"Forget the records. They're not worth a damn."

"But sir, you wrote them."

"No, not me, Voorzangler. I was another man entirely when I wrote those. That man is gone."

"Gone, sir?"

"Yes, Voorzangler, gone. As in departed. Exited the building. *Dead*."

"You look a little sick, sir," Voorzangler said, speaking slowly, as though to an idiot. "But . . . *you're not dead*. Trust me."

"Oh no. Thank you very much for the invitation. But I don't think I will. Trust you, I mean. I have better advisors now."

"Sir?"

"It's their understanding that our neighbors on Gorgossium, specifically that she-cur, Motley——" As he spoke of her, his features were overtaken by a rising wave of infiltrations, his muscles twitching violently, plainly not under Pixler's command. "*She's* apparently intending to cut off all natural light to the islands."

"How do you know this?" Voorzangler said.

"I'm looking at the screens, Doctor. This mass swarming of sacbrood is blotting out the skies. There will be a severe, even catastrophic, drop in temperature. Blizzard conditions on islands that have never seen a flake of snow. Crops will perish in the fields. Livestock will freeze to death. There will be massive loss of life in rural areas——"

"People can build fires," Kattaz said.

Pixler looked at the woman with naked disdain. "Go away," he said. "You offend me."

"Why?"

"I don't need reasons. Just go."

"Mr. Pixler, please."

"Oh don't whine, Voorzangler. I know what goes on between you two. I've watched you fawn over her. Love makes you look ridiculous, don't you see?" He glanced back at Kattaz. "Are you still here? I said go away."

Kattaz looked to Voorzangler for help, but his face was utterly blank, all sign of real emotion concealed. She didn't wait for him to come to her defense. Obviously he wasn't going to do so.

"I'm sorry I offend you . . . sir," she said in a monotone, and departed.

"So Mater Motley has herself an army," Pixler went on, as though nothing had happened.

"She does?" Voorzangler said. His gaze was on the screens filled with sacbrood now.

"Stop looking at the damn insects. They're just a part of what she's up to. Look at this."

He pointed to a cluster of screens showing both recorded footage of the stitchling legions, marching in shockingly precise lockstep as they assembled to board the warship, and live feeds showing those same warships carving their way through the dark waters of the Izabella; the only light supplied by the lamps, like blazing eyes, in the bows of the ships, and a host of smaller, airborne lights that cast a cold, blue-white luminesence as they flew around and above and behind the vessels.

"You mean the goons on the ships?" Voorzangler said. "They're just stitchlings. Rags and mud! They have no brain-power. Yes, she can train them to march, but I doubt they'll do much else!"

"I think perhaps she let you see the clowns so that you wouldn't ever think of them as soldiers. The Old Mother's quite brilliant in her way, you know," Pixler said.

"The Old Mother? Is that what they call her? Huh. She's a crazy hangover from the days of the Empire. I doubt she even knows what year this is."

"She may indeed be touched by madness, Voorzangler. On the other hand, that may be simply a performance, to have you believing she is harmless in her lunatic condition."

"Sane or insane," the doctor said, "she is not the real power. That was Carrion right from the beginning."

"Never underestimate a woman. After all, Old Mother has persuaded some very powerful allies to come over to her side. Powers I do not even care to name. They do not see the world as we do, in opposites. Night and Day. Black and White."

"Good and Evil?"

"They would find that particular idea utterly absurd."

"So these . . . beings . . . are her allies?"

"So she believes."

"But you don't."

"I believe she is useful to them at present. So they indulge her dreams of founding an Imperial dynasty—"

"Isn't she a little old to be having children?"

"You don't have to give birth to children in the world

of mysteries where that woman walks."

"I see."

"No, you don't. Not remotely."

"No. No, I don't."

"Good!" Pixler said brightly, laying a clammy, cold hand—a *dead* man's hand was all Voorzangler could think—on the doctor's shoulder.

"You can still admit to ignorance. There's hope for you yet, Voorzangler. Smile, Doctor!"

"I can't. I mean I will if you want me to . . ."

He tried to fake a smile, but it was a wretched sight.

"Forget it," Pixler said.

Voorzangler let the smile die a quick death, and went on talking: "Is the City in any danger?"

"Well, ask yourself: what do our sources tell us about her plans?"

"That she wants the Abarat in total darkness."

"But . . . Commexo City is still lighting up the sky."

"Exactly."

"So maybe we should placate her? Offer to dim them, maybe fifty percent? Just until she sends her warships home?"

"That won't fool her. We have to stand our ground or she will destroy this city and all that it's about to become."

"Which is what . . . ?"

"It's a conversation for a night without warships, Voorzangler. Go down to the dormitories. Speak to that milk-and-cookies woman."

"Mrs. Love."

Pixler looked appalled.

"Who in the name of all that's addictive called her that?"

". . . um . . ."

"I take it from your gormless expression that I did."

"Yes."

"Well, we'll fix it when this Last Great War is over and we've won the peace."

"You sound very confident, sir."

"Do I have any reason not to?"

"Wars are unpredictable, sir. We didn't know Mater Motley had an army of stitchlings until a few minutes ago. And . . . there's the matter of her allies."

"The Higher Powers," Pixler said.

"We have no idea who they are, is that right?"

"Put it this way. If I had some knowledge of them I'd tell you. Not the knowledge. Only that I knew it."

"You don't trust me any longer, do you?"

"Oh, Lordy Lou, Voorzangler. I *never* trusted you."

"What? *Why?*"

"Because you think too much and you feel too little. And that can bring Empires down."

Voorzangler studied the ground between his oversized feet for a long moment. "If I may remark, sir . . ."

"Remark away."

"I feel something for Kattaz. Something very real. At least I believe it's real. And it may seem foolish in a one-eyed, obsessive-compulsive scientist of advancing years to hold out hope for some return on my investment of devotion, but if it's foolish, then so be it. I stand by my feelings, however much a fool I may be."

"Huh."

Now it was the architect who looked away, staring at the screens without seeing them. When he looked back at Voorzangler, there had been a subtle shift in his features. Though he was still Rojo Pixler, something else—the same force, perhaps, that had infested his face with twitches—was present in him. It leaked a tiny amount of black fluid through his pores into each bead of sweat, so that they decorated his blood-drained features like immaculate black jewels.

Or, Voorzangler thought, like the eyes of the sac-brood.

"You know, just a few minutes ago I had decided I was going to put an end to you, Voorzangler."

"An end to me. You mean . . ."

"I mean I intended to kill you. Or more correctly, have you killed."

"*Sir?* I didn't realize you had such a poor opinion of my performance."

"Well, I did. But I've changed my mind. Your love saved your skin, Voorzangler. If you hadn't admitted to that, I'd have had you arrested and you'd have been dead two minutes later." He studied Voorzangler as he spoke, with a kind of detached curiosity. "Tell me how that makes you feel," he said. "Just tell the truth. Nothing fancy required."

"I suppose I'm grateful. I'm a fool."

Pixler seemed satisfied with this.

"There are certainly worse things," he said, apparently speaking from a profound fund of knowledge. "A great deal worse. Now go and tell Mrs. Love to wake the Kid. *Go on.*"

With a thought, the doctor had his disk on the move, dropping away from the high screens that he and Pixler had been viewing, and calling after Voorzangler as he descended: *"And be grateful you're a fool, Voorzangler,"* he yelled. *"You get to live another night."*

38

AN OLD TRICK

WITH THE JOHN BROTHERS at the helm of *The Piper*, the harbor at Tazmagor was soon out of sight, erased by the sea spray that was thrown up by the waters of Mama Izabella. Candy went into the boat's wheelhouse and consulted the very old charts—all of which were covered with notes about where the boat's owner had been successful in finding schools of ninkas, fool fish, and even the triple-beaked, ten-tentacled decapi.

"You know what?" John Fillet said.

"No, what?" said John Moot.

"I think our glorious leader has taken a liking to our new crew member," John Fillet said.

Candy kept her eyes on the chart, though there was very little information there of use.

"Don't know what you're talking about, Fillet," Candy said.

"It's not just Fillet," John Slop said.

"We all noticed it," said John Pluckitt.

"You can't keep much from the John Brothers," said John Drowze.

"It's none of your business," Candy said.

"I'm sorry," John Mischief said.

"You're all such gossips."

"The point is—" Mischief started to say.

"The point is whatever you think you saw, you saw wrong. Lordy Lou, the boy was going to stab you."

"So you stopped him by throwing your arms around him," said John Serpent. "Yes, we saw."

"I am not having any further discussion on the subject."

She stopped and turned to look directly at what she'd seen from the corner of her eye. *The Piper* was plunged into a thick fog, making the end of one Hour and the beginning of another. The light continued to dim, but the darkness wasn't black. There were shifting patches of blue and purple in it now.

"We're going to be coming out of the other side of this very shortly," Mischief said.

The brothers were back at the wheel now, their smiles erased. Fun time was over. Candy went to the wheelhouse windows to look for some sign of the coming Hour. But the windows were filthy with an accumulation of salt and bird droppings.

"Any sign of The Great Head?" Sallow asked her.

"I can't see anything. But I'll hang on tight. And you guys? Keep the gossip to yourselves in the future."

"So we were wrong?" Mischief said with a smirk that

defined his name. "You don't like him?"

Candy left the wheelhouse without answering.

There was a ladder that brought her up to the roof of the wheelhouse, and a railing for her to keep hold of, for which she was grateful. The swell was growing with every wave. The boat reeled and shuddered.

"Mind if I join you?" Malingo called up to her.

"Of course not," Candy yelled back. "Come on up!"

Seconds later, Malingo was standing at her right-hand side, hanging on to the iron railing as tightly as she was.

"If we're on the right course, we should be seeing The Great Head from behind," he said.

"In which direction?"

"Hopefully dead ahead."

"I can't see anything."

"Neither can I. But the fog is thinning, I think."

"Oh. You're right! I see it, Malingo." She laughed. "I feared the worst, but it's still standing!" Candy called down to Mischief. "I see it! Off the port bow!"

Mischief cut *The Piper*'s engines, sensing perhaps that everyone aboard needed to have a quiet moment in order to think about what lay ahead. The powerful currents met out of the boundary of the fog and into the murky twilight in which The Great Head stood. Even viewed from behind, The Head was an extraordinary monument, the towers that crowned its cranium so cunningly designed that they seemed to rise naturally out of the structure of the skull.

A bonfire was blazing on the top of the tallest of the

towers. It was not a natural fire. The flames were violet and silver and when they rose to sufficient heights they threw off lattices and other geometric forms, then briefly blazed as if being tested against the twilight sky. She watched the flames without even blinking, mesmerized.

"I think it's sending a message," Eddie said from the deck. "They look like sentences being written in the air."

"Really?" said Malingo.

"He might be right," Candy said, watching the flames closely. "Oh . . . wait. Yes. Look!"

She pointed past The Head. There was a cloud of roiling darkness laid along the horizon; its shadow, erasing all below as it advanced across the moonlit sea. The moon itself, two-thirds full, its face already touched by the seething fingers of darkness. And of course The Great Head, its huge, simple form—at least seen from behind—stoic, immovable. That was both its strength and its weakness, of course. It would not move, it could not move; and when darkness had come and gone, it would still be standing. Apparently it had occupants who lacked Candy's faith, however. There were maybe forty boats in the vicinity of The Head all in the process of making a departure.

"What are those idiots doing?" Malingo said.

"And where do they think they're going to go?" Candy replied.

Some of those departing had seen the approaching cloud and the sight of it had obviously made them reconsider their plans. Several boats, many overloaded with passengers, were turning around, or at least attempting to. The consequences were inevitable. Boats rocked and turned over, pitching their living cargo into the water.

There was a lot of panicked shouting and cries for help. There were some voices too, that did not express such terror and confusion. They did not shout, they sang: a great multitude of voices rising together to sing in Old Abaratian. It mattered not at all that Candy couldn't make any sense of the words. The majestic calm in the tune reassured Candy the way her favorite Christmas carol, "Silent Night," reassured her. She wondered if they knew the story of love being born in a stable, with shepherds and kings, and a bright star, high above, to mark the place, and for a moment, she wasn't on a boat drifting on an alien sea as a living darkness eclipsed the moon. For a moment, she was back on Followell Street, on a night long gone, before she'd come to fear the stink of beer on her father's breath.

"The moon's almost gone," Malingo said, monotone.

"You don't sound very bothered about it," Candy said.

"Well, what can I do about it? It's a big cloud, and I'm a geshrat with a fish-gutting knife I got from a stowaway, which I wouldn't know how to use properly anyway. I should give it back to him."

"No," Candy said very firmly. "You hang on to that. You might need it one of these days."

"One of these days? There aren't going to be any more days."

"Oh, there will be," said John Mischief. He'd climbed

up to share the view. "Clouds come. Clouds go. It's the way clouds are. You can't rely on them. They're too . . ."

"Flighty?" John Moot suggested.

"The very word!" Slop said.

"It's not that simple. This isn't an ordinary cloud. It can't be blown apart by a gust of wind. It's a living thing," she protested.

"How come you know all these things?"

"Because she's becoming a shaman," said John Drowze.

As Candy drew breath to remark that she didn't much like being talked about as if she wasn't there, she heard somebody call her name. A woman's voice. For a moment, she panicked. *Boa?* No. It couldn't be. She glanced around, looking for the person who'd spoken. The brothers, meanwhile, continued to discuss Candy's shamanic potential as though she wasn't even there, and the tempers on both sides of the argument were becoming ragged.

"If she's a shaman," said Slop, "then I'm an only child."

"He's right," said Fillet. "The girl's half crazy—"

"Only half?" said Sallow.

"You underestimate her," John Mischief said. "Yes, she's a little unpredictable, but that's what we need if the Abarat's to survive."

"She knows more than's good for her—"

"More than she knows she knows—"

Candy? Come here.

Meanwhile, the debate raged on.

"Fillet's right!"

"She's a sweet girl—"

"But all that power—"

"She can't deal with it—"

"And what if you're wrong?"

Pay no attention to their babble, Candy, the voice said.

You're not Boa, are you? she asked, knowing she only had to form the thought for it to be heard.

No.

Lordy Lou . . .

Please. We have very little time, Candy. You're going to have to step away from them for a minute or two.

Step away? Are you kidding? Candy replied. *I'm on a boat.*

We know, another said. *We can see you.*

When the second voice spoke, Candy knew who she was talking to. She scanned the water looking for some sign of the women of the Fantomaya.

Leave your chatty friends on the boat. Come and talk to us.

Where are you?

Fourteen paces off the stern. Come to us, Candy. Quickly. Mater Motley's seamstresses are after us. They're riding fever wheels, and they're moving fast.

What's a fever wheel?

If you see one you'll know and if you don't then you're blessed not to have the sight in your head.

Now that Candy knew where to look, she saw Joephi and Mespa. They appeared to be simply standing on the swell, illuminated by a light in the water that surged and then waned again in rhythm with the waves. Even at this distance Candy could see that the journey had taken a considerable toll on them. Their robes were dirty and tattered, and their faces and arms bloodied.

Come on, Joephi said, beckoning to Candy.

I can't walk on water.

Yes, you can, Mespa said. *Have faith in yourself.*

I'm going to sink.

Faith. Hurry!

She turned back toward Malingo and the John Brothers.

"I'll be right back," she said to them.

Then she climbed down the ladder. Legitimate Eddie was staring up at the bizarre bonfire blazing on top of The Great Head.

"There's one of them up there," he said.

"One who?"

"One of the eight. Gan Nug!"

He pointed and Candy looked up at the Head to see that there was indeed a tall creature there, his stylish clothes, high-coiffed hair and reptilian wings garishly lit by the pyre he tended.

"Any idea what he's doing?" Candy asked him, keeping up the same casual tone as she clambered over the side of the boat.

"Calling something up, I dare say," Eddie replied. "From the depths."

"Wait! Wait!" Gazza said. "What are you doing?

Where are you going?"

She looked up at him. The light from the swaying lanterns made his face seem to shift, the only steady thing his immense gold eyes.

"There's some friends of mine I need to talk to."

Gazza looked out across the Izabella.

"Are those women *walking* on water?"

"Lordy Lou, you ask a lot of questions. Yes."

"Witches?"

"I suppose so."

"You're one as well, are you?"

"Not really. I'm learning, but—"

Are you coming, Joephi said, *or are you just going to flirt with the boy?*

"They say you're a boy."

"The witch women?"

"Yes."

"If you want to talk to Candy," he hollered, his voice echoing off The Great Head, "then come to the boat!"

Come, Candy. Or if the boy has your heart, don't. Just make up your mind.

"I'm coming," she murmured, and set her foot on the water.

She tested her weight on the frothy water. The news wasn't good.

My foot's sinking!

"You're going to drown!" Gazza yelled. "Get back up here."

Are you barefoot? Mespa asked.

No, you didn't say anything about—

Isn't it obvious? It's you who's walking on water, not the shoes.

All right! No shoes.

She headed back to Gazza.

"Hold my hand."

"Finally, some common sense!" he said.

"Don't get excited. I'm just taking my shoes off. Keep hold."

"I'm not letting go."

"Oy. They bicker like man and wife," said Eddie.

"All right. I've just . . . got to . . . got to get . . ."

The sentence came out in fragments as she struggled to get the shoes off her feet, attempting not to lose them as she did so. She liked the shoes. They were Abaratian: iridescent blue, with little animals performing on them in a shoe sky circus. But it was an awkward maneuver to reach over Gazza's arm to get her fingers under her shoe to keep from—

Her left shoe slipped off and dropped into the water with a palliative plop. It sank instantly. The other shoe came off more easily, and for a few seconds, the last gleam of the smothered moon caught the animals prancing upon that perfect blue that no sky had ever been. She tossed it on deck.

"There," she said to Gazza. "I'm ready."

Then get on with it, Mespa said.

Candy let go of Gazza's hand and walked back to the

ladder, despite his protests. She set a naked foot, the left, down in the water. No, not in the water, on it. The surface wasn't entirely solid, but certainly enough to support her. She glanced up. Malingo was looking down at her.

"Tell me you're not going to walk!"

"Well . . . I'm a horrible swimmer," Candy said, "so . . . yes!"

"You're crazy."

"That's what I've been telling her," Gazza said.

She suddenly felt the water that had supported her foot softening.

Don't listen to doubt, Candy, Joephi said. *All great things come of paradox.*

"Don't worry," she said to Malingo as she took a breath and drew her gaze away from his disbelieving face.

"I'm not going to drown, Malingo. I'm not!"

"You can still turn back."

"No. I can't, Malingo. You know I can't. I've been preparing for this test since I arrived—No—since I was born."

"Utterly insane. The girl is . . ." Mischief muttered as he and the brothers joined Malingo in watching.

"I heard that," Candy replied.

Forget them, Mespa said. *This is when you prove your right to make history or drown in the water you want to walk on. You can. You are answerable only to your greater self, which in turn answers only to Creation.*

She looked down at the foot that was going to take

the step. If the Old Woman was to be unseated from the throne of the Midnight Empire then Candy had a part to play in that unseating. That, she understood. And if she was meant to play that part, she had to walk on water, and walk on water she would.

"I . . . am . . ." The water bore her up. ". . . going . . . to . . ." Yes! She could do this. ". . . walk!"

It isn't a dream. It isn't real. It's just your mind and Creation thinking together. Walking together.

You make it sound so simple, Candy said.

It's easier than drowning! Joephi said.

I'm not going to drown.

Then what?

I'll walk!

And so she walked. It wasn't as difficult as she'd expected. Every now and then she felt an eddy move against the sole of her foot, which was a little unsettling, but otherwise it was like walking on sand dunes: the rises gentle, the descents steeper. She kept her eyes on Mespa and Joephi all the way, and very soon she was close enough to see that the women were standing at the center of what appeared to be a vast spiral of fish: fish with luminous anatomies, some blue, some scarlet, some turquoise or gold.

The closer Candy got to Mespa and Joephi, however, the higher and tighter the curves of the spiral became, the smallest of the fishes being those that were describing intricate spirals directly beneath the feet of the women, offering their devotion to the Fantomaya, then descending through the center of the ziggurat toward a light far, far below that pulsed like a vast needlepoint heart.

"So," Candy said, "what's the news?"

39

LOOKING FORWARD, LOOKING BACK

"THERE'S A LOT TO tell," Joephi said, "and we don't have much time. We don't want the seamstresses trailing us here, to you."

"Why did you have to come here in person?" Candy said. "You were putting thoughts in my head when I was on the boat. Couldn't you have done that from a distance?"

"Believe me, we tried," Mespa said. Her once close-cropped hair had grown out since Candy had last seen her, and the severity of her features had been mellowed by a profound sadness. "But your thoughts were busy dreaming."

"I'm sorry. I had some family problems."

"Your father?" said Joephi.

"Yes," Candy said.

"The *father*," Joephi said. "Of course. The father."

It seemed Candy's reply had provided an answer to a vexing problem.

"Why didn't we think of him earlier?"

"Because he's a drunken half-wit," Mespa said bluntly.

"Was it my father you came to talk to me about?"

"Now that you raise the possibility, *yes*. We're looking for pieces of the big picture, and we're not doing very well. It's possible your father's important."

"Who to?"

"To the future," Mespa said.

"Are you sure there's going to be one?"

"Why would you doubt it?"

"Because Carrion said——"

"Wait," said Joephi. "Christopher Carrion spoke to you?"

"Yes. He was in Tazmagor when we passed through. It was he who told me to leave before things got any worse."

"What form did he take?"

"He's a mess."

"Is he dead?"

"No. He's alive. But only just. He said his nightmares saved him. They must have caught him at the last minute because I've never seen anybody look so sick and so *broken* before."

"Well, that's something to be grateful for," Joephi said.

She looked at Candy, expecting some echo of this sentiment, but Candy couldn't bring herself to celebrate Carrion's wretched state. The significance of her silence wasn't lost on either of the women.

"Ah, *Janda, Janda*," Joephi said, digging her fingers into her long, red hair, which was wet, and pulling it away from her face. *"B'yetta, B'yommo. 'Kathacooth, Monyurr—"*

"Calm down, sister."

"You say *calm down* as though our problem was the house catching fire. The fall of the Abarat is upon us, Mespa!"

"We will do our best to save it," Mespa said. Her eyes went back to Candy. "With the only weapon we have."

"A weapon against what? Who?"

"Christopher Carrion for a start."

Candy looked away from the women's faces down at the spiral that came to an end between them. A tiny luminous fish leaped clear of the water and turned three somersaults in the air before plopping back into the water to begin its long descent.

"You're wrong about Carrion," Candy said. "He's no real danger. In fact, he was trying to get me to go back to the Hereafter. He was afraid for me."

"You two have always had a strange relationship," Mespa said.

"We *three*," Candy said. "He loved her. And she used him."

"Carrion's incapable of love."

"Again, you're wrong," Candy said. She felt anger suddenly rise up in her, too fierce to be silenced. "You're very quick to make judgments, but you're not always right." The women said nothing, which was fine by Candy. "Boa is one of the real monsters," she said. "But you didn't see that. You were too busy accusing the *Bad Man*. The poor little

Princess, the *woman* couldn't be the wicked one, right?"

"That is so *pitifully* simpleminded—" Joephi said.

"Yes. It. Is," Candy said. "*You* should have known better."

"That's not—"

"What you meant. I know. But it's the truth. You put
that vile creature in me and left me to deal with her."

"We kept watch over you," Mespa said. "And we saw
your unhappiness. But it was no worse than the unhappiness of your contemporaries."

"Where are the rest of your friends, by the way?" asked
Joephi.

"Betty, Clyde, and Tom went to Babilonium. Geneva
is going to look for Finnegan Hob. He's somewhere on the
Nonce."

"He won't be there for long," Mespa said. "We see him
traveling to Huffaker with—"

"Princess Boa," Candy said, despondent.

"So it *is* true?"

"That we separated? Oh yes. I threw her out once and
for all."

Before either of the women could respond there was a
fresh escalation in the shrieks and prayers that were emanating from The Great Head.

"What's happening?" Candy said, looking past Mespa
and Joephi at the boats just outside the harbor. The water
there was seething and bubbling, she saw, the motion so
violent that it overturned many of the boats.

"This is *his* work!" Candy said, looking up at the figure on top of the tallest of the towers. "Gan Nug!"

"How do you know——?"

As she spoke the tentacles of what was perhaps a leviathanic Abaratian sea monster rose up out of the frenzied waters. The massive tentacles uncurled and instantly proceeded to demolish The Great Head.

"Oh no . . ." Mespa murmured. "All those people."

"We have to go," Joephi said. "Save who we can."

"We'll go together," Candy said.

"No," said Mespa. "If you want to be useful, stop Boa."

"How?"

"Use what you know," Joephi said. "And what you don't know, learn."

There was a great roar of destruction from The Great Head as tentacles, which had quickly curled around the towers that had been The Head's crowning glory, pulled them down. Now it all curled like a vast, breaking wave, stones and people raining seaward as the towers toppled. Any attempt at escape was a lost cause. What boats had not been overturned by the churning waters were now crushed by falling debris. None were saved.

The waters around the Yebba Dim Day were very quickly littered with the remains both of vessels and their passengers, all rolling in the bloody surf while the rain of stones continued to beat down upon them. As for Gan Nug, the summoner of this monstrosity, he and his uncanny bonfire still stood, hovering on the darkness, exactly where they'd been when they'd had the tower beneath them.

"Oh my . . ." Candy whispered. "I knew a woman and her two children who were in there."

The Great Head continued its collapse, as the tentacles of the beast searched the rubble, their huge scale not denying them an atrocious delicacy. They picked over the rubble carefully, plucking here and there some poor creature clinging to life.

Mespa suddenly looked up.

"Get back to your boat!" she screamed. "Run. *Run!*"

"What's wrong?"

"The seamstresses! They're here!"

She pushed Candy away from her.

"Go!" they shouted, and the two women of the Fantomaya raced away in the opposite direction.

Candy turned and looked toward *The Piper*. She could see Malingo, Eddie, and Gazza by the swaying lanterns hanging at the stern. Malingo was beckoning to her, and Gazza started to do the same. Candy looked back at the women, intending to say good-bye, but they had already gone. The only clue to their whereabouts was the sight of their pursuers: five women, their long hair streaming behind them, standing astride juggernauts of almost white-hot iron, easily three times as tall as their riders. Weaving between one another they chased their unseen quarry off over the Izabella. Candy watched a second or two then started to run toward the boat.

The same violent message was spreading out from the remains of The Great Head in all directions. It made the water beneath Candy's feet shake as she ran, the worst tremors so powerful she was afraid the sea was going to open up beneath her. It was the continuing destruction of The Great Head that was causing the tremors, she knew, but she refused to look at the horrors there. She kept her eyes fixed on *The Piper*. Malingo was beckoning to her, as was Gazza. It was his voice that she heard from above the rubble.

"*Come on!* Don't look back! Keep your eyes on me." He reached toward her, as though he had the power to stretch out and gather her back into the same arms from which he'd released her. *"Just run, Candy!"*

There was another sound now, audible above Gazza's voice and the noise of dying and destruction. She could hear the rising whine of the fever wheel, and the insane scream of the monster who was riding it.

She knew Gazza was right. She shouldn't look back. But she made the error anyway.

It was a smear of a sight, but it was enough to know she was in very serious trouble. The fever wheel was no more than ten yards behind her, its proximity making every bone in her body vibrate. On the seamstress who rode the fiery wheel, was an obscenely distorted face, her mouth a gaping black shriek, her hair streaming behind her like white paint thrown against a starless sky.

"Run! Run!" Gazza said.

Candy threw everything she had into it: her strength,

her anger, even her fear that this fast dash was a lost cause, that she'd never again feel around her the arms of those who loved her, or say to Gazza the words she knew she felt but didn't yet know how to say.

How cruel and stupid was that? To finally lay her eyes on a face she knew from some other sweet dream of life, sweet dream of love, but never get to say: *I know you, don't I? I've always known you.*

She. Would. Never. Tell. Him.

The wheel was going to kill her. A spray of scalding water caught her neck. It hurt. But nowhere near as much as the thought that she'd—

Never—

Ropes of unraveled fire arced past her and set the water ablaze where they fell, boiling it to columns of steam—

Never—

And now the seamstress's shrieks were added to the sum of terrors closing on her. There were fragments of words she'd either heard or even used herself, all dissolved in the vile torrent of noise pouring out of the virago:

"Sheeeeaaanammaaashinigajjandajamdannamandasighaphi- pheeenuuuurrrephriidddeaajardadchalajicfloatakaiemama- mee—"

The consonants and vowels so unendurable—like needles being driven into Candy's head—that it was all she could do not to add her own sum of screams to the cacophony—

"Never!"

The word came from Gazza.

Candy stared at *The Piper* through her agony and saw that he had lifted Eddie up onto his shoulders.

"NEVER!" he said again.

Then Eddie threw the machete. Candy saw it catch the light as it left his hand, then it was gone into the shadows, and all she caught was the noise of its approach—a quickening breath that for some reason surfaced through all the other noise—until it briefly appeared again as it passed over her head.

She couldn't help but see where it went, turning in time to see the expression on the seamstress's face change as she understood what she had raced with such eagerness to meet. The machete cut through her neck, and her head was thrown up toward the lightless heavens on a surge of scarlet.

Candy didn't linger to see it fall. Though the fever wheel had lost its rider it was still on the move.

She fixed her eyes upon *The Piper*—or more truthfully upon *one* of the faces among the many—and ran. There was a raw shriek from the wheel, and then a crash as it keeled over. Candy felt freezing water splashing against her back. She didn't look to see if the wheel had in fact fallen over. She just ran and ran until she was there at the boat, gasping. She reached up and found that the arms that had let her go were the first to catch hold of her again, and wrap her up tighter than anybody had ever held her before.

40

BONES AND LAUGHTER

FINNEGAN HAD BEEN ON the Nonce for a day, searching for a place that he had endeavored to find ever since the death of his Princess. He had finally discovered it, beneath the mountains of that Hour: the place where, according to the myth of the dragon families, their dying members went to pass the last portion of their lives. There they had perished, leaving their bodies to decay among the numberless bones of the worms who had come here to die over the centuries.

Now he was standing in that most secret of secret places, a cavern that had been fashioned over the millennia by the genius of water and stone into the likeness of a cathedral so big the city of Commexo could have comfortably fitted within it three or four times over. It was illuminated by the phosphorescence given off by a fungus that flourished on the bare architecture of the dead. They had spread to every corner of the caverns, laying a gray pallor on the air, which only served to add to the immensity of the space. But the scale of this vast cathedral was barely large enough to contain the immense numbers of dragon's bones that had collected here over the centuries, some laid here by mourners, carrying the corpses of dragon kings or common soldiers; some laid down by those who had owned them, and had made their final journey dressed in meat and scales, so as to lose them at least among the remnants of those who had gone before.

In places they were heaped like stained snowdrifts against the hundred-foot walls, in others simply littering the floor, broken by the passage of the centuries into splinters, the splinters into crumbs, and the crumbs to dust.

"That's a fine sight," Finnegan murmured to himself.

"Is that all it's about, Hob?" said a voice of age and pain. Its vibrations, breaking the bleak silence, brought tiny changes among the bones. Dust ran hissing from eye sockets of dragons dead in their mothers' wombs.

"Deetha Maas?" Finnegan said. He already had his sword and dagger drawn. "Show yourself."

"I'm right here," the ancient voice told him. "Look."

Indeed, something directly in front of him *did* move. It was so uncannily slow that it was several seconds before he could make sense of the form. When he did so he recognized instantly that he was looking at a creature that was, like himself, the child of a forbidden union. Finnegan had been born of a Father of Day and a Mother of Night. But Deetha Maas, the keeper of this ossuary, had been made from a far stranger marriage: that of dragon and man. For sixteen years Finnegan had been slaughtering members of the Dragon Nation, but he had always let Maas see that in some secret place he knew that he was taking the lives of innocents. And that in allowing their corpses to be recovered and brought to this place was his way of making peace with that fact.

Once, perhaps, Maas had been an intimidating figure. He stood eleven or twelve feet tall, even stooped. His head was a calamitous mismatching of the infernal reptile—the long snouted skull, the slitted eyes, the gold-green scales, the teeth in a barbed array in rotting gums—with the humanish parts, the most significant part the fact that he was standing upright on his crooked back legs. He had fashioned a primitive walking aid out of bones bound with strips of cloth, on which he leaned his entire weight only advancing with the greatest difficulty, each step exacting its price in pain. There were other subtler signs of his human aspect: small places where his scales gave way to areas of translucent skin under which a network of dark blue veins was visible, pulsing against his pale purple sinew, his dirty white hair, which grew down to his waist, and here and there portions of a beard in the same wretched condition, which sprouted from pieces of flesh between the scaly patches beneath his snout.

"I'd expected you to be younger," Finnegan said.

"I'm alive," Deetha Maas said. "That's some kind of triumph surely. I got to be one hundred and thirteen. And now I presume you have come to make sure I don't see a hundred and fourteen."

"You were the one who called me here," Finnegan reminded him.

"Yes. Well, we go back sixteen years, Finnegan. I thought with what's going on above we might never have another opportunity to meet face-to-face. So I seized the offer while it was there in the dust, so to speak."

"What offer?"

"From the true dispatcher of the message I sent."

"If not you, then who?" Finnegan said, raising his sword. It was a heavy blade, hard to wield with any great ease. Much broader, fuller, stronger men than Finnegan had attempted to use it and found it virtually impossible to wield. But Finnegan had its measure. It made him feel lighter on his feet to have it in his hand.

If—as he suspected—that this summons from Deetha Maas was a last attempt by the surviving dragons to kill him, he would not go easily. This was, after all, the night of Midnight's Empire. He'd seen all the stars go out as he'd made his way here. If this was not the end of the world he would be surprised—in truth, disappointed. He wanted an end to his loneliness and to his rage. And if it was going to be anywhere, where better than here? And who better to cure him of life than one of the very species who'd also cured him of hope and happiness? One last battle then, fought to the death, his own.

"I'm ready," he told Maas.

"I doubt that," Maas said.

"Death holds no fears for me," Finnegan replied.

"I didn't imagine for a moment that it did. But it isn't death that's waiting for you."

"What then?"

"Your love."

"I have no love!"

A spring of clear, sweet laughter appeared from behind a litter of bones and echoed around the ossuary. An elegantly dressed woman emerged from the shadows. Finnegan let his raised sword sink down under its own tremendous weight.

"Hello, Finn." Boa smiled.

41

DRAGON DUST

"Y OU CAN'T BE HER," Finnegan said. There was a tremor in his voice. "She was dead. I held her in my arms."

"I know. I was there."

"No!"

"I thought you'd be happy—"

"If you were real—"

"Do you remember the letter you found? Written by your grandfather from the battlefield of the Nonce, during the last war? The letter to your grandmother? You read a part of it to me."

"Go on," Finnegan replied. His voice was hushed now.

"I remember there was a part of it that made you angry because it was your grandfather's story about what happened after death. You thought he was wrong. It was a selfish letter, you said. Because your grandfather wasn't thinking about how it would affect someone who read it. You were so furious, you wanted your grandfather to know how you felt."

"Yes. I remember. I couldn't tell him, though, because he was dead."

The smile came back to Boa's face, bright as ever.

"You're trying to trick me, Finnegan Hob. You're trying to catch me out, aren't you?"

"I don't see how."

"You know he wasn't dead. He was alive when you read that letter to me."

Both members of her audience, man and dragon, gazed at her in astonishment.

"All right," Finn said. "It's you. I don't know how, but it is."

"I thought you'd be happier to see me."

"Well . . . you know . . . you were dead. I've lived thinking you were dead. Buried in that royal mausoleum on the Nonce. And you weren't."

"No. I was a prisoner. But I escaped." Her smile became laughter. "I escaped, Finn! And I'm back, to love you."

Finnegan tried to put on a smile but it didn't quite stick. "It just seems so impossible."

"Of course it seems that way. But then yesterday you wouldn't have thought you'd be seeing the stars go out, would you?"

"Is that why you're here? Are you responsible for that?"

"For murdering the stars?" she said. As she spoke there was a subtle change in her very being. Something caught fire in her, and threw off a garish light. It was in her skin, in her eyes, in her throat. "Do you think I'm capable of that, Finn? Of throwing the world into darkness?" She had lowered her head, like a wild animal preparing to charge. "Well . . . do you?"

"I don't know what you're capable of," Finnegan said. "How could I?"

"Because I'm your Princess."

"Stop saying that."

"But it's the truth. Look at me, Finn! *Look!* Am I not the same woman you were about to marry?"

"Too much the same," he said, half turning his face from hers, as though he might better break the spell of her perfection if he looked at her askance, and in breaking it, might see what hid behind her beauty. But it didn't work. He still had to ask her: "How can I believe what I see if I don't understand how it happened?"

"Touch me, Finn, and I'll tell you." She offered him a playful little smile. "I promise I won't turn into a monster when you touch me." She walked toward him raising her arm to proffer her hand. "Please, Finn. I'm begging you. I've waited a long time."

"Waited where? Who was holding you prisoner?"

"Touch me and I'll tell you. *Go on.* I came back so I could be with you, Finn. Where's the harm in a little touch?"

"I don't know."

"There is none," she said. "Here. Look." She took hold of his hand. "I'm real. I'm warm."

Finally, Finn smiled, his hand moving up over the

back of her hand, his thumb tenderly brushing the bone of her wrist. He could feel her blood pulsing through her veins. And, as promised, Boa told him everything, more or less. She told how while the wedding guests had been watching the struggle between Finnegan and the dragon, the women of the Fantomaya had reached into her dead body and claimed her soul, how they'd carried it across the divide between the Abarat and the Hereafter, and hidden it in the womb of a woman who was very close to giving birth.

"So this was all planned out?" Finnegan said.

"I really don't know, to tell you the truth. I don't see how it could have been. The Fantomaya just wanted to protect my soul, and when they saw a chance to hide it—somewhere no one from the Abarat was going to look—they took it. The child was born a few hours later. But you had already worked most of it out for yourself, hadn't you?" Boa said. "I saw the confusion on your face several times. You felt something for the girl but you didn't know what or why. I'm right, aren't I?" She took a half step toward him, her hand going up to his face. "There's nothing to feel guilty about," she said. "You weren't seeing her. You were seeing me through her. I was her prisoner. I had no defense against her. All I could do was stay locked up in that head of hers and watch her despicable little life go by year after year. Wondering what was happening here. Always, always thinking about you. Wondering who you'd married now that I was dead."

"Finn, it's all lies," Maas insisted.

"Then none of it can do any harm, can it?" Finnegan replied.

"You should be careful with your affections, Finnegan Hob. There is a greater wickedness close to you than the crimes any of the beasts whose bones we stand among may have committed. Some of them were weak. Some of them were stupid. And some had masters who demanded they do terrible things. But there were innocents here too. You know that, Finnegan."

"You're right. I concede it. I killed in anger. I killed in loneliness. I will make my peace with the spirits here. But not now. We have other problems right now."

"By other problems, you mean Midnight's Empire?" Maas said.

"Since when did it become an Empire?" he said.

Maas shrugged.

"I don't know that it ever did. That's just the way Mater Motley spoke of it. The darkness that's gathering. It's her work. She will see herself Empress of the islands if she has her way."

"Is darkness so terrible?"

"This darkness, yes. And it's spreading like the plague. I think a woman with your skills might know a thing or two, Princess," Maas said, turning to Boa.

"Don't listen, Finn. He's doing exactly what I told you he'd do. He's trying to poison our happiness."

"What skills, Maas?" Finnegan said. "What are you talking about? If you have something to say—"

"He has nothing to say," Boa said quickly. "It's all

dragon slime he means to coat me with. I've been in their jaws before, Finn. I know how they stink. The closest he gets to having any real humanity in him is when he dines on it."

"Nicely done, Princess," Maas said with sour appreciation. "Inflame his rage with talk of dragons and maybe he'll forget that he really doesn't trust you."

"Enough, Maas," Finnegan said sharply. "Just because the stars have gone out, and the world is likely to go with them, it doesn't mean I'll simply forgive every utterance that spills out of you. An insult is an insult. And trust me, Maas, one more word spoken against my Princess and your head will fall farther than any star."

Whether out of fear for his life or from a genuine sense of contrition, Maas laid his clawed hands, right over left, across his heart.

"Forgive me, Finnegan Hob," he said inclining that burdensome head, "I have been too long in the company of the dead. I have forgotten simple courtesies."

"Not good enough," Boa said.

She took hold of Finnegan's hand, and he felt a surge of cold power move down her arm and through her palm into his. It felt as though his arm was actually gaining muscle mass, and he was glad of it. There would be enemies out there in Midnight's Empire that had only risen up now because the circumstances were propitious: he would need all the strength he owned to protect Boa from their assaults. It wouldn't be easy, but with her help he would find a way to get them to a place of safety, assuming such a place existed.

"How do you feel?" Boa asked him.

"Good," he said. He shook the arm she'd touched as though it had been asleep all his life and was now waking up.

"It feels a lot stronger than it did before you . . . what did you do?"

"Just rolled away a stone," Boa said, "that had been between you and what was always in you. Take out your sword."

He did so, the blade making a sound like the chiming of a perfect bell as it slid from the sheath.

"It's never felt so light before."

"Nor has it ever been so sharp," Boa said, making a pass over the sword with her hand. A gleam of light ran up along the blade. "Now," she said softly, "use it."

"Use it to do what?"

"What it was meant to do. Kill."

"Maas?"

"Of course."

"He has no harm in him, my lady."

"I say he does, Finnegan. Trust me. Kill him. Then we need never to think of him again."

Maas made no attempt to move while his fate was considered. He simply waited, his hands still pressed to his chest.

"*Do it!*" Boa said.

"He has nothing left, Princess. Look at him."

"I'd forgotten how much hard work you can be," she

said. "You never could see what was right in front of you."

"You're right in front of me, Princess. And right now you're very hard to see. I'm trying. I really am. But there's something . . ."

"Of course," she said with weary irritation. "There's always going to be more of me to find. Or it would all get boring very quickly, wouldn't it?"

He opened his mouth to speak, but she was there before him.

"You're going to tell me this isn't the time for games, because 'very soon the world's going to end' and I'm here to say if it really is going to end then we may as well have some fun before it's all over."

"Agreed."

"Good. So let me have my fun."

"Doing what?"

"Finishing the job!"

"You're both crazy . . ." Maas said, the words passing around the boneyard like a rumor, gathering force with every echo.

"Very likely," Finnegan said.

"You think?" Boa said. "All those years locked away. All those years grieving. Making me crazy. Oh, I know crazy. I've had more than my share of crazy."

"It's over."

"Almost . . ."

"No, it is. Whatever's out there, we'll deal with it together."

"Finn, you've got to finish what we're doing here."

"It's done."

"But the dragon still has a head on his shoulders."

"I'm not killing him, Boa."

"Fine. Then I will."

"You don't want his blood on your hands."

"Don't tell me what I want," she said.

"These are powerful spirits, Boa."

"You're afraid of ghosts now?" she said, her contempt diseasing the air between them.

"Not fear. Respect."

"For what? For Maas?" She glanced toward the place where Deetha Maas had last been standing, but he'd moved.

"Come here, worm!" she said. There wasn't a great deal of volume in her voice but there was immense power there, and it instantly carried to every corner of the boneyard. *"I! Will! Have! Your! Lying! Head!"*

Maas had disappeared.

With every syllable Boa spoke her utterances grew in power, so that by the time she'd reached the fifth word the sound was causing the smaller bones on the slopes to shake themselves loose and tumble down the inclines like mobs of bones assembling in every part of the ossuary. The bones didn't just slide down the slopes. They skipped, they tumbled, they leaped and somersaulted. Nor did their motion cease when they reached the bottom of the slope.

Instead, they cavorted among the shards and the bone

dust, conferring upon the agitation they had carried down the slopes. As the clouds of dust rose into the darkness, they started to create unmistakable shapes, made from the dust's memory of the beasts it had once been. The dragons were returning! No matter how large they had looked or how complex their forms and colors had been, it was all encoded in every mote of dust. Each beast in every grain remembered; they were waiting in every particle of dust in their entirety. Their majestic shapes sprang up from death throughout the caverns—the iridescence of their scales, the gilded beauty of their eyes, and the purples and reds and greens of their massive wings.

"Maas!" Boa yelled. *"Why are you doing this? I demand you kill these things right now."*

"He can't kill what's already dead, Princess," Finnegan said.

"This is dragon magic. I don't like it. *Maas!*"

"I'm here," the priest said, though now it was harder to be sure the direction from which his voice was coming.

"Show yourself, *Maas.* Finnegan's not going to hurt you." In the same breath she dropped her voice to the lowest of whispers and to Finnegan: "Slice off the top half of his head. He's dangerous."

"You don't mean that."

"If you're too weak to do what has to be done—"

She raised her left hand, in which she was holding a brilliant blade.

"Maas!" she called out. "Where are you?"

She stopped in mid-syllable, and her eyes lost their hold on Finnegan. Her mouth couldn't hold the words she had yet to say, nor could her hand hold the knife. It fell from her fingers and as it did so Finnegan caught a smeared glimpse of Deetha Maas, standing behind and a little to the right of the Princess. He had his hand at the back of her neck, touching some vital place, injecting his magical Order of Silence into her.

"Please! Don't—" Finnegan said.

"Don't what? Gut her the way she was about to gut me? She fully intended to do it, you know. You were too weak. She wanted it done fast, didn't she? 'He's dangerous.' That's what she said about me. Doesn't that make you wonder? *Why* am I so dangerous?"

"Just let her go, Maas. I won't hurt you—"

"Don't you want to know her secrets, Finnegan?"

"Not from you I don't. Just let her go."

"You're going to have to see for yourself, then."

"See what?"

"Her little hideaway on Huffaker."

"Huffaker? She doesn't even like—"

"You can both go, courtesy of the powers of this place." The ghost dragons continued to roil around, their images rising up on all sides. "I think the dead must want to forgive you. They look at you with pity, Finnegan, for what you have to suffer. I know you think the suffering is over now that she's come back but you're wrong. It's just begun."

"Let her go, Maas."

"To Huffaker, both of you!"

Finnegan felt the air throb around him, and the forms of the ghosts became remote.

"Maas!" Finnegan yelled.

Then the cavern was gone, and he was standing out in the darkness of another island, another Hour. In that darkness there was only one source of light: it was coming from the crack of a door, a little way from where Finnegan stood.

Again, the air throbbed. And his Princess was suddenly beside him.

"The knife," she said, looking down. "It was in my hand!"

"Boa. We're on Huffaker. He said you used to come here." He glanced back at her, but there was too much darkness for him to see her. "Is that true?"

Boa looked and realized Finnegan was right. She sighed.

"Yes, love. It's true. And I suppose you had to see sooner or later, didn't you? Come. Let me show you my secrets."

They walked together through the darkness to the threshold of the door, where the light fell. There was no sound around them. Nothing moved. Nothing sang. It was just the two of them as they approached the door.

"Touch nothing," she said, and led the way inside.

42

THE FIENDS

IN THE MAP-MOSAICKED ROOM at the top of the Needle Tower, Mater Motley surveyed her creation, and was satisfied. The Midnight Empire she had planned for, labored for, lived for, now owned the Abarat from horizon to horizon, with the exception of the Twenty-Fifth Hour; though it was only a matter of time, she was sure, until that most perverse of Hours fell to her. Everywhere Mater Motley sent her remote gaze, it was the same triumphantly desolate story. Where there had been calm there was now chaos and violence. Where there had been celebration there was panic and terror.

On several islands she observed desperate attempts being made to provide some light to cure this darkness. Many, much to her satisfaction, ended in disaster.

On Hobarookus, for instance, she witnessed the tribal wizard of the Amurruz attempt to propel himself, accompanied by a number of warriors, into the smothering darkness overhead with the apparent intention of hacking a hole through to the stars. But the sacbrood were

formidably violent, despite the fact that they were imprisoned in a jigsaw of their own interlocked bodies and their
solidified excretions. After a brief, noisy encounter, a rain
of body parts fell upon the upturned faces of the Amurruz, marking the brutal end of that foolish act of bravery.

On the Isle of the Black Egg, the Chief of the Jala-
pemoto nation ordered the igniting of a pool of highly
combustible kaizaph oil—which offered a comforting
source of warmth and light for several hours, until the fuel
in the shallow pool had been entirely consumed. Then the
hungry flames followed the path of the oil into the seam
that fed the pool, which divided and divided as it spread
out across the plateau. Within half an hour cracks began
to appear in the ground, followed quickly by sinkholes,
gouting flame, which claimed the lives of thousands of
Jalapemotian inhabitants.

And while these exquisite follies played out, the fiends
came out of hiding. Mater Motley couldn't possibly have
witnessed all of their reappearances, but she saw plenty.
Creatures of every kind—bestial, grotesque, crazed and
infernal—they all came out of hiding. Some she knew
by name from her grimoires: monstrous descendants of
the Eight Evils who had first walked the Abaratian stage.
The devourers of ruins called the Waikami; the phantom,
Lord Hoath; the many-tongued beast, Morrowain; the
death's head creature know as the Depotic; the raging,
gape-mouthed monster simply called the Overlord.

And for every one beast she could name there were
twenty she could not: abominations that had passed the

ages hiding in the intricate systems of caves and passage-
ways that lay beneath the Hours, or in barrows and pits
where they had been buried permanently by those who
had fought them and believed them dead. Many had lived
out the ages in solitude and darkness, nurturing their
rage, emerging only when hunger drove them to risk
being exposed and hunted down; others had procreated
over the centuries, and emerged from their sanctuaries
with immense families, their grotesqueries multiplying
over the generations. A few had lived well: worshipped
in secret temples by Abaratians who considered them to
be the raw stuff from which divinities were made. These
fiends, made arrogant by years of worship, rose with their
legions of believers all around them: ordinary men and
women of the islands who had secretly been paying homage to these bleak-hearted deities over the years.

Almost everywhere Mater Motley's roving eye traveled it fell upon sights that would have sickened and
appalled a compassionate spirit, but that filled her with
a venomous joy. It wasn't only for herself that she felt
this joy. There were other eyes watching how her plan
to unknit the order of the Abarat proceeded: the eyes
of beings ancient and insatiable, whose presence she had
only glimpsed as a monumental, limitless shadow thrown
across or beyond what was neither space nor substance,
presence nor absence. At some time not far from now they
would show themselves, she knew. They would descend
out of their mystery and be seen, here in the Abarat. And
on that day she would be elevated to the highest throne for

the services she had done them.

Meanwhile, she had another order of business to observe: the arrests. Her stitchling legions had already reached many of the islands. Already Mater Motley had seen the arrests of hundreds of individuals who would have caused, had they not been arrested, conflict and rebellion in the future. She'd seen the possibility in the visions the Powers That Be had allowed her to witness, and it was a future she had vowed to keep from coming into being. On the dark side of Scoriae she had, many weeks ago, ordered a camp to be built where all these agitators and troublemakers would be kept. It was a rudimentary place. The huts that had been hastily built to have the arrestees stripped of their personal belongings—jewelry, wallets, expensive shoes—and their presence recorded did not keep out the cold wind that incessantly blew so close to the Edge of the World. The camp had very little healthy drinking water, and the supplies the inmates had been given to make soup with were laughably inadequate, but Mater Motley saw no purpose in giving comfort and nourishment to people she was going to have executed within hours.

Meanwhile, the number of arrests continued to grow. Every outsider, every radical, every dealer in visions and hope—in short, anyone who had ever stood against her in word or deed, or that she suspected of one day doing so—was taken from their homes and family without explanation, and interned in the camp at Scoriae.

The Old Mother was well pleased.

43

DARK WATERS

THE TASK OF RESCUING the survivors from the turbulent waters around The Great Head had quickly degenerated into chaos, as people struggling in the water converged on *The Piper* from all directions and attempted to clamber aboard. Within two or three minutes of arriving at the scene *The Piper* was carrying more than its limit of passengers, and listing badly to starboard.

"We have to get out of here, Candy!" Eddie said. "We're over the limit for passengers, Candy. They're going to sink us! Are you listening to me?"

Candy stood frozen in place.

"Okay, fine. Then I'll just go tell some drowned people we'll be joining them soon."

Candy continued staring off into the starless, moonless, cloudless sky, her body convulsed by little spasms.

"Malingo?" Eddie hollered. "I think there's something wrong with Candy. She's having a vision or a fit or something! Get over here, will you?" As he yelled he shoved his diminutive foot into the middle of the same brutish face of a man he'd shoved back into the water just a few moments before. "Can't you take a hint, mate?" he bawled. *"There! Is! No! More! Room!"* He put all the strength in his body into making sure that this time the man stayed down. "Who's at the wheel?"

"We are!" came a chorus of Johns from the wheel-house.

"We *have* to get out of here!" Eddie yelled.

"He's right!" Gazza shouted. "Much more of this and we're going to be flipped over."

"Just get this crawfiddlin' thing moving," Eddie said.

"There's people in the water right in front of us," Mischief said.

"They'll get out of the way when they see us coming!" Eddie yelled back.

"We can't just—"

"*Gazza!* Get to the wheelhouse and take over from that gaggle of idiot heads that some gene-deficient woman had the misfortune to carry to the tragedy of birth."

"You are despicable, you know that?" John Mischief said. "Nobody put you in charge here. You're just an actor."

"Oh no, that was just a role I was playing!" Eddie said. "I'm a man of action. I get things done. You and your brothers just talk, talk, talk. All the time. Talk, talk, talk."

The John Brothers said nothing. Except Serpent, of course, who couldn't help himself.

"Your time will come," he murmured to Eddie.

"Well?" Eddie yelled.

"I'm in the wheelhouse," Gazza hollered. "They gave up the wheel."

"*Good,*" Eddie said. "Now get us out of this mess."

"I'm working on it."

"How's Candy doing?" Eddie asked Malingo.

It wasn't Malingo who replied. It was Candy.

"Lordy Lou. She's still with me!"

"Who?" said Malingo.

"Boa. Who else?"

"She's here with you now? In your head?"

"No. But we're still connected somehow. She just pulled me into her head. I don't even think she meant to. I saw through her eyes for a moment. She was in some place filled with bones. Then—I don't know how—we moved on."

"Who's we?"

"She has Finnegan," Candy said. She put her hand up to her head. "I saw him right beside me. No, not me, her. Beside her. I'm all backward."

"You said they moved on?"

"Yes."

"Where to?"

"I don't know."

"Hazard a guess?"

Candy closed her eyes.

"Carrion built her a place to play . . ."

"Play?"

"Magic games. Oh—it's Huffaker!"

"And you think that's where she took Finnegan?"

Before Candy could reply *The Piper*'s engines made a guttural growl, and the boat surged forward perhaps twice its length before the engine made a second sound, far less healthy than the first, and the vessel shuddered to a halt.

"No!" Eddie yelled. "No! No! NO! This is not the place to lose power, Gazza! Get this hog-boned boat *moving*."

"Then stop cursing at us," said John Mischief. "And make yourself useful. There's nothing wrong at the helm. And the engine's still going. Something's jamming the propeller. Gazza, can you find out what it is?"

Gazza gave a quick "Aye, aye, Captain," and raced toward the propeller. Peering into the water he said, "It's just some piece of trash wrapped around the propeller. I'll cut it away and—"

The boat lurched. First to port, then to starboard, then to port again, this time so deeply it took on water. All the desperate creatures they'd tried to leave behind had swum in pursuit of them, and they, plus a hundred others, had grabbed hold of *The Piper*.

This time there would be no saving the ship. This time she was going down, taking everyone aboard with her to feed the fishes.

44

PARIAH

THE PIPER HAD PLAYED its last tune. Its boards creaked and cracked as one desperate soul after another sought to save themselves from the seething, bloody waters of the Izabella. They were already littered with the bodies of those who had died in the collapse of The Great Head or had fallen prey to the countless beasts that had risen from the depths with the Requiax. Terror had made them mindless and merciless, clawing at one another as they attempted to clamber up onto the boat, even though it was lurching wildly.

"This is the end," Malingo said. "Candy, I'm sorry. It shouldn't have ended like this. What am I saying? It should never have ended. I thought we would go on forever, I really did."

"It's not over yet!" Gazza said. "Look up! *Look up!*"

Everyone did as Gazza instructed. Nine or ten winged constructions that looked like the skeletons of vast birds, were circling high above *The Piper*. Their broad skulls were crowned with elaborately woven ziggurats of blazing bone, their wings, fully twenty feet wide, gilded by firelight.

And in the many ribbed bodies of these extraordinary mechanisms, lying flat along their midsections, were their pilots. One of which was Geneva.

"*Candy!* Be ready!"

"*Geneva?*"

"Of course!"

"*It is!*"

Candy could scarcely believe what she was seeing, but there she was, Geneva Peachtree, lying in the long cage of the bone-glider's body.

"I couldn't leave you to die!" Geneva yelled. "But I needed help!"

"You'd better be quick!" Gazza hollered. "We're going down fast."

"Geneva, be careful," Candy shouted. "Don't get pulled down! These people—"

"Smallest first!" Geneva ordered. "Malingo, pick up Eddie!"

"Now?"

"*Now!*"

What happened next was so fast and so extraordinary Candy could scarcely believe it was happening. Two of the fliers swooped down toward *The Piper*, as Malingo lifted a protesting Eddie up—

"Put me down!"

—first onto his shoulders, and then—

"I don't need help, geshrat!"

That was all he had time to say. The fliers were carrying between them a hammock, which scooped Eddie up like a fish in a net, lifting him into the air. Their burden was nowhere near heavy enough to prevent them from rising again with their catch.

"You're next, Candy," Geneva yelled.

"No, it has to be Gazza! I won't go until he goes."

Geneva knew she had no time to argue with the girl, so she didn't even try.

"Gazza it is!" she said.

"Wait!" Gazza protested. "Don't I get to have—"

"An opinion?" Geneva yelled.

"Yes!"

"No! You've only got one chance at this!"

Two more fliers swooped down, needing to drop lower this time, not only because Gazza wasn't raised up on Malingo's shoulders but because in the half minute since Eddie's rescue, *The Piper* had sunk significantly lower in the water.

"*Now* you!" Malingo said to Candy.

"No, I won't—"

"We heard that already," John Serpent snapped. "Don't be selfish, Candy."

"What?"

For the first time, Candy found all the brothers staring at her. "If we drown, it'll be a pity. If you go it's a tragedy. And you *know it*. We'll get Malingo, don't worry."

In that instant some combustible substance in the rubble of The Great Head erupted in garish flame, and its light illuminated John Serpent's face.

"Go," he said.

She nodded.

"I'm ready!" she yelled to Geneva. The words were barely out of her lips when the third pair of fliers swooped down and she was lifted up, and up, and up, into the safety of the sky, where the bone-gliders wheeled.

Some time later, every soul aboard *The Piper* was safely deposited back onto the lantern-lit northeastern shore of Ninnyhammer, where Candy found she had a host of reunions awaiting. The first Abaratian to have ever shown her hospitality, Izarith, along with her two children, was there. So was the munkee called Filth she'd met in the Twilight Palace, and the members of the Totemix. It was no accident that all the people she'd encountered along the way to this place and moment were here.

"We watched you from the first step you took into the Abarat," Geneva explained to her.

"When you say we, you mean—"

"All of us. The Kalifee."

"It's more than just us, though," said Izarith.

"Not many more," Geneva said quietly.

"Sad but true," one of the Totemix said. "We've known this Midnight was coming sooner or later. We've read the omens."

"So we started assembling a force—"

"The best of the best," Filth said, his fingers plunged deep into one of his nostrils.

"Appearances can be deceptive," Geneva remarked, catching the look on Candy's face as she watched Filth snot mining.

"Kalifee means troublemakers. Rebels," Izarith explained. "But we haven't managed to do much to defy Mater Motley. She's clever——"

"Or we're too stupid," said Filth. "Maybe a bit of both."

There were more familiar faces appearing, stepping out of the shadows into the lantern light: Jimothi, head of the tarrie-cats, and some faces she remembered from the crowded boardwalks of Babilonium.

"Why was the Mazathatt watching *me?*" Candy asked Geneva.

"We thought you were working for *her.* The Hag."

"Why?"

"You came from nowhere. But you had power," Izarith said. "It was no accident that I invited you into the house, I'm afraid. That was *me* chancing to take a long look at *you.*"

"And?"

"We knew immediately you weren't working for her. Evil stinks; you didn't."

"Thanks."

"But we still had questions," Geneva said. "We'd put together some pieces of the puzzle. We knew the Fanto-maya had been tinkering with your mind before you were even born."

"Doing what?" Candy said.

"Nothing that we didn't think necessary," said Mespa, who now also stepped out of the shadows with Joephi at her side. "We needed to keep you hidden from your lodger, and she from you. But it was a hastily conceived plan, and the magic was less than perfect."

"We were arrogant," Joephi said bitterly. "We thought our sisterhood was beyond error. Huh." She shook her head. "It shames me still."

"What do you mean: error?"

"It was poor thinking. Arrogance will do that."

"We thought we had your life under control," Joephi said. "But—"

"I changed," Candy replied.

"Yes. Oh yes. You certainly did. Watching you deciding to go back to that little boat at the Yebba Dim Day even though you knew it was almost certain death to do so. Oh yes. We were in error."

"Hence this moment with the good souls who fought the Hag in secret ways for years, and won little for their efforts."

"And died," Geneva said softly. "In ways only an abomination like the Hag could have conceived."

"She was the reason we had such doubts about magic. We had come to think that it corrupted everything it touched. Look what it did to your people, Candy."

"My people?"

"'Manity."

"Is that what you call us?"

"It's one of the politer terms."

There was a subtle undercurrent of laughter.

"And what magic did you do to us?"

"Gave you power you lacked the skill to control."

"Oh, that. Yes, I've seen some of that."

"You mean your father's cruelties?"

"Yes."

"If you can find it in your heart to pity him . . ."

Candy thought about this for a moment. "No," she said. "I can't."

"Well, that's honest."

"Was he always a man of vision?"

"My dad? Vision? Ha! You must be kidding. He likes beer, girlie magazines, kid's cartoons, beer, being mean, and beer. He believes in nothing."

"Well, he seems to have founded a religion."

"You call that a religion? What was it called? *The Church of Cold Pizza*?" Her audience looked at her blankly. "Never mind. 'Manity joke."

"We call it the Church of the Utter Void," Geneva said. There was laughter now. "Abaratian joke."

"Well, I don't worship there," Gazza said.

"There's a time for everyone . . ." Geneva said flatly.

"Are you preaching for the Church of the Utter Void now?" Eddie said.

"No. But it has its attractions, doesn't it? To have no more dreams you have to protect. To have nothing you love so much you live in fear of losing it. That wouldn't be so bad . . ."

"It would be death," said Candy.

"And would that really be so terrible?"

"Yes," Candy said. "Of course it would. I didn't just escape dying to go and give it all up because some preacher says it's better that way. We still remember the light. We still remember happiness. Well, don't we?"

"You make it sound very simple," Geneva said.

"Well, to me it is. I want the Abarat to survive all this darkness, and come back stronger than ever. But I need to tell you something that might be important."

"And what's that?" said Mespa.

"On *The Piper* I realized that I still had a connection to Princess Boa. I could see through her eyes."

"Oh, Lordy Lou!" John Mischief said. "Does that mean she can see through yours? Is she looking at us right now—"

"I don't think so."

"If she is, then she'll know where we are!" Eddie said.

"Eddie, calm down."

"Why didn't you say something before now?"

"Because the feeling came and went. I think maybe it was just there for a few seconds. Perhaps because I thought I was going to die. I don't know."

"Even if this feeling has passed," Geneva said, "Eddie's right. You should have said something the moment you had a chance! You shouldn't even be looking at me. *Don't look at anybody!* I can't believe you would be so stupid as to endanger our entire enterprise!"

"All right, all right!" Candy said.

She turned her back on them all, and stared up at the empty sky.

"There's no need to treat me like a total leper," she said more quietly. "I told you, Boa only came through for a few seconds. I don't know why. Whatever the reason was, I can't feel her presence any longer."

"Which proves absolutely nothing," Geneva said. "You know how sly she is. She could be behind your eyes right now and you wouldn't even know it."

"Well, she isn't."

"Candy. Think about it. How would you know whether she was or she wasn't?"

"Because I'm not the ignorant girl I was when I lived in Chickentown. Because I threw her out of me, and just because there's one little strand of her left in there doesn't mean she still owns me. But I understand. She's planted a little seed of doubt in you, and now I'm stuck with it." She raised her arms in mock surrender. "I'm going to not look at any of you. I'm just going to walk down to the sea and think. And if she is looking out of my eyes all she's going to see is blackness. Happy?"

And so saying she walked down to the water and looked out at the darkness, wondering as she did so if the darkness was looking back at her.

PART FIVE

STORMWALKER

A Man will always
Rise to the bait of
His higher self, however
Turbulent the waters it is
Cast upon.

—Anon.

45

THE BUSINESS OF EMPIRE

WITH THE MANY HUNDREDS of seam-stresses Mater Motley trusted and considered most experienced out among the islands leading the Death Squads, their task of gathering up any troublesome individuals who might be using the chaos to work on chipping away at the foundations of her Empire, Mater Motley's messenger of choice had become Maratien.

Twenty-two hours had now passed since the sacbrood had been released. In that time, Maratien had come to know the interior of the tower very well as she carried messages up and down its stairways. She had brought letters of supplication or surrender from those in power from across the Hours, all of whom had lately come to understand that they would forfeit both their territories and their lives if they did not pay their respects to the woman they'd once called the Mad Hag of Gorgossium.

Mater Motley made Maratien read the begging, self-serving missives aloud, but the Old Mother seldom had patience enough to hear more than a paragraph.

"Enough," she'd say.

And Maratien would do precisely as her mistress instructed, letting go of the offending plea near one of the windows where a gust of wind could carry it away. There were a few occasions when Motley confiscated a letter herself. These were all from sorcerers and wizards who claimed to have had some romantic liaison with the Old Mother. They were treated with particular contempt, snatched from Maratien's fingers and torn to shreds before the wind took them.

In the end, no claim—regal, religious, or sentimental—carried any weight.

There were only three letters that the Old Mother paid any attention to. The first was from one of the Old Mother's loyal seamstresses, who wrote to inform her that she had heard rumors that somebody who closely resembled Mater Motley's missing grandson, Christopher Carrion, had been seen on three islands: the Black Egg, Huffaker, and Ninnyhammer.

"I have heard, Lady Mother, that you believe your grandson may have left this world for that other at our soles. If you have proof that this is the case, then my information will be of little interest to you. But I offer it nevertheless . . ."

This letter Mater Motley kept for herself, making no comment upon its contents. She did the same with a letter from another of those seamstresses, whom she counted among her inner circle, who wrote to tell her she was optimistic that she would soon be able to report the arrest of the rebel, Candy Quackenbush, and asking whether, when that happened, was the girl to be brought to Gorgossium or taken to join the condemned souls in the camp on Scoriae? To this Mater Motley dictated a reply, which Maratien dispatched.

Mater Motley was of the opinion that when the criminal Candy Quackenbush was in custody, the girl was to be taken to Scoriae, treated like the common criminal she was, and executed as such.

The third letter, which the Old Mother studied very closely, was from the Captain of a squad of warrior stitchlings called skulliers. He was departing from the streets of Commexo City, where the skulliers, every one of them sewn up with war in its threads, were driving Commexo's forces to a harrowing defeat. But, the Captain reported, the architect of Commexo City then threw on to the battlefield a force she had not known existed.

"*He has legions of likenesses of that infernal child of his, the Commexo Kid. All of them are a perfect copy of the original (if indeed there ever was a living original, which I highly doubt). These legions came against us in swarms, with no weapons except their numbers, which I begin to fear are limitless. Knowing the importance with which you view the extinguishing of the city's lights, I am writing in the hope that you may somehow lend your own powers to those of your faithful legions. I fear the victory that is your right will not come to pass until the balance of power is tipped in our favor, and I can think of no more certain way of making that a reality than by your personal intervention to turn the tide of this battle. I believe with your presence here the struggle to extinguish this city and to hang the architect, Rojo Pixler, from a lamppost, will be quickly realized."*

The letter moved the Old Mother to action on the instant. She wrote some fifty letters on the air, and conjuring for each a wind to bear it away, let them go their many ways. Then, ordering Maratien to accompany her, she called down the ethereal staircase that led from the mosaic-laden chamber up to the roof of the Needle Tower.

"Stay close to me, girl," the Old Mother said. "I am about to let powers loose in whose path I would not want you to get caught."

"They would harm me?"

"They would kill you, Maratien. Take the hem of my dress. Why do you hesitate?"

"The dolls, lady."

"Souls. That's all they are. Enemies of our mighty intent. They're just afraid that you're going to take them from me. Go, grip the gown tight. Tighter still. That's it. Now don't move."

"I won't."

"Good. Trust me. You're quite safe. Take the visions as they come."

"I am ready, my lady."

"You must be brave and drink in all the visions I am

about to show us. They will exist but once. After my Midnight, they will be gone. For there has never been such a sight as this before, nor will ever be again."

So saying she pulled the collar of her gown away from her neck, exposing her clavicle. There was precious little flesh upon her, and the finely curved bone stood clear of her skin, which had a jaundiced hue. With a sudden burst of speed, she reached into her own flesh and caught hold of the bone, snatching it out of her body, apparently without any pain. A metallic tang attended its revelation, a smell of magic, which drew countless blends of darkness out of air.

"What's happening?" Maratien asked, her voice shaking, more with awe than with fear.

"I am calling together the nine parts of my beloved deathing ship, *The Stormwalker*, which was the labor of a hundred years and ten to build, all of it done in hiding."

"Why so long?"

"That will be plain, when you have sight of it," Mater Motley said. "Be patient, child. The pieces rise, even as we speak."

She spoke the truth. As soon as she had raised her summoning clavicle into the air, and her orders had gone forth, in nine places around the islands, all of them wastelands or wildernesses where nothing lived to know the secret that lay hidden in the earth there. Now the buried mysteries rolled over in their tombs of dirt and stone so that the ground cracked and gaped. Nine vast implacable forms, none smaller than a cathedral (and most much larger), slowly rose up into the air.

Two of the nine parts of *The Stormwalker* moved toward each other as they had been programmed to do before they were buried, their massive forms tumbling over as they converged, meticulously aligning themselves so as to fit perfectly with the other, the two becoming one. The new singularity formed the vast engine of the machine, the thunder of which rolled around the sky. There would be lightning to accompany it in time, spat from the underbelly of what would be, upon completion, a vessel three-quarters of a mile long—the Stormwalker Christopher Carrion had spoken of—so called because it would stride on legs of lightning.

Mater Motley called forth visions of the remaining seven parts resurrecting themselves, throwing off their blankets of earth and rising to greet the first morning of the Night. She felt the profoundest pleasure to witness the approach of the nine parts of *The Stormwalker.* Only she knew the genius that had brought the vessel into being. Only she knew that the forges in which its many metals had been melted together, in an alloy so black it made Midnight look like a blaze of Noon, had not been fired up in the Abarat, nor ever could have been. Only she knew that the minds that had aided her in its design and construction had been those of beings more remote from the islands than the stars. They were the Nephauree. *They* were from a place, or state of mind, called the Zael Maz'yre. It, and they, existed behind the stars.

But nobody in this little Empire of hers needed to know about any of that now. Just as the time had finally come for her to pluck forth her clavicle and summon up her deathing ship, so the time would come when she would let her true allegiances be known. The alien intelligences that lived beyond the mausoleums of the real had trusted her with their knowledge so that she might lay a road of blood out for them, where they could sit enthroned and dictate the nature of magic from here to the end of the world.

That, in essence, was the pact between them. The Nephauree provided the technical genius to design *The Stormwalker*, along with the armaments and war-machines. It was Nephaurite technology that would decide the outcome of the battle to preserve this darkness until it had done its dark work, and it would carry the day. With the islands under her thumb, the Empress would return the favor in kind. While she led the Abarat into an Age of Blood and Gold, the Nephauree would be preparing to draw down a curtain over all things beneath the stars. With their Empress, they had been so highly protected from all harm by their devices, they would be able to come and go from the islands with impunity.

Subjugated to their Empress's will, the people of the Abarat would not see the monstrous presences in their world. But, year on year, the work would be done: the land plundered and left fallow, the seeds sewn until the time of harvest was upon them. And with that harvest, the end of this foolish game of life. One last season of fecundity, and then Time no longer. Life no longer. And Death incarnate smiling in the silence.

46

TALKING OF MYSTERIES

CANDY HAD BEEN STARING out at the darkness, sky and sea for perhaps an hour, searching her thoughts for any sign, however small, of Boa's presence. She had found none. But that didn't mean she was cleansed of Boa's contagion. She *had* lived for almost sixteen years believing she was Candy Quackenbush and only Candy Quackenbush, never once realizing that she had another presence inside her head. How could she say with absolute certainty that this wasn't still true?

Of course she couldn't. That was the sickening truth. She couldn't know for sure that whatever thread of Boa had twitched into wakefulness when it had seemed Candy's life was over was not still lying in the coils of her mind.

And then, from the shore behind her, the sound of agitated voices rose up. What was happening? Something significant, that much was apparent. There was a sickening reverberation in the air and earth. She could feel the shake as it gusted against her face, and could hear the little pebbles at her feet rattling against one another.

Had she not been watching the twin darknesses of water and sky for so long she would not have seen what she saw next for her eyes would have been unable to distinguish one darkness from another. But they were far subtler instruments than they'd been at the beginning, and in the two darknesses, the one above and the other below, she saw to her distress a third order of darkness moving against the other two. Its silhouette was a puzzlement. What manner of creature was this?

A massive shape was moving across the sky, barely grazing the horizon. Even though its mass was entirely black, and offered no clue to its true structure, there was something about its slow, steady motion that told Candy it was gargantuan: the size of a city, at least. But this vast thing tumbled as it crossed the sky, presenting Candy with a subtly different silhouette as it did so. When she tried to imagine it, all her imagination could conjure up was something that resembled an immense geometrical puzzle. Its passage across her field of vision affected everything around her. The air reverberated. The pebbles rattled and became louder and faster. As for Mama Izabella, she lay smooth and glacial, every ripple and wave laying down in defiance to the passage of the immense traveler.

Behind her, Candy heard people asking the same questions she'd had in her head. Even though the mystery had passed from sight, people spoke in fearful whispers.

"What was it?"

"I heard no engines, nothing. A thing that size ought to make a noise."

"Well, it didn't."

"Then it's not Abaratian."

"And where was it going?"

It was Geneva who provided the answer to that.

"It was moving south-southwest," she said. "It's going to Gorgossium."

There was a surge of responses to this from the people in Geneva's vicinity. But there was one voice that was more audible to Candy than any of the others. It was the last voice she wanted to hear, but she wasn't all that surprised to be hearing it.

The Peachtree woman's right, Princess Boa said in Candy's head. *Whatever that was it's heading for Gorgossium.*

For a moment Candy contemplated the possibility of pretending she'd heard nothing, but what was the use of that? Boa knew she'd been heard. Ignoring her would be a waste of vital time.

I thought we'd parted, Candy allowed her mind to say.

You mean you thought you'd got rid of me, Boa replied. *You wanted me gone. Come on, don't say you didn't. You'd had me in your head all those years and you wanted me out.*

You're right. I did. And I still do.

Really? Isn't it just a little lonely in there? Come on. Of all people, you can own up to me. It's a lot lonelier in there than you thought it would be, isn't it?

I'm not going to invite you back in, if that's what you're after.

I asked you a question.

Yes, it's a little spacious in here, all right.

She felt Boa make a small smile of satisfaction.

Oh, you're never happier than when someone else is unhappy, are you?

Isn't everyone? They just don't admit to it.

What do you want?

Nothing. I was just checking in. I want to keep a connection between us. I might need your sisterhood one day.

I can't imagine that ever happening.

Who knows? We are each trapped in the blinding procession of linear time. There is no way to know what the future holds.

What about Finnegan?

What about him?

He's with you, isn't he?

What if he is?

Don't hurt him, Boa.

There was no reply to this.

Boa? Candy said.

Shall we change the subject?

He spent sixteen years avenging your murder.

Yes, so he's told me, more than once.

He loves you.

No, Candy. He loves somebody he thought *was me.*

Then let him go if you don't love him. Just don't hurt him.

What is this? Has the little witch-girl fallen in love with the son of night and day?

Not in the way you mean, no. I'm not in love with him. But

I won't see him hurt.

Empty threats, Candy. But don't worry. His heart's safe with me.

Yeah, I'm sure.

Moving on . . . You saw the thing in the sky, I presume.

Do you know what it is? Candy said.

During their conversation the huge dark form had moved all the way across the horizon, and was almost out of sight.

I can't be certain, but Carrion once told me something about a sky-ship, a Stormwalker. It walked on legs of lightning, he said, hence the name.

Yeah. He told me about it too. But I don't see any legs of lightning on that.

He did? Huh. Well, I think it's just a part of the ship. It was made in many pieces, all hidden around the Abarat. That way she could do what I think she's probably doing now—

Bringing all the pieces together . . .

So that her death-ship can walk the storm. I have no way of knowing for sure, but—

Suddenly, Candy glimpsed, for a moment only, Finnegan, through Boa's eyes. He did not look happy that he was finally reunited with his beloved. Far from it. His clothes were torn and bloodied, and his expression desolate. Though Candy saw him for no longer than a couple of heartbeats he looked up in that brief time, and even though there can't have been any visible sign of her presence in the secret chambers where he was Boa's guest or prisoner, it seemed that in that little time he looked at Candy. *Looked and saw.*

Finnegan . . . she thought, expecting that this tantalizing glimpse was most likely just another piece of Boa's manipulations.

And then Boa was gone, and the great room of Candy's head was hers again, and hers alone.

47

CONVERGENCE

"**S**HE WAS HERE, CANDY, wasn't she?"

Candy didn't turn to look back at Malingo. She just kept staring out at the darkness of sea and sky.

"How did you know?"

"Something about your body. It was different when you were together talking to her. And then I got used to seeing you as you. Just Candy."

"And when she came visiting . . ."

"I don't know what it was exactly. But it didn't seem to be a happy chat."

"I have to go to Huffaker, Malingo."

"Why? What's there?"

"That's where she's got Finnegan. And I don't think he's as happy in her company as he expected to be. Not remotely."

"How are we going to get there?"

"Not we, me."

"There is no *me*, Candy. There's only *we*."

"Oh, Lordy Lou . . ." she murmured, her voice close

to breaking. "What did you have to go and say that for?"

"Because it's true. You saved me from Wolfswinkel—"

"And now you're going to save me from the rest of the world?"

"If need be."

"Do you want to tell the others then?" Candy said. "I know they're all suspicious of me, and maybe they have good reason. You should tell them that what we saw out there was a part of a death-ship, a Stormwalker, Boa called it. Apparently it's two miles long."

"What? No. That can't be."

"Well we were just seeing a part of it, actually."

"And what is it?"

"Boa called it a death-ship."

"Oh, lovely."

"I don't know if anyone is interested in my opinion, but I suggest that the best thing everybody can do is just lay low. There are terrible things happening out there right now."

"I'm sure."

"But it won't last forever. We've got to remember that. The sacbrood are dead up there, or dying. And it's only a matter of time before they start to decay, and a rain of brood bodies will start falling."

"Well, that's something to look forward to," Malingo said dryly. "And then the stars will start showing through again."

"Oh yes. That will be welcome. But it's going to be a

grim, filthy mess, Malingo. Light or no light." She drew a deep breath. "I'm going to walk a little way along the beach. Make a glyph."

"I'll talk to the rest of the folks."

"Tell them I don't think Boa is going to cause any more problems, will you? She's gone, and I really don't think she'll be back."

"Famous last words."

"Well, I can hope, can't I?"

"That you can," Malingo replied. "That and not much else."

The pieces of *The Stormwalker* converged on Gorgossium like nine vast curses carved out of gleaming black destruction. They made the Izabella crazy as they converged on the island, churning her waters up until they were white and the shadowy air through which they passed was stirred up into an insanity of its own, its particles sticking against one another, causing trillions of tiny fires to ignite all around them.

Atop the Needle Tower Mater Motley turned her clavicle, the black, polished surface of which was an unmistakable echo of the nine pieces which had now come to a halt all around the island's perimeter. Like the air around the Needle, and the Needle itself, Maratien was shaking violently, out of sheer terror.

"What are you thinking, girl?" the Old Mother asked her.

"They're so huge . . . how do they stay in the sky?"

"It isn't Abaratian magic that made them," Mater Motley said. "*Or* that moves them. It is the technology of Those Who Walk Behind the Stars." She glanced down at Maratien. "Next time I go to them, you will come with me."

"To the other side of the stars?" Maratien murmured as though she was testing the words to see if they contained the truth.

"Watch now," the Old Mother said, raising the black clavicle higher than her head.

She uttered an instruction in a language that Maratien had never heard before. Something ignited in the marrow of the bone, and blazed from the hairline fissures, shards of flickering illumination that raced away in all directions. Time grew lazy, or so it seemed to Maratien. Her body lost its appetite for breath. The rhythm of her heart slowed to a funereal pace, from beneath the beat of which the noise of what might have been a thousand thousand thunders rose, one noise rolling into the next so that it became a single unbroken sound, its volume steadily climbing.

It was the sound of *The Stormwalker*'s energies she was hearing, she knew. There were lights coming in the nine parts of the ship: rows of tiny windows in one place, a vast sigil in another, as alien to Maratien's eye as the words she'd heard the Old Mother utter had been to her ears. There were other signs of how remote from anything familiar to her the device was. As the power of the engines climbed, and the lights within the parts multiplied and grew stronger, they shed their illumination in sections of the vast machines that had not been visible until now. What had looked like plain black surfaces from a distance now showed their true faces. They were etched with elaborate detail, black on black on black.

She had no idea what she was looking at; whether this was an external manifestation of *The Stormwalker*'s engines, or a vast manifesto of destruction, Maratien had no way of knowing. But her instinct told her that the Old Mother's claims to the origins of this massive creation were true. Maratien had been born into a family of sorcerers, and had been surrounded by books that chronicled the history of Abaratian magic from her infancy. But nowhere in the tens of thousands of pages, many illustrated or illuminated by artists of antiquity, had she ever seen anything that remotely resembled the monumental mysteries that were now assembled around Gorgossium. Though they had all halted without crossing the invisible boundary between sea and land, none of them were completely still, each in its own subtle fashion was preparing for the imminent convergence.

They did not need to wait long for the signal. Once again the marrow in the black bone caught fire, and again sheets of incandescence erupted from it, each striking one of the waiting pieces. The thunder of their energies suddenly rose a hundredfold. Then they proceeded to close in upon one another. As they did so, Mater Motley turned the black clavicle skyward, and a tenth sheet of brilliance escaped the marrow. Maratien followed its ascent, passing the incandescence and reaching its destination a second or two before the signal.

The Stormwalker didn't have nine pieces, it had ten.

The tenth lay against the top of the lightless sky, its very lean body resembling a spine along the length of which perhaps fifty pairs of multi-segmented legs were arranged, the limb on the left a perfect mirror of that on the right, the symmetric severity of their design touched now and then by tics and tremors. The bone's signal didn't cure the waiting spine of its agitations. In a matter of seconds, the tenth part went from being a vast stillness touched by flickers of lunacy to a mass of intricate shifts and unfolding that multiplied a hundredfold, then ten hundredfold.

"It sees me . . ." Maratien said very softly.

"Perhaps so," Mater Motley replied. "If it does, then it sees something insignificant. A fleck of living clay clinging to its Maker. Don't think—don't *ever* think you can understand it. You can't. You can't ever comprehend it, because you don't know the intelligences that made it."

The tenth part was now beginning its majestic descent from the top of the sky, and as it did the other parts picked up speed, still making adjustments in their positions so as to match more accurately the parts with which they were about to be knitted.

There was another sound behind the roaring of their many unknowable engines. There was a rising whine of power, which became sharper and harder as the pieces converged, and arcs of scarlet lightning leaped between the parts, and down from the descending tenth, to connect with the nine below: a spitting, blazing net of energies drawing them together.

Below them all, still raised high in Mater Motley's hand, was the beacon bone. The Old Mother kept her eyes turned skyward watching the convergence. But the moment that Maratien covered her ears and closed her eyes she knew.

"What are you doing, girl? I didn't bring you up here to have you whimper like a beaten child."

"It's too much."

"Too much? This?" She reached down, her fingers suddenly horrifically long, digging into the girl's hair and scalp. *"Open your eyes!"* she shrieked. "Or I'll have the lids off them, so you'll never close them again."

"No, please, Mother, please! I'm just afraid!"

"I said: OPEN YOUR EYES!"

"Please, I can't. Don't make me."

Mater Motley glanced down at the girl, with her face buried in the souls sewn to her gown. "Is that where you want to be, Maratien? You want to be wrapped up forever in a place you'll be safe?"

Maratien didn't open her eyes. She simply nodded and sobbed.

Mater Motley looked down at her with utter contempt on her face.

"You disappoint me, girl," the Old Mother said. "You bore and weary and disappoint me. But if that's what the child wants, who am I to deny her?"

"Thank you," Maratien said. "Thank you, thank you, thank you."

"Oh don't thank me too quickly, girl," the Old Mother said. "Wait a hundred years."

The fingers in Maratien's scalp dug farther still, plunging into her thoughts and memories, reaching down with her needle fingers in search of the part she would keep: the soul.

Too late, Maratien understood the significance of the Old Mother's words.

"No, Mother, please! No, I didn't mean. No, no, no—"

Her words dissolved into a single shriek as Mater Motley's fingers found her essence and closed around it. In desperation Maratien reached up and attempted to catch hold of the invading hand but before she could do so the will to act was taken from her in that same instance as her soul.

Out of the girl's head the Old Mother drew the girl's last light, delivering it into one of the countless rag dolls that were sewn to her gown, still awaiting a soul.

Mater Motley returned her gaze to the glories of the convergence that blazed above, allowing her hand to linger in Maratien's head only long enough to raise the puppet corpse to its feet, then let it go. Gravity did the rest. The body toppled backward, and dropped off the point of the Needle Tower.

Just as the ten parts of *The Stormwalker* touched and fused, Maratien's body met the ground. There it broke open, its pungent scent alerting scavengers from every direction to come partake of the feast while it was still warm.

48

SMILES

"WHERE ARE YOU GOING?" Gazza asked. He had appeared over the top of the sand dune behind which Candy was summoning up a glyph big enough for two.

"You're not supposed to be here," she told him. "I'm not even supposed to be looking at you."

"Well, I am and you are."

"Yes, so I see."

"So where are you going? I know what you're doing. I may be just a fisherman but I'm not stupid."

"I didn't say you were."

"You're making a glyph. You're flying away somewhere, leaving me—"

"I'm not leaving you. I'm going to find Finnegan."

"Oh, good. So I can come?"

"No. I didn't say—"

"You just said you weren't leaving me."

"Where's Malingo?"

"All right, if you have to go, at least show me how to make a glyph for myself so I can follow you. I will. I can do anything if I want something badly enough."

"I'm sure you could."

"And I want to be wherever you are."

"Gaz . . ."

"Is that wrong?"

"No. It's not wrong. It's just a bad time, that's all."

"You showed Malingo. He told me. *So show me!*"

"No!"

He ran down the slope of the dune at a rush, his pie-bald features bright with fury in the light off the solidifying glyph.

"You think I'm like all the rest, don't you?"

"I don't want you to get bent out of shape, but we don't have time for this, Gaz."

She turned her back on his stare.

"I'm not," he said.

Candy stared hard at the ground, trying to remember where in the glyph summons she'd been. She was tired, and her fatigue was starting to affect her ability to get things done.

"Not what?"

"I'm not like all the others," he said. He came around to the other side of the glyph so that she couldn't continue to avoid engaging his stare. "I'm not waiting for the miraculous Candy Q to come up with all the answers—"

"Well, that's good because I haven't got any! Sometimes

I think I don't have anything except . . . except . . . except . . . you're not to blame." Candy looked up at him through the skeletal form of the glyph, its lines solidifying in the air.

"You look like you hate me right now," he said.

"No," Candy said. "Not hate. Just . . . why now?"

"Why now what?"

"You know why."

"Do I?"

"Stop it."

"Say it."

"Say what?"

"What you feel. What we feel."

"So I'm not just imagining it?"

"Oh, Lordy Lou," he said, throwing up his arms. She couldn't tell who he was angry at. Or whether he was even angry. "*No*. You're not imagining it."

"So do you . . . ?" she asked.

"Well . . ." he said.

"*Because I do.*"

"Ha!"

Such relief flooded his face. He grinned the grin of all grins.

"You should see the grin on your face," he said to her.

"*My* face? What about on yours?"

The glyph finished itself while they were standing there, exchanging their grins. She sensed its stillness. So did he.

"Your magic's done," he said.

"I know."

"You want me to go find Malingo?"

"In a minute."

"We don't have much—"

"Half a minute?"

"No. A minute's good."

Before they'd been mortal enemies, Candy and Deborah Hackbarth had been friends. And two summers before, when on the first day back at school after summer vacation they walked home together, exchanging tales of summer, Deborah had one big story to tell. His name was Wayne Something or other and she'd met him in Florida, where she'd gone to visit her grandmother. Wayne was the *One*, Deborah had said; she knew so because it felt right when she said it, which she had, over and over, during that long walk home, and Candy, knowing that it was only a matter of time before the conversation would falter for a moment, and her best friend would sew the seeds of their enmity with the oh-so-casual: "And what about your summer, Candy?"

How times had changed! Perhaps the street had sur-vived the flooding of Chickentown by the Sea of Izabella and even now there were two girls sharing secrets as they wandered home from school, but Candy would never know. Not because Mater Motley's all-devouring dark-ness would devour her, though that was possible. But because she didn't care. She didn't want to go back there.

She could live and die here, under these troubled heavens, perhaps even staring at the troubled face on the other side of the glyph.

Then came the first shot. A missile was fired out of the west by a weapon of such power that the projectile it launched toward the shore punched its way through Hour after Hour before striking its target. The trail of fire it left on the air was still decaying when a second projectile was fired, this one aimed much lower than the first, barely clearing the shore as it screeched overhead.

When it landed, the force of the explosion was powerful enough to knock Candy to the ground. She got to her feet, gasping for breath, and raced up the dune. To her relief she saw that Malingo, along with the rest of the refugees, had sought shelter among the rocks.

She cupped her hands around her mouth and called to him.

"Malingo!"

There was no answer from the landscape, which was illuminated afresh when a third volley came shrieking through, this one so low it clipped the hill that rose beyond the shore, sending up a plume of debris.

"I have to go, Malingo!" Candy screamed. "Be safe!"

When she turned back to the glyph, Gazza was already inside.

"We're going together," he said.

She had neither the time, nor in truth the will, to argue

with him. They needed to be gone. Now. As she leaped into the glyph, the small, sleek gunship that had fired upon them appeared from the sea-mist that had, until now, veiled the sandy shore upon which they stood.

Behind it, Candy saw a vessel at least thirty times as big; its watchtowers and uniformed guards assuring its function. It was a prison ship, coming for them all. Candy willed the glyph into motion, but as it rose into the air, a fourth volley came suddenly from the west. It struck its target, and everything went dark.

49

OF THOSE WHO WALK
BEHIND THE STARS

THOUGH THE OLD MOTHER had not known when she would have need of *The Stormwalker*, nor precisely to what purpose it would need to be put to when that time came, she had laid meticulous plans for how things were to proceed. It was crewed by three hundred and fifty stitchlings, and another four thousand were in the belly of the ship: massive legions of warriors, ready and waiting to go. They weren't simple mindless cannon fodder. Far from it. They had been created to make war with the utmost ferocity and intelligence; war so terrible that once made would never be allowed to happen again, because the memory of its horrors would be so grim.

In addition, she had on board one member of that species who walked behind the stars. Its name was ninety-one syllables long, but it answered to Nephauree. The physical form it presented to her was an illusion: a thin wavering line of smoke-shadow, standing three times her height. Of its true form, she knew nothing. Once she'd made the error of demanding that she see it as it actually was, and the experience had almost made her ready to stab out her own eyes. The experience had been so traumatizing, she remembered nothing of what she'd seen, but she knew what lay just a few vibrations of vision beyond the smoke-shadow was a thing so vile, so repugnant, so utterly without beauty or virtue, that no mind could witness it and remain sane. It was an engine of venoms and despair.

The Old Mother was quite happy with this. She had no use for mercy or tenderness. She had given herself to the service of darkness and despair the day she had set fire to the mansion containing her entire family, murdering all those within, except for her baby, Christopher, whom she had raised after her own unholy fashion, educating him in all the joyless wisdom of her rotted heart.

But the teachings had failed. He'd fallen for Boa like a witless adolescent, giving her some of the most potent workings in Abaratian magic as tokens of his undying affections. Had Mater Motley not been more powerful she would have taken this betrayal of her trust more heavily. But Those Who Walk Behind the Stars had given her access to power that made Abaratian magic seem inconsequential. A power as old as Death itself was their muse. And what better proof of how inspiring this power was than the vessel in which the Old Mother presently traveled. *The Stormwalker* was full of the Nephauree's genius for death dealing. One such creation was a vast display of the archipelago, which floated on the air before her, with the internal systems and structures of each Hour all rendered visible, so that, should it be her will to destroy an island completely, the maps knew of their frailties and would know exactly where to direct the missiles.

She studied it now, a thirty-foot-long tapestry, which looked as though it had been painted on fog with pastel luminosity. The things that were darkness were only a piece of the knowledge the tapestry provided. It also showed her what emotions were rife in the Hours. A simple map might have shown her the shape of an island, but *never* the feelings of those who lived there. This schematic showed the glad news that the islands were drowning in panic and terror. Fiends held sway over the ruins of what had once been places of calm and delight.

There were monsters in Babilonium now, walking the boardwalks. And the Legendary City of a Thousand Fiends, a creature that stood half a mile high, and was home—as its name implied—to ten hundred fiends, had been seen moving in the unpopulated wastes of the Island of the Black Egg. Meanwhile, in the southwest, The Great Head was no more than rubble, destroyed by some monstrous being summoned from the deeps of the Izabella. The Council who had once met in its towers, and written the entire laws of the islands and kept the peace, were now drowned or crushed in the rubble.

All the while, Mater Motley's Arrest Squads continued to collect up anyone who was on the list of those whose names (and there were thousands) appeared on the List of the Empress's Enemies. They continued to be shipped to the camp behind Mount Galigali, where the other device that the Nephauree had devised for her was being constructed: the Great Eraser of Souls, which was designed to put an end to every individual who had ever raised their voices against her, or that her prophetic seamstresses warned her would do so in the future.

There remained only two thorns in her side, both of which she and her legions, supported by the fury of *The Stormwalker*, would deal with. One was the garish nonsenses of Commexo City, where the Kid ran riot. The other was the Twenty-Fifth Hour.

She would leave the Time Out of Time until the last.

"To Commexo City then," she murmured.

The Stormwalker heard her instruction. Walking on legs of lightning, scorching the earth black when it set one of its limbs upon an Hour, or boiling the waters of the Izabella to steam when it set one of its feet upon the sea, it turned its immensity toward Pyon, where Commexo City shone defiantly in the murk of Midnight.

50

OUT OF THE DEEP

"**M**R. PIXLER! MR. PIXLER!"

Voorzangler knocked on the door of Rojo Pixler's suite of rooms cautiously at first, then with his fist rather than his knuckles.

"*Please,* Mr. Pixler. *This is an emergency!*"

From within, Voorzangler heard what sounded like the motion of something heavy moving over the polished marble floor. Finally, emerging from this strange sound came the voice of Voorzangler's beloved genius, the creator of the original Commexo Kid, Rojo Pixler.

"I am well aware of the situation out on the streets, Voorzangler. I have legions of Kid Kops out there, doing their courageous best. But somehow I think a more *primal* touch is required—"

"There's a huge vessel—it's a mile long, I swear—"

"*The Stormwalker?* Yes. I can see it on the screens in here."

"It's Mater Motley, Mr. Pixler. She is calling herself

the Empress of All the Islands."

Voorzangler heard the sound of live reports from the streets of Commexo City, which the great architect was presumably viewing. Pixler had built the city from the wealth the Commexo Kid had brought it. It was the work of a true visionary to have made a city of everlasting light at an Hour where the darkness was very deep. The city stood at Three in the Morning. But nobody who lived in its bright streets feared the night. Until now.

"You don't care that this woman has a vessel capable of destroying the city—"

"She wouldn't."

"She's perfectly capable of killing everything you—"

"And the Kid."

"Yes."

"Don't forget the Kid."

"But before the Kid was *you*, Mr. Pixler. You are the creator."

"Am I . . . ?"

"Yes . . ." Voorzangler said, his voice a little less certain now, ". . . of course you are. Without you . . . There's nothing."

"The Kid?"

"*Sir*. You came before the Kid. The father must come before the son."

"Yes . . ."

"So the city, sir."

"Yes, the city . . ." He seemed to remember the words

he'd once believed above all things.

"Commexo City belongs to the Spirit of the Kid and always will."

"Good," Voorzangler said, relieved that the genius he worked for had not lost his grip on the order of things. "So what do we do about the . . . Stormwalker, sir? It hangs above us with all its firepower directed at the city. You don't want any harm to the Spirit of the Kid, surely."

"Absolutely not. This city must stand as a testament to the dreams of the Commexo Kid."

"Good, Mr. Pixler. So . . . What should I do?"

"What would you advise?"

"Me?"

"Yes, Doctor. What would you advise for the health of the Kid's city?"

"I don't think we have any choice, sir. We are either destroyed or we surrender."

"Do you think if I were to surrender to this Empress person she might come for me here?"

"I'm sorry, sir. What are you saying?"

"I'm saying that if she wants total supremacy, then it would be quite a coup for her, would it not? My priceless body in return for the safety of the city."

"Is that what you want to offer her, sir?"

"*I accept,*" Mater Motley said.

"Is that her?" Pixler asked, sounding quite puzzled.

"Yes, sir," said Voorzangler. "It is."

"How did she get onto our secure line?"

"She's not on the line, sir. She's here. With me."

"What?"

"I'm sorry, sir, I had no choice."

"Why didn't you tell me?"

"She forbade me, sir."

"And like the sensible coward he is," the Old Mother said, "he preferred to keep his one good eye rather than tell you the truth."

"I don't blame him," Pixler said. "No doubt he thought his little life was all he had. So losing it meant more to him than it would have if he'd known the truth."

"What are you babbling about, Pixler?" Mater Motley demanded.

"Once we witness the great certainties of the High Worlds and the Deep Worlds, once we know darkness absolute and breathe the truth of light, everything else— like life—seems inconsequential."

"You make no sense."

"Do I not? Well, the fault is surely mine, lady. I'm afraid I'm sick. Some strange contagion I picked up on my descent into the waters of the Izabella."

"You're not going to frighten me off with stories of deep-water plagues, Pixler. I fear nothing and no one."

"Oh, Empress, that's extraordinary! *To have no fear.* I want to look in your eyes and see that for myself. Voor-zangler?"

"Sir?"

"Will you escort the Empress into the library?"

"Of course, sir."

"I will be with you in just a moment, Empress."

The line was broken and went to black noise.

"He's no longer in contact," Voorzangler said. "He's never done that before. He's always been listening."

"Apparently not today, Doctor. Or he would have realized I was here with you. So take me to him."

"I can only go as far as the door. I've never entered the sanctum. It's his private world."

"Well, today you will accompany me, Voorzangler. I am your Empress. Serve me, and I will always be with you."

"Then of course I must obey you."

Voorzangler proceeded to make his way through the poorly lit rooms. The only consistent illumination was from the hooded lamps above the paintings that lined the walls.

"Pixler has very eclectic taste, Voorzangler."

"The paintings?"

Mater Motley paused to look at one of them: a very brightly colored canvas, depicting a simple white cottage, some trees, a small shed and a single star.

"Voorzangler?"

"Yes?"

"What is this atrocity?"

"I believe it's called *The Morning of Christ's Nativity*."

"Decadence. Look at it, showing off its colors. It sickens me."

"I'll have it removed."

"No need," Mater Motley said.

She raised her hand and the canvas was consumed by an invisible flame, the bright color blackening and blistering until every last fleck of color had been consumed, leaving the antique gilded frame to enclose a view of almost any part of Abarat at that moment.

Just a few paces farther on was another picture, its style and subject as agitated and violent as the first image had been calm and peaceful. It appeared to be a body hung on a grid of barbed wire, but the details were hard to decipher. Again the cremating hand was raised, and Voorzangler flinched. But Mater Motley simply pointed.

"Now that," she said, "I like." She looked at Voorzangler. "All right. I've had my fill of art."

She didn't linger in front of any other painting, but followed Voorzangler to the large room at the end of the passageway.

"You seem to have a problem with your drains, Pixler," she said as she stepped into the room.

"And with the lights . . ." Pixler replied from somewhere in the darkness. "Everything in here has failed, I'm afraid. Your . . . your . . . forces . . . Empress . . . have . . . taken . . . their . . . toll. My perfect city is no longer perfect."

"Forget about your city. It's you I need to see. Are there no lights in here *at all*?" There was an edge in her voice, more than a touch of suspicion. "Surely the chamber has a window, Doctor? The light from the burning city would—"

"Light . . ." Pixler replied, "would not . . . show you . . . anything your eyes would want to see."

"You would forbid me?"

"No. Of course nnnnot. How could I? You are the Empressssss."

"Then what's going on in here? I demand to know."

"If that is what the Empresssss wishes . . ."

"It is."

"Then . . . sssseeeee."

And suddenly there was light in the chamber, though it didn't emanate from a lamp. It was Rojo Pixler, himself, who was the source of this frigid light, though his human anatomy was merely the frail centerpiece of a living form that had taken over the entire chamber, an intricate filigree of lacy tissue that covered the walls and hung in lazy decay from the ceiling. A foul stench was in these layers of rotting tissue, which here and there clotted, forming sluggish creatures that were attached by pulsing cords of matter to the body of Pixler himself.

Mater Motley seized hold of Voorzangler, her fingers digging so deep into his body that he cried out in pain.

"A crude trap, Doctor."

"I had no knowledge of this, Empress," Voorzangler said.

"She . . . is no *Empress*," Pixler replied, his corrupted voice thick with contempt.

He rose up now, although there was little sign that it was the work of Pixler's limbs that allowed him to do so. It was the creature within whose body he was enmeshed that drew him into a standing position.

"I . . . ammmmm . . . a part of something greater now," Pixler said. "And I do not . . . ffffearr your DARK-NESS, witch." The light in the lace body flickered. "I . . . have passed eons in a deeperrrr darknesssss than your gray Midnight."

Again, the light flickered. But it didn't plunge the room into darkness. Instead it revealed, like a corrupted X-ray, the single vast anatomy of man and monster, exposing with appalling clarity how Pixler's bones were interwoven with the stinking substance of his possessor. Rojo Pixler, the great architect himself, had become a piece of a piece of something that existed in all its unknowable immensity somewhere in the depths of the Sea of Izabella.

He rose up off the floor, lifted up on fans of fluttering tissue that shimmered as they worked. Rows of wet-rimmed valves twitched and spat; soft spines swelled into clusters of vicious barbs, surges of power passed through translucent ducts from one body to the next, noisily spilling Requiatic liquids onto the marble floor when they brimmed over.

"A *Requiax*," Mater Motley said, her lip curling with contempt. "No wonder it stinks like a shore at high tide in here."

"And . . . what is *your* stench, Hag?" the Pixler-Requiax said. By now Pixler's body was ten feet off the ground, lit from below by the flashes of cold luminescence that spilled through the layers of tissue scattered everywhere.

"Tell your master to leash his tongue, Voorzangler, or else I will reach into that foul mouth of his and tear it out by the root."

Voorzangler attempted to form some response to this, but she was killing him with her grip, and he was losing control of his body. His tongue could only flop about in his mouth, unable to shape a single coherent word. His whole anatomy had been drained of life force, and was now so weak that if the Empress hadn't had her fingers buried deep in his shoulder he would have dropped to the ground and died where he fell.

But she held on to him, shaking him like a little one-eyed doll.

"*Tell him, idiot!*" All Voorzangler could do was shake his head in terrorized despair. "You thought to lure me into a trap, didn't you? With this . . . *fish*."

Again, Voorzangler shook his head, his control over his body seeming to become weaker with every passing moment.

"What do you want, fish?" the Old Mother said. "Are you hanging up there to terrorize me? Because you haven't a hope of doing so! Whatever you assume you have made yourself, you are nothing, fish. Bow down! *Do you hear me? Bow down before the Empress of the Abarat!*"

As she spoke she let her free hand drop to her side, presenting her open palm to the floor. This simple gesture caused her to rise up into the air, dragging Dr. Voorzangler, his body now in the grip of something very close to a full seizure, with her.

Others had entered the room now, and were witnessing these grotesqueries: Voorzangler's assistants from the Circular Room had followed him in, as had several seamstresses, but nobody made any attempt to intervene. This was a pitting of Higher Powers; everyone watching knew that. Anyone who attempted to interfere now would only earn themselves a quick death. So they all stayed close to the door in case things took a turn for the apocalyptic. And from there they bore witness.

"Bow down!" Mater Motley said again as she rose. "With your face to the ground."

There was no response from the Pixler-Requiax, at least at first. Then, very slowly, the creature began to shake its head. The weight of the great architect's brain distorted the soft bone as it swung back and forth, his mouth lolling open, allowing a stream of fluid that resembled molasses to pour forth. Its issue caused the stink in the chamber to become far, far worse: so vile and overpowering that three members of Voorzangler's staff turned and fled, puking, back into the passageway.

But Mater Motley had seen and smelled far worse. She was untouched by this whole performance. She was standing on the air at the same height as the architect now and raising her hand, presenting her palm to the enemy.

"You have one last chance to bend to me. And then I will make you do so, even if I have to break every bone in you to do it. Choose, fish. *Bow or be broken.*"

The shaking of the head slowed, and then ceased. Pixler raised his own hand to wipe from around his mouth the last of the noisome fluid. When the thing spoke again the corruption of its speech was over. The Requiax spoke now with a clear intention to sound as though Pixler had regained control, enunciating each word with almost absurd precision.

"You would find it hard to break bones that are so soft—" the thing began. As it spoke, the thing lifted its arms above its head, seizing the wrist of his left with its right, and twisting it around as though the bones were made of rubber. "—I can let the currents carry me and never break."

"So go back to your currents, fish."

"I am no *fish*, woman," the creature said. *"I AM REQUIAX!"*

51

FATHER AND SON

EVEN BEFORE THE FINAL syllable was out of the creature's mouth it flung itself at Mater Motley. She had anticipated that it would do exactly that, because as it reached for her, something that resembled a fan, decorated in purple and gold, snapped open in front of her. She blew on it: the lightest of breaths, motes of purple and silver clouded the air around the Pixler-Requiax's head.

Innocent though the weapon she had just called into service might have appeared, the innocence was a lie. It was that most guilty of things—a weapon possessed of the power to lay death down wherever its dart went. The purple and golden motes broke against Pixler-Requiax's face like tiny sparks. As he threw back his pierced visage, finely knotted cords of dark matter flew up out of the many wounds and rose to strike the ceiling. Cobs of plaster came showering down, like brute snow. But their descent merely presaged a far more bizarre descent. The knots of dark matter burst like overripe fruit. Out of their split skins came a rain of the Requiax's base matter; the raw sea muck from which its elaborate filigree was made. As soon as it fell on Mater Motley, it began to spread like a vine, insane with its own fecundity, coursing over her body in all directions; dozens of trails of the nameless stuff raced down her body, crisscrossing to form a foul-smelling net around her.

But it was her face that the Pixler-Requiax was most concerned to control, its matter wrapping itself around her skull from five or six directions at once.

"Idiot fish!" she said. "I've told you already. Why don't you pay attention?"

She reached up and caught hold of the spreading networks of muck that had already overtaken two-thirds of her face. Her merest touch leached the color from the chaotic network of matter. Then she tore it, ripping it away from her face. There was more of the matter to replace it, of course, and the wrapping and tearing, wrapping and tearing struggle might have continued for a lot longer had a thin, shrill voice, that of a young boy, not said:

"Pops?"

Somewhere in the midst of the Requiax, the remains of Rojo Pixler woke from his nightmare of possession and saw—much to his horror—the only thing he had ever loved, the Kid, *his* Kid, at the threshold.

"Not now, son!" he yelled.

"What's happening?"

"Nothing you need to know about. Now turn around and run!"

"Now what kind of cowardly lesson is that teaching the child?" Mater Motley said. She casually dropped Voorzangler, whose body was now inert, and reached out to the Kid. "Come here, Kid. I mean you no harm. Are you the last one standing?"

"No. *I'm the First.* The Original. *The Kid of Kids.*"

Pixler moaned to hear his own child condemning himself, but it was too late, the words were said.

"Oh, I think I need you in the Imperial Court, boy."

"I can't leave here, sorry. I gotta stay with Pops."

"I'm afraid your poor father is lost forever."

The copyrighted smile vanished from the Commexo Kid's face.

"No," he said softly. "My pops will live forever."

"No. He won't. Because your father has been taken over by something that found him in the deep trenches of the Izabella."

"Don't listen to it," the Pixler-Requiax said. "She's a liar. Always was. Always will be."

Mater Motley raised her now-empty hand, proffering it to the boy.

"Come here," she said, her voice all velvet and honey.

Her hands told a different story. The arm that reached for the Commexo Kid was becoming unnaturally long in its ambition to claim the child, its fingers also lengthening, their shadowy lengths sharpening into black points.

"Run, boy!"

"Pops! Help me!"

"Just *go*!"

The Kid started to race for the door. But Mater Motley's hand snatched at his hair, her fingers growing longer, joints multiplying. The Kid lost his balance and fell backward, allowing the Empress to drag him back toward her as he shrieked for his father's intervention.

"Stop her, Pops. She's stealing me! POPS!"

It wasn't his pops who replied, however. Or rather, it wasn't *simply* his pops. It was the hybrid creature made of Rojo Pixler and the Requiax. And it wasn't the Kid they spoke to. It was the woman.

"First you murder poor, stupid Voorzangler, who never did you the least harm. And now you go after my *firstborn*?"

The whole chamber shook, and the fractured marble on the floor split wider. Water started to pour up through it, its sharp, clean smell unmistakable. It was seawater that was bubbling up into Pixler's stinking chamber, and it was coming up with such force that it threw over several more slabs of marble.

None of this distracted the Empress from her intentions. Her long-fingered hand closed over his face from which his trademark grin had vanished, and he screamed into her smothering palm.

"Don't leave me with the bad woman, Pops!"

For those who had ventured over the threshold to watch this confrontation unfold, there was no choice now but to retreat and slam the door. It was either that or drown. The seawater was rising very rapidly in the chamber, the space itself repeatedly being battered furiously by the frenzied waters. The enemies fought with powers that invented some new crazed manifestation with every passing moment. Pieces of the bleached, dead matter fell away from Mater Motley's face like shreds of a papier-mâché mask, while new, mutated forms of the Requiax's matter rose up behind the Empress's head like a black wave curling and curling, preparing to break.

She was too interested in drawing the Kid toward her to even notice. Or perhaps she did notice and, in her supreme arrogance, was simply indifferent to the threat that the riding wave presented. Either way, she had her eyes and her attention fixed upon the Kid. Her arm, impossibly elongated, resembled a long, leafless branch more than a limb of flesh and blood. But there were no diminutions in its strength. With her hand still covering his face she lifted the Kid up, his thin legs with their cartoony shoes dragging through the seawater that was continuing to flood the room, the water rolling up against the walls, taking down the pictures that had hung there.

The waters were merciless with them, as they were with everything else that the room contained: the antique furniture, smashed to tinder; the walls themselves cracking as all that the room contained was caught up in the spiral of foaming waters.

The Kid had been pulled clear of the chaos, but Mater Motley knew that while she held the child—who was still shrieking for his father's help behind her hand—the Pixler-Requiax could not act hastily against her. One slip, and Pixler's firstborn went into the vortex. However tough Pixler's manufacturing methods had made his child, once he was caught in the battering waters he would not long survive.

"*Accept me,*" she said. "*Or the firstborn slips out of my hand.*"

She raised her forefinger from the head of the child, leaving him held by only three spiked fingers and her thumb.

The Kid knew his life hung in the balance.

"*Please don't let her hurt me! Pops! Don't! Let! Her—*"

"He's just a child," Pixler said.

"He's no child!" Mater Motley replied. "He's painted plastic, or whatever you make these toys from."

"He's *not* a toy. He has a fully functioning brain. He's able to feel love. And *fear.*"

"Oh, you mean these screams are the real thing?"

She lifted her middle finger from the Kid's face.

"Don't struggle, Kid," Pixler said. "Just be very still. Please, my boy. Very, very—"

Before he could again say *still*, something burst from the tumultuous waters beneath the Kid. Another portion of the Requiax, formed from its matter in the likeness of a vast double-thumbed hand, rose up out of the water and seized hold of Pixler's firstborn. The Kid's shriek became so shrill now that no child born from a womb could possibly have made the sound. This was indeed the shrill shriek of a machine.

The sound momentarily was so sharp and sudden that it made the Empress lose her grip. The Requiax's double-thumbed hand closed around the boy and quickly carried him away, still holding him up above the tumultuous waters.

"Open that door!" Pixler yelled, his voice—in its sudden, absolute clarity—unmistakably that of a man used to being obeyed.

And obeyed he was. The doors were opened instantly, the presence of the water in the room quickly subsided. The violent rush threw just about all those who'd been watching the confrontation off their feet, carrying them out into the passageway. There was still enough force in the water to give it the power to sweep the *Crucifixion* and Mater Motley's "Midnight Nativity" off the walls, dumping them in the same scummy soup in which the witnesses were being thrown around.

From every direction came the din of terror and destruction, as the invading waters of the Izabella carried Voorzangler's staff into the passageway, mercilessly tossing them about. The weakest of Mater Motley's stitchlings were simply torn apart by the force of the currents, the rest carried away. The dead doctor's staff shrieked and begged for mercy, but the waters granted no reprieves.

"Such noise!" Mater Motley complained with the offended airs of some highborn woman who'd never heard the din of suffering in her life. *"Enough of this! Enough!"* She

threw a glance at the doors. "Shut up, both of you!"

The doors did as they were told. It was something of a struggle, but they pulled themselves shut against the power of the departing waters. Then, without further instruction, the forces the Empress had unleashed in the room set about melting the lock, which sent up a column of sulfurous smoke. The job was quickly done. The lock was melted, leaving the chamber sealed shut.

The Empress took a moment to compose herself. Then she said: "Let's finish this business once and for all."

52

ATROCITIES

IF A STRANGER HAD wandered into the battle-scarred streets of Commexo City at about that time, they would surely not have been blamed for thinking they had taken a wrong turn somewhere, and found themselves in the clutches of a nightmare. Even though there were fires consuming many of the fine, fancy houses along the brightly lit boulevards, nobody was attempting to extinguish them. There were bodies sprawled on the streets and sidewalks, some apparently the citizens of this noble city, unarmed and dressed for anything but sudden death, killed by shrapnel or bullets and left to lie where they'd fallen.

There were sights even more terrible, that this wandering stranger would have found it difficult not to see, given how numerous such horrors were. And though they might have tried to look away, the scene and the tragic story it left half-told would be imprinted on their memory forever, so that even at life's end, when they no longer knew their children from a tree, they would remember being in Commexo City with the death-ship filling the sky, and the buzzing of the innumerable flies.

Inside the Commexo Building, there was another scene, just as profound. The drowned lay where the draining waters had left them. The Empress's seamstress attendants waited in the room, idly watching events unfold across the Abarat. The seamstresses were scarcely strangers to things fearful and abhorrent. They had been chosen by the Old Mother to accompany her into Commexo City because they had each in the course of their lives proved as unrepentantly vicious and enthusiastically cruel as she. Or at least very nearly so. But even they, who knew the bellies and bowels of the monstrous as well as heart and head, stood in mute awe and astonishment, seeing what atrocious glories their Empress's Midnight had called up out of hiding.

Some of these scenes the seamstresses knew; they were the stuff of nursery horrors. Queen Inflixia Grueskin was one such: she was the monstrous Queen of Efreet according to legend, who tended her blood garden where for centuries she'd attempted to grow the missing anatomy to fill the empty cage of her body. She was a terror to frighten children no longer. She was real. There she was, up on one of the screens, in all her ghastly splendor.

On another screen, a tree called the Brakzee, which was by reputation the oldest in the archipelago, had become a gallows from which hundreds of ordinary people had been hanged. This was not the work of some vile demonic force. The executioners had been, until the disappearance of the moon and stars, the neighbors of those they'd hanged.

Nor was the incident at the Brakzee tree an isolated case. All across the islands fear caused ordinary people to do monstrous things. One of the seamstresses, going from screen to screen to screen, thinking each time she'd found the worst horror, but then discovering something still more atrocious said: "This is the End of Everything."

It was Mater Motley who set her right.

"This is the end of *their* world. The purposeless ones who wanted only to live their lives. Their time is over. Midnight has begun. And out of their hiding places now come the Heirs of the Lightless Hour. See! They come to inherit this broken, bloody world and rule in my name."

On screen after screen, beings that the women had never seen before appeared from their sanctuaries: monstrous creatures that had never appeared in any bestiary of the Hours, nor ever would. Now they had a world to rule by the laws of chaos. A slothful slug lay upon a slimy rock with a raw tongue-tail and hooks for hands; a two-legged beast with a quadruped beside it, walked through a place on Obadiah where a deluge of fire rain was falling; two human-headed birds sat on a dead branch, debating the weather—

Suddenly, from out of the sealed Chamber, the Empress's command—

"To me! Women!"

A beat, then—

"NOW!"

The seamstresses had kept up a fine illusion of indifference for the benefit of Pixler's storm troopers but they had been ready for this moment.

Now eight of them, acting as though governed by one mind, returned through the littered passageway, throwing their collective will at the sealed doors. The hardened sealant on the inside cracked, and the doors were flung wide, pushed from behind by the weight of the water. The women were ready for its fall. They threw up a quilt of invisible patches around them, sewn together by their own hands. It was only woven fabric, like any other, but such lattices have strength in their pattern out of all proportion to the mild stuff from which they are woven. The doors smashed against the quilt and broke.

The seamstresses entered the chamber and saw what the exchange between their Empress and the Pixler-Requiax had come to. The combatants were still high above the ragged hole in the floor through which the waters of the Izabella continued to surge up, their ambition unquelled. The Empress was elevated by a pillar of seething darkness, while the frail form of Rojo Pixler was borne up by the fronds of the Requiax's continuously regenerating anatomy, which drew up with it countless lengths of woven water. Each carried, within its length, a cord of the Requiax's matter, through which the desires of its mind were communicated. The mind had one desire above all others: to see the monstrous woman standing in darkness before it dead. She was the enemy—not the greatest of them, to be sure. Other evil, vaster than her by orders of magnitude, was using her to gain a stronghold here in Time. That would not happen! She had to be brought down. The glittering cords of the Pixler-Requiax went about their labors, wrapping themselves around the pedestal of shadows on which she stood, and then rising through the soul-laden folds of her garment, forming a net of knotted sea around her.

"Get! It! Off! Me!" the Empress shrieked, appalled by this violation.

She couldn't get the rest of the words out. The water ropes had climbed her torso, and there was a noose of water around her neck. It tightened.

"No!" she said, and raised the hand she'd used to seize hold of Voorzangler, its fingers sharp and dark. Only this time it was onto her own flesh that she turned her piercing fingertips, sliding them down between her throat and the noose. She pulled the water rope off her gullet, far enough at least that she could get two words out.

"Free . . . . . . me . . . . . . "

The seamstresses were already raising their hands and speaking in old Abaratian the Eight Names of the Creatrix, which would summon to them the means to liberate their Empress.

"Giathakat."

"Juth and Junntak."

"Kiezazaflit."

"Enothu and Eyjo."

"Yeagothonine."

"Yuut."

"Yuut."

"Yuut."

Even before all eight had been spoken, motes of fire ignited in their hands, forming vicious instruments, far more effective at cutting than any knife. They exchanged no words. They knew their business. They came at the column of darkness on which their lady stood and cut at the silver-green waters of Pixler and the Requiax. The tools that had been the gift of the Creatrix were as efficient as they were strange. They lacerated the waters, like assassins in a world of throats. Back and forth! Up and down! The cords of water, severed, fell back into the churning flood that had produced them.

Pixler-Requiax roared his disapproval.

"You should have stayed out of this battle, women," he roared. "It's going to be the death of you."

The water was still pouring up out of the ground, weaving replacement ropes as it did so. They rose up suddenly—only two of them, but many times thicker than the cords that had climbed the column. They weren't interested in disarming the women. It was the seamstresses themselves these two ropes of water were eager to claim.

The ropes did not linger to choose which women to

take; they simply took, snatching two of the seamstresses from their cutting and summarily drowning them. The remaining seamstresses were too busy at their cutting to even notice that two of their number had gone. But the Empress did.

"Sisters! Take care!" she called to them. The meaning of her words was lost in the confusion. The ropes, having drowned two already, rose up to snatch another two.

"No, Pixler!" Mater Motley cried out, her voice heard at frequencies only living waters heard. *"They are just women."*

Pixler was not a man without compassion. His spirit, in the Requiax's cold embrace, saw that the seamstresses were indeed only women. They had let go of the instruments they had been cutting with. They wanted only to live.

We should show mercy on them, Pixler said, exchanging his thoughts with the Requiax.

Mercy? asked the Requiax, searching the grid of its mind for some clue to the meaning of the word. But it was like a piece of bone, or a flame. It had no need of mercy in its being. *I feel nothing in me, Pixler.*

No?

No.

Pixler could hardly blame the creature for what it had never known, or needed to know. He was the one who'd baited it with his lights and noise of his heart, drowning in the deep. He was the one who'd caused the Requiax to rise up and meet the sky. So it had no mercy to offer up? Such was its state.

"*Let go of my sisters!*" the Empress cried out yet again.

This time, Pixler and the Requiax spoke with one united voice.

"*This is its Absolute Midnight,*" it said. "*And in its darkness, your sisters must die.*"

PART SIX

THERE IS NO TOMORROW

Night comes down upon my heart
And smothers me with grief.
Let us take comfort before we part,
That at least our lives are brief.

—Anon.

53

FORGIVENESS

CANDY WOKE, AS SHE had woken so many times in the months of her travels in the Abarat, not quite sure of where she was at first, or how she'd come to be here, but figuring it out slowly, from the sights and sounds around her.

She was in the prison ship. She was down here in the bowels of the vessel with a large number, certainly upward of a thousand, of other arrestees. There wasn't very much light to offer her any details of who these others might be, but what light there was came from two ineffective lanterns that hung high above the mass of huddled prisoners, and swung violently with the pitching of the ship. They were plunging through some very turbulent waters, which caused the ship to creak and roll, and which was in turn causing no little pain to those suffering around her.

She could hear their minds, restless with fear and pain, letting their questions flow unanswered from their bruised heads.

Where are they taking me?

Was it something I did?

Will I get a trial?

She wanted to quiet their terrors.

"It'll be all right . . ." she murmured.

Who's there?

Who is that?

I heard somebody say—

"I'm going to put a light on," she said.

What is she talking about?

There are no lights.

She's crazy.

"Just *trust me*," she told them. Then, very softly, she spoke the wielding word for light: "Onazawaar."

A soft luminescence entered the air around her head, no more than the brightness of two candle flames. Then she gently willed it from her, and it spread like a pliant mist, lending its subtle brightness to the air. She urged it to be cautious. There was so much pain here; people who would not necessarily welcome the presence of an undeniable reality, however gently it was proffered. Even now, she heard thoughts from unhappy souls who had no desire to see what her kindly light was showing them.

Put it out! Put it out!

I'm dreaming. Don't you understand?

Put it out!

It's her. The girl from the Hereafter. She's the one who turned the light on.

Put it out!

"No!" A strong voice now; the first among all those she'd heard so far. "Let the light burn."

Candy sought out the speaker, and found him without any difficulty. He had a great cloud of red hair, with streaks of white in it. His square-cut beard was the same mingling of scarlet and white, his skin a bilious green. His voice by contrast with these excesses, was bland, colorless even.

"Don't be afraid of anything that your eyes tell you they're seeing," he said. His words carried farther than his volume would have suggested; a trick Candy knew from many an encounter with those who wielded magic. "Nothing here is real, children. I promise you that."

Even as he made infants of his congregation, somebody nearby whispered his name.

"It's Father Parrdar! The Prophet of Map's Vault."

"I am not your Father. I am but a child, like you. Afraid, like you. Fearing sometimes, as you fear." A murmur of recognition passed through the assembly. "Be calm, children. Our Father in the Hereafter hears our prayers. The Church of the Children of Eden will come to wake us, very soon."

Candy couldn't believe her ears. Once again, a murmur passed through the prisoners' ranks. This time, however, it was simply the sound of fearful people being granted some much-needed solace.

"None of this is real. How could it be?" Parrdar went

on. "What reason could there possibly be for so much suffering?"

It came as no surprise to hear affirmation by way of response.

"Yes, Father, yes! We *have* suffered in this nightmare!"

Parrdar went on talking as though nobody had spoken, but Candy could tell from the renewed force with which he went on speaking that his congregation's cries had been heard.

"The Reverend listens to our cries. The Reverend suffers as we suffer!"

Candy couldn't take it anymore.

"There *is* no Reverend," Candy said loudly.

"You be *quiet*," said a female who was sitting close by. She had more than a touch of Sea-Skipper in her blood, which gave her eyes the same silvery gleam that Candy had first seen in Izarith's gaze. "That's Father Parrdar talkin'!"

"I don't care who it is," Candy said, pushing herself up out of her dozy slouch. "A lie is a lie, whoever says it."

"He's not lying," another of the prisoners said, somewhere in the gloom.

"All right then, he's mistaken," Candy said. "But either way what he's saying isn't true."

"How do you know?" came a third voice.

The speaker was a large male; that was all Candy could see. But that was enough to make her very cautious. She had to be careful. She was tired, weak, and vulnerable. This wasn't the time to get into an argument with anyone.

Besides, they were all in this together, weren't they? All of them were prisoners on a dark ship under what was surely still a starless sky.

She made a small conciliatory gesture, raising her hands palms out to signify that she was letting the argument go. But the man in the darkness who had, Candy saw, a little question mark of hair rising from the middle of his head, wasn't willing to let go of the disagreement.

"I asked you a question," Question Mark said.

"Yes, and I heard you," Candy said, doing her best to remain calm and polite.

"So answer me."

"The pastor has every right to his opinion," Candy replied. She should have stopped right there. But no. She had to keep going. "Even when he's wrong."

She'd thought that willful, would-not-be-silenced part of her had probably been one of Boa's contributions; but no, it was pure Candy.

"He's *not* wrong," Question Mark replied.

He was getting up now, and Candy was starting to see just how big an argument she had got herself into. The man kept getting up and getting up and getting up, unfolding like an enormous accordion. He seemed almost as broad as he was tall. And as he rose, and spread, and rose and spread, he recited the Gospel According to Question Mark.

It was really very simple.

"The Father is Right. Always. He knows the Truth and

He speaks it in words we understand. Accept His wisdom and beg His Forgiveness."

At this point Parrdar himself entered the exchange.

"I'm certain she will—" he began.

"ACCEPT HIS WISDOM AND BEG HIS FORGIVE-NESS!" Question Mark said again.

Candy was standing up now. She could feel the rolling motion of the ship, not just as a passenger, but as an empath, sharing the ship's state of being just as her magic had allowed her to share the feelings of other human beings. She could feel the sea breaking against the prison-ship's bows just as Question Mark's bullying words were breaking against her face. She could feel the rhythm of the waves rolling against her ribs as the stares from all the people around her pressed against her. She could hear the murmur of their thoughts, foaming up like the waters.

"We're in this together," she said, shrugging. "We're all Mater Motley's prisoners. I don't want to get into an argument with anyone." She took a deep breath, swallowed her pride, and said, "I accept Father Parrdar's wisdom and I beg his forgiveness."

Even so, she couldn't keep from having her hands behind her back as she spoke, with her fingers crossed. It was a silly playground trick, to make a promise with your fingers crossed so that the promise carried no weight, but she couldn't help herself. She didn't truly accept Parrdar's wisdom or beg his forgiveness, but she was practical about things. That was also pure Candy.

"I forgive you, child," the Father said.

"Oh that's nice of you," Candy said, and for an instant she thought she'd overacted, and the Pastor would realize her sweetness was a mask covering a very different Candy.

But he was too in love with the power she'd given him to doubt that it was real.

He simply said: "The light."

"Do you want me to put it out?" she asked him.

"Not necessarily," he replied. "Do you have any control over it?"

"A little," she said.

"Then send it where it can do some good."

It took Candy a moment to work out what he meant, but only a moment. Then, being sure to make the task look as difficult as possible, she gathered up the light, which had spread around her, and willed it to go where Father Parrdar felt it could be most useful: illuminating him.

"That's better," he said as it bathed him. "I think we're going to get on quite well, child."

Candy started to say something by way of reply. But the pastor was already talking again, about how their Father in the Hereafter, who, along with his church, was coming to wake them from this terrible dream.

"Even now . . ." he was saying, ". . . he is coming to wake us. Even now."

54

THE EMPRESS
IN HER GLORY

Mater Motley had been known by many names in her long, bloodstained life. She had been the Visage, the Hag of Gorgossium, the Old Mother, and much else besides. But she had not fought her fate. She'd endured the time, knowing that there would come a Midnight when she would bestow upon her own head the only title that she had ever cared to possess: Thant Yeyla Carrion, Empress of the Abarat. Her first edict was to revenge herself upon Commexo City for the troubles its disobedience had caused her.

She was merciless.

The executions were a spectacle no one who survived that dark time would ever forget. For the first two hours following the dissemination of her edict, and its attendant death sentences, the Empress remained in the Circular Room, recovering those energies that had been depleted by her struggle with the Pixler-Requiax. After dispatching with her seamstresses, the Pixler-Requiax retreated to the depths of the Izabella, leaving the Old Hag to her Empire. And when she wearied of watching the sights on Pixler's shiny screens (What was the use of inspiring fear if you couldn't smell the sour stink of the terrorized?), she perched herself atop the blue-gray mummified hand on which she always traveled and took to the streets.

This tour of the surrendered city was the first and last time most of Commexo City's residents would ever see, in the flesh, the woman who had so very nearly destroyed their world. The people of Commexo thought of themselves as sophisticated, not without reason, and to their eyes the sight of this Empress, about which they had heard so many chilling stories, was surprisingly reassuring. To their well-bred gaze, the woman looked like a relic from some antiquated book of nursery tales. She looked ridiculously laughable, so they whispered behind their hands. She was old and unkempt, like a madwoman.

On this last point, they were not mistaken. The Old Mother was indeed insane. But it was not a powerless madness. Even her meditations on the scenes of destruction, which were caught by Rumor Spirals that moved around her, carried wisdom. At one scene of destruction she paused to study the ruins, and saw an orphaned infant lying blank-eyed amid the rubble.

"Oh, my pieties!" she murmured. "At every turn despair is new. Happiness is of a piece, yet was heard by all. And every hurt is its own world." Then, finished with her unrehearsed elegy, she turned to a nearby skullier and addressed him: "Soldier!"

"Me, Empress?"

"Yes, you. What's your name?"

"Hemosh, stitched by the seamstress Mezbadee, lady."

"And where is your mother?"

"Dead, Empress. She perished on the *Wormwood*."

"Ah. Well, Hemosh son of Mezbadee, do you see that poor little thing in the doorway there?"

"The babe, lady?"

"Yes. Bring it to me, will you? It pains me to see its distress."

"Do you wish to . . . hold the babe, m'lady?"

"Why do you sound so surprised? I was a mother before I was an Empress, Hemosh. And I will be a mother after I am dead, for there will be worms in my womb, will there not?"

"I do not care to think of life without you, m'lady. It breaks my heart—"

"You have no heart, Hemosh. You are just mud, living mud."

Hemosh looked conflicted.

"I don't understand, Empress. If I have no heart, why does the sound of the child's crying trouble me so?"

"I don't know, and I don't care, Hemosh. I am an Empress and you are nothing. Obey me."

Hemosh nodded and put his spear down on the ground. He took five backward steps, his head bowed, before turning and scrambling up over the rubble to the doorway where the infant still sobbed.

The sound it made was so very like a human voice. But it didn't look human. Its eyes were set above one another, its mouth also set on its side. As a result its head was long and narrow, and made to look longer still by the infant's ears, which were tall and pricked, like those of an alerted rabbit.

"Hush, little one," Hemosh said, reaching down to pick the infant up. Its wails faltered once Hemosh had gathered it into his arms. He rocked it gently, and its wailing ceased. "There."

Then he turned and was about to start back over the debris when the Empress spoke: "Don't bother to bring it back. Kill it where you're standing."

"Kill it?" Hemosh said.

"Yes, soldier. Kill it."

"But why?"

"Because I told you to?"

"But it's quiet now."

"Are you arguing with me, soldier?"

"No. I just wanted—"

"You are! You're arguing!"

A sudden fury seized the Empress.

In her rage the Empress stepped down from her hand, her skirts so laden with dolls, that when she did so the high-backed throne in which she'd been sitting was knocked over. She glanced down at Hemosh's spear, which responded instantly to her unspoken instruction. It rose up and turned in the air, so that it was pointing both at the stitchling and the infant who was still weeping in his shadow.

"M'lady, please. I meant no disrespect. I only—"

He got no further. The spear flew at him and the child, quickly silencing them both.

The death of the stitchling called Hemosh and the name-less infant didn't go unwitnessed. There were eleven other stitchlings surrounding the hand, eight of whom witnessed the scene. But so did many other citizens of Commexo who had come to this spot in order to see their destroyer for themselves. And as the account spread, the number of those who claimed to have seen the two creatures, infant and soldier, run through with the same spear, also increased. Some of these new "witnesses" also embellished the cruelty and vileness that the Empress had demonstrated. One claimed that the Empress had called the baby's soul to her and imprisoned it in one of the dolls sewn to her gown. These early additions to the account were within the bounds of believability. But as the story spread, and the additions proliferated, they became more and more outrageous. There were tales of the Empress's legions rising up against the Empress. Rumors that the dead soldier had reappeared, swollen to gigantic size. There were never any witnesses to these marvels, of course.

These rumors simply bred further enemies of the

Empress. There were enemies everywhere now. And she needed to be rid of them. So it was time, she decided, to stage the execution of the several thousand individuals whom she had already had arrested. With those enemies silenced, once and for all, she might reasonably expect Those Who Walk Behind the Stars to proclaim themselves happy. After all, had she not achieved all that she had set out to achieve? She was now the Empress of All the Hours, the Abarat beneath the thumb of her nail.

Standing next to her cherished hand in the ruined streets of Commexo City, the Empress unbent the first and last fingers of her left hand an inch, a tiny gesture that was nevertheless seen and understood by some observer in the death-ship far overhead. A hexagonal door opened in the belly of the vast machine and an immense light rained down upon her. She felt the power in the elevation beam pull on her, lifting her up. Though she very seldom took pleasure in relinquishing power to anyone, this was an exception. Being in the grip of the elevation beam was immensely pleasurable. She was perfectly content to let it have custody of her body for a few seconds, opening her arms and turning her palms skyward as the beam lifted her toward *The Stormwalker*.

When she was no more than her own body's length from the underbelly of the ship, she heard a cry rise to find her. It was intended for her attention, she had no doubt of it. Nothing so singular, so strange, was loosed without distinction or purpose. It quickly became more than a single cry; it turned into a litany of cries strung together, a churning murmur of lamentation, which in turn became a raw shriek of rage.

It wasn't difficult to decode the meaning of this. Commexo's citizens wanted her to be reminded that, although their city was now in darkness, its inhabitants were going to survive this dark time with their memories and their rage still very much alive. And they would find her, their cries promised, and finish the grim business she had begun.

Just in case their cries were not enough, they began to demonstrate one last proof of their fury. Some two hundred Commexians appeared from the darkness, converging on the small circle of light where the mummified hand waited for its turn to be raised up. But before the elevation beam could do its work, the Commexians descended upon the hand, fully intending to slay what was already a piece of something dead.

55

BELOW

CANDY DRIFTED OFF TO sleep. She let out a long, slow breath and let her dream-self slide out upon it and through the layers of timber and tar into the ship's skin of paint. It was red, of course, what a fine thing it was, to be red! To be the color of fire and blood and poppies and the setting sun.

She flowed from the prison-ship with dreamy ease, freed of all bodily concerns, yet in that freedom reconnected to all that was essential in her. All that was true and real and right.

She glanced back one last time at the prison-ship, where her second prison, that of her body, awaited her return. The nearest island was plainly visible to her dream sight, the waves blazing white as they met its shore.

The prison-ship was not far from its destination. A makeshift harbor had been built on the northeastern corner of Scoriae, lit by banks of acidic lights that were being buffeted by the gusting winds. There were two prison-ships identical to the one Candy had just left already using the primitive facilities the harbor provided. She could see lines of prisoners, all exhibiting signs of mistreatment, hobbling, some of them, others carried by stronger companions, as the Empress's stitchlings beat them with bludgeons to keep them moving; cruelty heaped upon cruelty, prisoners begging for a judgment from some Higher Power Candy no longer believed would intervene.

She threw her rage high into the air, where it tumbled over like brawling birds, then dropped back into the Izabella to carry her down. It was dark here, yes, but her presence drew luminosities to her in the billions; tiny motes of life attended upon her anatomy, formless though it was, and made of her a bright cloak that sank, bejeweled into the lightless deeps.

Now she had to put some force into her descent, but that was not so hard when the alternative was what she'd seen on Scoriae. Yes, she would have to go back there, of course. But not yet . . . Not quite yet.

Another ten minutes, Mama, please, before you bid me leave. Just ten.

The sea indulged her, and so on down and down she took her gown of light.

Such illumination was rare here, and drew curious eyes. She'd seen many of their species on her plate or for sale in a market stall. But the species she'd made meals of gave way very soon to others that would happily have made a meal of her, many were relatives of species she knew from the Hereafter, albeit much changed by the waters in which they swam. The hammerhead shark had become less hammer and more ax; the whale that moved with solitary grandeur below her housed a bright globe of much smaller fish, which seemed to propel it.

And still she descended, increasingly mindful of how soon she would have to return to the ship and her body.

Just another minute or two, she begged.

There were coral cliffs down here, though they seemed dead: their faces white with ash from the chimneys that vented volcanic fires, outposts of Mount Galigali's Empire. And then—seconds before she knew she must return to the ship—she was blessed with a vision. A tree appeared in her head, driving away the gloom: a living tree with lemon-white blossoms and a canopy so perfectly blue . . . She'd heard a poem once about that very thing.

> *Life was . . . something*
> *And dead the crew.*
> *And sinking the ship—*

No, no!

> *And holed the ship,*
> *And drowned the crew.*
> *But o! But o!*
> *How very blue*
> *The sea is!*

She was tempted to dive on, deeper still. And she wondered how far would she have to propel her thoughts before she had sight of the legendary Requiax?

Diamanda, Candy remembered, had called them: *the "enemies of love, the enemies of life. Wicked beyond words."*

Candy had asked where they resided, and Joephi had

told her that they were deep in the Izabella, where she hoped they'd stay. Diamanda had doubted that things would be so simple. She'd heard rumors that they were on the move.

". . . there are those who say that when they surface, it will be the end of the world as we know it."

Well, that had come true, already. So did this mean the creatures below her were now going to be walking the islands? She had to see them for herself. Just once, a quick peek. What did the enemy of life and love look like? She might never get another chance to find out for herself.

She willed her thoughts down into a darkness beyond all darknesses she had ever witnessed before.

Something down there knew she was coming. She could feel its vastness unfolding, its limbs or tongues or both, reaching up toward her thoughts, and touching them with a beguiling gentility. And as they touched her she remembered, for no reason she could fathom, something else she'd been told. Except that the subject hadn't been the Requiax. It had been a remark about the fact that magic seemed to be just about everywhere nowadays.

"It's going to take time to root out all the magic in these islands," she once heard somebody saying. "We've got a lot of books to burn, a lot of spirits to break——"

Then very slowly, the tentacles unknotted themselves, and there below her was the man who'd spoken those words, though he'd changed much since their last encounter.

"Hello again," said Rojo Pixler.

56

THE HAND IN FIRE

"*U*p!" THE EMPRESS YELLED to the door-keeper and his staff. "Quickly, *quickly*. They mean to harm the hand!"

The doorkeeper, Mister Drummadian, was already coming to greet his Empress on the broad walkway, which was automatically moving into position. She stepped off the air and onto the walkway. He had wiped the grin of welcome off his face at the first glimpse of his Empress's expression. Before he could even murmur a word of welcome she said: "Get your soldiers down there, Drummadian! *Right now!*"

"Yes, ma'am." He yelled an order to the Captain of the Guard. "You heard the order, Flayshak!"

Captain Flayshak, a gargantuan skullier stitchling with a uniform that barely constrained his six-armed torso, was on the task.

"I did indeed, sir!"

He summoned three of his stitchlings to his side with

a few sharp syllables in the old voice, and then simply plunged into the Elevation Beam with his fellow soldiers following behind.

"Who's doing the attacking?" Drummadian asked.

"Insurgents! Radicals! Working to undermine the Throne! I want them alive, Drummadian. I want to take my time with them to get the truth."

"I have every faith in Captain Flayshak, ma'am. He knows—"

There was a soft *whoomp* from the ground below, and a bloom of jaundiced light around the base of the hand.

"No, *damn them!*" the Empress shrieked. "I don't lose him too!"

Drummadian didn't understand what she meant by that, but he understood perfectly well the wisdom of silence. Besides, the Empress needed no further prompting from him to speak out. She seemed, to the doorkeeper's respectful eyes, to be a woman on the edge of insanity. Though her head was directed so as to allow her to look down at the ground, her eyes darted everywhere rather than look at the sight below. But then given that she seemed to feel some affection for the hand on which she was so often perched, it was little wonder she avoided sight of it. Drummadian turned his head away, and didn't even realize his Empress was demanding he act until her words began to slap him on the face like blows from a thorny stick.

"Bring the thing up!" she was screaming.

"Into the ship?" the doorkeeper said, plainly appalled at the notion.

"Yes! Of course into the ship! Quickly! Do you understand, you cretins! If he dies, so do you. You burn up the
way he's burning!"

"Oh, lady, no—"

"Then save him, you idiot!"

The doorkeeper became a blur of action, first slamming his fist against a large yellow alarm button, which
caused panicking alarms to whoop throughout the vessel.
Drummadian had very specific orders.

"All firefighters to the receiving bay. *We have an emergency!*" He then yelled down to Flayshak. "Extinguish the
fires by any means possible, Flayshak! You hear me?"

Flayshak yelled something by way of reply, but it wasn't
audible over the sound of the crackling fire from below.

"BRING HIM UP!" the Empress again demanded. "Did
you not hear my order, Mr. Drummadian?"

"I heard, m'lady," the doorkeeper replied. "And
your . . . the . . . he's on his way up to you, m'lady."

The engines of *The Stormwalker* were indeed already at
their churning labors, empowering the Elevation Beam
to lift the blazing hand up off the ground into the belly
of *The Stormwalker*. Waves of stinking heat rose up off
the hand as it threw itself around within the confines
of the beam. Drummadian's alarms had by now brought
responses from all directions. Pumps had been primed,
and numberless hoses directed at the massive burning
form.

"Get the water flowing!" Drummadian yelled.

He'd no sooner spoken than the hoses bucked and

spat, and foaming waters poured out of them. There was a tremendous hissing sound, and clouds of steam rose up from the Elevation Beam as the flames were dowsed. Once the hand was within the confines of the vessel, Doorkeeper Drummadian ordered the aperture closed and the beam shut off, which allowed the firefighters to concentrate their hoses on the hand with even greater force. The flames were quickly subdued. But the damage that had been done to the hand was horrendous. It was so weakened by the flames that it could barely stay upright on its fingertips. It tottered like a vast infant as the waters buffeted it.

"Enough!" Mater Motley yelled. "Do you hear me, Drummadian?"

"It's done, m'lady," the doorkeeper replied.

The hoses were shut off. The flow of water dwindled and died completely. Even without the water beating against it, the hand had difficulty standing upright. Its dead flesh blistered and in places burned away completely, leaving only blackened bone.

"Leave us," the Old Mother said very quietly.

The doorkeeper was plainly uncomfortable with the notion of leaving his Empress in such unpredictable company.

"Perhaps if I just stayed at the door."

"Out!" the Old Mother yelled. Then more quietly: "I won't have it watched while it suffers. You understand?"

"Of course," Drummadian replied. "Captain Flayshak,

you and your men—"

"Understood, sir," the Captain replied. At a nod from their Captain the firefighters departed. Flayshak waited at the door for the doorkeeper to join him, then they too left.

"I'll make this quick," Mater Motley said. "You've served me well. I'm sorry I failed to do the same. Be free."

She walked around the hand, counterclockwise. The crude circle her feet drew on the ground unleashed a wave of black energy, which converged on the hand. It knew what work it had to do, and summarily did it.

"Go," the Hag said.

The hand took the comfort it was granted. Its fingers folded up beneath it as it toppled sideways, collapsing in the filthy water. Pieces of burned matter broke off the thing, and struck the walls of the chamber. The hand twitched where it had fallen, and then the unnatural life force that owned it for so many centuries went out of it, and was gone.

The Empress did not linger to keep the company of the twice dead. She went directly to the bridge so that she could speed the vessel on its way to Scoriae. The enemies of her Empire were there, awaiting their executions.

57

A KNIFE
FOR EVERY HEART

CANDY'S EYES SHOT OPEN. She was on dry land; for that she was thankful. The last thing she'd seen was a glimpse of Rojo Pixler, or something that had once been Pixler, lurking in the depths of the Izabella. It had smiled at her hungrily and then reached for her with vast, tentacle limbs.

She was glad to be delivered from that vision.

"What island is this?" she murmured, hoping there would be someone close by to answer.

There was. Beaming with happiness, Malingo's face came into her field of vision.

"Malingo?"

"You're awake! I thought you'd really got away this time."

Candy offered a smile, back up at him; or at least she tried her best to do so. But she felt so dislocated from her body she wasn't entirely sure it was doing what she thought it was doing. All she knew with any certainty was that her eyelids still felt very leaden, and that despite the pleasure of seeing Malingo again, all that she really wanted to do was to feel sleep gather her up into its arms again and carry her away to some kinder time and place.

"No," Malingo protested. "Please don't leave again. I need you. We all need you."

"All?"

He looked away from her, and curious to see what Malingo was seeing, Candy pushed herself up into a sitting position.

"Lordy Lou . . ." she murmured.

They weren't alone. There was an immense crowd here, sitting or standing, most of them silent and seemingly alone, the whole assembly contained within a long rectangle of razor wire.

"From what I gather, there are about seven thousand of us," Gazza said from somewhere behind her.

She looked around at him. He was climbing up onto the top of the boulder followed by, much to Candy's surprise, Betty Thunder. Candy took a good look around.

"How come we get to sit on the only rock?" she asked.

"You're famous," Gazza said. "So we get the rock."

"Who are all these people?"

"We're all the Empress's prisoners."

"Is it just the four of us?"

"No. Eddie and the Johns are here too," Gazza said.

"What about Geneva? Tom? Clyde?"

Betty gave a sad shrug.

"We might find them, though," said Malingo. "Eddie and the Johns are out there looking for them and trying to find out why we're here. What we've all got in common."

"She doesn't like us," Candy said. "What more reason does she need? She's the Empress now. She doesn't answer to anyone."

"Everybody answers to somebody," said Gazza.

Candy shrugged and stood up to survey the crowd. Bonfires were blazing in dozens of places around the camp. By their light, Candy saw that the crowd here was just as diverse as it had been on the boardwalks of Babilonium. Though these were prisoners, not pleasure seekers, the familiar exuberance of Abaratian life was visible: the same dream-bright colors that had no name; the same elaborate configurations of feathered crests and fanning tails; eyes that looked like smoking embers and rings that were decorated with constellations of golden eyes. The only real difference was in the noise the crowd made, or rather its absence. The pleasure seekers at Babilonium had whooped and shouted and howled at the dusky sky as if to call it down to join in the fun. But there were no whoops nor shouts here. Nor were there tears. Just whispered exchanges, and perhaps here and there some murmured prayers.

"They're all watching the sky," Candy said. "Seeing the cracks opening up."

"Well, that *is* a good thing, isn't it?" Malingo said. "I saw a star just a little while ago. See it? Oh, and there!"

"She knew this would happen," Candy said.

"She knew the darkness wouldn't stay?"

"Of course," Candy said, momentarily forgetting she'd kept her conversation with Carrion a secret. She quickly added a defensive, "I mean, how could she not? She had to know that whatever creatures she put up there wouldn't live forever. Otherwise why would she have all the troublemakers locked up? It just makes sense."

"What's going to happen to us now?" Malingo said.

"We're going to get out of here," Candy said. "Before Mater Motley gets here."

"What makes you think she's going to come here?" Gazza asked.

"She's worked a long time to get all her enemies in one place. She can take us all out at the same time."

"*What?* There are thousands of us!" said Malingo.

"Yes. And we're hidden behind a volcano at the end of the world! Nobody will ever know if we're murdered here. But she'll want it soon, before some order is put back into things."

"How can you be so sure?" said Betty.

"I just am. I think I have come to understand her . . . a little."

"Well, I don't see how we get the six of us out of here," Betty said. "Maybe you and Malingo . . ."

"*No,*" Candy said.

"What do you mean *no*? Is six too many?"

"When I say all of us," Candy said, glancing back toward

the compound and all the souls imprisoned within it, "I mean: *All. Of. Us.*"

"There are stitchlings in every direction, Candy," Gazza said.

"Yes, and no doubt she'll bring more with her when she comes."

"Lordy Lou . . ." Malingo murmured.

"How many more?" Gazza wanted to know.

"What does it matter?" Candy said.

"I need to know what we're going to face," he said to her.

"I don't have precise numbers, Gaz. I wish I could explain it better, but I can't. All I can say I know she's coming, and that she'll have a knife for every heart."

She'd no sooner given her grim answer to his question than a commotion started running through the crowd. Candy tore her gaze away from her friends.

"What now?" she asked.

Candy walked to the edge of the boulder in time to see a blind man emerge in front of the crowd.

"Candy Quackenbush?" he said.

"Do I know you?"

"No," said the blind man. "I'm Zephario Carrion. I believe you know my son."

58

NOW, BECAUSE

CANDY SLID DOWN OFF the rock. Her visitor was standing with his back to one of the fires, so he was almost entirely in silhouette, except for his eyes, which despite their sightlessness had somehow drawn into them all the light being shed by the peeping stars. Either the cold, or simply fatigue, filled the old man's body with tremors. Only the starlight remained constant.

"I don't understand," Candy said. "What do you want?"

Zephario reached into the pocket of his baggy jacket.

"I used to make money by reading these."

Candy accepted whatever he was handing over to her.

"These are tarot cards, aren't they?"

"An Abaratian deck. I lost my old deck to the wind a long time ago. But I found another."

"These look different from the ones I saw in Chicken-town."

"They are. There are eighty-eight cards in an Abara-tian deck, not seventy-eight. And of course the images are different. Not all of them. Some faces are ever present."

Candy couldn't see the designs on the cards clearly from where she was standing; there wasn't sufficient light. But she could feel the visions on them, their vibrations moving through her fingertips, and they made her want to get a better look at them. So she moved out of the blind man's shadow, turning the cards down and out, so they were lit by the flames. Now she saw them, it was no wonder her fingers had felt their power. Such visions! Some of the images were beautiful, some were terrifying, some of them made melancholy music in her head, like the lost songs of things that would never come into this world or any other.

She was unable to take her eyes off the flow of images long enough to look back at the blind man, but he didn't mind.

"Lost forever," she said to herself.

"I didn't quite catch——"

"I've just always believed that nothing was really lost."

"Ah. If only . . ."

"So . . . you saw me here? In one of the cards?"

"It wasn't just one of them. You will wear many faces."

"I don't see me anywhere."

"Good. Only a fool thinks he sees."

"You're Christopher's father?"

"Quite so," he said with a strange calm. "Christopher . . . oh, my sweet Christopher . . . he was so small once."

Zephario lifted his hands, cupped side by side to show how small his beloved son had been. Candy took the opportunity to take hold of one of his hands.

"Here," she said. "Your cards."

"Please. You keep them. Use them. They are already mapped with what I've learned. Now you add your own journeys to mine and it's all part of the Thread."

"What?"

"The Thread. Do you not know of it?"

"No. But I do believe there is a pattern in the Hours; a hidden connection, which will show the greater order of things when the time is right."

"Ah," said Zephario, "you *are* wise. I want you to *live*, Candy. I want you to know the greater order, and if you wish to, pass it back to me, so that those among the dead who are lost—and there are many—find their way to the Embrace of Everything."

"Everything . . . that's in the air a lot, isn't it?"

"Yes, that or Nothing at All. It's an Age of Absolutes."

"What comes after this Age?"

"I've no idea. Why would I?"

"You must have asked the cards how this is all going to end."

"The cards don't tell the future. It hasn't happened yet. We hope that certain things will happen. But none of it's guaranteed. We may want one kind of future and get another kind entirely. My daughters used to sing a rhyme. All these years later I still hear it.

"There is no tomorrow,

There never——"

"Was," Candy said, picking up the rhyme immediately.

"Beg, steal or borrow,

Now, because——

There is no tomorrow

There never was.

Beg, steal or borrow

Now, because——

"We used to sing it too," Candy said. "Why tell me this now?

"Because now is all there is. And because you sense *her* too," he said.

"Oh," Candy said.

"She's not alone, is she?"

"No, of course not. She must have at least seven thousand stitchlings with her. That's what Christopher told me."

"Is he with her now?"

"I doubt it. She thinks he's dead. Drowned in the streets of Chickentown."

"But he isn't, is he? I came here to find you so that you could help make peace between us. I want to see my son, one last time before I die. He's all I have, lady. He's all that I have left to love."

"You might find loving him a bit difficult. He's no saint."

"Well, nor was I. When he was born I was one of the

most feared men in the Abarat. I thought that was something to be proud of, in my stupidity. I made it a point of
pride to burn every harvest I hadn't planted and tear down
every tower that I hadn't built. When I think of the harm
I did . . ." He paused, drawing a ragged breath. Whatever
memories his mind was seeing, they made him weep. ". . .
My son can do no worse. I was only forty-two when the
fire destroyed the mansion. It killed my wife, and all the
children except for Christopher. Forty-two! It's nothing,
forty-two. But I managed to fill up that little time with so
many shameful things. Terrible things. I just wanted to
tell Christopher there's still time . . ."

"Still time to do what?" Candy said.

"Heal those he's hurt," Zephario said.

"You can't heal the dead."

"You're quite the plain speaker, aren't you?"

"It's the truth."

"Oh, I don't doubt it. My son has done a lot of terrible
things. I see the stain he leaves behind him, on whatever
he's touched. Even on you."

Candy suddenly felt as though somebody had just emptied a bucket of sewer water over her head. How clear was
the stain on her that a blind man could see it?

"You do know it wasn't me he wanted, right? It was
Princess Boa. She'd been hidden in me all my life. I didn't
know she was there until . . . until I found the Abarat. Or
it found me."

"Are you sure?"

"About what?"

"Christopher wanting Boa and not you?"

"Yes. I know it," Candy said, nodding.

"I saw you in a vision once, while I was laying out the cards. I had no idea who you were, but you were talking to Christopher, who was lying down, barely able to lift his head . . ."

"That was back in Chickentown. Yes. He was very weak. I thought for certain he was going to die. He wanted to talk to Boa, and of course I let him."

"What did he want from her?"

"He wanted them to die together."

"And she was ready to go along with that?"

"No, I don't think she was. I can't be sure . . ."

"Even though you were sharing a mind?"

"Sometimes I couldn't find her. She hid from me. Even in my own head. Why does it matter?"

"Does he know that you and the Princess are—?"

"No longer together? Yes, he knows. I saw him, in Tazmagor. He came to find me . . . well, no, to find *her*, but in the end all he got was me. He came to warn one of us about what was coming."

Some tension that Candy hadn't seen in the blind man's face until now suddenly melted away.

"You know that for certain?"

"What? That he'd wanted to save my life? Or her life? Yes. Yes, I know that for certain. Why? Does it matter?"

"That he has a shred of goodness in him? That he cares

enough about somebody to put himself in harm's way? Yes, it matters a great deal. Only to me, perhaps. But then I'm the only one who has to live with the knowledge anyway."

"The knowledge of . . ."

"All the terrible things he did. The families he destroyed. The love he destroyed. I was a bad man before the fire, Candy. I'll be the first to say so. But I didn't teach him to murder people with their own nightmares. That was my mother's doing. The Mad Hag of Gorgossium . . . and now our Empress and executioner. She's there . . ." As he spoke, he pointed to the card that had surfaced in Candy's hands. She'd been sifting through them as they talked and one had drawn the blind man's attention. "My mother," he said.

The image on the card was one of heart-stopping terror. In a bare room, lacking even the most rudimentary comfort or decoration was a single occupant: a small unclothed figure stood looking at a window that filled most of the left-hand quadrant of the picture. Through it, staring down at him, was the vast bloodless face of a devourer, its teeth glittering.

"I don't think this is your mother," Candy said.

"It's a symbol, not a likeness," Zephario replied. "There is a difference. That thing at the window represents the power that allowed my mother to do all that she's done. It is Nephauree. One of Those Who Walk Behind the Stars."

Candy could feel cold emanating from the painted image. It made her head throb.

"It's Nephauree magic she wields. That's why she's been able to do so much harm. I pray my son has not made the same bargains with them."

"Why?"

"Because the price of that power will be a terrible thing to pay. I could perhaps persuade him to turn his back on the Nephauree if I could speak with him."

"Then talk to him."

"I need your help to do that."

"This isn't something I had planned for."

"I have no wish to put you in harm's way——"

"That's not what worries me."

"I have no money——"

"I wouldn't want it even if you did," Candy replied.

"Then what do you want?"

"We need to leave this place, Zephario."

"Well, that shouldn't be difficult. You have the power to make a glyph, do you not?"

"Oh, I do. And this one is going to be *very* unusual."

59

A WHISPER
OF INFINITUDE

T HE EMPRESS THANT YEYLA Carrion stood
at the fifty-foot-wide battle window of her Stormwalker
and viewed with immense pleasure and subtle satisfaction
the spectacle of the Ceremonial Assembly of the Imperial
Executioners. Everything was proceeding in an orderly
fashion. There were eight battalions of stitchling executioners, each a thousand stitchlings strong. The excess of
knives to hearts was intentional, a precaution taken in case
the number of condemned turned out to be significantly
larger than expected, or there was a failure to success-
fully kill among some portion of the executioners. Their
commander stitchlings were sewn with special symme-
try from remnants of finely woven fabric and the bleached
skins of scaly reptiles.

The Empress stood, admiring her steamstresses'
handiwork, when a voice, entirely unwelcome, interrupted her reverie.

"Hello, Grandmother."

The Old Hag bristled.

"Christopher." She didn't turn. She didn't need to. She saw his reflection in the window as he stepped out of the shadows. "This is——"

"Unexpected? Yes. I have new scars. But then you know that. You gave them to me."

As he spoke, a flicker of the old rage, the fury that had erupted from him on the deck of the *Wormwood*, reappeared. The nightmares caught the infection of anger, and became still more livid.

"I sense that you still harbor a measure of resentment toward me," the Empress said, turning to face her grandson.

He hardly resembled at all the despairing, forsaken creature Candy Quackenbush had met in the alleyway behind the marketplace at Tazmagor. Now he was wearing fine robes, new white linens that made a perfect screen for the light from the blazing ziggurat on Scoriae. And the nightmares in his new collar threw their own illumination up onto his face as they circled his head.

"Are my reasons hard to fathom, lady?" Carrion said. "With just a few words you could have saved me."

"You suffered. And so did I. But we recovered. We can still plan for the future." She looked past the interwoven strands of nightmares to find the glittering gaze of her grandson. "Now you should go."

"I don't choose to go now, Grandmother. I want to see why you're not going home to Gorgossium. I hear you tore my tower down——"

"I tore all of those ugly things down."

"Why?"

"Don't be angry about your tower, darling, please. I thought you were dead."

"You thought no such thing. You knew I was still living, just as you knew the soul of my Princess was hidden in Candy Quackenbush. You just see the things you want to see and disregard the rest."

The Empress offered no reply to this. At least not for half a minute or more. She just tapped on the window, watching her army. Finally she spoke: "You can take my tower!"

Carrion was genuinely shocked at the proposal.

"I can . . . take it?"

"It's yours. I'll have you escorted back to Gorgossium."

Carrion laughed into his night terrors.

"Oh, you are *very* clever, aren't you? You can't slip out of this so easily. I want to see what you've got hidden in Scoriae."

"Enemies, Christopher. Just the same old enemies. Only in an hour they'll all be dead. Every last one of them."

"Ah. Now I see. *A knife for every heart.*"

The Old Mother nodded, the weight of the years and the crimes and the betrayals heavy upon her.

"Yes, *a knife for every heart*," she confessed. "Are you happy now? I am about to do the last and bloodiest business of a very bloody time. You needn't witness it."

"No, but I will. You may keep your fine tower, lady.

I want to see this business to the very end. Then you can deny me no part of the spoils. For my hands will be as stained red as yours."

"Then come," she said. "But they all die. Understand that. All of them die, no exceptions."

"Of course not, lady," he said as though he had ever been the compliant student, learning the ways of the Empire. "What must be done must be done."

"You want *all* of them out in a *single* glyph?" Zephario said.

"There's no other way to do it. There are thousands of people here."

"It's impossible."

"No, it isn't."

"It's never been done."

"Maybe not. But that doesn't make it impossible. The two of us working together . . ."

"I'm no magician," he said.

"Well, then why do I get such a buzz of power off you?"

"Maybe it's the cards."

"*I'm* holding the cards, Mr. Carrion, so try again. We have very little time. Tell me about the Abarataraba."

"What do you know about it?"

"Not very much," Candy said. "I know what it isn't. It's not like the *Almenak*. It's not a guide to magic. I think maybe it's magic itself. Am I right?"

"Well, to an extent, yes. Wherever there's the Abarataraba, there is magic. A lot of magic."

"Is 'a lot' enough?"

"Enough to fuel the creation of a glyph to carry all these innocent people away from here before their executioners arrive? If I had an entire book, the answer would be yes. More than enough."

"But you don't."

"No," Zephario said. "No."

"You have a piece?"

"A piece of a page."

Disappointment crossed Candy's face.

"You have *one* piece of *one* page?"

"I know it seems like a small amount but it isn't. Each book had eight pages. Each page was square, and divide: eight horizontally, eight vertically."

"Sixty-four squares on each of eight pages. That's . . ." She closed her eyes to do the calculation in her head. ". . . that's sixty times eight . . . is four hundred and eighty, plus eight times four . . . is thirty-two . . . so that's . . . *five hundred and twelve*. What does that even mean?"

"It brings us back to eight again."

"How?"

"Five plus one plus two."

"Equals eight. Okay. So what's the big deal about eight?"

"If you turn the number on it's side, it's infinitude."

"Oh, that little squiggly sign. I suppose that is more or less an eight, isn't it? Where's this all going?"

"I only have a little piece. But it's a piece of an infinite thing. So it too is infinite. At least in theory."

"Your piece of paper. What does it say?"

"Nothing. There are no words in the Abarataraba."

"Then what's in it?"

"Squares. Lots of squares, filled with color. And it is in the energy between the pieces that the magic ignites."

"I want to see it."

"I'm not sure you should."

"What? Now you don't want to show it to me?"

"It's unpredictable."

"All right, but we don't have a lot of time. We agree on that, right?"

"Yes."

"So unless you—"

"All right, all right," Zephario said. "Just don't say I didn't warn you. I hope this isn't more power than you can handle."

He reached into his jacket and pulled out an envelope made of coarsely woven cloth, pressing it into her hands. There was a strange fumbling moment between them when it seemed to Candy that, even though her head was telling her hands to take the package, they were refusing to play along.

"The flesh fears it," Zephario said.

"Why?"

"Because the Abarataraba changes all that it touches."

"I'm not afraid of change," Candy said, her voice no longer playing tricks.

"Then take the magic wisely and regret nothing."

That sounded like good advice, even to Candy's reluctant hands. They accepted the envelope, and now resigned to the consequences, whatever they might be, they opened it up.

There was a piece of thick paper—perhaps four inches square—inside it. She saw red first, brighter than the hull of any ship she'd seen plying the waters of the Izabella. A blue current had caught it up, and it burst against one of the sides, shattering into blue and green. Not one blue, but a thousand, and green the same, every fleck of paint that the brush deposited a variation on the originating note.

"Be careful," she heard Zephario say.

She glanced up at him, but her gaze never focused on his face. It slipped over his shoulder, through the crowd of prisoners and up over the fence, slipping through the coils of barbed wire on top of the boundary fence, and out, across the wasteland that lay between the camp and the slopes of Mount Galigali. It ascended in a heartbeat, up the steep slope. Her eyes had no interest in studying the barren heights, however. There was something above the volcano that had claimed their attention.

There was a storm up there, vast and implacable, moving in with the obscene certainty of a blood-hungry army. There was thunder in it, but it wasn't a natural thunder, rising up to crack the sky then falling away again, muttering its complaint as it retreated. No, this was the churning thunder of an endgame machine; a funeral march played for those about to die. It neither cracked nor complained; it simply grew louder as its source approached.

"Oh, Lordy Lou," Candy said very softly.

"What can you see?"

"The biggest storm clouds I've ever seen. It's ridiculous how big they are. And that thunder."

"That's not thunder," Gazza said as he climbed down the boulder, the rest of the group following closely behind.

"Who are they?" Zephario quickly demanded.

"They're fine," Candy said. "They're my friends."

"Nobody's fine. Not around this much power."

"Well, it's too late."

Gazza was staring at the Abarataraba.

"It's so beautiful," he said.

"See?" Zephario told Candy. "What did I tell you? Give me the piece back."

"Let me look at it," Gazza demanded.

"*No*," Candy said. "We have to hurry. You see that storm? Motley's in there somewhere. Her and the stitchlings she's bringing to execute us."

"Mother . . ." Zehpario whispered.

With those two syllables, Zephario gained everyone's silent attention. It was Malingo who broke it.

"Are we supposed to trust him?" Malingo said. His nostrils were widening ever so slightly, as he suspiciously inhaled the scent of Carrion the Elder. "I've had bad experiences with Carrions."

"My mother has a lot to answer for," Zephario said. "And it will be up to you to make sure she doesn't get to keep her Empire. She's murdered a lot of innocent people to get it."

"We can talk about the future once we have it in our hands," Candy said.

"And how do we do that?" Malingo said.

"A glyph," Candy said with certainty.

"A glyph? How are we going to keep all these people from asking stupid questions and getting in our way?"

"Why would they get in our way?"

"Because they've never made a glyph before and we don't have time to explain."

"Just because it's never been done before doesn't mean it's impossible. We just have to spread the word. *Very* quickly."

Candy looked back at Zephario, who must have sensed her gaze on him because he said: "Go on. You're doing just fine."

"Mr. Carrion gave me a piece of magic. And we're going to use it to spread the gospel of the glyph. It's either that or waiting for the executioners to arrive."

"Well, that's an easy choice," Gazza said. "Let's spread the gospel."

60

ABARATARABA

On the far side of the camp, close to the fence that bounded the northern end of the compound, John Slop, whose head was positioned close to the top of Mischief's left antler, and therefore had the best vantage point of all the brothers, said: "Something's happening over on the rock."

"I said we shouldn't have wandered so far," John Fillet remarked. "Eddie? Did you hear what Slop said? Wait! Where's Eddie?"

"It's spreading . . ." John Slop murmured.

"*What's* spreading?" Mischief said.

"*Eddie!*" Fillet yelled.

"Please," Serpent said, "there's no need to make such a song and dance about it. Eddie's perfectly capable of—"

"Is anybody paying attention to these storm clouds?" John Sallow said.

"I've been watching them."

"*That's* the problem. That cloud."

"Sallow, it's on the far side of Galigali."

"Has anybody seen Eddie?"

"No."

"I'm warning you," said Sallow. "That's not a normal storm. It's spreading. *Look!* Even in the last couple minutes—"

"It's getting bigger," said John Slop.

"*What's* getting bigger?" said John Fillet.

"Candy's sitting on the rock, and she's giving . . . I don't know what she's got . . . it's bright. And it's being passed on. It looks like she's got a flame and she's just passing it on. And it's . . ."

"Spreading?"

"Yeah."

"We should just go back over there and see what it is for ourselves," said Mischief.

"Now you're just being sensible, John. Don't do that. You'll take all the fun out of things," said John Drowze mockingly.

"We can't go anywhere until we find Eddie," Fillet said.

"I see Eddie!" John Sallow said. "He's over there doing a scene from *Mythfit Unbound.*"

"How do you know it's *Mythfit?*"

"He's standing in a bucket."

"Ohhh," said all the brothers in unison.

The Abarataraba had begun its work. Even though there were almost two thousand people between the rock where Candy was sitting and the spot where the John Brothers were arguing, Candy could hear their circular exchanges quite clearly. She could hear too, Eddie's recitation of the speech from *Mythfit Unbound*:

> "And the world'll go on without me,
> This is certain sure.
> Should you choose to doubt me,
> I'll leave and close the door."

If she'd simply heard clearly that collection of voices, given the distance between them, and the number of people who were filling that distance, it would have been remarkable. But there was more. A great deal more. She could hear with the same extraordinary clarity the voices of all the people who were talking in the space between them. Not only was she able to hear them all talking as though she were standing a step away from them, but she was also able to make sense of every single voice, her mind a crowd of attentive Candys, giving to every speaker a slice of her mind's pie, for them and them alone.

There was, in addition to her many listening selves, one Candy who heard it all, and heard the pattern in the words, and gently, as the wind might carve a cloud with subtle gusts, moved each where she needed them to go, without their knowing she was present.

She wasn't alone in this endeavor. She had given Malingo, who had created a glyph with her before, the charge of guiding Gazza and Betty and the Johns while she kept Zephario Carrion to work with her. He would either prove to be their greatest ally or a complete liability. But Candy was spreading a vision, which Carrion had seen quite clearly before Candy had departed from the rock.

They would all have to work together to conjure a glyph so massive it would carry them out of this place of death before Mater Motley's vessel appeared. There wasn't time for doubt or weakness. Like all structures, their escape glyph would only be as strong as its weakest creator. Somehow Candy had to galvanize these sad, broken people, show them that there was a life after Midnight.

She was giving them all a piece of the Abarataraba as a touchstone, a way to hold onto the vision she had just shared with them.

But even when they had a piece of the Abarataraba's power to lend them strength, it was difficult not to succumb to despair. Everywhere Candy went she heard the same suspicion being offered up as to why the camp had been built in this particular spot. It wasn't that the Empress was trying to hide her atrocities behind Mount Galigali. It was something far grimmer. No more than three-quarters of a mile from where the camp was situated, lay the Edge of the World. The waters of the Sea of Izabella simply ended and plunged over the edge of the Abarat and into Oblivion. It was into those foaming waters, and then over the edge and into the Void, that all of Mater Motley's enemies, once slain, would go, to be carried away by the waters into the silent Abyss below.

It was here the maps of the Abarat ended. There was nothing documented beyond that point. No other worlds had ever been seen in that bleak firmament. Nor suns, nor moons.

Even Candy couldn't quite shake off the power of that

image; the knowledge that if she failed to make this glyph a reality then her body would be carried away with the bodies of everyone who'd been executed, and all that she had seen or dreamed of would go down and down into that pitiless void and be lost forever.

It *had* to work. That was the thought she needed to hold onto.

And she had reason to hope; tentative tremors of affirmation in the air, as the first of the people who had been touched by her vision of escape, and given a tiny but significant boost in their strength by the fragment of the Abarataraba they had been given, rose like signals above the heads of those who'd willed them to appear. She let a line of thought go out to the signal closest to her, from which it gained another spurt of strength and more on to the next closest, and the one after that, the vision gaining clarity as each connected with each. The path of her first thought was set now, and it had no further need of her, fueled as it was by the thoughts of all those it had already met on its way.

She turned around and sent a second thought on its way, out into the vessel that her vision and passion were inspiring; a vehicle built from the intersection of two magics. One was ancient and external. It was rooted in the essence of things: was a thing red or blue or gold? Was it earth or sky or water? Was it alive or dead or hanging in the balance, waiting to be judged? This was the primal power of the Abarataraba. The second magic was rooted in the limitless particulars of living beings, each carrying their hopes and doubts and rage to the furnace where the vessel of their salvation might be made manifest.

Here was the mystery of creation, played out on a field of dirt and desperation. Candy could see it, this mystery. It was happening all around her. Out of the common earth of living beings, fragile and afraid, came the extraordinary forms of a glyph beyond the conceiving of any single mind. She heard the voices of her fellow prisoners, daring to hope aloud; one voice whispering a second; two voices whispering a third, fourth and fifth: *I dreamed this. . . .*

We're not dead yet.
And we're
NOT
GOING
TO
DIE.

"The answer to *how* is to *do*," Candy said. "That's all there ever is. We're not scattered pieces. We're all one hope, one will, one dream."

The Abarataraba was alight in her own body now, throwing off hundreds of blazing notes, each trailing lines of light, sketching the glyph against the sky. It was a crude rendering, but it showed the congregation gathered below the scale of their endeavor. And rough though the sketch was, there was something potent in its chaos. It was a vessel, this glyph, designed to hold every kind of thing that the desire for freedom called forth: whether color, form, mark or meaning. However disparate the visions were—the glyph would somehow turn their energies to its purpose.

Some visions were painted in color that had the clarity of myth: their blues were as vivid as the skies over paradise, their reds redder than any blood-rose love had ever bruised into bloom. Others were nameless, eruptions of color behind color: iridescences and luminosities, stains and corruptions, in which the glyph found the phantoms of forms that bespoke their conjurers' dreams. A two-headed ax bound by ropes of smoke, another roped by rivers. A temple of carved divinities, each painted another unknown color, their heads crowned with the garlands of mercurial blossom and barbed cloud.

Candy felt a wind blow through the colors that she held, scattering them like the embers of an ancient fire, and she was astonished to feel a portion of her soul go with them, conforming not only into the shape of wind and flame but into a third shape, which was that of their antiquity.

Like all sacred works, it was both momentary and eternal. The intertwining of thoughts rising from the prisoners like branches from dreaming trees; the spinning prayers casting entreaties out to any thing in any heaven that might come to their rescue; the tiny fires that took a piece of Candy's soul for fuel as they went to find the Lighter of all fires, the Begetter of all winds, the Lover of all souls, and carry Its holy song back to lift the brimming vessel up upon Its music.

She was a constellation now, pieces of her soul speed-ing in search of Deity, while the sigils of her flesh, bone and mind were gathered up by the glyph's authority, and elegantly placed in the vast design where all the ley lines of its structure converged. She knew what she'd been called to do. For all its vast intelligences, the vessel had need of a pilot; and she had been called to duty.

"Lady?"

She was not alone: Malingo was rising to the left of her, Gazza to her right. And beyond them, and behind her, and in front, all the other authors of this vast device rose into its midst, their entrance instructing further reinven-tions, as though their very presences caused the system to convulse with bliss, turning every thought and breath and bead of sweat into an exaltation.

One part of Candy—impatient, doubtful, *human*—wanted the glyph to get underway, to carry them all off before their executioners arrived. But another part of her—a quieter, calmer part that was perfectly content to die if death was the price of enlightenment—took too much pleasure in the splendors visible from her place at the vessel's heart to let fear of what might come steal what she was witnessing.

"All are boarded," Gazza said.

And, as if on cue, the first blind burn of lightning came, turning Galigali into a black pyramid against a heaven of flawless white.

"Oh, Lordy Lou," Malingo murmured. "We're too late. *The Hag is here!*"

PART SEVEN

OBLIVION'S CALL

The Place is Where.
The Question How.
The Hours are When.
If Never, Now.

—Found written on the wall
of an abandoned asylum on
Gorgossium.

61

MISSING

"**G**RANDMOTHER?"

Mater Motley had put her hand, palm out, against the battle-deck window. Though her head was bowed, Carrion could see her anguished features reflected in the smoke-smeared glass.

"What . . . have they *got*?" she said.

"I don't understand," Carrion told her.

She, very slowly, looked round at him. There was naked disgust on her face, either at her own lack of foresight or at her grandson's stupidity, perhaps both.

"Do you not feel the barbs raking your skin?"

Carrion considered the question, looking down at his hands as he did so, as though to silently interrogate them.

"No," he said. "I feel nothing."

Then his eyes went up to his glass collar. Inside, he saw his remaining nightmares were behaving strangely. Depending on circumstances, they behaved in one of two ways. When feeling peaceable, they slowly swam around, warily studying the world outside their dreamer's collar. When they were aroused, however, either by rage or a desire to protect their maker, they would lash and thrash like electric whips, causing the fluid they all breathed to become milky and laced. But now they were doing something they'd never done before. They were perfectly still, the entire length of their bodies pressed against the glass, so as to be as close to their window as possible.

"Whatever it is you're feeling, my children are feeling too."

"Your *children*?" Mater Motley said, her expression of disgust souring with contempt.

"Yes, dearest Grandmama. I know you much prefer to burn your children and their children, but I take pleasure in the company of mine."

"You'd do well to remember that you were the one I kept from the flame, do you not?"

"It's never far from my thoughts," Carrion replied. "Truly. I know I owe you my life." The Empress's expression sweetened at this. "As I do my scars." And quickly soured again. "As I do my purpose. My very reason for living."

"And what is your purpose?"

"To serve you, lady," Carrion said.

He met her gaze, his eyes the color of the midsummer sea—a gleaming, glittering blue that concealed unfathomable depths: black, blacker, blackest.

All but one of his children that had retreated to the

inside of his collar had detached themselves, and were now looking at her. Did they understand the meaning of the conversation between the old woman and their master? Did they understand her contempt and his subtle mockery? It seemed they did. When he ceased to study her, they too looked away, returning their gaze as did he, to the new form out the window.

The vessel hawked up another limb of lightning, and spat it down upon the bleak flank of Mount Galigali. The force of the strike threw up a cloud of vaporized rock in the midst of which fell a hail of lava boulders, which would have beaten holes in a vessel less well designed than *The Stormwalker.* A number of them struck the battle-deck window, but for all her sensitivity to the nuances in the air, the assault of shattered stones didn't perturb the Empress in the least. She simply stared unthinking out at the billows of pulverized rock pressing against the battle-deck window.

"*Call in the Commanders,*" she instructed Carrion. "*Quickly now!*"

This time, Candy knew, there would be a kind of thunder to follow the lightning. It wouldn't be the rolling growl of burning air, but the boom of guns.

Mater Motley wasn't going to let her prisoners go without a fight.

"*Candy? Candy!*"

It was easy enough to identify the speaker: it was Zephario. But it was a lot more difficult to work out precisely where he was located. She had lost contact with him as the construction of the glyph had escalated, and she'd almost forgotten, in the heat of the moment, the deal that she'd made with him. He had given her the means to make this escape possible, in exchange for her attempting to connect him with his lost child. He had kept his side of the bargain, and now it was her turn. It had to happen *immediately*. There'd be no other time.

"Gazza," she said. "I'm going to have to leave you in charge of getting this glyph and everyone inside it away from Mater Motley. Do whatever you have to do."

"Where are you going?"

"To keep my promise."

"Are you crazy?" Gazza said.

"A promise is a promise."

"Even when you make it to a *Carrion*?"

"He can hear you, you know."

"I don't care," Gazza said. "He's going to get you killed. And I—" He growled, his brow in knots. "Why can't I—can't I?"

"We have to go," Candy said.

"I have stuff to say."

"Then say it."

"I love you," Zephario said.

"Oh?" said Candy. "Well, that's sudden."

"I'm speaking for the young fellow here."

"Oh," Candy said matter-of-factly. Then, comprehending, "*Oh*. You do?" she said to Gazza.

"Yes," Zephario replied again. "He loves you with every last bone in his body," Zephario replied.

Gazza smiled confidently. "There's more," he said.

"There's no time for more," Zephario said.

The look of confidence had gone from Gazza's face. His eyes looked at Candy, ashamed of the young man who stared out from behind them, unable to say the words.

"Zephario and I need to go," Candy said.

Gazza simply nodded.

"I'll be safe up there." They looked at each other. "I wish it was different," she said, staring at his sadness with her own. "You know what I mean—"

"Yes."

And his knowing was enough for her. Maybe there'd be another time, when things were different. But for now . . .

"I'll see you soon, then. . . ." Candy said, and with perfect timing the glyph released her, extending its own structure twenty feet or so, allowing her to drop down below, without injury, onto the shattered ground of Mount Galigali.

The Empress had begun to give her instructions. Time was of the essence, she let it be known. Time, and that the job be done flawlessly.

"In a few moments," she told her Commanders, "*The*

Stormwalker will emerge from the cloud of volcanic dust that the lightning limb has caused to temporarily blind the vessel. At which point," she went on, "I will have a comprehensive view of the site of execution. We should expect some minor attempts to resist. These people have foolishly tried to live by their own laws, refusing to obey the judgments laid down by their superiors. Obviously no Empire can sanction the presence of such individuals in its midst. They will—"

"Leave before their executioners arrive?" Carrion suggested.

"Do you find this funny?"

"No, Grandmother, I believe what you say is absolutely correct, and these iconoclasts should be executed. But—"

"But *nothing*. A knife for every heart, remember?"

"Of course."

"Well?"

"You have the knives, I realize. But regrettably the hearts have already departed."

"Impossible."

The vessel was emerging from the smoke now, and what Carrion could see was visible to a growing number of soldiers. The camp was empty. The prisoners had gone.

"Where are they?" she said, quietly at first. Then more loudly: "They were here! Six thousand, six hundred and ninety-one prisoners! The gates are still closed. THEY WERE HERE!"

"Two of them *are* still here," one of the commanders—a

small, gray-skinned stitchling called Chondross—pointed out.

"The compound is empty."

"They're not in the compound any longer, my lady," Chondross told her. "They're down there on Galigali." The stitchling pointed out of the window down at the boulder-strewn slope. "Do you see them?"

"It's Candy Quackenbush," Carrion said.

"Of course it would be her," the Empress said. "She was bound to be in this chaos somewhere."

"Who's with her?"

"It doesn't matter. Whoever he was, he shouldn't have gotten so close to her. It will be the death of him. I need a gunner!" she demanded.

No sooner had she uttered the words, than one stitchling called out: "Empress. I have the gunner ready at the bows. She has acquired your target."

"Gunner?" the Empress yelled.

The gunner's image appeared.

"Here, my Empress," she said.

"Targets," Christopher said.

"Ah, there you are," the Empress said. "Two stupid animals standing in our way. Thank you, Christopher."

"My pleasure, Empress. And my duty. Shall I have them killed?"

The image of Candy Quackenbush and her traveling companion came up on the Window. The latter had been extensively scarred—his face little more than a rigid mask of disfigured tissue; out of which he gazed blindly. Despite his maiming there was something in the man's bearing that caused Mater Motley to hold back for a few moments.

"I have the target in my sights, Empress. Shall I fire?"

"Wait . . ."

She brought the Window closer to her so as to better study the mask of scar tissue for some clue as to the face it had been, before its destruction by—

"Fire," she murmured.

It was a simple, stupid mistake. Gunner Gh'niemattah had been trained to respond to an order without hesitation. The syllable her Empress uttered was barely audible, but she responded to the sound of that one syllable by simply pulling the trigger.

It was impossible not to be astonished by the speed with which the girl from the Hereafter and the blind man beside her were erased by bursts of brilliance as each rocket found its target.

62

THE VOLCANO
AND THE VOID

CANDY, SITTING ATOP THE higher slopes of Mount Galigali, stared up at the immense expanse of *The Stormwalker*'s underbelly as it slowly passed over her. The immense machine seemed almost close enough for her to reach up and touch. The guttural drone of the vessel's massive engines made the scree on the slope dance a lunatic dance.

"It's time. Take me to my son," were the words Mater Motley had watched Zephario say to her.

He was right, Candy knew: this was the moment. The Prince of Midnight was inside *The Stormwalker* with his grandmother—and was there any place he was more likely to be on this night of nights, when old allegiances became clear, than with her? She had to get them both up into the great lightning machine before *The Stormwalker* destroyed them both.

And then, up out of the unsifted memories in her head, a word sprang onto her tongue: a word in Old Abaratian.

It had a flawless provenance. Candy had taken it from the sleeping mind of Princess Boa, back in the days when she'd used Boa as a living repository of magic. Boa had in turn learned the word from the same source she'd used for the wieldings and invocations, prayers and necromancing— her devoted Christopher Carrion. And who was Carrion's source? Of that, Candy had not the slightest doubt. Carrion had learned the word from his grandmother, Mater Motley, who was riding high in *The Stormwalker* over their heads.

Somehow that confirmed the rightness of the word she was about to utter. She had tracked it around in a circle, back to the Hag of Gorgossium.

She didn't even know what the word meant. But she knew this was the right moment to say it. It had four syllables:

Yet—

-ha—

-si—

-ha.

"Are you ready?" she said to Zephario.

"For what?" he said.

"I can't be sure, but I think there's going to be a staircase, made of smoke, and we're just going to climb it."

"Then I'm ready."

At that moment, though Candy didn't know it, the Empress of the Abarat was studying them in the Window—no, not them: Zephario—trying to work out what it was about the burned face that puzzled her.

"*Yet*—" Candy said.

Words of magic had to be spoken very cautiously, Malingo had once told her he'd read in Wolfswinkel's books. *They had to be pronounced clearly so that the forces that were being summoned into activity knew exactly what they were being instructed to do.*

As Candy spoke the second syllable—"*ha*"—the Empress looked up from the Window, suddenly realizing what element had worked such a terrible transformation upon the face on the slope below.

"Fire," she'd said.

Gunner Gh'niemattah had thought she'd heard her Empress's instruction. She had not aimed for one figure or the other, but for the rock between them. The rocket would blow a hole in the rock between them, causing the ground they were standing on to fold in on itself, carrying both of them down to their deaths.

"*si*—"

Gunner Gh'niemattah pulled the trigger. The charge in the gunner's launcher exploded.

"*ha*—"

The explosive charge slammed against the expulsion plate at the base of the rocket.

The phenomenal power of the weapon, which had been mounted on *The Stormwalker* so recently that the gunner had never had an opportunity to test it, completely blind-sided her. The whole launcher kicked so violently that the gunner was thrown back across the gunnery tower, her neck snapping at the same moment the rocket struck the flank of Mount Galigali.

Such was the power of the rocket's release that a ripple of its force passed through the entire Stormwalker. It juddered and rolled. As its motion settled, the Empress called forth five more windows to study the aftereffects of the rockets.

"What do you see?" Christopher asked her.

"A hole in the side of Galigali, and a lot of dust and dead rock."

"So they're dead?"

"Of course they're dead. The ground opened up beneath both of them. And down they went into the fire."

"What fire?" Christopher said, looking toward the window. "There's nothing left burning in Galigali, surely."

"I might have killed Candy Quackenbush, but I've resurrected Galigali." Mater Motley turned and walked back to look at the volcano. "So many resurrections. First Boa, then you, now Galigali."

"I was never dead, lady," he replied. "If I had been, I would have remained that way. Happily."

He didn't look back at her. He just kept staring at the ever-multiplying streams of magma as they coursed down over the volcano's flank.

"Stop obsessing on the girl! Did she really mean something to you?"

"Yes. She reminded me I'd been in love once. And that

maybe I had deserved to be loved in return." He stared past his grandmother at the wasteland visible through the battle-deck windows behind her. "She was quite a creature. Look! There! Her last miracle. She made them a glyph. That's how they got away. She made a glyph big enough to carry all of the prisoners."

"Impossible," the Empress told him.

"I'm *looking* at it," Christopher replied, pointing past her.

The Empress turned, following the direction of his finger, out through the battle-deck window.

Beyond the empty camp was a stretch of boulder-strewn wasteland, and beyond that, the Void. An empty darkness, into which was headed the immense glyph that Candy helped create.

"They've gone over the Edge of the World," one of the stitchling Commanders remarked.

"Indeed they have," the Empress replied.

"That's the end of them then," a second Commander said. "There's nothing to hold them up out there. They'll fall forever."

"How did she do that?" Mater Motley said to herself.

"Does it matter?" Carrion said. "She's dead. She won't be doing it again."

The Empress responded as though he hadn't spoken.

"The amount of *power* that takes. Where did she get it?" She talked very quietly, almost to herself.

"They don't seem to be falling," Carrion said. "Are

you sure that's the Edge of the World?"

A copy of the *Almenak* had already been brought out, and the map in it carefully studied. Christopher went over to the Commanders and snatched the copy away to scrutinize for himself.

"Of course none of the information in these wretched *Almenak*s is reliable," he said. To the north of Scoriae, the Sea of Izabella fell away into a featureless darkness, along the edge of which was written: *This is the Edge of the World.* Beyond the edge, etched in white letters against the blackness were four letters, widely sprawled:

VOID

"They *will* fall," one of the Commanders said.

"Forever and ever," said Motley.

"We should go to the very edge then," Carrion said. He was smiling now, genuinely pleased at the prospect. "I want to see what this Void looks like."

"I already gave the order," the Empress said. "We'll be waiting for them if they attempt to turn around."

The Stormwalker had taken one lightning stride, and was about to take a second, moving the two-mile-long vehicle over the deserted camp toward the Edge of the Abarat with extraordinary speed.

"I see no sign of her glyph falling," Carrion said.

"It *will*," his grandmother said. "There's nothing out there to hold it up. See for yourself." She directed Christopher's attention to the port side of *The Stormwalker*. There, beyond a stretch of solidified lava, the Izabella rushed on toward the edge of the world, where it fell away, throwing up churning clouds of spray.

"Impressive," Carrion said.

"Yet her glyph still flies," the Old Hag groaned. "*How? Where does power like that come from?*" She glanced at her grandson. "Did she ever talk to you about these powers?"

"The girl? No. But I have a theory. . . ." he said coyly.

"I'm listening."

"The blind man who was with her. I knew him. Not the face, of course. There's nothing left there, but . . . the eyes. Something about the eyes . . ."

"Don't be coy. Talk!"

"It's ridiculous," he said, "but . . . I remember them from a dream. I was just a boy, and they looked down at me. Then he whispered something to me . . ."

"*What did the man say?*"

Carrion's gaze slid in his grandmother's direction for a second or two. Then he looked away.

"He looked down at me and he said, 'I love you, Little One.'"

63

PIGS

"*Y*ETHASIHA."

The stairway of fog had understood very well the urgency of Candy and Zephario's situation. It had formed beneath their feet, and instantly closed up like an accordion, lifting them up into the belly of *The Stormwalker* through an open door that then closed very quickly, protecting its passengers from the explosion that peppered the hull on which they were sprawled with a number of projectiles that struck it like bullets.

They were alive. The breath had been knocked out of them, and they were a lot closer to the Hag of Gorgossium than either of them would have wished, but they were alive.

"That was quite a word," Candy said. "I've never wielded something that moved so quickly—"

She stopped, silenced by the sound of two low-ranking stitchling soldiers engaged in a fierce exchange as they opened an iron door that brought them into this portion of the hold. Judging by their banter, the Old Hag's seamstresses had devoted considerably little time to their mental capacities.

"There's Quagmites on this vessel. I swears."

"You and your Quagmites, Shaveos," the other stitchling said as it sniffed the air. The sound of its voice changed suddenly. "*Huh*. You right. You right."

"See! You smells it too?" said Shaveos excitedly. "That's a Uman Been. I told you I knows it, Lummuk!"

"How'd you know what a Uman Been smells likes?" Lummuk wanted to know.

"I were on the *Wormwood*, whens it went the Hereafter."

"You saw that Chickumtomb?"

"I did. I saw all that drownsd."

"Were it horrible?"

"Oya. It were Viley!" Shaveos said gravely. "I was trown out the ship. I ended up in . . . I forgets. I still got the paper!" Candy heard the sound of the stitchling rummaging for something. "Here. Hold my knife," he said.

This probably wasn't a bad time to snatch a look at the enemy, Candy thought. She peered out from behind the tarpaulin-covered crates where she and Zephario had hidden and got a clearer look at stitchlings than she'd ever had before. There was an intelligence in their behavior, though not in their speech, that she hadn't expected to see in the sacks of walking mud. And she noticed that the mud didn't simply fill the sack, the way dirt might, rather it pushed out of little holes, as though it was constantly in the process of reinventing itself. There was something in the weave of the sack that then crawled all over the stitchlings' forms, repairing any larger tears by crudely restitching the thread. They were, quite obviously, as she had been, Two In One: the thing occupied, and the occupying thing.

These two stitchlings in particular were chaotic, asymmetrical beings. One had an arm that ended in something more like a lobster claw than fingers, while the other, thanks to some seamstress's whim, had no less than four hands at the end of one arm, two pairs set palm to palm, and no hand at all on the other arm.

Lobster Arm was apparently Shaveos, because it was he who now brought a tattered piece of folded paper out of the jacket of his mud-and-blood-splattered uniform. He pulled out a pair of spectacles with both lenses cracked, and peered at the map.

"This ams the place," he said proudly. "The place I fell from *Wormwood*."

"Whoaya now!" said Lummuk, obviously skeptical. "How's that certain? What that sign sayings?"

"Sign? It sayings '*Fort Com*'!"

In less stressful circumstances, Candy might have found some humor in the stitchling's error. He had an advertisement for the Comfort Tree Hotel in his hand.

"Was there battles?" Lummuk wanted to know.

"Was there battles? *Was there battles?* Nine Peep-Holes was killed just from by frights! And it was all the Uman

Beens that was doin' the crazies. I din't do nuffin! I was just . . . smellin' 'em."

"And you smell 'em here now. That's how comes you knows, huh?"

"Yeps."

They both inhaled.

"Oh yes," Lummuk said. "I smells it."

"Give me my knife back," Shaveos demanded. "I'll cut-sem!"

His knife was, in fact, a machete. He felt the heft of it, and even in the shadows Candy could see the sick smile of pleasure that came onto his face as he did so. This was a weapon he'd used. She knew it. The evidence was there in his lipless smile.

"Ready?" he said to Lummuk.

"I was stitched ready," Lummuk said smugly.

"We gotta be ready for thems to come at us all at once. They's vicious, these—"

His remark was interrupted by what was unmistakably the grunting of a pig. A very large pig, its grunting encouraging more noise from pigs in its vicinity.

"Oh! Piggie wiggies!" said Shaveos. "Look a' 'em!" He pushed Lummuk aside. "I sees me some piggie wiggies, I does, I does."

"What ams you doing?" Lummuk wanted to know.

"I wants to hug a piggie wiggie. And then maybe takes a bite. Just one bites."

"Fooly fool! Thems not your piggie wiggies to hug and

bites. Thems the Empress's piggie wiggies!"

"She don'ts gives care how many piggie wiggies she's has. What you think, she come up down every morning to countsem?" Shaveos replied, pulling open the cage door. He reached in. "Come on, you. You looks delish!" He talked to the pig as though he might have spoken to a baby, in a singsong voice. "Come come, piggie wiggie. Pretty piggie wiggie." The charm didn't last very long. When the pig failed to respond to his request, he quickly lost his temper. *"Come, you vilely porkund!"* he yelled, throwing the cage door open. *"I needs my belly filled all up! Wally on, porkund! Wally on!"*

He reached in to grab the hog with both hands. The creature squealed as it was hauled out by the stitchling and lifted up into the light. It was a big beast, its body striped orange and blue, except for its head, which was that of an albino, its flesh stark white, its eyes bloodred with long white lashes. Though it retained some porcine snout, its features were flatter than those of an ordinary pig, making the animal look almost human.

"Oh, yous is a *gorgeous.* Yous is! I could . . . I could—"

Apparently besieged by his own appetite, Shaveos opened his mouth, which was lined with rows of dagger-like teeth—and bit down on the animal's neck. The pig's squeal became even shriller. Candy kept her eyes fixed on the struggle between the diner and his dinner. It was seconds away from catastrophe, she sensed. The pig was too strong, and the stitchling too concerned about his empty belly to notice. Keeping her eyes locked on the two devourers, she caught hold of Zephario, tugging on his arm to let him know the moment of departure was near.

But before Candy could say a word, the pigs broke free, all of them squealing now.

"Backs! Backs! Dumdum poogoos!" said the fooly fool.

"Aw. Now lookee what youms done!" hollered Lummuk.

"We should move. Now," Candy said.

"Good plan," said Zephario.

Pigs were jumping and scrambling under them and scrambling to free themselves of two stitchlings' grips. The chaos was good news. It distracted the stitchlings long enough for Candy and Zephario to reach the door. Their luck, however, quickly ran out. At the last minute, Shaveos flung his claw about wildly and accidentally entangled itself in Candy's hair. The stitchling turned to see what it had snagged. Its face went slack.

"Uman Been!" the stitchling said.

He turned Candy toward him, and she was treated to her first close-up view of a stitchling's face. It was a mixture of genius and crudity: the stitches were large and uneven, but there was an uncanny realism in the way it moved. This was no simple brute. The Todo mud that gleamed in his eyeholes, forming his shiny-wet eyes, had intelligence in it.

"I knows yous," Shaveos said. "Chickumtomb girl! Candy Quackenbush!"

It said her name with remarkable clarity. But the words had barely escaped his lips when Candy felt a wave of force, like a narrow wind, rush past her. The air ignited all around her, just for a second, then the ring of light and power passed her by, closing like an iris as it did so. It struck both stitchlings in their chests. They loosed a shock of rage and pain. Shaveos's claw went limp, freeing Candy's hair from its grip.

She instantly turned to look for Zephario.

"Are you all right?" she asked him.

He was reaching into the interior of his jacket, mumbling to himself as he did so.

"Can I help?" she said, reaching toward him.

Though her fingers didn't touch him, she sensed how close they were, and retreated from him with guilty haste.

"That power surge," she said. "It was you."

Behind her, Shaveos bellowed:

"Candy Quackenbush. She ams here!"

"Oh, great," Candy groaned.

"Cargo Hold Nine! Cargo Hold Nine!" shouted Lummuk.

"I'll killser!" said Shaveos.

And so saying, he stood, picking up his machete as he did so, and ran for Candy, swinging his machete in the air.

She saw the machete coming, and tried to throw herself out of its path through the door into the next hold. But the thresholds of the doors between the holds were abnormally high, and she stumbled. She might well have cracked her shinbones had she not reached out and caught hold of the door frame. Shaveos swung at her again, and this time she might have perished had he not lost hold of his dinner. At that moment, a pig a charged into him, knocking him over, and taking Candy with him in the process.

Candy was shoved aside by the stitchling's bulk. She lost her grip of the door frame and fell back among the pigs. There were several seconds when all Candy could see was a blur of wet snouts and curly pink tails, then she sat up, in time to see Lummuk stagger away from Shaveos, whose machete was buried deep in Lummuk's head: so deep that the blade was entirely hidden for several inches of its length before its painted end could even be seen.

Shaveos reached out and caught hold of the machete's handle as his companion toppled backward. This had two consequences. One, it stopped Lummuk from falling backward; indeed it pulled him back into an upright position, where he teetered for several seconds, while Shaveos twisted the machete this way and that, attempting to free it.

Candy was watching Shaveos's face when he finally worked the blade loose. She saw his expression shift from frustration to pleasure—there! The blade was coming free!—only to decay seconds later into puzzlement, more than puzzlement. Fear. And Candy knew why.

It was only common sense.

She saw Shaveos try to push his machete back into the hole he'd just unstopped, like a man with a fat cork trying to fit it back into the narrow opening of a bottle from which a djinni was escaping. It was a lost cause. Still he pushed, and as he did so the mud from Lummuk's head leaped at him. So fast. So horribly fast! Tentacles, black as the stitchling's eyes had been, but shot through with smears of vivid color that had surely never been in gray-brown muck mined on Gorgossium. Shaveos knew he was in trouble. He let go of the machete and instead used his free hand to stem the flow of mud.

"Lummuk! Shaveos ams sorry! Accident! Oopsies! Lummuk! She ams to blame! The——" He drew breath and yelled: "CANDY QUACKENBUSH!"

The mud that had once been Lummuk didn't care about his explanations. It continued to crawl up Shaveos's arm, leaping over his fingers, and then—just as Shaveos drew breath to yell Candy's name one more time, Lummuk oozed into his open mouth.

Candy shook herself out of her trance of curiosity and turned to Zephario.

"We should get——" she started to say.

But the blind man had already gone.

64

NO PLAN B

"**W**HY HAVEN'T WE FALLEN out of the sky?" Gazza said.

"Maybe because we haven't stopped moving?" Malingo suggested, though there was precious little conviction in his reply. "How far have we come?"

Gazza looked back over his shoulder. "Oh, Lordy, Lordy, Lordy," he said.

"What's wrong?"

"We're a lot farther from Scoriae than I thought we were."

Malingo got to his feet and turned around to look back through the glyph's semitranslucent walls. It was a beguiling, rapturous spectacle, with layer upon layer of figures, their colors shimmering toward the stern of the glyph. There were people in all directions, some assembled in groups, many solitary. But he resisted the temptation to study them too closely. He needed to focus his attention on the northern coastline of Scoriae.

Gazza had been right. They were indeed a lot farther from Scoriae than he thought they'd be. If he squinted, he could just see the area of flat ground where the internment compound had been located, and beyond it, Mount Galigali, which was no longer the inert rock it had been for as long as any of these people could remember. A gaping hole had been torn open in its flank, and liquid magma blazed from the wound, hawking up phlegm-fire to spit at the sky.

"Galigali's gonna go bang," Malingo said.

"Hasn't it already?"

"I think it's got more destruction in it than the few fireworks we've seen so far."

"Really? Funny, I feel like Galigali right now. I'm going to go bang. But a good bang. No . . . a *great* bang," Gazza said.

"Oh? What's brought this on?"

"Not what, Malingo, *who.*"

"Oh, *her.* What was it that got ya? Her eyes, right? Blue, brown. Blue, brown."

"But each time, a different blue."

"A different brown."

"Lordy Lou," Gaz said.

Malingo's smile withdrew, only lingering in his eyes.

"I didn't realize. I'm sorry," Gaz said.

"What's to be sorry for?" Malingo asked.

"You don't look very happy now. I didn't realize—"

"We geshrats seem to always want more than fate has given us."

"That's not just a geshrat problem."

"No?"

"No. When you like something . . . even love something . . ."

"Or even love, yes."

"Yes. *Love.* That's the word." His voice got louder with every syllable. "Why not use it?"

"Perhaps more quietly?" Malingo said.

"Why? She makes me happy. *Crazy-happy.* And I know I shouldn't feel this way, but she's . . . I don't know . . . hypnotizing me with those eyes. Blue, brown. Blue, brown."

"You *do* sound crazy. Be careful," Malingo warned him. "Everybody can hear what you're saying."

"Fine by me," Gazza said. "I've got nothing to hide." He raised his voice to be sure he could be heard by everyone in the glyph. "*I love the girl* who brought us together, Candy Quackenbush. None of us would still be alive if it weren't for her," he reminded them all, his voice coming back to him in mysterious echoes off the vaulted ceilings and the nine-sided chambers. "But we're not safe yet. The Stormwalker that's waiting for us back there is even bigger than our glyph, and it contains an army of stitchlings: one stitchling for every one of us. *A knife for every heart.* That's what Mater Motley has planned for us. But we're free and we're going to stay free. The problem is there's seven thousand knives they haven't used yet."

There were murmurs of assent from all directions, high and low, port and starboard.

"Does anybody disagree?" Gazza yelled.

He let the silence play out for a few seconds, to give any dissenting voice a chance to be heard. But there were no objections raised. Candy was the heroine of the Hour.

"All right," he said, smiling. "So then it's agreed. We have to go back. We're—"

"Wait."

The voice of a woman came from somewhere on the starboard side.

"Before we turn around, there's something everybody should know. The vessel the Empress has come after us in is a death-ship. It's called a Stormwalker. I saw copies of the plans for its construction. It could blow us out of the skies in a heartbeat."

There were murmurs of suspicion:

How did she see plans for a thing like that?

Whose side was she really on?

"I wouldn't be here if I wasn't on the side of what's right," the woman said. "I want Mater Motley brought to trial for murder. My brother, Kaltu Mothrass, was tortured to death by her and her seamstresses."

"Why?"

"We don't have time—" Malingo started to say but the question had been asked and the woman was already answering it: "I'm Juna Mothrass. My brother and his wife, Geneva Peachtree—"

"Wife?" Malingo said quietly to himself.

He had spent many hours in Geneva's presence since they had all banded together around Candy, but not once had he heard Geneva make any mention of a husband, which would have sounded odd under any circumstances, but was particularly strange when the husband you were talking about was one of the most famous revolutionaries of Abarat. Malingo needed to be certain that this woman was who she claimed to be.

"So, Juna——" he said.

"Yes?"

"——do you know Geneva well?"

"Very well."

"Well enough to tell me which book she knows by heart from beginning to end?"

The fact that Malingo had presented Juna with such a demanding question had a murmur of anticipation to make the colored compartments of the vessel churn, color flowing with color, creating hues that only existed in the ethereal or metafictional dimensions.

"Of course," Juna Mothrass replied without hesitation. "The *Testaments of Pottishak*. She knows every word."

"Is that the right answer?" Gazza said.

"Yup," Malingo told him. "She knows Geneva. We should listen to her."

"I don't know much," Juna said. "All I can say with any certainty is that if we try to come at the vessel from either side, we'll be blown out of the sky."

"So what do you suggest?" Gazza said. "Are we supposed to leave Candy on that island? Look at it! Look!"

He had picked, quite by chance, a particularly

opportune moment to direct everyone's attention toward Scoriae, because two and half seconds later the top of Mount Galigali, which had been a shape so recognizable it had been used on Ž500 paterzem notes without need of identification for many years, blew off. A column of liquid stone poured heavenward, blackening a sky that was only just beginning to clear the dirt from the sockets of the stars when the flame turned into an oily-black smoke that blinded them again. Meanwhile, titanic shovelfuls of infernal cinders rolled smoking down the slope, pitched so far by the force of the eruption that some of them flowed down onto the beach, where they rolled into the water, throwing up clouds of steam.

"I think there's only one way to go," Juna said.

"And where's that?" Gazza said.

"We go straight at The Stormwalker."

"You mean fly straight at that thing?"

"That's suicide, surely," said somebody else.

"On the contrary. I think it's our only chance because it's the last thing she'll expect. She thinks we're frightened of her."

"We are," said John Slop.

"No," said Gazza. "We're not. And if we admit to fear, then we're already lost."

"So what's going to stop us colliding with her?"

"Nothing. We *will* collide with it! And push it back, directly into the mouth of the volcano."

"Is the glyph strong enough to survive the impact?"

"I don't know," Juna said. "We're only as strong as our will to survive."

"All right," said Gazza warily. "Let's call that Plan A. Who has a Plan B?"

There was a very long silence, which Malingo eventually broke.

"Apparently there is no Plan B," he said.

"Well, that keeps it simple," said Gazza. "We fly straight at *The Stormwalker* and take our chances."

"What will they do? What will they do?" The Empress paced back and forth in front of the window, watching the glyph. "They can't stay out there forever."

"Maybe they're not out there," her grandson said.

"What nonsense are you talking? I can see them with my own eyes."

"Who knows what's really out there? We could be one great big mirror. We could be looking at a distorted version of ourselves."

"I've never heard of anything so ridiculous. I have access to every form of magic in the Abarat. And I have moved on to search other worlds for new sources of power."

"Are you still keeping all that a secret, Grandmother? Because it really isn't much of one is it? Not any longer. I followed you as far as the Starrish Door—the one that leads to the Zael Maz'yre—years ago."

"No," the Empress replied coldly. "You couldn't have."

"Oh, don't fret yourself. I got no further than the door. How could I? All those choices. Doors *with* doors. And within every door, a destination. Of course I had no idea which one you'd taken, and of course I was deathly afraid of choosing the wrong one. Who knows where I would have been delivered? I was afraid I'd never find my way back. So I left, and went back to my work, and never—"

"Hush!" she said sharply.

"What?"

"We have visitors."

The monotone in which she spoke was a voice Carrion had learned to despise—no, to *dread*. It was worse than anger, that voice. Anger had a beginning and an end. Even if it went on for weeks it would run out of fuel eventually. But the nullity from which this voice arose was his grandmother's permanent state of being. It was her speaking from the grave into which she had been born, as she was fond of saying; the hole of dirt, worms and despair, which was the lot of all living things.

This was the harsh, unforgiving law that Carrion had been raised on. And every time he saw that look on his grandmother's face, and heard the almost metallic harshness in her voice, the brutal lessons of his childhood came back to him as though her needle had only pierced his lips yesterday.

"Well?" she said.

"Well what?"

"Are you going or not?"

Christopher had drifted further into memory than he'd realized. He'd missed a piece of the conversation, it appeared. He knew from childhood it wasn't wise to lie.

"I was distracted. Memories. Nothing important. You have all my attention now."

"Good. Because we have a problem and you'll have to fix it. I need to stay here in case they make a move."

"What's the problem?"

"Don't you feel it?"

"No."

"Look."

She pointed to the ground, and threw down one of the wieldings he especially loathed. This was one of the Nephauree's specialties, Carrion suspected: a violation of spatial geometry and physics alike. Though he had not moved a step, he now felt the ground shift beneath him. When his eyes dropped to the bare marble he was no longer standing on solid ground. But everything had shifted. The place where Carrion was standing now dropped away steeply, as it did on the opposite side, where his grandmother was standing on a steep slope, staring down into the depths of the ship. The floors and walls between the battle floor and the hold had been erased, essentially, by the power of the Nephauree's magic.

There was chaos down there. Pigs were running around, squealing wildly. And in the midst of the pigs were two stitchlings. One of them was grievously wounded, a machete buried in its face. Mud continued to leap up out of the wound, its matter creating a gathering on the chest of the second stitchling, who lay sprawled on the ground.

The Empress took a steep step down the chaotic wall of the pit.

"*You!*" she said.

It was neither Shaveos or Lummuk who replied to her. It was the third entity down there: the one squatting on Shaveos's chest, that looked up and spoke. Its face was still a work in progress, invisible fingers pushing the mud of its features around two holes for eyes—a slash of a mouth. But for all its crudity, it knew how to make words.

"What do *you* want?" it said, its voice a raw rasp.

"I want some respect from you, to start with! Do you know who you are addressing?"

"What makes you think I'd care?" the mud replied.

"Carrion?" the Hag said. "Go down and fetch me that skinless piece of filth. Carrion?"

Only now did she look up at the place where she'd last seen her grandson. He was no longer standing there.

"Carrion?"

"*Carrion!*"

"*CARRION!*"

65

LULLABY

CANDY DIDN'T SEE ZEPHARIO ahead of her at any time during her pursuit, but her instincts told her she was on the right track. They also told her that she needed to pick up her pace otherwise she was going to lose him, even though he was the blind one and she the sighted. Luckily the old man had left a trail of air tinged with magic: drifts of color like chalk dust the color of his robes, falling away through the murky air. They weren't, she thought, accidental. They only appeared at places where she might very well have made a wrong decision: turned right instead of left, or chosen the wrong one of several doors.

But even with the assistance he was giving to her, the space between them was getting bigger. And she certainly would have lost him eventually if help hadn't come to her from a most unexpected source.

Mater Motley.

It was the Hag herself whom Candy heard call out:

"Carrion? Carrion! *CARRION!*"

Candy halted for a moment, and waited for the voice of the Hag to echo off the walls all around her. When they finally died away she heard the sounds of footsteps. It was Zephario she thought she heard, his running slowed by fatigue, but still moving fast. He was nearby too, just above her.

She risked everything, and called to him: "Wait for me, Zephario," she said. "I'm coming. Just let me catch up with you."

She had found the flight of stairs he had climbed—the pastel dust that he'd left behind him was still in the air, fading as it fell—and she went after him, climbing the stairs two or three at a time. Halfway up she met a cloud of spice-and-honey smoke rolling down the stairs to meet her as she ascended. By now, she reasoned, the Hag was fully alerted to Candy's presence. Stitchling troops were being sent to arrest her; and given her ignorance of the vessel's layout, and the stitchlings' familiarity with it, she had little hope of evading them.

She was almost at the top of the stairs. The atmosphere up here was very different from the atmosphere below. The lights in the hold had been the Commexo Company's version of utilitarian supermarket lighting. It simply made things blandly visible. But the light that was illuminating the air at the top of the stairs was something else entirely: a blue-gold haze that dropped in lazy loops from a kind of ziggurat of candles in the center of a room so large that even thousands, perhaps tens of thousands of candles burning could not illuminate the walls of the room. It was some sort of altar. A place of worship for some thing Candy had no knowledge of. It was really only then that Candy understood how truly vast the craft that they had entered actually was; and the inconceivably immense orders of power that were being generated to keep it in the air.

"Zephario?" she said, her voice apparently never reaching the walls of the space, because no echo came back to her. "Zephario, where are you?"

"I'm here," he said, and her eyes, following the sound of his voice, found him standing no more than thirty yards from her, standing so still in the flickering light of the temple that her gaze had slid past him several times without noticing him. "But you don't need to stay with me any longer, Candy. You got me here. You did what you said you'd do."

"I said I'd get you to him," she said.

"To who?" Christopher Carrion asked.

For the second time she followed the sound of a Carrion's voice in this place. And for a second time, found the one she was searching for just a short distance away. Candy couldn't help but notice his startling transformation. He looked nothing like the festering alley urchin she'd encountered in Tazmagor.

"You shouldn't be here, Candy. This is a sacred place. At least the Hag thinks so."

"Sacred to whom?" Zephario asked him.

"The ones who give her the power she's got. Who helped her build this Stormwalker," Carrion replied. "Those Who Walk Behind the Stars."

"The Nephauree?" Zephario said very softly.

"Yes . . ." Carrion said, his voice carrying a fresh measure of respect for this knowledgeable stranger. "Do you also have dealings with them?"

Zephario didn't answer the question. Instead he said: "She deals with the Nephauree?"

"Yes. What does it matter to you?"

"You have to stop her. The Nephauree? *They're* at the heart of this?"

"What?" Carrion said, faintly irritated now. "What are you talking about?" He didn't give Zephario time to fail to reply. He looked directly at Candy. "Do you know what he's talking about?"

"No. Not really."

"But you brought him here."

"Yes."

"Why?"

"Because he had to see you."

"All right. Again: *why?*"

"He's your father, Christopher."

There was a long, brutal silence when everything that eyes could express flickered in Carrion's gaze. "That's not possible," he said. "My father is . . . not . . ." The words slowed as they emerged. "Not . . ."

"Not a blind, broken old man dressed in filthy rags?" He sighed. "I would have preferred to have come before you in a more noble state, I will admit. But we take what we are given, when it comes to the clothes upon our backs. And I trusted you had enough of your mother's heart in you to look past the rags to the spirit."

He lifted his hand, as though to touch his son's face, even though they were ten strides or more apart. Despite that distance, Carrion flinched behind the wall of glass and the circling nightmares as though he'd felt the touch.

Zephario sensed his response.

"You're angry," he said.

"No," Carrion replied. "Just doubtful."

"I wouldn't have brought him here if I wasn't certain," Candy said.

Christopher turned his baleful gaze on Candy. "Speaking of bringing him here, how did you do that? My grandmother thinks she saw you die on Galigali. And I saw the place where you were standing erupt moments later. So why aren't you dead?"

Though Carrion asked the question of Candy, it was Zephario who replied.

"We left the mountain before the death sentence could be delivered. You don't need to know how. But you can be certain the power she used to carry us away wasn't got from a bargain made with destroyers of worlds, like the Nephauree."

"How do you know what they've done, old man?"

"You still don't believe me, do you?"

"That you're my father? No. I'd know you. Even after all these years . . ."

"Why? You never saw me. We three survived the fire. But you were so small, and so traumatized by being in the middle of all that death . . . hearing them all." The strength in his voice began to falter. He drew several quick, shallow breaths, but they failed to carry him through the terrible truths that awaited utterance.

"Your brothers and sisters, your own mother . . . burning alive . . ." His voice was shaking, but so was his entire body. Candy wanted to somehow help him tell this terrible story, but how could she? There was nothing in this vast burden that she could carry for him. It belonged solely to this tragic father, who could only pass it on in his own anguished fashion to his already wounded son. "I sometimes wondered when I looked at you, how or why you even held on to life. Why?"

"Wait!" Carrion said. "Now I know you're lying. You said I never saw you just a moment ago. Now you say you looked at me."

"Oh, I looked at you, child," Zephario said. "Many times. But only when you slept. I wanted to get my fill of you, as any father would."

"The fire didn't blind you?"

"No. I blinded myself," he said. "She made me crazy, your grandmother, and I poured poison in my eyes to kill my sight."

"Why did she make you crazy?"

"Because she found me one night in your nursery, holding you sleeping in my arms, singing to you."

"Nobody ever sang to me."

"The 'Lullaby of Luzaar Muru.' You don't remember it?"

He began, in that shaking voice to sing:

> *"Coopanni panni,*
> *Coopanni panni,*
> *Luzaar Muru.*
> *Copii juvasi*
> *Athemun yezoo.*
> *Coopanni panni,*
> *Coopanni panni*
> *Luzaar Facheem*
> *Mendonna quasi*
> *Wemendee bazoo . . ."*

Candy had no idea what the words meant, but she had no doubt that she was indeed listening to a lullaby. The simple melody, even sung by a voice so close to breaking, was still calming.

She allowed her eyes to stray, very cautiously, toward Christopher. The look of triumph on his face, having caught Zephario out in a lie, had vanished. So had the doubt. Very softly he said what might have been the two most important words Candy had heard him say. Perhaps that he had ever said.

"I remember."

Something essential had changed in him, Candy saw, the greatest evidence of which was the behavior of his nightmares, which no longer circled his head, but lay acquiescent at the bottom of his collar. Not dead, but simply robbed of any belligerent purpose.

"Why didn't you show yourself to me, Father?" he said. "Why only hold me when I slept?"

"I wasn't a pretty sight, believe me. The doctors told me if you even saw me, so badly burned, it might be too much for you. That you'd just give up on life. So I only held you when you slept. But that stopped after she caught me. No more singing 'Luzaar Muru' to my baby. I should have left that night, because in my heart I knew she would win the battle for your soul. She wanted a true servant of her will, whose mind she knew as well as she knew her own, because she'd shaped it. And she couldn't afford to have anyone else taint her perfect apprentice. So she had to rid herself of me."

"But you knew——"

"Of course I knew."

"Still you didn't leave."

"You were all I had. All that was left from a tragedy I thought I'd caused. It never occurred to me that my own mother would kill her own grandchildren. No, I thought it was me. All me. And the only sacred, beautiful thing that had been saved from what I'd done, was you. So how could I abandon you? How could I give up my times holding you while you slept? I couldn't. So even though I knew she would try to take my life sooner or later, so that she could own you completely, I stayed close. And I was always ready for the moment when her assassin came. I knew how to defend myself against any blade she might hire to dispatch me. What I didn't consider was that there might be no blade. That she would be poisoning me slowly. Sewing seeds of madness in my head, so that the assassin who almost took my life was myself."

He stopped. His voice had become so thin, so insubstantial, that it was barely louder than the sound of the candle flames gathering.

"You know the rest," he said.

"How did you live?"

"I somehow found my way back to myself, when I began to read the cards. Piece by piece I put my memories back together, though I'd forgotten almost everything."

"Even me?"

Zephario finally began to walk toward his son, and this time Carrion didn't flinch. He simply stood there, waiting for his father to approach.

Candy searched Carrion's features, looking for some sign of what he was feeling. But he was either letting nothing show or was not certain what he felt. Either way his face was blank, his eyes as empty as those of his father's.

Candy had learned to become aware of how the feeling in the air changed when magic was at work, and it was at work now. Its source was Zephario. He was wielding the same power that he had wielded in those terrible moments on Mount Galigali, when he'd done something that had plucked them from certain death.

But what was he using it for now? What purpose was the magic serving?

She got her answer as Zephario came within reach of his son, and lifting his right hand, touched the collar. His fingers didn't pause upon contact with the glass. They passed *through* it, their motion not slowing even an instant as they slid through the divide and into the mysterious fluid that Carrion and his nightmares lived upon and within. The nightmares raised their heads a little at the intrusion of the fingers, but quickly seemed to decide that, since their master saw no harm in them, then why should they, and lay their heads down again.

Zephario's fingers reached out and touched his son's cheek.

It seemed to Candy that in that moment, in that touch, all the suffering Zephario had spoke of—all the waste, all the anguish, all the death—poured out of the father and into the son. Memories Carrion had kept hidden all these years, even from himself, finally surfaced; and he remembered what it had felt like to be in the heart of the fire—

Features, which had moments before betrayed nothing, suddenly wore every agony carved on a living face. His mouth was drawn down, his brow became a mass of anguished forms, the traces of veins across his temples began to swell and throb, while the muscles of his jaws clenched.

"Oh, Father . . ." Carrion said. ". . . this *hurts* . . ."

"I will let you be," Zephario said.

He broke his contact, and withdrew his hand from the collar, leaving the place where he had entered and exited unmarked.

"It all makes sense now," Zephario said. "I never understood why the cards wanted to look for a child I knew would never care for me. And now I see why. The idea of seeing him again strengthened my heart. But it wasn't the real reason I took this last journey. It was so that the blind man might see a terrible hidden thing."

"The Nephauree," Carrion murmured.

"You knew all along?"

"That she worked with them?" He looked up at his father out of the maze of pain he had discovered and Candy knew that the Christopher Carrion who was watching the world now would never have been able to make sense of his father's fears until he had been made to remember the fire. Now he was reconnected to the horror of the burning of the Carrion Mansion, in all its terrible particulars. It wasn't some ancient tale of a cruel thing done in a cruel time. It was living memory of the dying. The stench of burning hair and flesh and bone. The sound of screaming silenced as those who were crying out inhaled fire. It was a crime committed by the woman who taught him not to feel, that could never be forgotten or forgiven.

But what he knew, she knew. It had always been like that between them.

"I'm sorry, Father," Christopher said.

"There's nothing to apologize for, son."

"You don't understand. I just didn't want the Hag to feel it. But your pain—my pain—was too strong. I let it slip away. *She* felt them!"

"What does that mean?" Candy asked.

"She knows he's here now," Christopher said. "She knows I've seen my father's face. And she is *very* unhappy."

66

LOVE, TOO LATE

THERE HAD BEEN NO dissenting voice from anywhere throughout the glyph. The plan was simple: tell the ship where it was to go, and return with all possible speed to Scoriae.

"How?" said John Mischief.

"Good one," said John Slop. "How?"

"Easy," said Gaz. "We *think.*"

"We just have to think to make it obey?" Malingo said.

"I hope——"

Suddenly, the glyph responded to its creators' instructions without a moment's hesitation. It sped even deeper into the Void and then—when perhaps it sensed that it was so far from Scoriae that it was no longer visible, even to the keenest eye—it swung around.

"See?" Gazza said. "Here we go! I just hope wherever Candy is . . ."

"Do you think she knows we're coming?" Malingo said.

"Yes," Gazza said. "She knows."

—ᘯ—

Events of great significance were happening out there, Candy knew. But what? She *had to see.*

"Window. Window. Window," Candy said. "Carrion? I need to get to a window."

It took a moment for the request to pierce Zephario's anguish. Again, Candy had to say: "A window."

"What about a window?"

"I have to find one."

Zephario didn't waste time with more questions. He reached out, open palmed, and touched the wall.

"I'll wait with Christopher until *she* comes. You go, Candy. There's nothing more you can do. *Go on.* I'm ready for her. It's going to be quite a reunion."

Even so, Candy paused. She wanted to be there when the Hag finally came face-to-face with the two men she had almost destroyed, but who had each survived, against all expectation. Candy, however, wasn't here to watch. She was here to do some good.

"Go!" Zephario said. "I'll find you again, somewhere. If not in this life, then in another."

She didn't like leaving him, but she knew she had to. She'd done what she could; now there was other work to do. Exactly what that work was she didn't know, but her instincts told her it would all become clearer if she could just look out at the island. Perhaps they weren't even over Scoriae any longer, but had drifted off out into the Void.

She got to the top of the next flight, and found

herself surrounded by doors, all identical: gray, metallic, unmarked. She had no idea where she was in the vessel; all she had to rely upon was her instinct. It had served her well before and if she was lucky it would do so again. She just had to focus—

It was no sooner said than done. A door opened in front of her and she was running down a corridor, calling as she ran:

"Come on, windows. Come *on*! I'm here. Where are you?"

The corridor divided. Again she chose. Again she ran.

"*Windows*. Come on. *Where are you?*"

There were noises coming from all around her: through the walls, up from the metal gratings under her feet, and down from the tiled ceiling: shouts, roars, squeals, screams.

And thundering behind it all, the roar of the engines that fired up the storm on the legs of which *The Storm-walker* trod. She could run forever in this place, she knew, and never find—

Wait! A window! She sensed its presence like an open eye in the sealed brutal prism of this monstrous place. There was a door to her left. She opened it, moved through a passage to a second door, which again she opened. It brought her into a large chamber filled with what looked like suits of armor made for giants. She threaded her way between them, and came, finally, to the window. She was looking out into the Void.

Directly below her she could see the very edge of the

Abarat: the limits of reality. Beyond that there was only Oblivion: a gray place that had neither depth nor detail, simply an unending nothingness.

"Must be a different window . . ." she murmured to herself. "Can't be this. There's nothing to see."

She was about to turn when she realized her error. There *was* something out there in the nullity. And oh, Lordy Lou, it was coming at *The Stormwalker* at such speed, and so directly, that she had almost missed seeing it.

The glyph was coming out of the Void, set on a collision course with *The Stormwalker*. There would be no error in this. Her friends, no doubt assuming she was dead, were coming back to greet their executioners with a death blow of their own—

Mater Motley had seen her son through Carrion's eyes, and had realized two things in the same moment: the first, that Zephario was now here in the sacred Temple of the Nephauree, and second, that the madness she had driven him into after the fire (some pitiful shreds of a mother's love, incongruous though it was, had kept her from murdering him) had now been driven out of him. She knew without a moment's thought whose handiwork this was: the witch from the Hereafter had touched him, damn her. It seemed every time Mater Motley encountered the girl she found another reason to despise her.

Well, no matter. It was all easily solved. Finally she would do what she should have done years ago: kill him.

Nothing vicious. Just a quick execution to get him out of the way. The neatness of the solution pleased her. She was at the door, already thinking about how she was going to slaughter him, when she heard one of the stitchling Commanders say, "Empress?"

"Not now."

"*Empress.*"

"I said *NOT NOW!*" her voice almost bestial this time.

She turned to reinforce her point, but her gaze never reached the Commander. Instead it went to the window, or rather the formless Oblivion beyond the window, and to the shape of a vast blade being flung out of that Oblivion.

At that moment, staring at the glyph as it hurtled toward her vessel, Mater Motley was given a helping of a kind of gruel she had not tasted since her childhood: helplessness.

"I hate you . . ." she said. "You and all the worlds." But her hatred was not enough to stop the glyph. "They mean to strike us," she said, her voice dead.

"Then it will break apart," one of the Commanders said.

"You can't break something that isn't solid, you imbecile. It's made of magic and hope. Damn her. *Damn her.*"

"Malingo? Gazza! I love you! Don't do this! Can you hear me? It's Candy! PLEASE SAY YOU CAN HEAR ME! STOP RIGHT NOW OR YOU'LL KILL YOURSELVES!"

—ᴟ—

"She said she loved me."

"Who did?"

"Who'd you think, geshrat? *Her!* Candy! I heard her say she loved me."

"I'M IN *THE STORMWALKER*!"

"She said——"

"She was in *The Stormwalker*. Yes, I heard her this time," Malingo said.

"She's alive!" Gazza said. "She's in *The Stormwalker* and she's *alive*!"

"But that's terrible! She'll be killed."

"No. Not my Candy," Gazza said, with unshakable confidence in the wisdom of his beloved. "She's clever. She'll think of something."

In the Temple of the Nephauree, where Candy had left the father and the son, the great roar of *The Stormwalker*'s engines ceased the moment the vessel touched the Void. The temple was the wellspring for every bit of magic that kept *The Stormwalker* aloft, and for a few seconds the conditions of space itself—cold, silent, dead—took possession of the temple. Denied the air to feed their bright flames, the candles were instantly extinguished, every last light pinched out at the same instant.

Though both the silence and the darkness were utter, the two Carrions knew that something had entered the temple: something that even they, who lived lives steeped in nightmares, had no desire to see or hear. One of the Nephauree had crossed from its hiding place behind the stars and was here, in this place.

A primal terror clutched at father and son. Instantly, the sound of the engines came roaring back. But in the few seconds of its absence, its volume had risen by orders of magnitude. It wasn't the sound of the vessel's engines themselves that were so loud: it was the sound of the vessel itself. *The Stormwalker* was reverberating.

"The ship's shaking, Gazza!" Malingo said.

"I don't feel anything," said Gazza.

"Not the glyph. *The Stormwalker*. Look at it. It's rocking around. What's she making it do?"

"*Lordy Lou . . .*" Gazza said. "I think we're causing it. We're pushing a piece of the Void in front of us—"

"How can an empty place have pieces?"

"Maybe it's not empty at all. Like space isn't really space. It's full of stuff. Gas. Dust. Bits of—"

"Wait!" Malingo said. "Did you feel that? Now *we're* shaking."

"I think it's trash from the Void," Gazza said. "It's breaking up against the 'Walker, and it's flying right back at us!"

There was evidence that his theory was right. All but invisible energies were seething in the air ahead of the glyph. The garbage of Oblivion swept ahead of the glyph's broom, breaking like a wave against *The Stormwalker* then thrown back at the glyph again.

"What happens now?" Malingo said.

"Your guess is as good as mine," Gazza replied. "There's no turning back. That I *do* know. In ten seconds we're going to hit. And then——"

"We're all going to die," Candy said, her tone quite matter-of-fact.

She hadn't moved from the window. Where was there left to go? She was looking over the Edge of the World, with Oblivion ahead of her, and with nothing behind except a world of melting stone. She was better off where she was, staring at the glyph that she'd helped bring into being. It was a freedom machine. It would strike the Hag's Stormwalker so hard it would fling the death-machine back the way it had come.

In the Temple of the Nephauree, in the company of the unseen Other, Zephario Carrion held his son in his arms, quietly singing to him the "Lullaby of Luzaar Muru."

> *"Coopanni panni,*
> *Coopanni panni,*
> *Luzaar Muru.*
> *Copii juvasi*
> *Athemun yezoo.*
> *Coopanni panni*
> *Coopanni panni*
> *Luzaar——"*

And then the two vessels struck.

67

YAT YUT YAH

GAZZA'S THEORY—THAT THE detritus of the Void, the trash of Oblivion, had somehow gathered up in front of the glyph as it speeded back toward Scoriae— was confirmed when the glyph hit *The Stormwalker*, pressing it closer to the gaping emptiness. The Empress's vessel began to shudder, the motion minor at first but rapidly escalating, intensifying the assault of the detritus upon *The Stormwalker*. The ship's dark armor cracked in places, and jagged pieces were torn away, their tumbling departure over the surface of the machine stripping away further pieces.

"*Candy?* Where are you? CANDY!" Gazza cried.

Gazza called out to her over and over, but now there was no answer. All he could do was watch the terrible spectacle of the machine in which she was trapped coming apart. It would not be destroyed quickly, he knew. The death-machine had been built, after all, to be a womb of storms. Not only to contain such birthing, but to channel their forces and to walk upon them. It would not succumb easily.

Even so, she was *inside*.

And she wasn't answering him, even though he kept on calling.

"Candy? Candy? Candy?"

Standing at the window still, watching the collision, the Empress delayed going down to meet with the visitor she knew had entered the temple. The Nephauree were quickly offended; even now she should have been hurrying down to find out what this one wanted. But there was another piece of business more pressing still.

Candy Quackenbush.

The girl from Chickentown had been nothing at the beginning. Just a stupid adolescent who'd fallen off her world into the Izabella and been washed up on the shores of the Abarat. Insignificant, she'd thought; a nobody, who would somehow find her way to the Hereafter again, or would perish quickly in a world that she did not understand.

But she'd been mistaken. The girl was an enigma sealed up inside a conundrum with a tribe of puzzlements, nonsense and contradictions. And she had an uncanny knack for self-preservation, even when circumstances were not promising; even when Otto Houlihan, the Criss-Cross Man, one of the most successful assassins in the Abarat, had slipped and fallen before her.

There was no time for any more fumbled attempts. The girl simply had to die, *now*, in the chaos and confusion of this battle. Nobody would ever know how she'd died, or why. And as to who should do the job, she had no doubt about that. She would. Though she was an Empress now, and should have been above such squalid labor, she was the only person she trusted to do the job—the glyph, the state of her Stormwalker, even her guest in the temple— none of it mattered right now. All that mattered was to kill Candy Quackenbush. The girl was an abomination, a freak, and she would be dead within the hour. Only then, when she was looking down at the girl's dead face—tasting her eyes and heart and liver—could she be certain that the First Empire of Midnight could begin.

The room where Candy had been standing, for reasons known only to those who had constructed *The Stormwalker*, was coming apart from both above and below, the metal panels of which the walls were constructed, buckling as though they were little more than pieces of tinfoil. Cracks spread across the window from left and right. Candy backed away from it, fearing it would shatter, and stumbled across the floor—which was collapsing in sections even as she crossed it—to the door. The door frame had cracked, however, and the door had been wedged closed. She wasted perhaps ten seconds trying to force it open before deciding that physical force wasn't going to work. She was going to have to use the magical kind.

Many years before, her curious mind had plucked out of Boa's private grimoire—for no other reason than that it was easy to remember—a wielding called the Cri Naz At. The spell was nine syllables, three of which were contained within its name.

Focusing her gaze upon the much-beaten door she recited them now.

> *"Cri Naz At*
> *By Tu Hu*
> *Yat*
> *Yut*
> *Yah."*

The syllables formed the image of a mallet in her head. Four syllables for its head, the other five forming its handle, which she held tight in her mind's eye, her fingers wrapped around *Tu Hu Yat Yut Yah*.

The words slammed into the door, and a ragged crater four feet wide appeared in the metal. A shock of pain, all the sharper because it was completely unexpected, ran up through Candy's hands and arms. This was something new completely: she was making a weapon with a spell, and literally wielding it. Now at least she understood what she was doing.

She gripped *Yat Yut Yah* even harder, and swung it with much greater force. This time, however, she was no innocent. She was entirely in the weapon—her thoughts, her news, her sinew, blood and bones. She was the bridge between the syllables and the force that it wielded. She was what turned words into action, into a force that would not be denied.

She slammed the syllables against the door

—*Cri Naz At By Tu Hu Yat Yut Yah*—

—and it flew apart!

Mater Motley heard the noise of the door breaking apart, but it would have meant nothing to her in the cacophony if it hadn't been attached to a surge of power from the level below; a magical signature that she instantly recognized. The girl was right there, just a few walls away. She called out to her. If she knew that Quackenbush was close by, then surely the girl knew of her presence as well.

"I'm coming for you," the Old Mother said.

In the Temple of the Nephauree, Christopher Carrion, ravaged by fear, whispered a flame into being. It was little more than a flicker, but it was enough to offer him a view of the ziggurat of extinguished candles.

"*What are you doing?*" Zephario murmured, his whispered voice carrying, despite the cacophony.

"*I have to find the door.*"

"You don't want to see the Nephauree. Trust me."

It was too late. The flame was already multiplying, leaping from wick to wick as it ascended the ziggurat, swelling to fill the temple with yellow-gold light.

From the corner of his eye—far off across the vastness of the temple—Christopher saw something no larger than a door that was opened just a crack onto a dark place. Then something that lived in that dark place threw the door open, and flowed through it, instantly swelling to become a vast incoherence, which possessed no sign of an anatomy whatsoever.

Gazing upon the Nephauree would certainly have been the death of him, but for the fact that at that very moment the blind man chose to act. He reached into his jacket, and seeing the iridescence that Zephario pulled out if it, the Nephauree unleashed a razor wire shriek that made blood pour from the blind man's ears, nose and mouth.

It wanted what it saw in Zephario's hand: *a last fragment of the Abarataraba.* And being the creature it was, it knew only one certain way to secure what it wanted. It would kill.

Sightless though he was, Zephario saw death.

Out of the Nephauree's meaningless form came a horizontal flight of steel needles. The spears came within a hand's length of Zephario's skull, then they were casually deflected, blazing briefly in complaint, then flying out in all directions, dying as they fell. Even so, the Nephauree had not given up on the thought of capturing the errant shred of the Abarataraba. It unleashed another torrential shriek, which were orders of magnitude more distressing than the first. Zephario reeled away from its source though he knew he had no hope of outrunning it, nor indeed had any desire left in him to avoid his execution.

He had done all he could, made his farewells. He was

ready for his trial by breath to be over, and in some place far from time and corporeality, have bright death finally begin.

With his back turned to his slaughterer he didn't see the second descent of needle spears. And their piercing, when it came, was not as painful as the shriek of their maker had been. But the shriek was not silenced. It went on and on, his face streaming with fresh flows of blood from his eyes, like tears shed for the fact that he was not yet free. In his dying throes, he did the only thing he thought would make a difference: he sent the last fragments of his power to the girl, Candy Quackenbush.

"You've got nowhere left to go," Mater Motley said.

Candy glanced back over her shoulder. The Empress of the Abarat was standing behind her, ten yards down the passageway. Everything was vibrating, much of it violently: the walls, the ceiling, the rivets in both. Only the Hag was still, uncannily still in fact, in perfect focus in a shaking world. Every detail of her dress was fixed, every doll hanging in there, each one of them a soul she had stolen, a prisoner: their suffering her constant pleasure.

"Yes is the answer," Mater Motley told her.

"I didn't ask a question," Candy said.

"You were wondering whether I'm going to lock up your soul in one of my little dolls." She smiled, showing her small gray teeth and mottled gums. "The answer is yes."

68

DELIVERANCE

"**G**AZZA . . ." SAID MALINGO, sounding slightly concerned.

"Yes, I know. *The Stormwalker*'s pushing back."

At that moment *The Stormwalker* responded to the immense pressure it was under. Its violently vibrating form shifted a little to the left, and then turned at great speed. It shifted ninety degrees, its starboard flank suddenly facing the Void-cloud.

Presented with a larger target, the Void's detritus threw itself forward with fresh insolence. The trash struck *The Stormwalker*, pushing it farther back.

"Oh, Lordy Lou! *The Stormwalker*'s moving again!"

This time there was no doubt that it was the pressure of the Void-cloud, not *The Stormwalker*'s engines, that was moving it. The death-ship moved suddenly and swiftly, turning a full hundred and eighty degrees as it flew, its massive engines laboring to regain some control, but without hope. The vast ship had too much momentum to be slowed.

The only thing that would stop it was the only thing that stood in its path: Mount Galigali.

"The volcano!" Gazza yelled. "It's going to hit the volcano!" He was up now, trying to find his way out of the maze of the glyph. "We need to dissolve this thing. Now."

Once again, everyone was in accord.

Barely taking his eyes off the vessel, Gazza stumbled out of the glyph. The vessel had behaved impeccably: carried its creators from their place of execution and into Oblivion itself, only to return them to Reality without losing a single passenger. But now the short epic of its life was over. Its energies were dissolving into the sulfur-stained air of Scoriae.

There were many among the disbanding seven thousand who took a moment to offer a prayer of thanks to the glyph in its dissolution. But neither Gazza nor Malingo were among them.

They, like Eddie, the John Brothers and Betty Thunder, had their eyes fixed on Galigali, which *The Stormwalker* was seconds from striking.

Mater Motley had been in the act of reaching to tear a hole in Candy's body when the vessel lurched. But she still put self-preservation above her desire to kill, and instead caught hold of a door frame to keep herself from being thrown to the floor.

Candy however lost her balance and fell, awkwardly and painfully, slamming her head against the wall on her

way down. She tried to get up again, but the tumultuous motion of the vessel hadn't ceased. The passageway
was no longer solid; it shook so violently Candy's eyes
couldn't fix upon anything long enough to focus.

Candy hadn't realized how hard she'd hit her head
until she tried to get up again. Her brain seemed too small
for her skull, and her legs shook. When she reached out
to touch the wall she found her fingers were completely
numb.

"Not good," she muttered.

She wasn't the only one who'd lost control. So had
The Stormwalker. It wasn't just shaking and reeling, it
was *moving*. And moving fast. She could feel its helpless
speed, the way she'd felt in the car when her dad was
drunk and driving like a madman, and all she wanted to
do was close her eyes. It was that terrible memory—of
her father—that made her defy her numb, weak body
and *get up*. She was just in time. As Candy rose, Mater
Motley reached for her a second time.

"No, Dad!"

The words came out so suddenly and so loud that the
Hag paused for the briefest moment.

That was time enough. Zephario's magic, finally
reaching its destination, came up through the floor off to
Candy's right, and her first absurd thought was that somehow a bright bird had been trapped in the death-ship. The
idea lasted a moment only. Then the colors melted into
a single exquisite iridescence, and she felt lightness—in

both senses of the word, of luminescence and of weight.

Candy saw Mater Motley's iron hand reach into her body. But the vision was short-lived. Her gaze quickly went where her body had already gone, leaving the Hag to grasp vainly at the space where Candy's body had been only moments before. Candy had only time enough left to see Motley's rage: her gray-white face suffused getting paler still, while the black of her pupils spread to extinguish every last gleam of whiteness in her eyes.

She'd lost again. Candy was gone. Small though the fragment of the Abarataraba was, it was big enough to reverse the route that had carried her aboard the vessel in the first place, melting all that lay in the way of her escape: ceilings and floors, creatures and cargo, all parting like smoke when Candy approached.

The Abarataraba pulled her out of the vessel, and for ten, eleven, twelve seconds Candy was held in the air, suspended only a few feet clear of *The Stormwalker*'s speeding underbelly, as it continued to hurtle toward destruction. The ground was a jagged grid of lightning, discharged by *The Stormwalker* in a desperate attempt to slow the vessel down. If she landed in its midst, it would have been the death of her.

So the Abarataraba kept her in the air until the vessel had passed overhead completely. Only then did it guide her down to the ground. And now, as she looked back across Scoriae to the island's northern shore (her sight sharpened by the power blazing in her cells), she saw a reason to smile. There was a large crowd of people—she knew it to be around seven thousand—all running in her direction, from the Edge of the World. Beyond them, the last remnants of the glyph were losing every last glimmer of solidity as its final passengers disembarked. It had done its work, and now dissipated, back to the ether from whence it had been borne.

The moment of calm was indeed brief, interrupted almost instantaneously by a din of destruction that shook the ground on which Candy was standing. She turned so quickly she had time to see *The Stormwalker* plow nose first into the crater where the peak of Mount Galigali had once been, now a ragged wound spitting fire and stone hundreds of feet into the air.

There the vessel came to rest. In a happier world all would have been put right. The evil-doers delivered into an all-consuming fire, and those who had been saved from execution free to return to their homes, lives and loved ones unharmed.

But this was not that happier world.

69

FOR EVERY KNIFE, FIVE HEARTS

INSIDE *THE STORMWALKER*, ZEPHARIO lay in the darkness and listened without fear to the steady slowing of his pulse. He was dying. Very soon his laboring heart would start to miss beats entirely, until finally, it ceased. There would be light then, and in that light he would see his family again, whose innocent souls had preceded him by many years into paradise. He had always imagined that place to be a garden—a garden where no flower ever withered, nor was any fruit corrupted by an invading worm. There his beloveds lived in bliss, beyond the reach of any hurt or harm. And he would be there with them soon. Very soon.

But even as he lay in the darkness, and the time of his deliverance from life drew closer, so too did the Nephauree. And it was not about to let him slip away into that peaceful place where his children played, at least not without one final violation. It prodded him with pushing until he rolled over onto his belly. He moaned. The slivers pressed against his back, but this time their intention was not to move him but to weave their substance into his cells, to press their presence into him, in four or five places.

He could not resist them. There was no strength left in him. What did this last cruelty matter, anyway? It would only quicken the approach of death to have his body invaded with such alien matter. Or so he had imagined. But no. The deeper the Nephauree's matter invaded his flesh the more strongly his heart beat. And further from him the bright, beautiful image of the garden receded.

"No . . ." he murmured. "Let me go to them. Please I have no wish to live."

"What you wish is of no importance to us," the Nephauree replied. "We have need of you alive. So you will live."

There was pressure exerted on him now, raising him up, his body's weight causing him to sink back upon the spines, until they transfixed him completely, and emerged from his chest and abdomen. He was helpless, more puppet than self-willed being.

Thus, carrying him before it, the Nephauree departed the temple in search of worshippers, leaving Christopher Carrion in darkness.

Mater Motley could taste her own blood. She had caught her tongue between her teeth when *The Stormwalker* struck the volcano. But apart from that minor harm, she was unhurt. She got to her feet. The vessel was apparently lying on its side, because the closest she could find to a horizontal surface was what had been one of the walls of the passageway a few seconds before. She walked to the nearest door, sick with rage that the girl had once again slipped away. No matter. They were at the Edge of the World. There was nowhere now for the little witch to go.

The nearest door, she found, was above her. It was heavy, but it took only a flick of her will to tear it off its hinges. Then she spoke—

"Yet—

-ha—

-si—

-ha."

—and ascended the smoke steps that formed in the air before her. What lay on the other side of the door was a spectacle of destruction so widespread that she might have taken pleasure in it had it not been her own Stormwalker that had been so demolished. She didn't linger, however. There were noises that might have been death-moans of wounded giants coming from all directions, the last complaints of the vast machine as it sank into the melting pot of Mount Galigali's crater.

There would be other death-machines in time, she knew. *The Stormwalker* had been but a hint of the glorious engines of destruction the Nephauree were capable of conceiving. She had seen some of them with her own eyes when she'd first ventured beyond the Starrish Door to find them, risking soul and sanity in doing so. But thinking of them now, of their power, and how many of their secrets they had shared with her, gave her weary limbs fresh strength. She climbed on, turning her back on the source of heat, and watching for a glimpse of the sky to appear through the smoke. There was cooler air coming from somewhere nearby. She followed it, her trek finally bringing her out of the carcass of the broken vessel and out onto the steep flank of Galigali.

She discovered that she was not alone. Dozens of stitchlings had escaped the conflagration, and were standing under the night sky, a sizeable number of them on fire, apparently indifferent to the flames. They certainly felt no pain. None of them even moaned.

She began to roughly assess their numbers, but it was a lost cause. They continued to emerge from every part of the wreckage, their will to live—even in the face of traumatic maimings—unquenchable. Many had horrendous wounds; some even crawled out of *The Stormwalker* without legs to bear them up. But though these gashes gave the Todo mud the opportunity to escape its confinement in these crudely sewn bodies, it seemed to be loyal to the form it had taken, to the individual each had become.

They clearly knew that they had their Empress in their midst, for when she emerged from the wreckage, they were waiting for her, standing around the lava pit, indifferent to the blistering heat. When she rose with the air above the wreckage, they let out a moan she had not known they were capable of making; a low note of celebration as though to lift her to Divinity.

"You good loyal soldiers," she said. "You will have countless proofs of my love in return for this moment. I will lift you higher than any creature that calls itself alive, for you, though made of mud, are worthier."

The stitchlings' great moan rose up again.

"Now listen all. This Night is not yet lost. Look at them, down there! They are trapped. Oblivion is at their backs, Galigali's fires at their front, and us in between." She laughed. "Now, we are no longer eight thousand strong. So you will have to take four, maybe five hearts instead of just one. So, five hearts it shall be! March, my soldiers, march!"

A voice, far quieter, yet infinitely more disquieting than Mater Motley's, spilled forth from within the wrecked vessel. It said only one word:

"Wait."

Although Candy was at the very bottom of the slope of Galigali, she could, thanks to Zephario's magic, plainly see and hear the events taking place at the volcano's turbulent crest. The Nephauree was emerging from a tear in the side of *The Stormwalker*; it looked like a fluid stain spilling forth through the gaping hole. As it moved, the air it trod upon trembled; as it spread, it parted like two enormous pieces of torn smoke. And to her horror, Candy saw that the entity was carrying before it a living trophy, Zephario Carrion. He was wounded. Blood soaked the front of his

robes. And yet as the Nephauree moved, Zephario continued to show faint signs of life. Despite all that his body had
plainly endured, he was still alive.

The Nephauree emerged from the wreckage entirely,
and Mater Motley bowed her head before it. The clotted,
textured forms within the being responded by assembling
at its core, their heads coming together in the midst of the
alien's amorphous stain, so that collectively they resembled a black sun, from which hundreds of frayed tentacles
seemed to sway in the grip of the Nephauree's abstracted
energies.

Having paid her respects to the creature, Mater
Motley turned from her ragged army—its numbers still
swelling as more burning stitchlings appeared from the
wreckage—and whispered one simple order to them.
Candy heard the Old Hag's imperative all too clearly.

"Kill everything."

70

NOTHING BUT STONES

Candy watched the burning, muddled army shambling down the slopes of Mount Galigali, with their Empress wearing her gown of souls leading, and the drifting form of the Nephauree both behind them and above, the nearly dead body of Zephario hanging in the shadowy air like a terrible trophy. Unsummoned, fragments of a song she'd heard first in Babilonium came to her head. A meaningless little nonsense, which she sang quietly to herself as she watched the army coming:

> *"I got a cold in my nose,*
> *But it comes and it goes.*
> *I got a cold in my brain,*
> *Which nearly makes me insane.*
> *I got a cold in my toe,*
> *That I can't get to go,*
> *I got cold,*
> *Cold,*
> *Cold . . ."*

And while the monsters came, she stood there, watching, knowing that she had no hope of stopping them. She looked back at the crowd that had emerged from the glyph, and saw that Malingo and Gazza had started to walk toward her. Gazza beckoned to her. She glanced one more time at the approaching enemy. They were still five minutes away, perhaps. But no more than that.

She turned and started to run toward Malingo and Gazza. Gazza was close enough to call to her now.

"Are you all right?"

"I don't know," she said. "I don't think so."

He opened his arms as he approached her, and hugged her tight. She gave as good as she got, which only made him hug her more. Malingo put his own arms around them both, which nobody objected to.

"What do we do now?" Malingo said.

"We have to defend ourselves," Candy said. "We've no other choice."

"I'm all for a good fight," Gazza said, "but we don't have a hope against those things. Look at them! They're burning and they still keep coming. No legs, so they crawl."

Candy looked back toward the volcano. The approach of the stitchlings was indeed terrifying. Though a few of the most traumatically wounded creatures had finally perished on the slope, the greater number continued their shambling descent.

"The Abarataraba's all used up," Candy said. "There's

still some magic in me, but there'll be no more glyphs, I'm afraid."

"What about getting off the island by water?"

"There's no chance of that," Malingo said. "Izabella just pours away over the Edge of the World. If we got into the water, we'd go with it."

"There's going to be a lot of killing," Candy said grimly. "We have to make a stand here."

"We were all brought here to die anyway," Malingo reminded her. "At least this way we have a chance."

There was another eruption from the heart of Galigali: this one so violent it blew the front half of *The Stormwalker* apart. It did not draw Mater Motley's gaze off the condemned, however. She simply kept walking down over the smoking slope.

"I wonder what happened to Christopher?" Candy wondered aloud.

"He's there," Malingo said.

"I don't see him."

"I did, I swear. He was a little way back from all the rest, but he was there."

Candy looked up at the approaching army with fresh interest.

"You're sure?" she said.

"Absolutely."

"Huh," Candy said. "Three generations of Carrions." She looked at Gazza and Malingo. "I guess we'll go meet them together."

71

AN EXECUTION

CARRION HAD THROWN UP a low-resolution Distraction Shield to keep the stitchlings he was moving among from noticing him, but it scarcely mattered. They had their attentions entirely fixed upon those they were about to execute. So after a while he simply let the wielding lapse, knowing that they neither saw him nor would have cared if they had. It was only when Carrion realized that the girl from Chickentown had started to walk back toward his grandmother's army——the expression on her face completely defying interpretation——that he repowered the shield and once again slipped out of sight.

In his invisible state he had a little time to get his thoughts in some kind of order. He no longer knew where his loyalties lay, or even whether there were any advantages to having loyalties. He had obeyed his grandmother's instructions for many years, doing servile work much of the time, and what had that got him? Death and a bitter resurrection on a stony beach. And love? Ha, love! That had been even more cruel than loyalty. True, it hadn't killed him. It might have been kinder if it had. Instead it had left him looking like a fool, having been tricked out of every piece of magic he'd ever learned and then left without so much as a kiss by way of compensation. He'd grieved. Oh, Lordy Lou, how he'd grieved. But more, he'd *raged*, the anger blazing about his heart, so that he'd had to stoop to murder in order to extinguish it.

But even that hadn't been the end of the anguish. Fifteen years or so later, the girl from Chickentown had come into his life, their paths crossing by accident, or so he'd thought. She'd been washed into the arms of Mama Izabella, carrying—again by chance; again, so he'd thought—only to find that Candy Quackenbush of Chickentown, Minnesota, carried inside her the soul of the Princess whose manipulations and infidelities had left him stripped of power and love. Now Boa's soul no longer occupied the girl, but it seemed not to matter. She still acted as though she could stand up against his grandmother! But she was wrong. This wasn't the same Hag of Gorgossium any longer; the vicious old woman she'd faced on the *Wormwood*. The Empress was a different order of power. Why didn't the girl understand that? Why didn't she see with her own eyes the scale of his grandmother's ally, the Nephauree? Didn't she comprehend how incendiary a place this had become? Not because there was a volcano spitting air and earth around them, but because three generations of the Carrion dynasty were assembled for the first time since the fire that had wiped the future of that dynasty away, and returned all the power to the oldest surviving member of that family, in whose shadow he, the youngest, had been doomed to live?

Right now this was the most volatile place in the Abarat. And however much Candy might have learned about magic from Boa, she was still, at root, an ordinary creature of the Hereafter, strong of will, no question, perhaps even extraordinary in some regard. But she was still merely human, the shadowy places at the back of her mind still haunted by the beasts that had stalked the apes from which her kind had risen up. She would never be free of that fear, Carrion thought. And that would always leave her weak when facing Midnight.

And yet still she stood there, defying his grandmother, defying her own fear. Perhaps, just perhaps, she *was* something new. The next kind of woman, this girl.

Such a pity, if that was so, that she was going to die.

The two armies met. The Empress looked at Candy without any visible emotion.

"What do you want?" she said.

"I came because I saw Zephario in pain," Candy said. "He's your son. Doesn't that make you a little merciful?"

"No, girl. I cleansed myself of mercy before I went to meet the Nephauree. I knew they would smell it upon me."

"So you feel nothing for him?" Candy said.

She had no conscious notion of why she was even asking questions, but there *was* a reason, of that she was dimly certain. This was family business, and like all families the Carrions had their secrets. Whenever the members of her own family had got together, it had always ended with curses and fistfights. Perhaps there was some secret here that might yet change the way this fatal game ended.

"Oh, I do feel *something* for him," Mater Motley admitted. "Something like maternal affection," she went on. "Or as close as I could ever get."

"Really?" Candy said. Now she was confused. What was the Old Mother admitting to?

"Yes, really," the Hag replied. She reached down and caught hold of one of the ragged dolls that hung from the front of her dress. "I want his soul here," she said. "Close to my heart."

Candy said nothing. The Hag hadn't finished, she sensed. So she still had something of significance to say. When she finally spoke, it was only to say five words:

"He won't be alone there."

That was it, Candy knew. That was the heart of it, in those words somewhere.

He won't be alone.

The Hag had such a terrible malice in her face. Such a profound perversity. But why?

He won't be—

Candy looked down at the doll, then back up at the Old Mother again, hoping to study the woman's face a

little while longer. But Mater Motley was already turning away from her so as to focus all her energies upon the
broken figure of Zephario.

"Look at you; so old, so broken. I held you once,
against my breast." She began to walk back toward him.
"Die now," she said softly. "Give up your soul to me."

She very slowly reached up toward him, as though
she was capable of pulling his soul out of him. By way
of response Zephario let out an anguished sound, something between a howl and a sob, the cry of a man losing
his mind.

It was more than Candy could bear. She couldn't just
stand there and let the Hag go on tormenting him. She had
to do *something*. What that something was she had not the
remotest notion, but she had will, and she was free to use
it. Whatever choices fate put in her head or heart or hands
she'd use. Anything to stop the suffering.

She started to move toward the Hag, who was far too
busy enjoying the anguish of her own flesh and blood to
bother looking back over her shoulder.

"Stop that!" Motley said to her son. "It won't do any
good. I'm your mother, Zephario. I brought you into the
world and now I'm going to remove you from it."

Every despicable word of this quickened Candy's step.
She would do whatever she could to make the Hag regret
her cruelty, she swore to herself. But that was more easily
said than done, wasn't it? Fate hadn't provided her with
any means to bring Mater Motley to her knees. She was up

against the Empress of the Abarat with bare hands. But if that was how it had to be, that was how it had to be.

Without even thinking about what she was doing, she leaped, the very last traces of the Abarataraba's magic lending her jump power it would never have had without it.

Without looking, the Hag turned, striking Candy with the back of her hand.

"Creeping up on *me*, girl?" She struck Candy a second time, and having nothing with which to shield herself from the blows, Candy was knocked to the ground, the breath beaten out of her. *"I am so thoroughly sick of you,"* she said, kicking Candy with unrestrained venom. *"I'm going to kick you until your heart stops beating."*

She proceeded to make good on her promise.

"You." She kicked.

"Stupid." And again.

"Little." And again.

"Nobody."

"Stop it!" Malingo yelled.

Candy saw him from the corner of her eye, stumbling forward to put himself between Candy and the Hag's assault. He distracted Mater Motley long enough to give Candy time to draw breath, but his intervention cost him dearly. The Empress cast a glance toward two of the stitchlings nearest to her and snatched the blades they were carrying out of their hands. Candy used the drawn breath to tell him:

"Run! Malingo! RUN!"

But even if he'd been willing to abandon Candy, which he wasn't, his death sentence had been written. The blades came at him from left and right. Candy heard him cry out, just once, then the blades cut at him with horrible speed, slicing his head from his neck, his hands from his wrists, his arms from his torso—Candy's horror and fury left her speechless, which was no bad thing. Not a scrap of her energies was wasted on words. All of it went straight from her heart to her hands. She reached up and grabbed hold of Mater Motley's crowded skirts, hauling her aching body to its feet.

She had killed Malingo.

Her beloved Malingo, who had said he would be with Candy forever, Midnight or no Midnight. But the Hag had taken him from her. Snatched him away with a casual gesture, as though his life was worthless, his love was worthless, as though his body was no more than a slab of meat and she the butcher, casually cutting it up—

As she climbed, Candy found Mater Motley's gaze, and for just a fraction of a second she saw the Hag recoil, her high regard for her Imperial Self shocked when it met such an intensity of hatred as it found pouring from Candy's eyes.

It wasn't enough, of course, to prick the Hag's vanity.

She had killed Malingo.

No death was too terrible to revenge such a slaughter. Candy wanted to turn the Hag's bones to blazing wood and her blood to gasoline, to watch the Old Mother consumed by the very element she'd used to kill her own flesh and blood all those years before. But she didn't have sufficient magic to make such an execution happen. She'd have to do whatever damage she could do with her hands and fingers: gouge out the Old Mother's vicious eyes and tear her lying tongue out by its rotting roots. She'd start with the eyes—

But the Hag wasn't in the mood to die today. She reached up and caught hold of Candy's hand, her grip so tight, and tightening still, that she plainly intended to grind Candy's finger bones to dust.

With one hand holding Candy firmly, she reached out with the other. Her Imperial dignity was once again intact. And so was the power that accompanied it. She murmured a syllable or two, and one of the wide-bladed knives that had taken Malingo apart came to her outstretched hand. She closed her fingers around the sticky handle.

"I've had more than my fill of you, Miss Chickentown."

So saying, the Empress raised the knife high above her head.

Candy refused to give the old woman the satisfaction of seeing her afraid. Instead she kept climbing, grabbing hold of whatever she could find, whether it was antiquated fabric of the dress or one of the dolls. Her bruises ached and her head throbbed, but not once did she take her eyes off Mater Motley's turkey-neck throat, even as the knife came whistling down.

72

TRUTH

THE KNIFE DIDN'T REACH her. Eighteen inches from Candy's skin, it struck something: an object that was completely invisible yet sufficiently solid to shatter the blade as though it had been made of ice.

"Who did this?" Mater Motley demanded. "Who did this?" She glanced down at Candy. "It wasn't you, so don't even try to claim it was." She thrust her hand over Candy's face and pushed her away. Her presence here, dead or alive, was suddenly of no interest to her. Somebody here had blocked the Imperial will, and she wanted to know who.

She turned her black gaze on those in her immediate vicinity, staring very hard at each dirty, scorched stitchling for a moment to assess their chances of guilt.

"You, was it? No. Too stupid. You? No. Your brains are burning. You perhaps? No, another cretin. Is nobody proud enough to *own* this act?"

Silence.

"Are you all just mud and cowardice? EVERY? SIN-GLE? ONE?"

Finally, a weary voice said:

"All right, don't give yourself a fit, you old boneyard. If it's all that important to you . . . *I did it.*"

The crowd of stitchlings parted, a figure emerged from behind a flickering Distraction Shield.

"You," the Hag said.

"Me," said Christopher Carrion.

"Why must you always *defy* me?"

"Oh, Lordy Lou. I didn't want you to kill the girl."

"And again I say: *why*? You had a reason to protect her when she had your Princess in residence. But *now*?"

"I don't know," Carrion said. "But please, don't . . ."

The Hag thought for a moment, then grinned.

"A favor for a favor, then?"

Carrion's thin lips curled.

"What do you want from me?"

"Tell your father, Christopher," Mater Motley said. "Tell him how he'll be welcomed."

Candy turned this phrase over and over in her head and watched Carrion's face very closely. Her belief that there was indeed a mystery here, some family secret that was teetering on the rim of revelation, was deepening. She still had absolutely no idea of what it was. Her one clue was that the Hag had made that bizarre remark that after death her son would not be alone.

Was there somebody else held prisoner in Mater

Motley's dolls? Another soul—or *souls, perhaps? Yes, it was several*—she knew it the instant she thought it—and they were all being held prisoner in all those wretched little dolls made of filth and rags.

Suddenly, she *understood.*

"The *children!*" Candy said. *"Oh God, she's got all the children!"*

Mater Motley didn't respond at first. She had already moved with unnatural speed to stand in front of Zephario and had begun to sing a death lullaby to him. But Candy's outburst silenced the slaughter song.

"Shut her up," she ordered Carrion. *"Quickly,* you fool. Shut her up!"

"What's she saying?"

"It doesn't matter what she's saying! *Just SHUT HER UP!"*

For a few seconds the Hag unglued her gaze from Zephario and threw Carrion a look, which briefly lit up his face with a burst of stinging, bitter green light, as though she'd just plunged his head in gangrenous waters. This was a new trick and it was only with the greatest effort that he succeeded in controlling his revulsion.

"Did you not hear me?" the Hag was saying.

"Yes," Carrion said.

He didn't need another lesson from his Empress. This newfound ability to render his own sanctuary poisonous was a terrifying escalation in her skills. He had no choice but to grovel. He stumbled toward Candy, his head roaring from the toxins still in his system, telling her as he did so: "You should have gone when I told you to. Now *I* have to kill you."

"Have you heard a word I've said?" Candy asked.

"Not one more word!" Mater Motley instructed.

She's afraid, Candy thought. *I've got the truth!*

The sudden certainty gave her voice power.

"Carrion, listen to me! She's got your brothers and sisters!" Carrion looked at her through the strangely stained fluid in his collar with a look of puzzlement. "In the dolls. She's got all your family right here with her."

"SHUT HER UP!"

"Your father thinks they're in paradise. It's what kept him sane. But it was a lie, Christopher. Just another of her cruel, vicious lies. She's had their souls all along."

"In the dolls?" Now he started to understand.

"In the dolls."

"And *my* mother too?"

"Don't ask me. Ask——"

Carrion was already turning on his grandmother.

"Is it true?" he demanded. "Well, is it?"

"Haven't you slit her throat yet?"

"I asked you a question."

"You really want to know?"

"I asked, didn't I?"

"Oh, you know me. I'm frugal. Nothing ever goes to waste. Not when it can be turned into power. I wasn't going to let all those souls fly off to paradise when I could use them, *here, close to me*. They're family, after all. My flesh and blood. They wouldn't even have existed if I hadn't endured the gross befoulments of the womb. I even let them sense one another, which does help them to hope. And they *yearn*, of course, for what they will never see again, never touch again, even though they're so very close to one another." She ran her bony fingers over the dolls as she spoke. "And the longer I keep them, the deeper the yearning gets."

As Candy watched Carrion listening to this she thought she caught a glimpse of something she'd never seen in his eyes before. She'd seen him dangerous and despairing, loving and lost. But this, this was a singularity. Hatred.

"Why didn't you tell me?" he said.

"What business was it—*is it*—of yours?"

"*They're my brothers and sisters.*"

"You never knew them. Why should you care? You never cared before."

"I thought they were in a happier place."

"Well, who's to say what they feel?"

"They feel *everything* . . ." Candy said.

"*Shut up,*" screeched the Hag.

"*They feel everything—*"

"I will—"

"*—because they're connected to everything.*"

"—KILL YOU!"

"*There'd be no power in them if they weren't,*" Candy continued, unmoved. "*You only drain off what comes through them. But it comes from everything and everywhere."*

"The girl speaks the truth," Zephario said very softly.

Candy glanced up at Carrion's father, who was staring down at his son through his blind, bleeding eyes.

"Must I show you?" he said to Christopher softly.

There was no answer forthcoming from Carrion.

"Then I must."

Strands of pale creamy mist were appearing in the fluid like a blindfold, concealing the innocent blue in his eyes as well as the nightmares, black at their center.

This had to be his father's handiwork, Candy thought. Not that Carrion had resisted it. Zephario was showing his son a glimpse of the world they had both lost: of Carrion's brothers and sisters, whose laughter, shrieks, tears and prayers he had many times imagined he'd heard.

"Your mother stayed in the house until the very end," Zephario said. "I had to drag her out of there myself. That's how I got the burns. I started to melt in the heat."

"This is absurd," the Empress muttered.

"You know it's the truth, Mother," said Zephario. "This is how it was, Christopher. Do you see? *Do you see* what your beloved grandmother did?"

Candy couldn't, of course, share the vision, but she didn't need to. She knew perfectly well what Carrion the Elder was sharing with the Younger: his mother, in extremis. Carrion had told Candy once that it was the first image he remembered, though at the time he'd no knowledge that it was his own mother he'd been watching die. She'd just been a screaming column of fire.

"I've seen enough, Father," Carrion said.

Weakened by the visions, he blindly struggled to get to his feet, unable to see anything but the horror he was being shown.

"Father," he said again, more violently this time. "*Please*. I've seen your memory now." He got to his feet. "I believe you."

And as he spoke the words, the clouds cleared away. Carrion's eyes had never looked as blue as they did now, nor his pupils as black.

73

SOULS

Oh, so slowly, Carrion raised his head. His purified gaze was fixed on Mater Motley.

"I see you now so clearly, Grandmother," he said.

"The clarity of your eyesight is of no importance to me," the Empress said.

"My brothers and sisters—"

"Are dead."

"—should be in paradise."

"Well, they're not. Nor will they ever be. They're part of the power that raised you so high."

"Let them go."

"No."

"I can make you do it."

"You could try," the Empress said. "But it would be your last act."

"So be it," he said.

As he spoke he came at her, throwing some wielding ahead of him as he did so. It exploded in her face like a ball of spiked darkness. He didn't give her so much as an instant to recover, but grabbed at her throat, apparently intent on throttling the life out of her. He carried her before him, stumbling back among her stitchlings.

Candy had seen the two of them meet head-to-head like this once before, on the deck of the *Wormwood*. She had no interest in watching the struggle play out again. Her concern was for poor Zephario. He was still pierced by the Nephauree, but he clung to life. She went to him. The temperature of the air dropped several degrees as she got closer to the Enemy of All Living Things: an unnatural chill that drove ice needles into her ligaments and marrow, making every step she took more difficult than the one before. But she would not be dissuaded.

Sensing her pain, Zephario raised his head. When he spoke his thoughts, it was a whisper of a whisper, the last exhausted murmur of a man using every sliver of strength to hold on to life.

The Abarataraba is still in you, he murmured.

I don't feel it, Candy replied

It's there. You would never have gotten so close without it. Not much of it, but—

What does it mean?

What does what mean?

Abarataraba.

. . . roughly translated, it means . . . Pieces of Life.

Then take them back. The Pieces of Life. Finish this. Set them free.

There's a door in your head that Diamanda made when she put Boa's soul into you. It's not wood and hinges. It's just a way into your being.

I know this door.

Then open it. Quickly.

I did it already.

Lordy Lou, so you did.

Will this hurt?

It won't be my soul coming into you that will pain you, Zephario said, *it will be my coming forth from you again.*

Why?

Because I will enter you through a single door, which you opened. But if I am to free all the souls, I must exit through many.

You mean doors that haven't been made yet.

I'm sure there's a better way, but we don't have the time—

Funny that. We live in islands of Hours and we never seem to have time enough for anything . . .

Here I come.

Instantly Candy felt the nerves in her head twitch. And Zephario's life force came into her. It was strangely comforting, an odd sense of familiarity. Not the same as Boa being there, of course, but close enough. She felt Zephario's anger turning her strength to its purpose, empowering her to face the monster.

The Hag had not even noticed her short exchange with Zephario. She'd been too busy fighting with her grandson. Unlike their battle on the deck of the *Wormwood*, in which the two of them had been equally matched, the balance had now plainly shifted in favor of the Hag. She had the wielding powers of the Nephauree at her disposal, and Carrion had nothing in his arsenal that was a match for them. Candy turned just in time to see Carrion drop down upon the ground, which was a chaotic mass of smoking fissures. The nightmares in his collar were writhing insanely, bleeding darkness into the fluid around his head. Whatever she had done to him, he had no fight left. The blow she landed would be the end of him.

"Empress?" Candy said. "I'm still here."

Motley turned as she spoke. "Don't worry, girl. My son's dead, and my grandson's almost gone. You're next."

Candy felt Zephario's power moving through her as the Hag's contemptuous gaze settled on her. The power divided as it did so: two becoming four, four becoming eight, eight becoming sixteen. He'd warned Candy it would hurt, and he'd not lied. The pieces of his divided soul coursed through her body in defiance of all anatomical constraints, burning their way like tiny fires through marrow and muscle, nerve and vein. Their passage was rapid, but before they could escape her, the Hag saw something in Candy that made her suspicious.

"What have you done?" she said.

She didn't wait for an answer. She raised her hand, around which the air was already becoming denser as she summoned up a murdering spell. She would have let it fly a moment later had Carrion not caught hold of her arm. He lacked the strength to hold on to her for more than a few seconds, but that was all the time Zephario's fragmented soul required to disperse itself throughout Candy's body.

The instant he was spread, he burst free. The sting of his soul's departure was almost more than Candy's consciousness could endure. But she held on, despite the pain, and her anguish was rewarded with an extraordinary vision: the flight of soul-shards.

Seeing the motes speeding toward her, the Hag panicked. She wrestled her hand from Carrion's grip and directed her murderous spell at the pieces of Zephario's soul. But Zephario had outmaneuvered her. By dividing himself as he had into so many parts, he presented not one place to strike, but many. And while Mater Motley was still attempting to free herself, Zephario's soul-pieces found what they'd traveled so far to find: his family.

As each of his children woke to the presence of their father, the filthy little doll in which its soul had been sewn up burst open as though a small explosion had been ignited in each. One by one, the dolls hanging in grim rows across the front of the Empress's gown blew apart, as the son or daughter inside woke up to the proximity of Zephario.

Candy could not know, of course, what that moment felt like: soul liberating soul liberating soul. But she saw how it looked clearly enough, and it was no gentle business. Small though the dolls were they burst with astonishing violence, their coils of ragged cloth like entrails bursting from poorly sewn anatomies, as something both more abstracted and more real was set free.

If there was any way to distinguish one child from

another, or the children from their mother, Candy couldn't see it. They were simply points of brightness that burst from their squalid prisons, weaving around one another in front of the Hag as if to taunt her with their long-awaited freedom, then forming a cloud of ecstatic light that rose as its numbers swelled, the motion of the motes so fast that the trails they left upon the air seemed to form something that was almost a solid form: a ragged globe of threaded light, glorious in celebration of their reunion.

The effect upon Mater Motley was catastrophic. Each time one of the dolls came apart, her body convulsed, the scale of the motion mounting, so that she was quickly reduced to the status of a doll herself, helpless in the grip of forces she could not control.

It was not for want of trying. Twice she had attempted to summon up wieldings to drive Zephario back, but the violence with which she was being thrown around robbed her of the breath to finish them. Once only did she manage to utter four words, her eyes upon Candy as she spoke them:

"I WILL FIND YOU," she said.

It was an uninspired response to the exquisite complexities of all that had come before, but Candy knew the viciousness of the woman cursing her too well to take the words lightly. Yes, the Empress of the Abarat had been cast down from her place of power. And yes, the souls she had most prized had been set free, the remnants of their prisons hanging off her dress, gutted.

Yes, she was weak at that moment, and could perhaps have been destroyed.

But none standing or lying or kneeling there knew how it might be done. Minutes before she had been the very image of Imperial power, descending the flank of Mount Galigali with an army of burning assassins following upon her heels. Now she was in tatters. But she was still too dangerous a creature, and too unpredictable, for anyone to attempt to put her out of her misery.

In truth it was this most inward of wounds that saved Candy's life, for after Zephario's soul-passage through her body, Candy's strength was utterly depleted. Had the Hag simply picked up a stone, she could have effortlessly beaten Candy's brains out there and then and destroyed her nemesis in a heartbeat.

But the Empress couldn't bear the idea of being seen in this broken, humiliated state, even though she'd won. The only memory of her she wanted anyone to take away from this battle was of her triumphant descent down the slope of Mount Galigali.

So, in a manner of restraint and decorum befitting a true Empress, she turned her back on the girl from Chickentown and very quickly made magical arrangements for her exit. She cast her eyes toward the bright place overhead where the comet of Carrions had briefly sundered the air and departed, leaving only a glimpse of that paradise to which they had gone, visible behind the door through which they'd passed.

The Empress was, of course, no longer wracked by the convulsions that the dolls had caused. All that unpleasantness was over. She could form words of summoning, sufficient unto the task of calling forth from the lava crust beneath her feet seven petals, enclosing her in a sheath of mottled gray and black, like a toxic flower that had yet to blossom. Only as it was about to close up, completely concealing Mater Motley from sight, did she utter one final instruction to the Other in her midst, in a language eons older even than Old Abaratian: the ancient mind-words of the Nephauree. Candy didn't need to know the language to understand what the creature had been told. The sounds of the words conjured pictures, which appeared with appalling clarity in her mind's eye. She saw the ground crack. She saw rushing water. She saw the Void.

Then the petal shroud closed around Mater Motley, and sealed her up completely. And having done so, folded itself upon itself, and was gone. The moment the Empress was out of sight, every eye in the Abarat witnessed the appearance of what Midnight's hand had cancelled: the light. The sacbrood fell from the sky, withered, and turned to ash.

It was a momentary triumph, for the Old Hag had left the Nephauree in her stead, asking of it one last favor: make sure that those many thousands who had witnessed her presence here did not live to tell of what they had witnessed.

74

THE HAMMER
OF THE NEPHAUREE

"CANDY . . ."

Gazza was there, standing a little distance away from her, as though he wasn't entirely certain that whatever he'd just witnessed happening was finally over, now that she was out of the fugue state that had put such a strange expression onto her face.

"It's all right," she said, looking up at him. She let him study her a while, to reassure himself that he did indeed have his Candy back with him. "*I'm* all right."

"That thing . . ."

"The Nephauree?"

She glanced back over her shoulder. There were little bursts of brightness in the clots in the cloud of the Nephauree, as though its vast gaseous intelligence was speaking to itself, turning over possibilities.

"She instructed it to leave no witnesses," Candy said.

"So now it's going to kill everybody?"

"I would think so. If you were Empress of the Abarat

would you want anyone—even a stitchling—to be able to report what they'd just seen? Poor Malingo. He's already gone. I'm afraid we're going to be following him very soon."

"You're not giving up?" Gazza said. He sounded appalled. "You, Candy Quackenbush? You can't give up. What about the people whose lives you saved? The people here, thousands of them."

"They . . . saved themselves."

"Well, perhaps. But you showed them how to go on . . . and why."

He looked away from her and attempted to clear his own eyes of tears with a quick wiping of his cheek.

"Please, Gazz . . ." she said.

"None of this was an accident, Candy; you meeting me, us coming here. I know you think you just brought more bad things here than good. And maybe Malingo *would* still be alive. But maybe he'd still be waiting for somebody to find him, and show him how to escape the wizard forever. You told me once, do you remember, not to think always of how something can happen. Only know they do."

"I've got nothing left in me, Gazza. I couldn't conjure a peanut, never mind a glyph."

"We can still find a way out of here."

"I don't see how. We're trapped."

Behind them was the Void; in front of them the liquid fire of Mount Galigali, and to either side of the island the spumy waters of the Izabella, pouring off over the Edge of the World into Oblivion. Candy was right. There was no way out.

Meanwhile, the Nephauree was responding to Mater Motley's last instruction; its virtually passive state became suddenly activated by the prospect of slaughter. The eruptions of light within each of the clotted areas threw out filaments of light, like lines drawn between constellations in the roiling darkness of the Nephauree's internal universe.

As each line found its destination and moved on to the next, its brightness intensified, as though some vast mathematical equation was being solved in this geometry; a theorem concerned, paradoxically, with the ordered escalation of chaos. The speed with which the calculations took place continued to increase; it was only a matter of time before it reached critical mass.

"We're not just going to stand here and look at it, are we?" Gazza said.

"No."

"So we're *going*?" Gazza said very quickly and softly.

"Yes."

"Turn and run?"

"Better not to run, I think. We don't want to draw attention to ourselves."

"Got it," Gazza said.

But the stitchlings, having been betrayed by their Empress once again, despite her promises of high remuneration, were beginning to understand that the Nephauree intended to massacre them as well, and took flight.

The Nephauree knew not where to begin its work of destruction. Finding a small window, together Candy and Gazza began to retreat, step after slow step over the baking earth. They had taken nine steps when the connection of black constellations ceased. The roiling motion in the interior went on, but now the darkness was being drawn toward a single place in the configuration. If the thing had an eye, then perhaps this was it.

"It's watching us," Candy said.

"Yeah, I get that feeling too."

"Maybe we should . . ."

"Stop moving?" Gazza suggested.

"Yep."

They stopped. It didn't seem to help much. The eye continued to draw in strands of darkness from all around it. The point was very soon going to be reached where it could get no darker, nor any denser. Then surely, its killing power would fly.

The darkness flickered. Candy glanced at Gazza, and as she did so one of the stitchlings to the right of the creature lost its nerve, and turned to run. The Nephauree turned too. Not its entire body, just that little part within which the dark-amassing eye was set. A brief glance, sending a blur of shadows forth, and the stitchling—which had been one of the bigger brutes—was gone, as though the darkness had simply devoured it. Candy and Gazza turned and ran. And it hurt. Oh, how it hurt! Though the channeling of Zephario's soul had been traumatic, and Candy's body ached just about everywhere, it was, strange to say, a *good* hurt, a pain that made her aware of how alive she was, and how good it felt to be alive.

That was something worth running for, wasn't it? To have more life, yes, more time to see the miracles of the Hours, and to help heal its wounds, more time to keep the company of the young man who was running as hard as she was beside her. All this raced through her mind as her body, filled with fury and gratitude, carried her over the broken ground—all this, and one other thing: the mystery of the Twenty-Fifth Hour, the Time Out of Time. There was a mystery being guarded there about which she knew nothing, except that it existed, and that she would never know the Abarat until she had solved it.

So much still to do: to explore, to solve, to *feel*. She couldn't die yet!

But it was hard ground to race over, and they would have stumbled several times if each had not had the other to keep them from falling. They had a third companion, though Candy had not yet glimpsed it yet. One of the Abaratian seagulls had apparently decided to keep them company as they ran. Candy could hear its huge wings flapping somewhere overhead, and once she thought she saw it for a moment but it was such a brief glimpse—and what she saw was so large and preposterous—that she assumed her hallucinating senses were playing tricks. There was no doubt that the bird *was* keeping up with them, however. The more distance they were able to put between themselves and the Nephauree, the louder its wingbeats became. Finally, Candy slowed long enough to glance back. It was hard to judge how far they'd come.

The landscape had changed, even in the short time they'd been running. The wind had shifted, and the smoke from the volcano was drifting north, toward the Edge of the World. It obscured almost completely the remains of *The Stormwalker*, along with most of Mount Galigali's northern flank. It only thinned out as it came close to the Nephauree. Or was it that the smoke had been consumed *by* the creature? That made sense. There was a jaundiced taint to the Nephauree now, as though it had somehow inhaled all the sulfurous filth in the cloud, and plucked up by its own devices shards of white-hot stone that hung like nascent stars in the Nephauree's universe.

She took all this in—the smoke, the stolen yellow tainting the Nephauree, the bright white stars—in one brief glance. Then, realizing what she had *not* seen, looked again.

The stitchlings had gone. The burning ones, the ones that had just a flicker of fire here and there, and even those that had emerged from the wreckage whole: all of them, gone. The Nephauree had destroyed them all. Now the Nephauree had nothing left to delay it. Candy and Gazza were its only targets. And after them it came.

Candy didn't look back a third time. She didn't need to. She could feel the motion of the alien as it closed in on them; a profound disturbance in the ground over which she and Gazza were running.

There were people coming to meet them from the crowd of survivors at the far end of the island. And leading that crowd was John Mischief, arms outstretched. The gesture was optimistic, but the expression on his face was not. Even at this distance Candy could see that Mischief's eyes were looking past Candy and Gazza. He was looking at the Nephauree. And he could see something terrible beyond words was about to happen.

"Bad news," the bird said. "It's attacking."

Candy's heart jumped, hearing the voice of the creature.

"Malingo?"

She slowed her run looking for the bird and, failing to find it, stopped entirely. Suddenly, down it swooped to hover in front of her. It was indeed Malingo. Or rather his head, the wound of his neck closed up and the leathery outgrowths on either side of his head flapping to keep him in the air.

"You're alive!" Despite their desperate situation she couldn't help but laugh: "Ha! Look at you!"

"This is how geshrats are born," he said. "Heads with wing-ears. Our bodies are replaceable. I'll just grow a new one when this is all over."

"You never told me."

"You never asked."

"Well, that's the strangest thing I've ever seen," said John Moot.

"I disagree," said John Serpent.

"Of course you do!" said John Mischief.

"Hey! I'm glad Malingo's alive too," Gazza said, "but we still have a problem."

The Nephauree was no longer pursuing them. It had halted, twenty yards or so from Candy, Gazza and Malingo. Though Candy had seen countless images of power in her journeys through the Abarat, she'd never witnessed anything quite the equal of this. It was immense: a looming mass of contradictions. Despite its gaseous-liquid form there were places where the clotted darkness had a steely sheen to it, and others where it seemed the fine lines she'd seen drawn on its darkness had been etched there on countless previous occasions, an intricate matrix of line upon line upon line, darker even than the darkness into which they'd been scratched.

"Oh dear," said John Fillet.

"What's it doing?"

"Nothing good," Candy said.

There was an insistent downward motion to the darkness now, the force of its substance pressing upon the solidified lava. It cracked open: jagged ruptures in the ground, which rapidly spread toward Candy and Gazza. There was nothing mysterious about either the motion of the fissures or of the light blazing out of them. The fissures were under the control of the Nephauree and they opened onto the molten magma that ran beneath the island.

Their way back to Mischief and the rest of the survivors was now denied. The widest of the fissures—seven feet wide and getting wider—had clearly been created to cut them off from their friends. They were being herded toward the northwestern corner of the island, where the waters of the Sea of Izabella became a roaring-white frenzy as they plunged helplessly on past the coast of Scoriae and over the Edge of the World. There was no real shore. The black lava rock simply sloped a little steeper before it met the panicking waters as they went to meet Oblivion.

The Nephauree was a stranger to itself, its mind a shadow on the wall of a chamber where the worst atrocities one living thing could visit upon another were commonplace. All it knew was the processes of fear, and how to multiply them. In the case of the young witch and her friends, it simply drove them back toward the waters until they were trapped between two unpleasant deaths: to be plunged into the white waters of the Izabella and drowned, or to drop into one of the fissures and be cooked alive.

At least, this had been its master plan. But the fracturing of the ground wasn't proceeding as speedily as it had planned. There were more urgent claims upon its time right now than watching the little witch perish. It had come here to witness the elevation of the woman Mater Motley, into whose hands its species' priests had put great power, for reasons more to do with their own Grand Designs than in service of her Imperial ambition. But she had underestimated the enemy, despite the elegance of her plotting.

The battle had been messier than the Nephauree had anticipated, but it had been won in the end. Even so, the priests who had dispatched the Nephauree here would not be pleased with the way things had gone. The sooner they had this news, the sooner they could make whatever strategic changes they judged appropriate. So the Nephauree could not afford to linger any longer. It needed this business with the girl and the fisherman over with, once and for all.

It needed to break the ground more effectively. And for that, it already had a plan. It willed its body to exude two horns of matter, into which it rerouted the darkness that had been dropped into its bowels. Now that same weighty darkness climbed up into the "horns" it had formed, turning them into vast hammers.

And down they came: two hammerheads of darkness that slammed into the wounded ground! Instantly, a fresh network of fissures appeared from the place where its hammerheads had landed. They zigzagged toward Candy and Gazza, separating them from the Johns, and causing every crack that had already gaped between the Nephauree and its victims to become even wider, creating a network of new fissures that drove the witch and her friends back and back and back, until they were at the top of the narrow shore that led down to the water's edge.

The Nephauree lifted its hammerheaded horns again, reaching up even higher than it had previously, and brought them down like a judge slamming down his gavel to pass the final sentence. The shock wave it sent made the ground gape everywhere, causing the tiny parcel of shore where the witch and her friends stood to be separated from the rest of the ground.

"We're in trouble," was all Candy could say.

Then the waters tugged at their little portion of ground with so much strength that it could no longer resist the demand. It parted from the rest of the shore with a violent shudder that threw Candy and Gazza to their knees.

Then the current caught it, and it was borne inexorably toward that place where the Sea of Izabella was lost to Oblivion.

75

THE END OF THE WORLD

THE WATERS OF THE Izabella did more than simply carry the fragment of shoreline toward the limits of reality. It spun the makeshift vessel round and round, rocking it from side to side as it did so. But none of these chaotic maneuvers were sufficient to prevent Malingo from coming in to land on the slippery surface, with only the tips of his wing-ears to prevent him from sliding straight across the water-slickened surface to be dumped in the crazed surf on the other side, where he would certainly have drowned. Luckily Candy saw him slide past her and instinctively reached out, grabbing hold of one of his flailing wings, halting him before the worst could happen.

Not that there wasn't an even more calamitous fate awaiting them all, just a few seconds away. Though the actual spot where the waters fell off into the Abyss was veiled in spray, there was no doubting its proximity. The closer the suicidal current brought them to their final moments, the less noise the waters made, their roar and rush fading as they dropped off the Edge of the World.

"You could still fly back," Candy said to Malingo.

"Why would I want to do that?"

"Because we're going to die!" Gazza said, sounding thoroughly furious. "I'd give my right arm for a chance to get off this damn rock."

"Oh, really? And leave your lady?"

Gazza blushed.

"I knew it!" said Malingo.

"I knew it too," Gazza said, looking to Candy. "From the moment I saw you. Don't ask me how, but I did. I love you, Candy," he said. "I'm glad I finally said it myself. I know it's a bit late, but there hasn't been a lot of opportunity, with one thing or another."

Candy smiled at him.

"What's *that* supposed to mean?" Malingo said.

"What?"

"You're just *smiling* at him."

Any further words were drowned out by a vast silence, as the roaring sound of the waters' chaos was stilled suddenly and completely, and the gray-blue mist that veiled the place where the waters actually fell away, cleared.

The currents that had carried the fragment of Scoriae to that place now vanished, for here the sea herself gave up possession of all form and will and power, and were tossed over the End of the Abarat, broken into innumerable beads of water, illuminated for a few seconds by the firelight, then extinguished. What had been, in the Reality from which the beads of water had now departed, an irresistible force was now no more than a million million drops falling away into the Abyss.

"This is it," Gazza said.

Candy thought, *After this, there'll be no more magic, no more visions, no more love, or hope or——*

"No, *wait*," she said aloud. "Wait!"

"Who are you talking to?" Gaz said.

"I want more!" she yelled into the Void.

"More what?"

"Everything!" she told him.

"Why are you smiling?" Gaz said.

"We're going over the Edge of the World!" Malingo said. "If there's some good news, tell it, before we're gone forever."

"Later," Candy said. "I'll tell you later."

They had run out of sea. The piece of land lurched and began to fall. But before it fell, Candy had time to look back toward the shore of Scoriae, and saw with heartbreaking clarity, John Mischief and his brothers. They were all watching her from a place so close to the water's edge that every fresh surge of water threatened to carry them all away. Indeed, they almost seemed to be inviting that very fate, so close to calamity were they standing.

"Go back!" Candy yelled to them, though she very much doubted her words were audible.

John Mischief cupped his hands to either side of his

mouth and the brothers tried yelling something in unison. But the air refused to carry the sound; the silence between shore and sea went unstirred. Then the little scrap of Scoriae tipped, and over the Edge it went, going where so much of the Sea of Izabella had already gone.

Down and down and down—

The John Brothers shouted the same word at the same instant: her name, of course.

"Cannndddeeeee."

It did no good. It changed nothing. The waters carried Candy, Gazza and Malingo away, and down they went, out of the John Brothers' sight.

"She's gone!" Mischief shouted.

"She can't have," said Fillet.

"Well she has!" Mischief raged.

"But . . . but . . . she was going to make everything all right," John Moot whimpered.

"It never would have worked," Serpent said. "A thing like the Nephauree is beyond anybody's power to resist. It'll kill us all now."

Serpent turned to look back at the Nephauree. For once his worst expectations were wrong. Those Who Walk Behind the Stars were departing. Promises were baubles with which ephemeral beings distracted themselves. The Nephauree had their own, far more important dealings. The beast had already swung its massive form around, and it was now moving off through the smoke toward the volcano. Its motion drew still more sulfur out of the churning air, and the Nephauree's color deepened again, to a dazzling yellow. Then, as though it had drawn a massive surge of power from feeding off the smoke, it quickened its step, throwing open its cosmic robes as it did so, and like a dark sail filled by a following wind, it swelled up, and stepped off the ground, climbing the filthy air so quickly that in less than ten seconds it had gone from sight completely.

"Well, that was anticlimactic," Serpent remarked.

"Only you, Serpent," said John Fillet, "would complain because our executioner left!"

"I'm only saying . . . it's a bit—"

"Shut up, Serpent," Mischief said. There was deep rage in his voice. "Don't you understand what this means?"

"Oh," said Serpent after a pregnant pause. "Lordy Lou."

His voice, for once, was scoured of every last drop of sarcasm or insincerity.

"She's dead," said John Drowze.

"Not dead," John Moot said.

"Yes, Moot: dead."

"We don't know for certain," John Pluckitt said.

"For the first and probably the last time, I agree with Serpent," Drowze said. "It's no use denying what we saw with our own eyes."

"And what did we see?" John Slop said. "Not very much, it seems to me. I certainly didn't see them die."

"You're clutching at straws, brother. They went over the Edge of the World."

"That they did," Drowze agreed.

"They fell, no question," John Moot said.

"They're probably still falling," Fillet said.

"So what happens to them?" Slop asked.

"She'll live," John Serpent said with uncharacteristic enthusiasm. "If anyone's capable of surviving falling over the Edge of the World, she is."

John Mischief had lost his rage, and had gone back to contemplating the scene beyond the shore. Nothing had changed. The Izabella still rushed toward her dissolution, the fine spray that blurred the place where her waters fell away, which had briefly cleared and now concealed the place again.

"What are you looking at, Mischief?" Moot wanted to know.

"Everything. Nothing," he replied.

"Well, that's a waste of time," Moot said. "We've got things to do. Important things."

Mischief continued to look at the sea.

"Such as?" he said.

"Oh, come on, Mischief," Moot said, "you know as well as I do."

"Can't think of anything."

"Well, we got a body to bury for one," Sallow said.

"That's a pleasant prospect."

"Then there's the Eight Dynasties to deal with."

"We can't do that on our own."

"We had a life before she came along," John Fillet reminded him.

"Yes, John, but we were *waiting*," John Mischief replied. "Weren't we? That first day in the Hereafter was about more than a stolen key. We all felt that, *didn't we?*"

"Yes . . ." said John Serpent. ". . . of course we did. I admit to it. I had a sense of . . ." He scoured his vocabulary for the right word. ". . . of *imminence*. That something of consequence was about to happen."

"And then she came into our lives," Mischief said. "And she changed everything."

"Everything?" John Serpent said.

"Everything," Mischief replied.

76

AND BEYOND

F ALLING AND FALLING AND falling through utter emptiness Candy, Malingo and Gazza quickly lost track of time; and—with no means of judging how far they'd fallen—of space too. The same colorless undifferentiated space to their left and to their right, and above and below. It didn't even offer them the hope that darkness had offered: the chance that hidden somewhere was life, purpose, meaning. There was just a gray banality; a vast absence through which they tumbled without any way to judge the speed of their fall, or even, at times, whether they were falling at all.

They said nothing.

What was there to say, when there was nothing but nothing around you? There was no view to remark upon, no moon was rising, no trailing stars, nor sun departing, the sky in flames. Nor was there sky for it to fall from.

And still they fell.

Or perhaps only thought they fell. Dreamed it, perhaps.

Whatever the reason, it didn't change their circumstances. To fall was—

to fall was—

to—

—fall.

Suddenly, there was something out of nothing. A flash of blue and scarlet, which instantly enveloped Malingo, and snatched him out of sight. Luckily he yelled his head off at this abduction and his long, loud cry appeared in the bland air, as though he'd scrawled it in a long trail of silver smoke. It was the first solid, or virtually solid, thing any of them had seen since they'd gone over the Edge. It wasn't much of a lifeline, but it was better than the absence. So Candy caught hold of the silver strand, hoping that it wouldn't go to nothing in her grip.

No.

It was solid.

"Grab hold of me!" she yelled to Gazza. He had his hand around her ankle before the words were out of her mouth.

Three thoughts came into Candy's head at the same time, each demanding priority: one, that she hoped Malingo didn't stop yelling; two, that they might not fall forever after all; and three, that she should have known, the moment she saw the mirrored word Abarataraba, that if there was a mirror of the islands along the horizontal axis, then it stood to reason that there'd also be one on the vertical. If to the left, then to the right. If above, then below.

While her thoughts fought, she pulled herself, hand over hand, along the length of the braided cry. She could see the length of it receding from her grip, and could fix her eyes upon the spot, no more than three hauling-lengths away, where it went from sight. What else could she do but follow her hands to the place, and find out the why and the how of it?

And then—Lordy Lou—Malingo stopped yelling. Candy felt the cord slacken, and let out a panicked yell of her own, which instantly formed a turquoise ribbon in front of her, like her breath on a winter's day, before fluttering away when she stopped her cry.

She wasn't going to let their chance to get out of the Void slip away. Whatever was on the other side of the wall of murk, it couldn't be any worse than falling forever into Oblivion, could it? She forced her body to reach, *reach— go on, fingers! Go on, hands!*—beyond the end of the cord, which was already slipping up and away, carried by a gust of wind that smelled like lightning and pineapples.

Her fingers went now, disappearing completely. Her hands searched, probing through the Void . . . and touched something on the other side of the Wall of Nothingness. It was moist and warm, as though it had been painted by a loaded brush, and as soon as she touched *whatever it was*, *whatever it was* reached toward her with the same urgency. Dozens of boneless feelers as thin as string wrapped themselves around her hands and wrists.

"What's in there?" Gazza wanted to know.

"I've no idea," she told him. "But it's alive. And it's

got hold of me. It's pulling."

"Does it hurt?"

It didn't, she realized. It was a tight grip, but it didn't mean her harm.

"It's all right," she murmured.

"What?"

"I said: *it's all right.*"

She saw a gleam of bright columns ripple past her face.

"What was that?"

The word *that* went by. It was written in turquoise on a strip of air the color of mangoes.

"Malingo?"

The three syllables came out of her mouth, and flowed in purples and blues in a woven streak of sound and color.

"Yes?" he said.

"I'm not afraid," she told him.

Again, her words poured out in a woven stream of color: red, purple, blue. . . .

"Oh, will you look at that. Words like ribbons."

And out the words came.

Words like ribbons.

Green and yellow and orange.

"What's happening?" Malingo said. "I just saw my name fly by."

"I know." She reached out toward the source of the tentacles. A gust of wind blew from the place where her hand was. She felt it on her face. She heard it telling her, as winds will:

Come away. Come away.

It carried the words off toward Oblivion.

"No, thanks . . ." she said very quietly, so quietly that the ribbon was translucent. "We've got somewhere to go."

She reached out as far as her muscles and joints would allow, and grabbed hold of whatever tentacles were growing from the Other Side.

Something there understood the sign she was sending. And it pulled. Candy didn't have time to offer further word to Malingo. It all happened too fast. Suddenly there were bits of color rushing at her, tiny bits, and with them, the briefest fragments of sound. Nothing made sense. It came too fast and it just got faster.

Color, color, color . . .

Note, note, note . . .

Color, note. Color, note.

Col—

No—

Col—

No—

Suddenly, nothing.

A long, empty, gray hush.

But she wasn't afraid. She knew how these things worked now. Everything was a mirror.

If prisons—

O!

—therefore liberty.

It's started.

If seas—
See it?
—therefore shores.
Hear it?
If silence,
Yes!
Therefore song.

And they were in another world entirely.

Hopelessness is reasonable.

But nothing of worth
in my life
came of reason.
Not my love,
not my art,
not my heaven.

So I am hopeful.

—Zephario Carrion

So Ends
The Third Book of Abarat